M000093728

STILL HARPING ON MY DAUGHTER

Enjoy the ride
Much love

Mom

Still Harping on my Daughter
Copyright © 2019 by Marc S. Silver

This is a work of fiction. Names, characters, and incidents are
used fictitiously. Any resemblance to actual persons, living or
dead is but an illusion, and almost entirely coincidental.

Cover and Interior Design by Lance Buckley

www.lancebuckley.com

All rights reserved. No part of this book may be reproduced
or used in any manner without written permission of the author
except for the use of quotations in a book review.

ISBN: 978-1-7330512-0-0

STILL HARPING ON MY DAUGHTER

MARC S. SILVER

Special thanks to my kind sister Sandy, for her encouragement and her determination to plod through early versions of this book. To Haley White and Kelie McIver, for their wise, thoughtful, and honest feedback. To David Himes and Lyssa Connelly for their great book cover ideas. And to my editor, Ruth Strother who got me the rest of the way.

For my wife Kathy who makes it all possible.

"Within you and without you..."

-GEORGE HARRISON

PART ONE

CHAPTER ONE

THESE BLAZES YOU MUST
NOT TAKE FOR FIRE

I am a proud ham-and-egger; a journeyman actor. I've had my moments in the big time, but all in all, being in my sixtieth year I prefer the occasional theater gig to the stress and strain of big-time TV and all that Hollywood mishegas. I am content, have a supportive wife, a nice home, a yard, and a cat. I watch my weight and get yearly physicals. I might have shrunk an inch this year. I could have sworn I was 5'9", but I've lost an inch somehow. At any rate, I'm drinking less and eating a more reasonable diet in hopes of prolonging my contentedness for as long as possible.

I just started a summer Shakespeare gig with a company that I've had a great working relationship with for the last seventeen years. This year we're doing *Hamlet*, the world's most celebrated tragedy, and I'm playing Polonius, the funny old guy. The actor playing Hamlet is excellent, and the woman cast as my daughter, Ophelia, just breaks my heart—she's so sweet and sad. We just had our first table read. I love first table reads. I've become very good at them. In fact, I tend to peak at the first table read and then it's all downhill from there.

In any case, I'm looking forward to another fun summer doing Shakespeare in the park. But then something happens.

As I said, I consider myself to be content. I'm not struggling with any kind of crisis or anxiety or psychosis (though others may not back me up on this). I am also not a particularly religious person. There's a Chanukah show a buddy and I wrote that we perform during the holidays, but I'm more of a cultural Jew than a religious one. Frankly, the existence of God is not something I pay much attention to. I've always felt religion to be responsible for more than its fair share of suffering in the world, and the more distance I keep from it, the better. Now, I'm not so sure.

It's about two in the morning, and my wife, Kelly, and I are in bed. She's a great sleeper, and I'm an insomniac. Her snoring makes things worse for me. I've mentioned it to her a few times, but she doesn't believe me. I've thought about recording her for proof, but that just seems cruel. And as a content person, I am hardly ever cruel. So, as she gently and peacefully snores away like a baby rhino, I am staring wide-eyed at the ceiling thinking about God knows what.

And speaking of God, this is when the dresser catches on fire. A great roaring blaze, Halloween-orange and chimney-red, from the dresser top to the ceiling. Weird swirling images appear inside the blaze: cats wearing saddles with turtles riding on their backs, groaning people with very bad skin eating sand in the desert, a choir singing Mozart, and then a giant face appears with a striking resemblance to Mel Brooks. I am horrified and gasping, afraid I might have a heart attack, and then the giant face begins to speak.

"Steven Harold Goldfarb?" asks the face in an authoritative but not unfriendly tone.

"Actually, it's Harold Steven Goldfarb," I cautiously correct.

"Are you sure?"

"Positive," I reply, my name being the one thing I'm certain of at this point. "Maybe you got the wrong address."

"No," the face responds, then pauses momentarily. "I see what happened—clerical error."

"Excuse me, but who are you?" I ask the giant face in flames who more or less knows my name.

"Who do you think?" the face challenges back.

"God?"

"Who else?"

"*The* God?" I double-check.

"The one and only."

He stops talking. I can't tell if he wants a bigger reaction on my end. It's silent for a few moments before I build up the courage to continue.

"Well, what do you want?"

"Listen carefully, Harold," he begins before interrupting himself. "Do you like the fire effect, by the way?"

"It's a little startling," I say.

"Well, that is the point," God responds. "If there's any charring on the furniture after I'm gone, a little Murphy Oil will take it right out, I promise."

"Is this really happening or am I dreaming?" I say more to myself than to him. It doesn't matter because God is already onto another subject.

"Have you ever considered Harold Steven instead of Harold Goldfarb? It might be a better stage name for you."

"I did, but there was already a Harold Steven in the union so I stayed with Harold Goldfarb."

"Oh, too bad."

"Appreciate the suggestion, though."

"Anyway, here's the deal…are you sitting down?"

"Well—"

"I'm kidding, Harold. Lie there. You're fine, relax."

"I'm trying to," I say.

"You have to impregnate the girl who plays your daughter, Ophelia, in *Hamlet*."

"I have to *what*?" I say, springing up to a sitting position on the bed.

"Her child by you will save the planet from annihilation."

"But I'm old enough to be her father!"

"Well, what can I tell you? That's the deal," God says, seemingly disappointed with my less-than-pleased response. "The child from your union with this actress is the only hope for humanity's survival."

"Hold on for just a cotton-pickin' second here!" And for the record, I've never said *cotton-pickin' second* before in my entire cotton-pickin' life.

"And you have to do it by June 19 or else it will be too late," God sneaks in as a last-minute disclaimer.

"That's in two weeks!"

"Good luck."

"This is impossible," I say while flopping back down next to my snoring wife.

"You're an actor, aren't you? Turn on the charm."

"I'm an *old* actor."

"Nah, you still got it."

"Why me? I'm not even that good! Did you see my Iago?"

"Look, it's complicated," God says. "Don't ask me to explain; it makes me vengeful. Just have a little faith, get some rest, and jump on it in the morning."

I look up at him, nauseated.

"Poor choice of words, but you know what I mean. I'll check in from time to time and see how you're doing."

"This is insane," I protest one more time.

"What can I tell you—the Lord works in mysterious ways," he says. And with that, the fire vanishes.

My wife had managed to snore through the whole thing. My stomach seems particularly disturbed by what may or may not have just happened, and I run into the bathroom to throw up. When I come back out, I notice the dresser top is definitely burned and warped, and I'm pretty sure Murphy Oil isn't going to cut it.

CHAPTER TWO

THERE ARE MORE THINGS
IN HEAVEN AND EARTH

Most mornings my wife leaves early for work. She always kisses me on the top of my head before she goes. Her reasoning is that in case there's an earthquake or a killer asteroid, at least she got a chance to say goodbye. A lovely, if slightly morbid, sentiment. Whenever this happens, I always pretend to be asleep. I'm not sure why. Sometimes I wonder if other unstable actor-type husbands with dependable hard-working wives do this as well.

The morning after I saw God, Kelly kisses me on her way out of the bedroom, as usual. I am awake for this, as usual. After wallowing in my what-kind-of-lousy-husband-am-I guilt for a moment, the previous evening's escapade floods back into my consciousness, and sleep-deprived as I am, I get up to tackle the day.

My morning stagger to the bathroom is more unstable than usual; I have to steady myself on the dresser, which I notice is no longer burned and peeling. In fact, there is no evidence of a godly visitation at all. Not a scratch, not a smudge.

"But it was so real," I mumble to myself just as countless other lunatics have mumbled on their way to take a morning piss.

I sit on the toilet, because standing takes too much effort at this point, and try to make sense of it all. Maybe it's some kind of late midlife crisis. I never really had one when I was middle-aged, so better late than never? But no. I am a content person. This religious hallucinating kind of thing doesn't happen to contented people, does it? Maybe it's a brain tumor. Or the lack of sleep is finally catching up with me. Wouldn't the smoke detector have gone off? And why me? I'm just an old stage actor for Christ's sake. Why not Chris Pine or Ryan Gosling?

But it was so vivid. It had to be real. Maybe something did happen, and like Moses I've received a message from God, and humanity's very survival depends on what I do next. I think about Isaac and what God asked Abraham to do. So, comparatively, I guess this isn't so bad.

"I must be crazy to think this really happened!" I shout to no one in particular.

"I must be crazy to think that it didn't!" I yell back at myself.

I take a break from all this arguing and decide to read the morning sports section, have a little coffee, and maybe take a walk. I do my best thinking on walks. And since my brain is whirling and I'm not scheduled for rehearsal this evening, I'll have all day to wander around and try to figure out what the hell is going on.

———

It's a beautiful, cool morning in Glendale, bright and clear and perfect for my morning constitutional. My neighborhood is just below the Verdugo Hills; a great place to walk with lots of pretty scenery. I always walk uphill toward the mountains, so it's a decent workout for an old guy. Sometimes I'll catch sight of deer, and the coyotes confidently stroll through the neighborhood with very little fear of humans. There're always Missing Cat posters on telephone poles. Those cats are not missing, though. The coyotes make a very good living here in Glendale.

Lots of other people in my neighborhood go for walks, too, and I know them and their dogs. There's the pretty stay-at-home mom in yoga pants who speed walks with a double stroller. The old Armenian man with the Yorkshire terrier who tried to bite me once. The dog. Not the Armenian. The shirtless college athlete who runs by me as if I were standing still. He sweats profusely and listens to loud music on his headphones. You can hear him coming from a block away.

They probably know me as the guy who mumbles to himself. In my defense, I'm usually running lines. The rest of the time, it's true, I blather like a madman. Like on this particularly fine Glendale morning as I try to figure out if I am crazy or if I have been chosen by God.

The last time I tried talking to God before now, I was eight years old and President Kennedy had just been shot. I remember praying and asking God to take me instead. That was probably the noblest moment of my life. I would make no such offer today, not with the people we've got in office now. God never got back to me then, and I'm doubtful that he'd get back to me now.

As I get to the top of the first hill, the endorphins kick in and I start feeling alert and energized. Out of the corner of my eye I catch sight of a strange, dark image. Startled, I quickly turn to face it. In the middle of the street, not ten yards from where I'm standing, is the biggest bird I have ever seen. It's at least six feet tall, standing on a dead raccoon, and picking at it with an enormous beak. I have been walking these hills for over twenty years, and I have never seen anything like it. An oversized buzzard or a hawk, maybe? An eagle?

"What in the holy hell!" I croak. With all those years of Shakespeare, you'd think I'd come up with something a little better than that.

The bird, or whatever it is, stops its flesh ripping to stare at me, a piece of meat still dangling from its bloody yellow beak. So piercing is the stare, that I let loose a little urine. That's how shook I am.

"Are you a sign from God?" I ask, trying my best to seem unintimidated.

The bird screeches and extends its wings—twelve feet of wingspan, possibly more. It rises into the air and lands again on a masonry wall in front of the corner house across the street. Staring at me with its huge golden eyes, it screeches one final time then rises into the air like a freaking pterodactyl and flies off in the opposite direction until it disappears from sight.

"What in the holy hell!" That's still the best I can do, but it's a much better line reading this time.

I continue my walk, charging up another hill and muttering to God under my breath.

"What the hell was that thing? How am I supposed to interpret that? What is going on here? You come in my bedroom telling me to do all this ridiculous Old Testament begetting weirdness. What am I supposed to think? What am I supposed to believe? Jesus Christ, God! I've got a serious moral dilemma here. A little help. I mean—what the hell!"

An old woman walking her poodle crosses the street to avoid a confrontation with a madman. I've seen this woman many times before and have even scratched her ugly poodle under the chin, but I guess she wasn't taking any chances.

I'm getting a good workout, anyway. Charging up and down hills at a much faster pace than my usual. I make my way up to Brand Park, where I come upon a strange scene by the Japanese gardens. An organization of turtle lovers has assembled for its annual turtle run for charity. A big plastic circle is laid out on the grass as a makeshift floor. In the center of the circle are a dozen or so turtles behind a starting gate. The gate is lifted, and people scream for their turtles to run across the plastic circle and onto the grass. By the looks of the prize booth, the owner of the first pet to get across gets a large, green cuddly stuffed sea turtle. I consider staying to enjoy the race, but then I notice the little toy cats sitting in saddles strapped on the turtles' backs, like the image in God's dresser fire. Except in God's version, things were reversed—the turtles were riding the cats. Close enough to freak me out, though. I back away slowly, and then hightail it out of there, jogging the whole way home.

First time I've jogged in fifteen years.

I'm totally winded and nearly dead by the time I get home. As soon as I walk in the door, the phone rings. It's the stage manager for *Hamlet*. Our lead has strep throat so he wants to change the rehearsal schedule. The stage manager wants to know if I can come in that night and work all my scenes with Ophelia.

I'm not the smartest man in the world but if that ain't a sign, I don't know what the hell is.

CHAPTER THREE

SAY, WHY IS THIS? WHEREFORE?
WHAT SHOULD WE DO?

I am not brave. I understand that about myself. I'll do everything possible to avoid confrontation. As an actor, I prefer all my dramatics to be on stage. But God, apparently, came into my bedroom and set my dresser on fire. So suddenly I am being forced to confront some very difficult stuff. I choose to do this in the shower.

As I lather my hair with my wife's expensive fruit-scented shampoo (rather than my cheap stuff that I ran out of last week), I mull things over for the hundredth time. I focus on how intriguing the parallels of my current situation are to the plot of *Hamlet*. He also struggled with a task he received from an otherworldly creature—in his case, his father's ghost. He went back and forth about whether killing his uncle was truly vengeance for his father or just plain murder; debated whether his dad's ghost was from heaven or hell. As we all know, things didn't turn out so well for the melancholy Dane.

My gut has been telling me to side with God and get this over with. *Hamlet* probably would have had a very different ending if Hamlet had completed what was asked of him in the first place. Besides, I asked God for signs, and he gave me three in a row: a bird-monster, turtles riding cats, and strep throat. What else do you need? And I do kind of like his style, kind of easygoing for a God. And I liked his sense of humor: "What can I tell you—the Lord works in mysterious ways." That's a pretty good line. Besides, even if I'm wrong and God turns out to be some cosmic joker, or this is really the devil or some demon trying to trick me, shouldn't I take a risk anyway to save the planet? Am I capable of being brave enough and having enough faith to take a stand for the greater good? No, I'm pretty sure if there's a way out of this, I'll run like a gazelle.

I really need to tell my wife about all this, but logistically that's not going to be so easy. In the summer when I'm doing Shakespeare, our schedules are such that we pass like ships in the night. She works during the day, and most of my stuff is in the evening. We can go a whole week without seeing each other, and this isn't something I want to talk about on the phone or through email. It might have to wait until my day off on Monday, which buys me some time because I have no idea how I'm going to explain this to her. "Honey, God told me that I have to have a fling with this twenty-three-year-old cutie so that our child can save the world. Isn't that great?"

This is going to be a nightmare.

Our sex life, as with many couples our age, has diminished over the years. We are more of a partnership now. Best friends, really. It does trouble me, though, because I'm afraid that I may not have been as good a lover as I should have been. Or maybe at a certain age couples just stop fooling around because it gets too awkward and funny looking. We never talk about it—although we probably should. After all, sex is an important part of a healthy marriage—I'm sure I read that somewhere.

Maybe if I shaved my back?

I get out of the shower and catch sight of myself in the bathroom mirror. Old and wet and sagging all over. I normally try to avoid such a confrontation by opening the medicine cabinet at such an angle that when stepping out of the shower I can steer clear of this vision of decaying manhood. But this time I forgot. And now I'm looking at my reflection like he's some stranger I have no desire to know. Someone that I might even like to harm. What happened to my hair? It's falling off my head and then sprouting again in the most ridiculous places. Look at those ears! That nose! Those tired, defeated eyes. Even if I could build up the nerve and approach this actress with God's outrageous proposition, one look in the mirror tells me all that I need to know—it's going to take a lot of charm.

Thousand Oaks is a sleepy little bedroom community about forty-five miles north of Los Angeles. That's where the Shakespeare festival is located, on the campus of a small private university. My green Prius and I take the back way to get there. The 2 freeway to the 210 to the 118. The 118 is a longer route to Thousand Oaks but less congested and a much prettier drive than the 101. It's early evening, but there's enough light to still see the beautiful rocky peaks and green hillsides that line both sides of the freeway, and you're bound to see some interesting wildlife en route. Birds, mostly—hawks, buzzards, owls—and an interesting assortment of road kill. I keep an eye out for something that might resemble the bird-monster, but there's nothing even close. I do see a car fire on the opposite side of the freeway and rubberneck to see if Mel Brooks's face might be in there somewhere. It isn't.

As I walk into the rehearsal hall, I find the director, the stage manager, and the young man who is set to play my son, Laertes, seated at a table, already absorbed in discussion. The director is one of my favorites, Tom English. A tall leading man–type with a mischievous edge that makes his work really interesting. I've worked with him, both as an actor and as my director, several times over the years. He's the best. I've worked with the stage manager, Ira Talorowski, several times as well. He is not so tall and handsome but very efficient. A little insecure, but a very sweet guy. The actor playing Laertes is someone new to the company, Richard Ramirez. I'm sure if God were to visit him, he'd suggest a different stage name. Isn't Richard Ramirez the famous serial killer? Anyway, he's a nice kid. Very handsome, Latin, about a foot and a half taller than me, and full of energy and enthusiasm. Why we were cast as father and son, who knows.

They wave me over, and I join them at the table. They're talking about why Laertes is so anxious to leave town and be out on his own. Usually I'd enjoy the discourse, but this evening I am too apprehensive to take any pleasure in such deep analysis of the Bard's intent. I am too busy thinking about how good-looking this kid is. If anybody were going to have an affair with my daughter—I mean the actress playing my daughter—it'd be him, and certainly not me. It is a bit deflating, especially after being abused by my reflection in the bathroom mirror.

Right as I'm wallowing in self-pity, the actress playing my daughter enters the hall, Portia Clearwater (even God would like that stage name). She has pale skin, beautiful raven hair, and is not much more than five feet tall. Apparently, the Polonius children come from different mothers. As she moves gracefully toward us, the world freezes for a moment—four guys completely captivated.

She sits down and we all shake hands and nobody seems to care that she's about fifteen minutes late. Tom explains that tonight will be a table read with discussion. Our first scene begins with Laertes and Ophelia. Portia starts to read, and I am immediately under her spell. She is so genuine and innocent that I feel like my heart will burst. I want to protect her and take care of her, like the daughter I never had. That's all well and good for my character, Polonius. But the prospect of trying to sleep with this girl in real life…Oy!

Union rules dictate we get a ten-minute break after eighty minutes of rehearsal. It's not really necessary (we're not digging ditches here), but it gives me a chance to have a little one-on-one with Portia. I approach her as she is nibbling on some of the peanut M&M's Tom had brought in for snacks.

"Howdy!" I offer, trying to be charming yet nonthreatening.

"Hi!" she says. And even that simple *hi* is exquisitely honest and kind.

"I…I love what you're doing with Ophelia," I say. "It breaks my heart."

"Oh, thank you so much," she responds. "Your Polonius is so funny. I didn't know he could be so funny."

She thinks I'm funny! At least I've got that going for me.

"I have to find a balance," I say, hoping I sound like a serious, professional actor. "He has his funny side, but I don't want him to come off as a goofball either. He is a counselor of the court, after all."

"Oh, I don't get goofball from him at all. He's a little dotty but definitely not goofball."

There's that smile again. Oh my God.

"That's good to hear," I answer. "I mean, he's stern with Ophelia, but I don't want to make him harsh with her, you know?"

I sure hope I sound like I know what I'm talking about.

"Yeah, I mean if you're too harsh," she says, "then why would I get so upset later when you die?"

"Exactly! Besides, you are so sweet and gentle, I couldn't be mean to you. I couldn't stand it." I give her my most charming smile. At least it used to be charming. I'm not sure what it looks like now. "You are going to be great in this," I add, taking her hand for emphasis.

"Thank you. You are so kind. That means so much to me, really." She blushes.

Then there's an awkward silence, and I realize I am still holding her hand. I drop it immediately and change the subject to something more casual. "So, where are you from?"

"Salt Lake City."

"That's Mormon country, isn't it?" I dumbly ask.

"It is," she answers. "I'm Mormon."

"How interesting!" I exclaim with way too much enthusiasm to be sincere.

Luckily, Ira calls us back to the table. At least I broke the ice with her, even if it ended a little awkwardly. I've known a few Mormons in my life, and they're all lovely people. Much like Portia, they're kind and sweet and family oriented. They seem well-balanced, too; certainly not bitching and moaning all the time like most of the Jews I know. They don't drink, though, so I won't be able to soften her up with alcohol. I can't believe I'm even thinking this way. Am I really going to do this?

I'm not exactly sure what Mormons believe in, but I'm hoping that Portia might buy my story more readily than someone from one of the major religious groups. Aren't the Mormons the ones who believe Jesus lived in the United States? Maybe it won't be too much harder to convince her that God came to my bedroom and told me to have sex with her in order to save the world.

Yeah, this is going to be a piece of cake.

CHAPTER FOUR

TO SLEEP,
PERCHANCE TO DREAM

Driving home from Thousand Oaks at night can be a little spooky. A fog tends to roll in, even in the summer, and visibility can be dramatically reduced. I'm creeping along with the wipers going and the defroster cranked up. Thankfully, both are working. Usually things like the defroster don't function so well with the Prius I'm driving.

I'm feeling tired but energized from rehearsal. I like these kids; so open and talented. When I was their age, I don't think I could have navigated Shakespeare nearly as well as they do. I've done a lot of shows with this company, but this production has the promise of being the best one yet.

I'm reveling in it all, thinking about Portia's raven-black hair and her sensitive and vulnerable Ophelia, when something big flies over the car, very low and close just as I'm merging onto the 118. So fast— *whoosh*—and then gone again, vanishing into the fog. I try to convince myself it's only an owl and not the bird-monster from before. I hold my urine, though, you'll be happy to know.

By the time I get home it's midnight, and Kelly is already asleep. I fix myself a drink—scotch with a splash and a twist, two ice cubes. I really shouldn't drink during the week anymore, but I'm too amped up to sleep. I turn on the TV (to get my baseball scores), sink into the La-Z-Boy, and take a sip. Macallan eighteen-year-old single malt scotch. My wife gets me a bottle every year for my birthday. Might be the death of me but what a way to go.

Our black cat, Squeak, jumps onto my lap, purring like a motorboat, and I can almost pretend for a moment that all is right with the world.

But eventually the sports news turns to background noise and the weight of what needs to be done becomes too much for me to ignore. I put down the foot rest, and the cat begrudgingly vaults from my lap. I shut off the news and stagger my way toward the bedroom doorway. I look at my wife peacefully sleeping and start to cry.

I turn from the bedroom. Squeak watches me, anticipating more La-Z-Boy time. He squeaks (hence the name), but I am feeling too morose. I amble through the house—checking bills, turning off lights, turning on lights. I check emails, lose a game of scrabble to my computer, and then, hardly able to keep my eyes open, wearily head to bed.

I want to wake up Kelly and tell her everything, but I watch her sleep instead. I lie down next to her, her slumbering face turned toward mine. She's been working out and going to Weight Watchers lately, and she's really looking great. Kelly takes good care of herself, and it shows. She seems impervious to time. No wrinkles, no bags under her eyes, I don't know how she does it. Probably because she's such a great sleeper. I'm marveling at her face as if I'm seeing it for the first time. Her skin is so smooth and clear, like a baby's. I wish she would open her eyes. I love her eyes most of all; sharp and clear, and they tell you everything about her intelligence, her humor, and her heart. I'm lucky to have her, and what a fool I'd be to lose her. There is nobody I'd rather be with, that's the truth. She is my rock, and I have loved her like crazy for thirty years. We never had kids, but we're okay with that. I think we are, anyway.

She lets out a little snort, and I find it charming and kiss her on the cheek. She mumbles something about macaroni and cheese. Since the dieting started, she often talks in her sleep about food. Sometimes she makes eating noises, as if she's enjoying the stuff in her sleep that she can't eat in real life anymore. I kiss her again and then, in record time for an insomniac like myself, I fall into a deep sleep.

My dream that night is horrific: A blazing sun beats down on a city in ruin. Crumbled buildings are covered in sand and ash. A multitude of starving people with ugly sores eat sand by the fistful while bird-monsters swoop in to feed on the dying.

Our future if I should fail God's assignment?

I abruptly awake and then get up for another scotch.

CHAPTER FIVE

CONSCIENCE DOES MAKE
COWARDS OF US ALL

My wife leaves the house at six in the morning. Immediately after, Squeak comes into the bedroom and starts howling at me, which is part of our usual morning routine. After he makes certain I'm awake and getting out of bed, he slinks over to his favorite chair and falls asleep for five or six hours. Why he does this, I have not a clue. Most mornings I think about strangling him.

I recently was talked into joining a neighborhood watch group on social media. It has about three hundred members, so I get posts all day long from nervous stay-at-home moms warning me about all the alarming things going on in the neighborhood. Usually it's nothing—people asking about missing cats (dead, coyote-eaten cats, actually) or to get a recommendation for a good gardener or an honest carpenter. But lately, stuff is starting to get serious. There's been a rash of robberies in the neighborhood, several cars have been vandalized, and there's actually been a few home invasion break-ins where the homeowners have been beaten and robbed at gunpoint. I guess you can't really blame the moms for being nervous.

It freaks me out that my wife is home alone at night with no protection. I keep a baseball bat by our bed, and we have a house alarm, but these neighborhood dramas make me think about getting a gun. I'm hesitant about this, though. Sometimes in the dead of night, as I lie staring at the ceiling, home invasion scenarios materialize in my head. In those scenarios, I'm always prepared and unafraid and can ruthlessly dish out what the bad guys deserve. I even enjoy the suffering that I cause. The intruders become my victims, and I make them beg me for mercy before finally putting them out of their misery. Anytime these fantasies start, I can't stop them until the entire scene plays itself out: I catch them, torture them, and kill them. I always come out of these imaginings ashamed and frightened by the Dirty Harry side of my personality, but if I ever find myself or a loved one threatened by violence, I hope he'll show up. Because frankly, the Harold side probably won't be worth a damn. Anyway, that's probably why I shouldn't get a gun.

I'm on my third cup of coffee, which normally relaxes me, but my brain is refusing to cooperate. What I need to do if this message from God is real, and I have to get this girl pregnant in order to save mankind, is to stop pussyfooting around and man up about it already. But how?

I can't possibly charm her into having sex with me. At my age and with this face? I'd be charming us right into doomsday. No, if I'm going to save the world, I'm going to have to get Dirty Harry mean about it. Take the bull by the horns and get 'er done. No more Mr. Nice Guy.

A sudden wave of lightheadedness comes upon me, and the room does a kind of half spin in conjunction with my stomach. I've had vertigo before and what a nightmare that was. I make a plea to the God I'm still not convinced I believe in.

"I've got enough going on here already. I'm begging you. No vertigo, please!"

I sit still for a moment, hoping the sensation will pass. It does, thankfully, but the wave of grief I feel in its place is overpowering. I could never be disloyal to Kelly. The very idea of it is making me sick. The more I think about Portia, the more I long for my wife, and the more I want to escape this whole situation. Thankfully, a knock at the door rescues me from these morose contemplations. I should check to see who it is through the peephole, especially with everything going on in the neighborhood, but I don't.

It's a good-looking guy in a nice suit carrying a briefcase and some informational brochures. He smiles at me, and I think, *great, another Jehovah's Witness.*

Not even close.

19

"Hi, my name is Seth," he says in a friendly tone. "I'm with the Kabbalah Center of Los Angeles. Have you heard of us?"

"Yes," I answer. "Actually, I submitted something to you guys a while back, a Chanukah show I wrote with a friend that we thought your group might be interested in. We never heard back from you, though."

"Really?"

"I do not lie."

"I bet that's how you got on my list." He smiles. One of those creepy, religiously self-righteous smiles.

"Ah, I bet you're right." I nod my head and wait for him to continue.

"So, you're an actor?" he has managed to deduce.

"I am."

"A lot of actors are studying with us now." He responds with a knowing grin.

"Madonna was into it, I hear." Why am I indulging this person? Why am I talking about Madonna? Maybe I'm happy to have the distraction.

"You'd be amazed how popular the movement has become," he says with the same creepy smile.

"I am amazed and know not what to say!" I try dazzling him with some Shakespeare, but he doesn't seem familiar with the line from *Midsummer*. He blinks. "Do you study there yourself?" I continue.

"Yes, actually, I converted to Judaism about two years ago and got interested in the Kabbalah. My wife is Jewish. I was Mormon."

"You're kidding me."

"I do not lie." He chuckles.

"I just met a Mormon girl," I say. "Funny."

"Do you know anything about Kabbalah?" he asks, getting back to business.

"It's sort of Jewish mysticism, isn't it?"

"The Kabbalah means different things to different people, but what the center is trying to do is to take the core principles and make them understandable and relevant to everyday life."

"That makes sense," I say and then pointlessly add, "Relevant is important."

"Our students can apply these spiritual tools to improve their own lives and by doing so, make the world a better place. Why don't you come down for a free introductory seminar? We have one every Monday night."

I start to answer, but he cuts me off, continuing with his speech.

"I think you'd be impressed. A lot of the confusion and uncertainty you might be struggling with, believe me, the Kabbalah can put things in perspective."

"I've always been curious," I say truthfully. "But right now might not be the best time for me. My nights are booked; I'm in rehearsal for a show."

"Mazel tov! What are you doing?'

"*Hamlet.*"

"Polonius?" he asks.

"How'd you know?"

"Just seems like you would be," he says. "Great part!"

"Are you an actor, too?" I ask, confident that he is.

"I used to be. Didn't work out."

"That's okay," I say reassuringly. "There's more to life."

"That's what I've found." He beams, his smile now morphed into something more genuine than what he had offered before. "Can I leave you a brochure?"

He says this while already starting to pass me a professional-looking booklet, which I accept and begin thumbing through half-heartedly.

"Are you okay?" he asks.

I look up. "What do you mean?"

"You just look a little troubled."

I don't answer him. I'm actually a little perturbed by the question.

He finally gives up on waiting for a response. "I do hope you'll come down. I have a feeling that our meeting here today—that it's important. Sometimes, reality isn't what it seems to be."

It hits me. Maybe, with his Kabbalah powers, he already knows something. No, of course not. That would be impossible.

"I'm interested," I say, trying to sound encouraging, "but I have some stuff to take care of first." Now I'm anxious for the guy to leave.

"'Our ego will always try to convince us that our work can wait another day, but every opportunity has a spiritual expiration date.' That's a quote from our founder."

"Brilliant," I say while closing the door and suddenly finding him particularly annoying.

"If you need us, we'll be here!" He blurts out one final thought as the door shuts on his hopeful, smiling face.

The Kabbalah Center going door-to-door, looking for Jews. Seth is going to have a short day in Glendale, the capital of all things Armenian. I drop the brochure on our entryway table, quite prepared to never give the Kabbalah Center another thought for the rest of my life. Then I stumble through the house, past Squeak, who is still passed out on his favorite pass-out chair, enter the bedroom, and fall face-first onto the bed, where I remain for the next several hours.

CHAPTER SIX

STILL HARPING ON
MY DAUGHTER

Back on the 118 North heading to rehearsal, I'm feeling completely clueless about who I really am. I've somehow become a stranger to myself; discontent and disconnected. I might be having an actual anxiety attack. My heart feels like it's about to leap out of my chest, my left leg won't stop shaking, and I'm starting to lose feeling in my arms from my elbows to my fingertips because I'm gripping the steering wheel so ferociously. Or else I'm having a heart attack.

My Prius suddenly lurches. It's a very weird sensation. If you have one or have ever been killed by one, then you know what I'm talking about. The car just suddenly accelerates and then feels like it's going to stall. The lights on the instrument panel blink on and off just for a second, giving you the feeling that you no longer have control of the vehicle. This is obviously quite disconcerting, especially when you're doing seventy-five on the freeway and having an anxiety attack.

There was a rash of runaway Prius accidents a few years back. Toyota said it was because of loose floor mats. They even did a bogus floor mat recall, which was complete bullshit. There is something seriously wrong with these cars. It's like driving a computer that is having emotional problems: sometimes it won't start, headlights go on and off by themselves, and the touch screen control panel and the CD player will or won't work depending on the mood of the car. I've complained multiple times about the car's erratic behavior when taking it in for service. They always tell me they can't find anything wrong. But I'm pretty sure when I die, this car will have something to do with it.

Can't beat the gas mileage, though.

I walk into rehearsal, and the hall is abuzz with energy. The entire company is present and excited to dive in. I say my hellos and participate in some chitchat with the folks I haven't seen since last summer. I see Portia from across the room flirting with Richard Ramirez, and judging from her exuberant giggling, she seems quite infatuated. She catches me watching her, and we exchange pleasant smiles.

More and more the youthful exuberance and sexual energy at the festival is making me feel my age. I've been with the company since its inaugural season, and at some point I've morphed from a young novice actor to the elder statesman for the company. I'm the second oldest member of the cast this season, which I take comfort in; at least I'm not the oldest. In past seasons, I'd take it upon myself to help out with personnel issues or other situations where the actors might need an ambassador to the management. I now serve on the board and have even been given an Associate Member title, though I have no idea what that means. In any case, I'm one of the few actors who has some sway with the decision-making processes of the company, and people seem to respect that.

Ira, who especially enjoys this part of stage managing, calls for everyone's attention at a volume akin to an actor projecting to the back of a 50,000-seat outdoor stadium. Midway through an excessively detailed reiterating of the company rules, Tom politely interrupts him in order to get the rehearsing part of rehearsal underway.

I have known Tom for a long time. He was also there, performing alongside me, back in the early days. Now he's one of two artistic directors for the company, the other one being the original founder. Tom and I were probably both in consideration for the position, but I must assume the higher-ups eventually reasoned him smarter, younger, and more talented than me. They aren't wrong. I've watched Tom develop his talent over the years, and he is now, aside from being a very good actor, one of my favorite stage directors. There are few people in the world who I invest as much trust in as I do Tom English.

Tom has decided to open the play with Hamlet's father's funeral. He's blocked the scene so that the corpse is brought in under a sheet on a bier, while the rest of the ensemble filters onto the stage in mourning robes. A priest character will recite a prayer from upstage center, and then the rest of us will sing a funeral dirge. The ingenuity of this is that Tom wants the sheet covering the corpse to be pulled back at the end of the song, revealing the food for the wedding of Claudius and Gertrude. Certainly gives weight to Hamlet's later line, "the funeral baked meats did coldly furnish forth the marriage table."

Tom's blocked the scene so that my character is to enter from stage left, arm in arm with Ophelia. I walk over to take my entrance position, and then Portia joins me there and takes hold of my sleeve. Her touch is stimulating and irritating all at once. We do this entrance movement several times, with Tom tweaking various characters' positions until he is satisfied with how the final stage picture looks. The more we repeat the blocking, the closer and tighter Portia clings until I think I might pass out from the anxiety of what I have to say to her.

Ira yells for a ten-minute break. I decide to seize the moment, yanking Portia's arm and pulling her away from the others.

"I have to talk with you."

"What's the matter? You're hurting me."

"I have to tell you…" I start, but the words suddenly stick in my throat.

"Tell me what?" she moans, looking terrified and confused.

"Do you believe in God?" I ask as a drop of sweat burns my eye causing me to blink rapidly like a crazy man.

"Yes."

"Do you believe God can speak to us?"

"Yes," she repeats, looking more and more worried for my sanity.

"Good!" I tighten my grip a little. I'm going for it. No turning back now. "He spoke to me. I wish that he didn't, but he did. And now I have to tell you something that is going to sound terrible, but I need you to keep in mind it's from God, not me. Do you understand?"

"I think you should let go of me," Portia says, approaching a full-out panic.

"God said that we have to—" I stop myself. I'm in trouble here. I'm trying to be tough and straightforward, but my Dirty Harry side works much better in my late-night fantasies than in actual practice.

I hold her tighter, trying to figure out the right words.

"You're hurting me. Please let go, Harold," she says.

"God said that our child will save the world from annihilation!" I finally blurt out in one breath.

"What are you talking about?" she whispers slowly, almost one word at a time.

Helpless and embarrassed, I somehow manage to continue. "God said that we have to be intimate within the next two weeks or else the planet and all of mankind will be doomed!"

Portia yanks herself away and takes a step back. She pauses for a moment, stunned. I see the tears well up in her eyes, and then she turns and runs away from me.

It is at this point I remember we aren't the only two people in the hall and suddenly realize that everyone is shooting daggers in my direction. I must have yelled that last plea to Portia at an Ira-calling-for-attention volume. I'm suddenly rendered into idiocy, unable to speak. I can only wag my fool head from side to side and shrug my shoulders like the village idiot.

After what seems like an eternity, Tom walks over to me. With a bemused but bewildered look on his face, he studies me curiously for a moment before he speaks. "What the hell happened, man?"

I still can't put together anything to say. I just stand there slapping my arms against my sides like a seal at Sea World.

"It's not a stroke or something like that, is it? Tom asks, with an inflection that indicates he'd prefer this as long as it meant he would have a logical explanation for what just happened.

"It's…hard to explain," I finally manage.

His face shifts to a harder, more determined expression. "Why don't you go home, Harold. I think that might be the best thing right now."

"Yes," I say.

I hang my head as I gather up my water bottle and keys and script. The room is totally silent. I don't look, but I can feel them all watching me.

"Will somebody write down my blocking for me?" I ask Tom on my way to the door.

"Sure, don't worry about that," he answers, now looking at me like I'm a dangerous stranger with a bomb tied to my back. "You okay to drive?"

His concern for my safety almost makes me feel normal again. What a guy. "I'm really sorry about all this," I say and then begin to slink away.

When I get to the door, I turn back to offer an apology to the company. The way they're staring at me, the shock and disgust and, worst of all, the disillusionment on all those young faces. I am again left completely speechless.

———

On the foggy drive home, I pound on the steering wheel while shouting at God. "Why don't you strike me dead now and get it over with? You've ruined me! Please, just leave me the hell alone!" Then I beat the shit out of the passenger seat.

I get home and storm into the bedroom, where my wife is sleeping. I get into bed and shake her by the shoulder.

"What's wrong?" she asks, groggy and yet very startled. "What happened?"

"We have to talk," I say. "I've been going through a very hard time and I need to grab onto something here. I'm scared and I'm sorry about things that we haven't said to each other."

"I'm sorry, too," she says. "I'm here for you. I love you."

This feels like the greatest thing in the world. I can't remember the last time I heard anyone tell me they loved me, Kelly included.

"I love you, too," I reply, leaning in to kiss her. I consider telling her everything from my conversation with the burning dresser to my humiliating display at rehearsal this evening. But her kiss lingers, and suddenly she is kissing me harder, wrapping her hands around my back and pulling my body close to hers. The next thing I know, clothes are being torn off. Like we're horny teenagers in the back seat of a car. It's been such a long time since we've been intimate, and her body some-how feels familiar and new all at once. We're at the age now where sex requires pausing every once in a while to allow for back spasms and knee pops, but in spite of these limitations, it's just as satisfying as when we were both young and discovering each other's bodies for the first time. In some ways, it's better. I'm getting an opportunity to make love to the woman who first stole my heart as well as to the woman who has faithfully put up with me for the past thirty years.

When we are finished, she rests her head on my chest and places her hand directly over my heart. I wrap my arms around her.

We sleep like this the entire night.

———

She tries kissing me on the head before leaving in the morning. This time I don't pretend to be asleep. Instead, I move my head up so that I can kiss her back.

After she leaves, a dream I had during the night comes back to me: I'm walking into the living room of the house Kelly and I had before this one. All the cats I've ever owned are in the living room foyer being attacked by hundreds of snakes. They're being bitten over and over again. I run to get a broom and start sweeping the cats and snakes out the front door. I watch through the stained glass inset in the door as my cats writhe in agony and the snakes slither away into the bushes.

Squeak starts howling at me from the foot of my bed.

CHAPTER SEVEN

LOSE THE NAME
OF ACTION

I'm sitting at the dining room table drinking coffee, cup after cup, trying to relax. I'm a mess, mortified by my humiliating encounter with Portia, yet thrilled with what I was able to share with my wife afterward. God's plan to save mankind and my future with the Shakespeare Company are both in serious jeopardy. I look up at the ceiling and put my hands together, because that's how I've always seen it done, and try to make up with God.

"God, can you hear me? It's Harold Goldfarb. I could use a little input here. I'm assuming you know what happened last night, so I won't dredge all that up again, and I'm sorry if I might have said some stuff to you that I shouldn't have, but this is not going well. I think you picked the wrong guy. I'm wide open if you have any suggestions—or a replacement. In, um, your name I pray, amen."

I wait for a few minutes in silence. I'm sure God is a busy man. I think about getting something to eat while waiting but then decide it might be disrespectful, and I'm probably in enough trouble already. So I sit, staring at the ceiling, twiddling my thumbs, and then the voice that visits from time to time begins to whisper in my head. The voice has a Kentucky gentleman's accent. He visits mostly when I'm under stress and feeling indecisive. Sometimes the voice urges me to do something stupid and self-destructive. Other times he just berates me. I'm not sure why it's a southern accent. Maybe it's from when I was doing a civil war version of *A Midsummer Night's Dream* in Tennessee and got one of the worst reviews of my life—"Goldfarb is stiff and awkward and obnoxiously over the top. His accent is more South Jersey than Deep South, and every time he comes on stage, the audience would collectively cringe" or words to that effect. Maybe the voice is a remnant from that.

Well, bless your heart. Just look at ya'. Crazy as a Union soldier with chlamydia! You don't even know what's going on here, do ya', son? Your brain is as slow as molasses, and you've got the courage of a draft dodger hidin' in women's clothing. We're gonna eat you alive, boy, and I cannot wait to see the look on your face.

He starts laughing, the low chuckle of someone who has smoked cigars since childhood. I shake my head to clear the sound of his voice. That usually works. Note to self: check WebMD about hearing degrading voices.

The phone rings. I run to get it.

"Hello, God?"

"No, Harold, it's Tom."

"Sorry. I was expecting somebody else."

"Listen, Harold, we have a problem."

"Yeah," I say sadly. "I thought that we might."

"I spoke with the board, and I think for both you and the company it might be best if you didn't do the summer this year." His voice hangs in the air for a moment as I let the words deflate me. "Harold? Did you hear me?"

"Yes," I say barely able to find the breath and get the words out of my mouth.

"I'm sorry, Harold," Tom says sounding not very sorry at all. "But because you're a board member, we might have a lawsuit here, and with the sexual harassment laws in this state, we really don't have a choice. Oh, and just so you know. Portia is from a family of lawyers."

"Do you think they'll defend me?" I ask.

"Defend you?" Tom's voice protests. "I think they're going to crucify you. What are you talking about?"

The voice chuckles in my head.

"Oh," I say. "I thought maybe—I don't know what I thought."

"Because we fired you, the company may be off the hook," Tom continues. "But that doesn't mean you are. Portia's father is really pissed off, Harold. You better lawyer up."

His words feel like a punch to the gut. This whole thing might actually go to court? How will I be able to convince a lawyer to even take my case? What's my defense? "I was only trying to implement God's will, so come on you guys, give me a break?" And poor Portia! What must she be going through now? Enough to make her want to get the justice system involved, apparently.

"But I didn't really do anything to her!" I suddenly blurt out. "Sexually, I mean. Did I?"

Tom exhales before speaking, then answers me as if he is explaining a very simple concept to a dim-witted child. "All it takes is a sexual suggestion. All you have to do is make her feel uncomfortable. And that's exactly what you did. There might be an assault charge involved here, too."

My heart does something weird in my chest, and I have to take a deep breath to get things moving again. "Assault?"

"Harold, I don't know what's going on with you, but get some help, man."

I wish I could explain everything to him. I wish I could start at the beginning and lay out every single detail, and even, perhaps, ask for his advice. But I know it will only make matters worse. So instead I just say, "I'm sorry."

"I'm sorry, too, Harold. Goodbye."

"Tom?"

He hangs up before I can say anything else. Then the voice chimes in again with another piece of advice.

Why don't you dive off a sharp cliff, Harold? Do everybody a favor.

I walk into my office instead. The desire to get away is so strong that if I resist it, I feel I'll truly go mad. I write a letter to my wife explaining as much as I can. I tell her I have to get away for a while to clear my head. I go to the backyard and pick a rose from one of Kelly's bushes. I leave the rose and the letter on the dining room table. With a heavy heart, I throw some things into a bag, say goodbye to Squeak, get my keys, and walk out the door. I have to come back again, though, to make sure that the back door is locked. And that I didn't leave any lights on. And I also forgot my sunglasses. And my wallet. I hope Kelly will understand what I need to do, even though I'm not so sure myself. Hopefully, the man who returns to her will be a better man than the one who left.

Sorry, God, wherever you are, but I'm outa here.

CHAPTER EIGHT

THOUGH THIS BE MADNESS,
YET THERE IS METHOD IN'T

After being fired, deserting a loving wife, failing a famously vengeful God, and setting oneself up for prison time, one should have a good breakfast, don't you think? I decide to stop off at the little coffee shop at the Roosevelt Golf Course in Griffith Park. They make a nice breakfast at a very reasonable price.

From there, my plan is to head north. That's where my California adventure began many years ago, and I think that by retracing my steps, I might find the better version of myself that I've misplaced up there. Maybe if I can rediscover the person I used to be, I might be able to better handle what's happening to me now.

I park the Prius (it turns off after the third try) and take my suitcase with me as I walk toward the coffee shop. I just don't trust the Prius to be alone with my valuables.

There is a corrugated metal awning and some picnic tables between the coffee shop and the starter's building, where golfers check in to get a tee time. When I arrive, I come upon a scene unfortunately not uncommon in Los Angeles these days. A homeless woman has staked out the picnic table closest to the water fountain. She has all of her stuff laid out on the table: plastic bags, dirty-looking towels and clothes, and plastic water bottles that she's filling at the fountain and then packing into her sacks. She is very thin and wiry. Her skin is dark and wrinkled from the sun, making it impossible to guess her age or nationality. Despite the 90-degree weather at 10 a.m., she wears a filthy ski hat, a bulky sweater, and nasty-looking sweat pants covered in dirt, bodily fluids, and God knows what else. There are a few older Korean men there with their heads buried in Korean newspapers, trying to pretend that she doesn't exist. As I start past her with my suitcase, she surprises me with a friendly smile. I stop for a moment. She mumbles something to me. It's either a language I don't understand or just the incomprehensible gibbering of a crazy person. Much like the Koreans, I decide to ignore her and head into the coffee shop.

There are just two other customers inside, an older couple who ignore each other as they slowly eat their eggs. I take a booth by the window, where I can watch the goings-on of the homeless woman. She moves quickly through her routine of packing and unpacking her bags with the water bottles she has already filled from the fountain. When she comes across a bottle that doesn't fit properly, she takes it out, places it back on the table, puts her hands on her hips, and argues with someone unseen about what to do next. Then she gets to work again, moving stuff more and more violently from one bag to another.

One of the Korean men looks up from his newspaper. Another one gets up and moves to another table farther away from where she's conducting business.

Here inside, the waitress has made her way over to me. She is a nice Armenian lady who has been working at the coffee shop ever since I first started coming more than a decade ago. I think she's actually the owner now but still works as a waitress since it's such a small operation.

"How are you, my friend?" She greets me with a wide grin. "Good to see you," she says as she puts a menu on the table for me.

"Hi." I hand the menu back to her. "I think I know what I want. Can you make me that egg sandwich with the ham and the lettuce and tomato?"

"Sure." She nods. "Do you want fries with that?"

"Do you have the fruit today?"

"Sure, it's even fresh." She winks. "Coffee?"

"How about some orange juice?" Since I knocked back an entire pot back at the house, I figure that was enough coffee for one day.

"No problem, my friend," she says with a warm smile but then notices the woman outside leaning into the fountain and filling up another water bottle.

"Oh no, not again!" she cries, storming out to confront the woman, the menu still in her hand.

I am not able to make out their conversation from inside, but I can tell by the way the owner is gesturing and waving the menu at her that she's telling the homeless woman to leave. She finally gives up and stomps back inside and gets on her cell phone.

Outside, the homeless woman has begun throwing stuff, sneering and growling like a cornered animal. The old Korean men reading their newspapers remain unfazed, but I'm getting concerned about how bad this is going to get. The starter, built like a marine sergeant, bursts out of the building on the other side of the courtyard and tries his method of getting her to leave: he screams at her at full volume. Him, I can hear from inside, loud and clear.

"Get out of here! Do you want me to call the police? Go on! Get!" He sounds like he's yelling at a stray cat to get out of his yard. The homeless woman stands her ground, though. She doesn't leave; she just starts throwing more stuff around and growling even louder than before. The starter finally gives up and heads back to his station.

"Ketchup or mayonnaise on your sandwich?" The owner is at my table again.

I jump when she speaks, being startled away from the scene outside.

"Can I get a little mayonnaise on the side?" I ask as I turn my attention back inside and take a sip of the orange juice she has just handed me.

"Of course," she says.

"Does she come here a lot?" I ask, gesturing toward the patio.

"Yeah, it's not good," she answers. "She's not right in the head." The owner furrows her brow and watches the homeless woman as she starts picking up some of the belongings she's thrown about. Abruptly, the owner shrugs her shoulders and turns back to me. "It's sad, but what can you do?"

"What will happen to her?"

"The starter will call the park police, and they'll come and take her. But they can just hold her for twenty-four hours, and then she'll come back."

As she's explaining this, the cook comes from the back of the kitchen and makes his way toward my table as well. He's a friendly-looking Mexican with a terrific mustache. By now the older couple across the room are also invested in the situation going on outside, nodding sadly at everything that's being said.

"We feel bad," says the cook. "We give her food and some soda sometimes. Poor lady." He shakes his head and frowns, as do the rest of us. "It's not right. There's no place for these people, so what are they supposed to do? She's sick in the head."

"We can't have her here, though," says the owner. "Last time she took off all her clothes and used the drinking fountain for a shower. That's not very appetizing for our customers."

"No, that's not good," I agree.

By now, the homeless woman is stark-raving mad and probably getting ready for a water fountain shower, I imagine. Does she know that the police are coming for her? That they'll take her away? Is that part of her plan? To get a cell with air conditioning for twenty-four hours so at least she can deal with her demons in a reasonable temperature?

The park police come. The homeless woman doesn't put up much of a fight. She gathers up her stuff, and they escort her to their nice police minivan and take her away.

I get my food and eat it, but I'm not really tasting very much. I can't stop thinking about the look the homeless woman gave me when I first arrived; that little smile and whatever it was that she had mumbled to me. Like she knew me. Like we were connected.

There but for the grace of God go I.

CHAPTER NINE

TO THINE OWN
SELF BE TRUE

As I walk back to the Prius, I feel a great loneliness, as if I'm disconnecting from the world and there is no turning back. Does the homeless lady feel that, too? Or does she function in a reality so far removed from the norm that no one can reach her ever again? Is that where I'm heading now, too? Is that why she smiled? Is that what she recognized in me? Will I be showering in water fountains and quoting Shakespeare to imagined audiences? Will I be, like Hamlet, driven to madness by an unreasonable request from a questionable source and then proceed to destroy the lives of everyone I've ever loved?

I torture myself with these questions while trying, unsuccessfully, to get the car door to open. That's another thing about the Prius. The car comes with a remote key, and when you touch the door handle the car doors are supposed to unlock on their own. Maybe I put off a weird electrical energy or something, but the doors often refuse to unlock for me.

I'm slapping and squeezing the door handle, torturing myself with unanswerable questions and devolving into my usual mumblings and profanities when I become distracted from this latest exasperation by the faint sound of ethereal music playing in the distance, somewhere deep in the park. The car doors suddenly unlock without any groping or cursing on my part. I throw my suitcase in the back seat, get in the car, and push the start button. The Prius miraculously starts up on the first try. I pull out of the parking lot with the windows rolled down and attempt to follow the music, which I'm not entirely sure is real or only in my head.

I drive slowly with one hand on the wheel and my head out the window like a golden retriever on a joy ride. The music grows louder. I come around a bend in the road. There, in an open grassy area, people stand in a circle holding hands. Maybe thirty of them. The music is coming from a portable sound system. Now that I can hear it more clearly, it sounds less ethereal and more like something from a B movie soundtrack. Like when somebody dies at the end of the film, and their soul floats up to heaven.

I get out of the car and move a little closer. There are men and women from different cultures and nationalities, all well dressed, all with heads reverently bowed. Children are playing and running around the outside of the circle, but that doesn't distract the adults from their communion. They all sway from side to side in unison, seemingly connected to one another as well as to something beyond.

As I get nearer, I can hear some chanting and others offering up some hallelujahs. I wonder if the God who set my dresser on fire is the same God they're in touch with now. I move in even closer and begin to feel it, the energy that is pulsating in that circle. I've never felt anything like it—pure electricity. I'm within fifty feet of the circle when the hairs start to stand up on my arms and the back of my neck. How amazing it is that people can come together like this and be rewarded for their courage and faith with this kind of peace and connectedness. How beautiful for them to be able, in turn, to send that energy out into the world. Even though the whole thing seems cultish and strange, I envy them. And despite my sarcastic and judgmental nature, I want to be a part of it.

As if on cue, three of the members within the circle simultaneously turn to face me. The chain of clasped hands is broken and a space is provided for me to join them. They all smile and wave me in. I feel my body being drawn to them, but something prevents me: a resistance, like being stuck in mud up to my knee caps. I can't move forward; I can only move back. This results in me feeling like I'm going to fall, so I take a step backward before I lose my balance. The instant I do, the three people turn their attention back inside the circle, and the opening they've made for me is gone.

"I wanted to!" I shout, my voice drowned out by the music and chanting. "I really did!"

But they're all back in a trance as if I had never happened along. I see some other people approaching the circle from different parts of the park. Maybe they will be worthier than I.

I get in the car, wondering how much more abuse I can possibly take. It's like auditioning for a part in a tiny fifty-seat theater for no pay and not even getting a callback. I'm fully expecting the Prius to add a little more to the pile. But instead it starts right up.

I look at them one last time through my rearview mirror when the voice in my head offers another suggestion.

Too bad, son. But, you're just not good enough. Not even for those voodoo hee-haw characters. Just get it over with already. You know that you want to.

I crank up the air and get myself the hell out of there.

CHAPTER TEN

THOU CANST NOT THEN
BE FALSE TO ANY MAN

"God? What was that all about? That might have been a very meaningful experience. Why did you stop me? Maybe I would have found a little contentment with them. Did you ever think about that? I am capable of making up my own mind, you know. And with all due respect—*free will my ass!*"

I'm ranting like a madman again, and my thoughts are running around my head like a broken record. An hour before, I was positive about heading north, and now here I am befuddled and bewildered yet again.

I should find out where Portia lives and force myself on her in the middle of the night and be done with it. I'll probably spend the rest of my life in jail, but at least I'll have the satisfaction of knowing that I did God's work. Maybe he'd appreciate it enough to shoot me a winning lotto ticket or at least just leave me the hell alone for a while. But seriously, how could I force myself on that poor kid? It's ridiculous. I could never do a thing like that...could I? Besides, I don't think I could perform physically under that kind of pressure anyway, so, forget all that Dirty Harry crap. And come to think of it, maybe this whole running off to Northern California thing isn't such a great idea either. What if I get up there and find out that I was the same schmuck then as I am today? That'll really send me over the edge. Somebody hit me with a brick.

I start to wonder why the voice hasn't shown up yet to add a little more self-destructive noise to my overactive brain.

I'm sitting back here just watching the show, son. You're doin' just fine without me.

Ah. There he is. Son of a bitch.

I need to talk to somebody real and human. Someone who isn't God or that Colonel Sanders guy in my head. Somebody who won't think I'm crazy and call the park police.

I need to talk to Jerry.

I've known Jerry since we were in Hebrew school together. He's my oldest friend in the world and the only guy I know who's had weirder shit happen to him than even I have. Jerry will listen. He won't jump to conclusions about my mental state, and he'll give me some advice that I desperately need. So I go to see Jerry and hope that maybe we can get a lunch in before a horde of Mormon lawyers descends from the salt lands.

I drive to North Hollywood in surprisingly light traffic, park the Prius across from Jerry's apartment building, and sit for a minute, trying to compose myself before I head inside. Good old Jerry. We began our show business careers together, back when we were young and full of hope. We had a comedy and music act. We'd get on a bus from New Jersey and ride into New York City and start knocking on bar doors, visiting nightclubs, and going anywhere else people might gather for a good time, and we'd try to get ourselves hired. We were fearless then. We eventually did get some gigs—the Village Gate, the Bitter End, and the Catskills. Yup, I'm that old.

Jerry and I eventually went our different ways. I got more into acting, and Jerry became a very good stand-up comic. We've always stayed in touch even though we don't see each other so often anymore. Girlfriends came and went, until I eventually settled down with Kelly. Weight was gained and lost and gained again. Drugs and alcohol were consumed and abused. Jerry got into some trouble back when we were younger, but he joined Alcoholics Anonymous and really cleaned up his act. He's been clean and sober for over twenty-five years now. He is a talented, funny man, and I love him like a brother.

Aside from the showbiz stuff, there are other interests that Jerry and I share. There were some pretty weird things going on in New Jersey when we were growing up. Some UFO stuff and some supernatural things that bonded us in sort of a brotherhood of the weird.

I call Jerry's landline on my cell to let him know I'm parked outside.

"Hello?" He answers like I'm the landlord calling about past due rent.

"Hey, Mr. Geeg, it's me."

I call Jerry Mr. Geeg, and he calls me Mr. Geeg. I don't remember when or how that got started, but it's a tradition that spans decades and will likely carry on until one or both of us are dead.

"Hello, Mr. Geeg! he says. "What time is it?"

"About eleven thirty," I say reading the clock on the dashboard that I haven't changed for two time changes now. If you're patient enough, all things have a way of coming back around.

"A.m. or p.m.?" he asks.

"I'm outside the building, can I come in?"

"I'm still in bed. You're outside the building?"

"Listen, man, I need to talk. I'll buy you breakfast."

He yawns. "Oh, okay, Mr. Geeg. Give me two seconds."

We hang up. I cover my suitcase with some loose newspapers in the back seat to deter any potential thieves. I get out of the car. It takes me three attempts to get the Prius to finally lock, then I walk across the street to his building. The gardeners arrived only moments before me; they're cranking up their obnoxiously loud mowers and blowers just as I head toward them. Crap is flying everywhere. I make my way past them to the security gate, guarding my eyes and face from the debris. Jerry lives in one of those two-story, single-bedroom apartment buildings. He has a studio on the first floor. I ring his apartment on the gate intercom.

"Who is it?" He answers, sounding like a ninety-year-old Jewish grandmother.

"It's me, who else would come visit you?" I say, sounding like a ninety-year-old Jewish grandmother's ninety-five-year-old boyfriend.

He rings me in. I walk through the narrow courtyard toward his apartment, passing a fountain and two propane barbecue grills. A pigeon sitting on one of the barbecues coos at me, reminding me of a routine Jerry and I used to do. Jerry does a great pigeon impersonation.

I get to his apartment and the door is already ajar.

"Come in," says the ninety-year-old Jewish grandmother.

Jerry is sitting at his desk looking as if he did, indeed, just get out of bed. He's wearing a big T-shirt and a pair of boxer shorts, his greasy hair pointing in several different directions. Jerry is large, and the apartment is small. There is always a clutter of junk, books, and magazines, and everything smells like cigars.

"Sit down, Mr. Geeg!" He motions to the leather easy chair across the room from him. "What's going on?"

"Mr. Geeg…I need some help." I drop into the chair. "There's been some pretty strange shit happening in my world."

"More than usual?" He smirks.

"I got fired from the Shakespeare festival."

"Fired, they can't fire you, can they? You're the main guy over there!"

"They can and they did. But that's nothing compared to the rest of it."

"Wait a minute." Jerry gets up, pulls back the curtains, lifts open the window, and yells out to the gardeners. "Will you shut the fuck up out there! I can't hear myself think for Christ's sake!" Jerry slams down the window, pulls the curtains closed again, and goes back to his chair at the desk, picking up our conversation as if his outburst had never happened. "Go ahead. Do you want some coffee?"

"No, let me just—"

"Maybe we'll get something after this, if you want. I should take a shower, though. Do you think I should take a shower first?" He tucks his head to his armpit and sniffs.

"I don't know, Mr. Geeg."

"I should," he says, pulling his head up and wrinkling his nose. "Sorry, go ahead."

I begin to launch into my story just as Jerry grabs a bottle of vitamins from the shelf above his computer desk and shakes it. "I gotta get some more of these. Maybe when we go out, we'll stop at the store."

I am sure I look like I want to kill him. He grimaces, trying to get a grip on his compulsiveness long enough for me to get through my story. He puts the bottle of vitamins back on the shelf.

"I'm worried about you, is what it is," he explains and then tries his best to give me his full attention.

I take a deep breath and tell my tale, all the God stuff and the signs I've seen, the giant bird-monster and the homeless lady and the circle of praying people in the park. I tell him what has happened with my wife, what happened with Portia at rehearsal, and my confusion about what I should do next.

"So, do you think I'm crazy?" I ask when I'm finally finished.

"I know you're crazy," Jerry says. "But that doesn't mean that I don't believe you."

"Thanks, man." I am relieved by this.

"Remember that time when I saw that thing in the woods by the Hollywood Sign?" he asks.

"Yeah, I remember." He had sworn on his mother's life that he came across a part-bear, part-badger monster one day on a hike up in the hills. This was ages ago.

"October 1982, 11 a.m." Jerry has an uncanny memory for dates and times. "I mean, I was very stoned, but I wasn't alone, remember? I had a witness."

"James Burton. Of course," I say. The characters are all well-known and now the stuff of urban legend—even if it's just between Geegs.

"Right." Jerry gets a dreamy look as he recounts the memory. "We hiked up there and got stoned, and then we sat down in that nice piney area and there was a cool breeze coming through the trees, and then we heard all the crashing up on the hill."

"Didn't you call the zoo later to see if anything escaped?" I ask him. But of course I already know the answer.

"Yeah," he says but doesn't elaborate on that particular detail. "That thing, it scared the hell out of me. It was ripping up trees and throwing stuff into the air, and it was coming right at us. We got out of there so fast…I never knew I could run like that. I'll never forget any of it." Jerry shakes his head at the memory.

"Weren't you doing mushrooms, too?" I ask, knowing full well he was.

"Pot and mushrooms."

"Breakfast of champions," I say.

"But it happened," he continues. "James and I both saw the same thing. And I thought that when I told you, you wouldn't believe me. That you'd think I was hallucinating and just tell me to go sleep it off. But you didn't."

"I could tell that something happened," I say. Which is true. There was something about the way he told the story back in 1982 that made me know it wasn't something he was making up.

"Just like I can tell now that something happened to you." Jerry gives me a reassuring smile, knowing himself how good it feels to know someone believes you. No matter how weird. No matter what.

Hallelujah. I am not alone in this whole mess.

"So, what do you think I should do?" I ask.

He takes a half-smoked cigar from the ashtray and fires it up.

"I think you should call that girl and apologize. Tell her that you just wanted to make sure that she's all right. Tell her you had a death in the family or your dog's gone missing. Tell her anything, but you need to smooth that shit over with her and her father, and then you should go talk to a lawyer."

"She probably won't talk to me, though."

"Leave a message so there's a record, even better." He puffs on the cigar.

"Do you think I should leave town?" I ask half hoping he'll talk me into staying.

"I think you probably should." He blows out several perfect smoke rings.

"But what about God's deadline?"

He considers. "The deadline is just unreasonable. Let God try it again next month with somebody else. He's God, I'm sure he's got options."

"But what if there is no option. It's either me, now, or else…the end."

He rests the cigar on an ashtray and leans forward, looking me earnestly in the eye. "Let this all air out for a minute and catch your breath. You need some time to sort it out, that's all. Something told you to go north, and that's what you need to do."

I nod. I knew he'd give me what I needed.

"But stay in touch with Kelly," he continues. "Not on the cell phone; they trace that shit. Use a pay phone or get a burner. You don't want to lose her or you'll wind up like me when you grow up." With this, he leans back in the chair, a small frown on his face.

"Do you think they'll come after me?" I ask.

"You know what?" He picks up the cigar again and gestures with it while he's talking. "Forget talking to a lawyer. You don't even know if anything you did is a crime. You just said some crazy shit because your dog died and then you went on a vacation." He takes a long drag, proud of his reasoning.

"And then if something happens, I just say, 'Oh, I'm sorry, I didn't know there was a problem, officer?'"

"Exactly," Jerry says. "And then you come back and whatever it is, it is." He nods his head several times as if in agreement with himself. "You should do that, I think."

He's right. I could just play dumb. I've done it many times before, on stage and off. It's good advice, but I can't help thinking that God is not going to like this plan very much.

Jerry puffs on his cigar for a moment and then cryptically adds, "There's something else going on here, Mr. Geeg. Something we're not seeing yet."

"I'm getting the same thing," I agree.

"I'm a little jealous, to tell you the truth," he says. "This should have happened to me. I could have used something like this." He puts down his cigar and places his hand on his stomach. His eyes grow large and then he burps.

"I'd gladly switch places," I offer.

"Next time you talk to God, bring up my name." Jerry stands. "How old did you say this girl was?"

"I don't know. Twenty-three, maybe?"

"Jesus." He motions for me to get up and gives me a short hug. "I'm a little nauseous, excuse me. I shouldn't smoke so much on an empty stomach." He lumbers toward the bathroom, stopping along the way to pick a piece of lint from the carpet.

Jerry is compulsive about lint. He lives in a chaotic mess of an apartment, but there is something about lint on the floor. He has to pick it up. Ever since he was a kid he's done that. Lint on the floor. Lint on somebody's shirt sleeve, lint in a stranger's hair. He is obsessive compulsive about lint. He enters the bathroom and closes the door behind him. And like that, I am alone in his smoke-filled apartment starting to feel a little nauseated myself.

"Close the door on your way out!" he cries from the bathroom.

I walk over to the bathroom door. "Are you all right?"

He doesn't answer me. I knock a couple of times. "Would you call Kelly for me? Because you don't think I should use my phone, right? Tell her I'll be in touch soon...Okay Mr. Geeg?"

Still he doesn't answer, so I leave, closing the front door behind me.

CHAPTER ELEVEN

BE THOU FAMILIAR,
BUT BY NO MEANS VULGAR

I get to the Prius and find the door unlocked. Either I didn't lock it when I arrived, or the car unlocked itself when I was visiting with Jerry. I want to punch the Prius, but I don't. I'm afraid of how the car might retaliate.

I get inside and check the glove compartment. I keep a cast list in there in case I run into trouble on the freeway. Portia's number is on the list. I stare at it for a while. Jerry was right. I should call and at least try to smooth things over. Even though, in this moment, I can come up with a thousand reasons why I shouldn't.

Portia has two numbers listed, her home and her cell. Nobody answers their landlines anymore because of all the phone solicitors, so I figure I'll call there so I can leave a groveling apology on her voice mail rather than actually speak to her.

As her phone rings, I prepare my plea for forgiveness. She surprises me when she picks up.

"Hello?" She answers in an alarmingly fragile voice.

"Portia?" There is a silence, so I continue. "I just wanted to say I'm sorry. I've been under a lot of stress lately and I didn't mean to scare you and I feel terrible about that."

Nothing comes back from her, so I keep on groveling.

"Portia, I've been having very bad nightmares, and I don't know what I was thinking. I mean, I really thought that I had to, that we had to—I mean, I like you very much but not in an improper way. In a healthy way. Portia? Are you there?"

She is still silent.

I can tell from the timer on my cell that the call is still connected, so I continue once more. "They fired me, so I won't be around anymore. I hope you stay with the show. I know that you'll be great in it. Anyway, I won't bother you again."

I stop again, hoping that she'll speak up and say she understands and that she forgives me. She doesn't, so I try to wrap things up.

"What I said and did was wrong, and I'm very sorry." I'm about to disconnect when she finally answers.

"I can't talk about this now," she says.

I hear a male voice in the background. "Disconnect the call, Portia."

"Please don't call me anymore," she says. And then she hangs up.

I feel about sixteen years old and stunningly inept. I assume that the other voice I heard was her father's. He probably just arrived from Utah with a gaggle of Mormon lawyers who are excitedly plotting my doom. I'm pretty sure that I'm royally and eternally screwed.

Suddenly, I'm exhausted. Like I've been drugged. The plan is still the same—I am going to leave town and head north.

But first, I need a nap.

CHAPTER TWELVE

GOD HATH GIVEN YOU ONE FACE,
AND YOU MAKE YOURSELF ANOTHER

I head all the way back to Glendale and drive to Brand Park. By now it's early afternoon. I find a shady spot under a giant pine tree and park the Prius. I can barely keep my eyes open. I actually fell asleep for a second at a traffic light on my way here—that's how tired I am.

I roll all the windows down to get some circulation and then push the button to turn off the car. The Prius cooperates. I search around for the lever that reclines the driver seat and find instead a cast list from last year's festival under the seat. I played Shylock that year. It was one of my better performances, and I didn't assault a single ingénue.

I finally find the lever and put the seat back. It reclines all the way down, just like my La-Z-Boy at home. I have a momentary kind thought about the Prius. The next moment I'm fast asleep.

A loud boom startles me back from a sound sleep. I search around again for the seat control, this time finding a piece of Good and Plenty candy. I think about eating it but throw it out the window instead. I get the driver seat back up to its original position. Another boom. A giant pine cone rolls off the roof on the driver's side and drops into the road with a heavy thud. I put my head out the window to take a look. It's the biggest pine cone I've ever seen. It occurs to me that another missile might be following the last, so I quickly return all body parts to the safety of the vehicle. A squirrel is sitting on the hood of the car, looking through the window at me. He flicks his tail and then jumps off, running after a friend of his, both of them chattering like crazy as they chase each other up a tree.

That's when I hear the screaming.

"No! Stop it! *Help!*"

Close to where I'm parked, a man has just made a grab for a young woman's purse. She is hanging on for dear life, refusing to let go. It's a violent tug of war. The man keeps yanking the strap of the purse harder and harder. The woman falls to the ground, still clinging to her bag.

"Somebody help me, please!"

It looks like he'll rip her arm off, but she won't let go.

I get out of the car and pick up the two giant pine cones, then rush over to where the confrontation continues to escalate. I don't think he sees me coming. She does, though. I hit him on the back of the head with one of the pine cones. He stops, lets go of her bag, and turns to face me with a shocked expression on his face. He is big, about the same size as Richard Ramirez, the good-looking kid who's playing Laertes at the Shakespeare festival. In spite of his size, I'm feeling surprisingly unafraid.

"Get out of my park!" I shout at him. I don't know when I decided this was my park, but I don't hesitate to do what's necessary to get him to leave. I throw a hard pine cone jab and hit him square on the nose. He stumbles backward, blood gushing down his face. I take a menacing step toward him, and he runs away, probably more confused than frightened. I go immediately to the aid of the young woman.

"Are you okay?" I ask and kneel down beside her.

"Yes, I think so. Thank you so much." She begins crying, her small body shaking like a leaf. "I had just been to the bank, and I'm on my lunch hour and…" She can't finish the sentence.

I guesstimate that she's in her late twenties or early thirties. She has a sweet face underneath the lines of melting mascara.

"Do you want me to drive you home? Do you want to go to the police?"

"No, my car is here, I'll be fine."

She lets me help her to her feet.

"How can I ever thank you?"

"You don't have to thank me. I should be thanking you." I'm starting to get a little emotional myself all of a sudden.

She tilts her head to the side and looks at me perplexed. "Why should you thank me?"

"Uh…" I can't explain it to her. "I'm just glad I could help, that's all."

I escort her back to her car. She has a Prius. Poor kid. We shake hands, then she leans forward and kisses the top of my hand that she was shaking. It's like somebody hit me on the head with a pine cone, but in a good way.

"Thank you again," she says. "We need more people like you in this world."

I smile and move away so that she can pull out of her parking spot. I watch her drive down the hill, and I'm suddenly thinking about my father.

A long time ago, just after my parents had retired and moved to Florida, I had gone to visit them. They were at the pool in their apartment complex with some friends. There was a discussion about how tough you had to be to make it in the world. My father and I were standing by the pool. He was still in very good shape in those days. I never could beat him at tennis, even when he was in his seventies. So, my father whispered to me semiprivately, "Are you tough enough, Harold?"

"I'm pretty tough," I say.

"Yeah? I don't think so."

I was naturally hurt by this, but I let it go. He wasn't going to, though.

"Why don't you push me into the water? Just throw me in the pool and show me how tough you are."

By now he was speaking loud enough for everyone to hear. He started taking off his watch and rolling up his sleeves. I didn't understand. Was he challenging me or trying to teach me something? He had never done anything like this before.

"I don't want to push you in the water," I say.

"Go ahead, Harold, I dare you." He got right up in my face, nose to nose. His chest puffed out like a rooster's.

All other conversation around the pool had stopped, and everybody was watching, waiting to see what would happen next. I was confused. Maybe this was something he was doing because I was an actor and not a doctor or a lawyer or a factory foreman like he was. Maybe he needed me to prove something to him, that I wasn't a wimp and that I'd be okay in the world.

"I can't do it. I don't want to," I finally answered, feeling the judgmental stares of his friends decimating my self-esteem.

He picked up his watch and started tightening it around his wrist again.

"I didn't think so," my father said.

I pick up my pine cones and shake them toward the sky.

"Did you see that, Dad? How was that? Tough enough for you?"

I head back to the Prius, pine cones in hand. I sit in the car for a moment, taking in what just happened. Crows begin making weird chattering noises in the pine trees above me, and a breeze abruptly comes through the park, causing everything to whisper and sing. I feel content. For the first time since all this started happening.

I start the car, rested, rejuvenated, and ready to drive north.

At the park entrance I see a big hole in the ground with a cardboard tube inserted into it. I'm not sure what the hole is for, but my nap dream suddenly comes back to me with a vengeance: I was going into the bathroom to use the toilet. It is dark, and I turn on the bathroom light to see that the toilet has been moved off its mounting and pushed all the way to the other side of the bathroom. The hole in the floor and the sewage line are exposed. Noises come up from the hole; groans and whispers and voices crying out for help.

There was a time when my dreams were funny. I used to laugh in my sleep.

———

I stop to get some gas for the Prius. I go to the place right down the hill from the park; a little more expensive but worth it for the convenience. I get out of the car to pump the gas and clean the windows. It's been a long time since I've been on a road trip, and I'm starting to get excited. It feels less like I'm running away from something and more like I'm running to something. I'm beginning to feel a little better about things and smile at the pretty young woman in cutoffs gassing up next to me at the other side of the pump. My friendly smile does nothing for her, however, and she quickly turns away. Sixty-year-old guys become completely invisible to pretty young things in cutoffs. So much for my budding positive attitude.

I browse through my CDs to find some good traveling music (assuming the Prius will cooperate and let the CD player work).

A homeless guy who haunts the neighborhood makes his way through the station lot, pushing his loaded shopping cart full of junk before him. Los Angeles might be huge, but the neighborhoods themselves are small. As such, he knows me and my car. Every time I see him, he approaches me and talks my ear off until I find a way to escape. He's always smiling, full of energy, and happy to see me. He speaks very little English, mostly Spanish, and smells like he lives in a sewer. He parks his shopping cart in front of the Prius and comes up to the driver's side window.

"*Hola, amigo! Hola, papito!*" he says with great enthusiasm.

"Hey, there he is!" I respond, pretending to be excited to see him. He always calls me *papito*. I don't know why.

He puts his hand in through the window, and I shake it. Then he straightens up and launches into a monologue in his own special language, part Spanish and part I have no idea what. He gestures wildly, and for added emphasis he makes the occasional rude gesture that sets him off into disturbing fits of hysterical chortling.

As he rambles on and on, possibly insulting me and calling me horrible names, I nod my head in agreement with whatever he says. Being an actor, I've learned the art of listening, or at least how to act like I'm listening. What I'm really thinking about is how often this kind of thing happens to me. If there is a beggar on the street, they will beg to me. I draw them like a magnet. If there is a woman distraught, she will cry to me. If there is a man guilty and in need of confession, he will confess to me. Lately, I prefer to stay home rather than have to deal with this stuff.

Finally, when I can pretend to listen for not a moment longer, I interrupt him. I hold up my hand to temporarily silence him. "My friend, I have to go. I have a big trip to make."

"*Si, papito*, you have to vamoose? *I comprende, si señor.*" He holds up a dirty index finger and jaunts over to his shopping cart. "*Uno momento, uno momento…"* he repeats continuously while he digs through his stash of junk. He finally finds what he's looking for and brings it back to the window.

I see in his hands a large stuffed penguin. It's dressed in a yellow rain-coat and rain hat, and it's possibly the cutest stuffed animal I've ever seen.

"For your little girl," he says in perfect English. "You give to her for me, *si?*" He hands the gift over.

"What girl?" I ask. "I don't have a girl."

He winks and smiles a giant and nearly toothless grin but says nothing else. He gets his shopping cart and goes on his way, waving wildly and singing something familiar. Maybe it's a children's song. Maybe it's something I've heard before in a Mexican restaurant. In any case, he turns the corner and disappears from view.

What little girl? Who is this guy?

My cell phone rings. I have that Sherwood Forest ringtone, and it always makes me jump a little. This time it makes me jump a lot.

"Hello?"

"This is Joe Clearwater. Portia's father." His voice is stern and low.

"Oh! I'm so glad you called," I say, though I don't know if *glad* is really the word I'm looking for.

"Mr. Goldfarb, I'm talking to the DA out there in Ventura County, and you are very close to being charged with assault and battery. In the meantime, we will be filing a restraining order against you. You will be served within ten days—"

"Mr. Clearwater, let me just say I'm very sorry about all of this."

This seems to catch him a little off guard. He pauses for a moment before getting back to his no nonsense, I-can-crush-you-like-a-bug tone of voice. "Mr. Goldfarb, you can appear in court to contest the restraining order. If you don't, you will by court order be forbidden to see my daughter or to be anywhere in her vicinity for the next five years."

"I have no intention of bothering her or you ever again, Mr. Clearwater. I promise you that."

"I have spoken with the Sheriff's Department, and they will be coming out to visit you at your home."

"They're coming to my house?" Kelly will be already freaked out enough because I've run away from home, and now she'll have to deal with the cops? I truly am a terrible husband.

"They will make sure that you understand the seriousness of what you've done."

"Mr. Clearwater, I do understand how serious this is. But I never meant her harm."

"I don't care."

I decide to try another tactic. The full truth. Maybe if he knows everything that happened, he will at least think of me as insane more than intentionally violent. "I know that you are a Mormon," I begin. "I don't know exactly what you believe about God, but—"

"I believe you are a dangerous crazy person, and you should stay the hell away from my daughter. If you do not, I assure you, Mr. Goldfarb, I can make your life a living hell. That's what I believe." With that, he hangs up.

I start the Prius and head north.

CHAPTER THIRTEEN

HOW DANGEROUS IS IT
THAT THIS MAN GOES LOOSE

I've been on the road less than two hours when the Prius lurches again—just to let me know who's really in charge. The CD player has been steadily working since I left Los Angeles, so yes, Virginia, there is a God or a Santa Claus or whoever is performing the miracles these days. Seems only fitting to blare Tom Waits's "Goin' Out West" while speeding through the Grapevine. Something about his voice makes me feel everything is going to be okay, especially when I get to sing along—"I'm gonna change my name to Hannibal or maybe just Rex." I know his stuff so well, I can do harmony to Tom's melody without even thinking about it.

The phone rings through my Bluetooth connection, interrupting my personal serenade to the Prius. The dashboard screen doesn't show who is calling, but I answer anyway out of habit.

"Hello?" I answer apprehensively.

"Mr. Geeg!"

It's the other Mr. Geeg.

"How's it going?" he asks.

I tell him about Portia's father and how he's hoping to file battery charges.

"And they're taking out a restraining order," I add.

"I figured they'd do that, but a battery charge? They'll never get a battery charge." Jerry says this as though he's suddenly an expert on the American judicial system. "You didn't hit her or anything, did you?"

"I grabbed her arm and I held her." As the words come out of my mouth, I envision Portia's terrified eyes pleading with me to let go.

"That's battery? That's not battery," Jerry says. "Maybe he's just trying to scare you."

"Well, it's working."

"You should talk to a lawyer," he says definitively.

"You said *not* to talk to a lawyer!" I yell.

"Yeah, but that's before he called you!" he yells back.

"Well, I'm on the road now, anyway," I say settling back to a normal volume.

"Where are you?"

"I don't know. I'm on the 5..." I wait a moment until I see the next green sign on the side of the freeway. "Coming up on Lost Hills."

"I should have gone with you, Mr. Geeg."

"I appreciate it, Mr. Geeg, but I think this is something I have to do on my own."

"I'm sorry I disappeared into the bathroom before. I was feeling weird," he says.

I know by his voice he isn't just referring to his stomach issues.

"It's okay," I say. "I understand."

"Do you still want me to call Kelly for you?"

"That would be great. Tell her to try not to worry. I'll fill her in when I call later."

"Use a pay phone. Shit, we probably shouldn't be talking, either."

"I think it's all right."

"You'd be surprised what these people are capable of."

"What people?"

"The people who listen. You know...those people."

"Oh, *those* people."

"Exactly," he says conspiratorially. "Anyway, let me know what happens out there. I think her father is bluffing. It's going to be all right, Mr. Geeg."

"Okay," I say, not fully convinced he's right.

"If you talk to God again, tell him I said if he needs anybody else pregnant, I'm available."

"And if you think of a lawyer—"

"I'll talk to a few cops that I know from the cigar shop."

"Cops?" I'm screaming again. "You're going to talk to cops about your friend on the run?"

"They're LAPD. They don't care about what happens in Ventura."

"Oh, okay…" I am somehow satisfied by this. "Goodbye, Mr. Geeg."

"Goodbye, Mr. Geeg."

With that, the call ends and Waits is back on at full volume. I turn the stereo down and drive in silence for a while.

I suddenly feel very alone, like back when I first came to California. I was nineteen and going to work with a brand-new theater company in the Napa Valley. I knew nothing about the Napa Valley or about the company, or hardly anything about theater for that matter. I wasn't sure what I was getting into, but I was game. So I guess I did have some courage once—way back when.

I turn off the air conditioning and roll down the windows, letting the fresh air whip around in the car. I change the CD, and miraculously the Prius continues to oblige. Dr. John sings "Big Shot." I crank it up loud and drive for quite a while this way, my mediocre voice rising to the heavens, and my thinning hair flying in the wind. I start to feel good again, and although incarceration is looming, I begin to feel oddly free. Then I get hungry.

I come upon a freeway rest stop in a town called Coalinga. I spot a pancake house kind of place, pull over, and go inside. The moment I step through the door, I feel like I've traveled back in time. They haven't done a thing to this place since at least the '70s. The décor, the booths, the servers—it's a period piece. The few scattered customers look like the hippies did when I first came to California. It's almost as if the place were waiting for me, unchanged through the years. Like a *Twilight Zone* episode. On my way out, I'll probably turn around to look back, and it will all be gone. Nothing left but a haunted, empty parking lot.

The waitress lumbers toward me dressed in the same colors that are on the walls, booths, and the building façade—an orange dress layered over a fluffy yellow blouse with a perky pink apron tied around her waist. She looks way too old for the job, like she, too, has been here since the '70s. Her name tag says Del, and she has one of those little retro carhop hats pinned crookedly to her badly dyed hair. Del skips the pleasantries and gets right down to business. She hands me a menu, also right out of the '70s and unhealthy as hell.

"What can I get you, sweetie?" She asks in the raspy rumble of a hundred thousand cigarettes.

There are pictures accompanying the food descriptions. I point to the first thing that looks edible.

"I'll have the California Club, please."

"Fries with that," she says as a dull statement rather than a sincere question. She's just going through the motions. Like a bad actor with a bad script—she couldn't care less.

"Can I get fruit?"

"We don't have fruit," she sighs.

"Well, what do you have?"

She sighs again. "Fries, potato salad, coleslaw, or you can have pancakes on the side."

"Pancakes with a club sandwich?"

She shrugs and looks past me, through the window, and out to the road. The expression of loss and weary resignation on this woman's face; it's a mesmerizing sadness. She hacks something up and gets back to business, tapping her pencil impatiently on her order pad.

"So, what's it gonna be?"

"How about we forget about the side? Just the California Club, very little mayo, on wheat toast." I close the menu and add, "If you would be so kind."

She is unimpressed with my manners. "Drink?"

"Water."

Another sigh. "The water is no good here."

"Diet Coke, then."

She grabs the menu then turns and lumbers away the same way that she lumbered in.

There is a girl drinking coffee in the booth across from me—long blonde hair, thin, wearing bell-bottom jeans and a tie-dyed shirt. She's probably near Portia's age, early twenties. A good-looking kid. She has her cell phone out and is texting somebody.

That's the only thing that breaks up the whole *Twilight Zone* period piece thing for me—the cell phones. Everyone in the place is doing something on their phones, even if they're with somebody else. The temptation is strong to take my own phone out for a quick game of Candy Crush, but I resist the urge. I instead sit quietly, observing the talented thumbs flying with impossible speed over tiny little keyboards. Skills acquired from countless hours of ignoring the present and real in favor of the more comfortable distance of cyberspace. Everybody is busy building walls these days. On our borders and in our heads. Creating our own little cocoons, our private little force fields to protect us from one another. Yes, I have truly matured into the "old fart" that I had promised myself I would never become. Shows you what I know.

A young man with long hair in a leather jacket storms into the restaurant. He also looks like he's straight out of the '70s—a rocker type verging on the early punk scene of the '80s. He scans the place, looking for someone he is clearly pissed off at. He sees the girl in the booth across from me and leans in on the table in front of her.

"What the fuck, Diane!" he says loud enough for even the chefs in the kitchen to hear.

"I don't want to talk about it," she whispers, not looking up from her phone.

"You don't have to say nothin', but you're coming with me." He straightens back up, expecting her to obediently follow his orders.

"No, I'm not." Her voice is a little louder this time, but she still avoids eye contact.

"Nobody runs out on me, you fucking whore."

This finally snaps her away from the device in her hand. She looks him dead in the eye and screams loud enough for the chefs in the next town over to hear. "Don't call me that!"

He grabs her arm and starts yanking, "Come on, let's go!"

She struggles to get him to release her. "Stop it!"

"You lied to me, bitch!"

"I had to, you stupid shit. What did you expect?"

"Come on!"

"Let go! I can't live like this anymore!"

Even in Coalinga, even in the middle of freaking nowhere—like a magnet—this stuff comes to me.

No one in the restaurant does anything other than dumbly watch, except for the few jerks who are taking pictures on their phones.

And then the long-haired man in the leather jacket slaps the young woman hard. The entire room fills with a shocked silence as she raises her hand to her cheek.

"Fucker!" she screams in what has to be the loudest decibel a human person can reach.

He grabs her again and starts yanking, this time pulling her out of the booth one forced centimeter at a time.

"I'm going to kill you, bitch!"

"Go ahead and kill me then!" She takes a swing at him and lands a good punch. "I don't care anymore, you fucking junkie!"

He backs away momentarily to reset his jaw then lunges forward and grabs her in a violent bear hug, yanking her entire body out of the booth. She continues in explicit vocabulary at full volume.

I grab one of the syrup bottles from the rack on my table. Then I walk over and crack the guy over the head with it. He freezes for a moment, boysenberry syrup and blood creeping down his long hair. He lets go of the young woman, and she falls back into the booth. He turns around to face me, a murderous look in his eye, but then he drops like a stone. I'm still holding the handle of the syrup bottle; shards of glass shattered on the floor all around me. I drop the handle, like how Michael Corleone drops his gun in *The Godfather* after he shoots those guys in the Italian restaurant.

The woman named Diane gets out of the booth and kicks the man in the ribs. He groans, which is a relief to me since I wasn't entirely sure that I hadn't killed him.

"We should get out of here," she says.

"We should?"

"Can I go with you?" she asks, not looking particularly thankful or relieved by my act of bravery.

"Uhhh…" I manage.

She musters up more urgency. "He's going to kill me," she says, her eyebrows furrowed like a puppy.

I'm convinced. "Okay, let's go."

I tiptoe out of the carnage and grab my keys from the table I had been sitting at. We leave the restaurant holding onto each other. As we exit the front door I look back, hoping that the whole place might have disappeared. It hadn't.

"Thank you for saving my life," my new road trip partner says.

"Sure," I say, "no problem."

CHAPTER FOURTEEN

WHAT IS IT BUT TO BE NOTHING ELSE BUT MAD

Besides skipping out on a California Club sandwich, we had left a long-haired man syrupy, bloodied, and moaning on the restaurant floor. Even in Coalinga, preserver of the '70s, that has to be some kind of felony. I resist the urge to look back to see if anybody is chasing us. Jelly-legged but determined, we manage to make it to the Prius without any interference.

Of course the Prius refuses to cooperate. It takes three attempts and one *motherfucker* before I finally get the doors to open. Once we're both inside, I just take off—back on the freeway, heading north. Neither of us speaks for a few minutes, mostly, I think, because we're both trying to process what has just happened. Right at the point when I think I better say something, she says something instead.

"So, what's your name?"

"Harold." I leave it at that. Probably best not to tell her my last name.

"I'm Diane," she says, which I already know from all the screaming. She extends her hand, and I pull my hand away from the steering wheel to shake it.

"Nice to meet you." I almost laugh after saying this—considering the circumstances.

"I'm heading to San Francisco," she says. "Are you going that far?"

"I'm going just north of there, actually," I tell her. "Napa."

Diane nods her head a few times and purses her lips together, apparently pleased with my travel plans. "Do you mind dropping me off in the city?" She leans back in her seat, already more relaxed. Like she knows I'm going to say yes.

I do. "Sure, no problem."

She lets out an audible sigh, an unmistakable sign of relief. "I can't thank you enough. I don't know what I would have done."

She pats my shoulder as you would a loyal old dog. I'd be insulted except that it feels good to be appreciated. I look at her and smile. She smiles, too. Then tears begin welling in her pretty green eyes. She is so young—too young to be in this kind of trouble. My fatherly side resurfaces. If I had any regrets before about what I had done, I had none now. I'm glad I helped her.

"So, who was that guy?" I ask.

"That was Travis." She turns away from me and looks out her window. "He used to be my boyfriend."

She starts sniffling, trying to hold back her emotions, then begins searching through her pockets. I instinctively lean over and open the glove compartment, where I always keep a small packet of Kleenex— something I learned from Kelly.

"Thanks," she says as I hand her the tissues. She pulls out a couple from the package, quite delicately, but then blows her nose like a truck driver. I decide I like this about her. After a few more honks, she puts the wad of used tissues in my passenger seat cup holder, then she starts telling me her story. They always do.

"So we both moved down from Redding to San Francisco to get into the music scene, but then we got hooked up with these drug people, and he started dealing. All kinds of stuff: crack, pills, heroin. I don't even know what he was doing." Diane's voice shifts, and she looks as though she might start crying again. "Everything changed. He changed. He was using a lot, and he started getting mean and wanting me to do things that weren't right." She shudders at the memories.

"Like what kind of things?" I ask.

"Like helping with the business, ya' know?"

I shake my head. I don't know, so she elaborates.

"Running, making connections, flirting with the clientele. Partying for the sake of the business. You know what I mean?"

"I think I do now, yes."

"We had some close calls and a lot of threats. It's very competitive out there. People get protective about their territories, you know?"

"Dangerous stuff." Great, I nearly murder a drug dealer and then kidnap his girlfriend. As if I wasn't dealing with enough already.

"Yeah, so we had to get out, and we came to Coalinga. I thought maybe it would get better if we got away from everything, like maybe it would get back to normal, like when we first hooked up. But it got worse. Coalinga is a weird place. There's a big state penitentiary and a lot of trafficking going on. People found out where we were, and he got crazier and crazier. I don't even know who he is anymore."

"How old are you?" I ask.

"Nineteen."

"Where are your parents?"

"My father is in jail and my mother is dead."

"I'm sorry," is all I can think to say.

"It's nothing to be sorry about. Just is what it is," she says. I get the feeling this is her go-to answer whenever discussing her parents.

"I'm still sorry for you, though," I say.

Diane tears up again, then changes the subject. "Anyway, I'm starting over. I want to act and see what I can do with that."

I decide to play it cool and let her discover in her own time about what I do for a living.

"Do you have a place to go?" I say instead.

"I have friends that will put me up." She kicks her legs up on my dashboard and fully reclines in the passenger seat. I'm glad to see she feels so comfortable with me already, especially after all she's been through.

We drive in silence for a bit. I try a CD. When that doesn't work, I try the radio. No luck. After passing a few more miles of empty fields and conservative-bent billboards, I decide to ask her something that's starting to really trouble me. "Do you think Travis will come looking for you?"

"My friends can take care of him," Diane says, peering out the window and then looking up at something in the sky.

I sort of want to know if she means *take care*, as in not allow him near me, or *take care*, as in put a few bullets in his head and then chop up his body in little pieces and bury him in the usual place. But I'm scared of what the answer may be so I just say, "Those are good friends."

"I should have left a long time ago," she says, regret heavy in her voice.

"Do your friends know that you're coming?" I ask.

"I sent a text at the restaurant."

"So you were about to head off to San Francisco from the restaurant?

"Yeah."

"Did you have a car there that we left behind?" I ask.

"No, I was going to hitch into the city," she says matter-of-factly. "I've done it before. I don't drive."

I decide it'd be best to appeal to our commonalities rather than act like an old fart and lecture her on the dangers of hitchhiking.

"I used to hitch too," I tell her. "When I first got to California. I was nineteen, just like you. Came to find my fame and fortune in show business. That was a long time ago."

Diane perks up. "Are you an actor?"

"Yup." So I couldn't resist.

"Cool!" she squeals. "Where are you from originally?"

"Born and raised in New Jersey."

"Really? That's so cool."

"Actually, it was freaking freezing!" I say for some reason. The ridiculousness of the joke combined with our absurd circumstances makes me start laughing. Soon she is joining in, too. It's great to see her light up a little.

About a minute down the road, the laughter dies down, and she's staring out the window again.

"You're a good kid, Diane. I hope things work out for you, I really do."

She turns toward me and smiles. "Thanks, man. I appreciate that."

Just as I'm thinking about how nice it is to have a road trip buddy to take my mind off my problems, I get to worrying again.

"Hey, do you think Travis—do you think he'd call the police about what happened?" I try to ask this as casually as I possibly can.

"No way will he call the police," she says. "If he did, they'd probably throw him in jail and beat him up some more."

This gives me momentary relief until suddenly a bigger worry hits.

"Does he have friends that might help him?" I know I sound way less casual this time, though I am doing my best not to seem frightened.

"I doubt it. Do you have a gun or anything in case?"

"I have pine cones."

"What?" Her eyebrows shoot upward.

"I don't like to use them, but I will if I have to."

As she tries to figure out what I'm talking about, an even worse realization strikes. What about all those people taking pictures with their cell phones? What if someone got a shot of me smashing that bottle over his head? What if they got pictures of my license plate? Travis doesn't need to go to the police if any of the people from the restaurant go there instead.

I'm working myself up into a pretty good lather when the phone rings.

"I don't have to take that," I say, meaning I don't *want* to take that.

"Go ahead," Diane says. "I don't mind."

Before I can stop her, she presses the accept button, and suddenly the call is live.

"Hello?" I say tentatively.

There is a pause, as if it's a telemarketer calling. I'm about to disconnect when she finally speaks.

"Harold?"

I know it's her before she even gives her name.

"It's me. Portia."

This time I pause like a telemarketer.

"Hello? Are you there?"

"Hi...yes, I'm here," I say uneasily. "Hi, Portia."

Diane looks at me, wondering what's going on.

I shake my head, to let her know it's no big deal.

Portia speaks again. "I have to tell you something. Do you have a minute?"

"Well, I'm in the car," I say. I don't know what this has to do with anything. I'm worried about what Portia might say in front of Diane, though. I'm worried what she might say, period.

"Let her talk," Diane mouths to me.

"Sure, go ahead," I say, though I'm still pretty sure it's a bad idea.

"Harold." Portia clears her throat. "I'm sorry about my father. He's very upset about all this. But I don't think you are a bad person."

"He wants to press charges," I tell her.

"I'm trying to stop him. I don't think you're crazy, and I don't think you're dangerous."

"You don't?" What a relief. Wasn't expecting that at all.

"I think God really did talk to you, Harold. Because…"

Another pause. Diane and I look at each other, her eyes widen in anticipation.

"He talked to me, too."

I'm surprised and more than delighted by this news, as weird as it might be.

"He said," she continues, "that I should do whatever you ask me to do. That it's why we are both here."

"Where?" I ask. Just to be sure.

"On Earth."

"Oh…"

Diane darts her eyes back and forth between me and the Bluetooth speakers.

Portia exhales, "So, if you want me to—"

I stop her before she blurts out what I think she is going to say.

"We can't, Portia. It wouldn't be right."

"I don't think we have a choice, do we?"

"Listen," I begin in my most respectable, most fatherly voice possible. "Let's back off this and breathe a little bit, okay? There is something off about the whole thing. I think neither one of us is thinking clearly right now."

"No, I've never been so sure of anything in my life! We have to be brave."

"No, we have to be smart."

Diane shifts uncomfortably in her seat.

"But if we don't, if we don't sleep together, we will be responsible for everything bad that happens. To the entire world."

"I'm married, you know?"

"Nobody has to know," Portia whispers slowly and deliberately this time.

"Ha! Heard that one before." Diane cracks involuntarily. She immediately covers her mouth with both hands and cringes.

"Who's that?" Portia asks. Diane slinks into the passenger seat as if trying to hide.

"Nobody. It's okay." I shrug at Diane, she shrugs back. No offense meant, none taken.

"Are you still doing the show?" I try to change the subject.

"Yes, I'm living on campus if you want to see me."

"I don't think that's a good idea—" I start.

"Or I can come to you."

"That's even worse," I say.

"We have to do this, Harold. It's our destiny."

I don't know what to say anymore. Diane gestures wildly for me to say something, anything, rather than let Portia's words continue to hang in the air. I just can't think of anything. Finally, Portia speaks again.

"I'm going to talk to Tom about having you come back to do Polonius."

"You don't have to. Please, everything is fine. We'll talk later." I want so badly for this conversation to be wrapped up so I do just that. "Goodbye, Portia."

I reach to the dashboard to turn off the phone. She gets in one last urgent cry before I hang up.

"We have to do this, Harold. God said we do!"

I look over at Diane. She is staring at me with those big green eyes of hers, but she doesn't say anything. We drive in silence.

A few moments down the road, Diane starts laughing. I'm not sure if she's laughing at me or just trying to release some weird shit before her head explodes. She calms down after a moment or two and then looks me over, a crooked little smile still lingers on her face. "I thought my life was a trip, but holy shit, man!" Then she gets immediately serious. "So, you talk to God, Harold?"

"He talks to me," I clarify. "I think. I'm not completely sure."

"And God told this girl to have sex with you? And vice versa?"

I nod. "Our child is supposed to save the world."

"Far out, man," she says.

"It's kind of a long story," I say.

"I've got time."

She gestures at the road sign ahead. We still have a couple hundred more miles before we're even in the Bay Area. I'm hesitant, but seeing how Diane's reaction this far has been mostly delight rather than terror, I decide it might feel good to talk about it a bit.

"I think it has to do with lack of sleep and confusing the message more than anything else." I start with, in order to make clear that I'm not some sort of religious nut.

"Or maybe you really are chosen for something really important. Maybe you're some kind of angel or something."

I want to assume that she's joking, but there is absolute sincerity in her tone.

"I'm not even religious," I say.

"You saved me, didn't you?" She smiles, and I realize that I just might be perceived as heroic to this kid. It's flattering but not particularly well deserved.

"I just happened to be there," I say.

"Have you saved other people? Before today, I mean?"

When I stop to think about it, I guess I have saved random other people throughout my life. Like the woman in the park. Diane reads my face and continues on before I have a chance to answer.

"Maybe you're an angel, but you just don't know it yet."

I shake my head. "All I know is I'm running away."

"Well, that makes two of us."

We both look out at the stretch of road ahead.

"I'm trying to sort one thing out and all this other stuff starts happening," I say.

"Like somebody is trying to give you a clue? About who you really are?"

"Is that what it is?"

"That's what it sounds like. Anyway, we're on the road to find out." Then she sings, a la Cat Stevens. "Ooh, baby, baby, it's a wild world…"

I'm surprised a girl her age would make that reference. More than that, I'm impressed.

"Do you know him? Cat Stevens?"

She shrugs. "I know a lot of shit about music."

I sing a verse this time. "Ooh, baby, baby, it's a wild world, it's hard to get by just upon a smile…" Diane throws in a harmony, and it's not half bad.

"Amen to that, brother," she says.

"Amen, indeed."

She laughs and shakes her head as she slides back into her reclined seat. She looks me over and then says with absolute certainty, "You're a fucking angel," as if she's figured out a big secret and is willing to bet all her money on being right.

CHAPTER FIFTEEN

THE TIME IS OUT OF JOINT.
O CURSED SPITE THAT I WAS BORN TO SET IT RIGHT!

Diane knows the way into San Francisco from the 5. Good thing, too, because the Prius's navigational system is refusing to cooperate, and I have the worst sense of direction on the planet. We get off the freeway at Mission Street. It's an interesting area, a little cleaner since I had last been here but with the same kind of independent San Francisco–specific vibe—quirky and slightly weird but in a good way. All the buildings are painted in bright, bold colors. In Glendale if you painted your house like that, you'd be fined and publicly humiliated. The weather in San Francisco is the best part, though. Nice and cool even in the summer. Diane directs me over to Market Street, then to an apartment building that is next to a fish market.

"This is it," Diane says with a touch of apprehension.

I pull over.

"I'll wait," I tell her as she opens the car door.

She looks back at me. "For what?"

"Just to make sure you get in okay."

She leans over and kisses me on the cheek. "Thanks, Dad."

I know she's teasing, but I detect a hint of wistfulness in her voice, as if she really does wish I were her father. I chuckle and try not to let her see the mist filling up my eyes. I wouldn't mind having her for a daughter, either. She jumps out of the car and runs up the steps to the building. At the same time, my phone rings.

"What the hell are you doing?"

It's Kelly.

"I—"

"Where are you?" I turn down the volume on the speaker and try to explain.

"I'm in San Francisco—"

"Oh my God, Haarold. You are freeeaking me ouuut! Do you know that?"

Kelly dramatically extends certain words when she's upset. This is how I can decipher when I'm in deep shit.

"I'm sorry—"

She interrupts again with a stressed-out sigh. "Just tell me you're okay."

"Don't worry. I'm fine. Did Jerry call?"

"Yesss, Jerry called," she says as if I should know better than to even ask that question. "He sounds as worried as I am. Just tell me what the hell is going on, Harold."

"I have to find something up here," I say.

"What does that mean? What do you have to find?"

"I don't know yet. I don't think I'll know until I find it."

She sighs again, even more exasperated than before. "What's with this girl in the letter? Did you do something that I need to know about?"

"Absolutely not. I would never!"

"But you got fired for this thing that you would never?"

"It's complicated, Kelly. I promise I'll explain when I get back.

"The police came to the house," she says quietly.

"Shit."

"I wasn't home yet. They left a card. You need to talk to a lawyer, Harold."

I know she's probably right, but I don't want to hear it right now. When I don't respond, she continues, her ire rising.

"I think it's a bad idea to leave town when all this is happening. It's going to give people the wrong idea, Harold."

I understand her concern. If word gets out about any of this—if the gossip hounds in her office start thinking that I'm cheating on her? Even though it's not true, they'll make life miserable for her.

"Nothing happened with that girl," I reiterate. "I just tried talking to her, I promise—"

"Jesus Christ!" she suddenly yells. I'm preparing to really get ripped into, but instead she moans and then takes in a deep breath as if reacting to a sudden sharp pain.

"What's wrong?" I ask. I'm hoping that it's just some elaborate buildup to a great insulting punch line that will make me feel like absolute shit. But instead she cries out in pain

"Shit, it really hurts!"

"What hurts?"

"I've been having these crazy cramps and terrible nausea all day long."

"Maybe you have the flu?" I suggest.

"I'm going to see Dr. Bloom tomorrow. Something isn't right."

Now I'm freaking out. I can't stand it when Kelly doesn't feel good. I get crazy about it. Probably got it from my mother, who would nurse a sick child by running around the house screaming and cursing God for bringing sickness into her home. If Kelly is getting sick because of what I'm doing—or if her getting sick is part of the big picture that's developing here—I wouldn't be able to live with that. I try to shake off this feeling of dread and attempt to stay calm for both our sakes.

"I'll be home tomorrow for sure," I promise.

I look up and see Diane still on her phone. She looks back toward the car and throws her hands up in the air as if she also isn't sure what's going on.

"You're going to call them, right?" Kelly asks.

"Who?" I say, distracted.

"The police, Harold!"

"Okay, okay, give me the number."

I look for a pen in the glove compartment and find a napkin to write on. Kelly repeats the number and the officer's name to me, grunting through her words with what sounds like increasing agony. I want to help her, to soothe her, but I spy Diane walking back down the stairs and toward the car.

"I'll be home soon," I assure her again. "I have to go," I say, trying to get her off the call before I have to explain who Diane is and what she's doing with me on my escape to Northern California.

"Be careful, Harold. Please," she says, her breathing becoming more labored.

"I love you. I'll explain everything. I promise."

Just as I try to push the button that will hang up the call, Diane reaches for the door handle and slides into the car. I motion for her to be quiet, but she doesn't see me.

"Nobody home," she says, slinking into her seat. I cringe, knowing Kelly is still on the line.

There is exactly one second of excruciating silence before her voice blares through the speakers.

"Whoooo is thaaaaat?"

Diane's green eyes widen to the size of saucers.

"It's nothing! It's okay! It's just Diane…I'm giving her a ride."

"It's nothing!" Diane repeats. "He's way too old for me!"

It's true, but it still stings.

"Sorry," Diane mouths silently.

"Harold," Kelly says in a quiet calm that I find particularly disturbing. "If you're not home very soon, I don't know what I'm going to do." Then she hangs up before I can explain anything more.

"Your wife?" Diane asks.

"Yeah."

"Bad timing, I'm sorry."

I change the subject. "Nobody home?" I ask.

"Yeah, they're not picking up. Probably went away for the day or something. Can I go with you?"

"With me?"

You're going to Napa, right?" I've never been there. Do you mind? You could drop me off on the way back. I won't cause any trouble, I promise."

"Uhh…" I say with complete conviction.

"Great!"

The kid is quick. She enthusiastically takes my *uhh* for an okay and contently slumps back into her seat. What am I supposed to do? I can't exactly leave her here on the street. Besides, to have some company for the rest of the way, a partner in crime (quite literally in this case), no offense to Tom Waits and my earlier sing-a-long buddies, but it's gotta beat traveling alone, and it might even keep some nasty voices out of my head.

There is a gas station at the end of the street, so I pull in to gas up the car. I know that I complain about the Prius all the time, but it did get us all the way from Los Angeles to San Francisco on one tank of gas. I give the car an affectionate pat on the back. "Nice job, buddy. You did good."

"I'm going to use the head," Diane announces as she hops out of the car and starts stretching like a cat.

"Get us some snacks or something, will ya'?" I reach out over the roof of the Prius and hand her a ten. She jogs toward the quickie mart just like a nineteen-year-old might. Equal parts sexy and awkward.

Squatting on the sidewalk near the door of the store is a young man with knotted hair in a filthy raincoat caked in soot. I get the sense he's staring at me, so I look away, busying myself with swiping my credit card and going through the steps of filling up the gas tank. I look his way again in hopes he's turned his attention elsewhere by now. But no. We lock eyes and suddenly he is up and bounding toward me with fast, aggressive steps. Three feet or so from where I am, he abruptly stops. I'm about to open the car door to retrieve a pine cone when he starts hissing at me like a snake. Then in a very low, harsh whisper, he speaks.

"I know who you are. I'll kill you if they tell me to. "

Then something distracts him. He looks up and quickly does a full circle, scanning the sky before turning his attention back to me. He sneers and then bolts away, as if his life depended on it, out into traffic, and then he is gone.

I look around to see if anyone else was witness to what had just happened. No one. The station is oddly still and quiet for being smack in the middle of one of the biggest cities in California.

"What in the holy hell!" I shout to no one in particular.

Diane gets back from the restroom, and I decide not to mention what happened. I take my turn in the bathroom and splash some cold water on my face to compose myself. I look in the mirror and assure myself that in just a short time I will be sitting in wine country with a gigantic glass of cabernet and all will be well. Relatively, at least. The self-talk improves my mood considerably.

CHAPTER SIXTEEN

SAVE ME, AND HOVER O'ER ME WITH YOUR WINGS, YOU HEAVENLY GUARDS

We get back on the road, snacking on Fritos and trail mix, and eventually make it to Highway 29—the main road to and through Napa. It looks exactly the same as the last time I was here almost four decades ago. Just two lanes, one for coming and one for going. Beautiful vineyards and century-old brick winery buildings line the way. Livestock graze, and there are walnut and almond orchards and farm houses that probably date back to the 1800s. I've heard over the years about how much the wine country has been built up with high-end restaurants, hotels, and tons of tourists, but everything looks the same to me. We get off the freeway and drive into a town called Yountville, my old stomping grounds, where the Napa Valley Theatre Company once was. Amazingly, the old brick building where the theater used to be is still there. So is the bar where we hung out after shows, and the coffee shop where I pretty much lived when I wasn't at the theater. The VA hospital and the old country store are still there, and the quiet streets and the single-family homes all look exactly as I remember them. I want to stop and explore it all, but I have my mind set on making St. Helena before it gets too dark. Something is calling me there, and if I wait, I fear that I'll miss it.

We continue north into the valley.

St. Helena is where I was introduced to some of the best people I have ever known. It's where I learned about what's really important in life but perhaps have forgotten somewhere along the way. St. Helena also had some of the best wineries in California: Beringer, Charles Krug, Mondavi. They used to have free wine tasting tours that I took full advantage of, sometimes several in a day. Unfortunately, because of the hour, Diane and I probably won't get in any wine tours today, but I do fill her in on my adventures in Napa. It gushes out of me. I hardly take a breath, as if it happened yesterday. It was the first job I had when I came to California. Eighty dollars a week, plus room and board. I was easy to please in those days.

"Look, cows," I point out, in case she missed it.

"Moo," says Diane.

"Kick me or something if this gets too boring."

"I will," she promises. "Go ahead."

"Okay, so all the actors and staff stayed at a place called the Ranch. It turned out to be a big theater commune of vegetarian hippies run by lesbians. It was tucked away in the middle of a vineyard surrounded by magnificent rolling hills just like these here. And for a city boy from New Jersey, let me tell you I felt as though I'd landed in paradise. I saw things that I had never seen before—like avocados. I saw lesbians having sex, nude pool parties, and I had my first taste of California marijuana, which knocked me for a loop. Actually, come to think of it, I saved a guy from drowning, my first day there. So add another one to the list."

"See? I told you," Diane points out.

"He was this stoner guy. I went outside to get some air, and I see him lying naked on the bottom of the pool. After I manage to drag him out of the water, the first thing he says to me is 'Whoa, just thought it'd be cool to lie down on the bottom for a while and chill.'"

Diane has a puzzled look on her face.

"It was the seventies. People just said things like that."

"Anyway, besides all the naked partying, and the rescuing, the work load was intense. We actually had to build the theater. When I first got there, there was nothing. It was just a big empty warehouse. My East Coast director friend who hired me didn't bother to mention that. We spent fifteen hours a day between rehearsals doing grunt work. We were actors, builders, designers, we did it all—and I met some of the weirdest, most interesting people I have ever known."

"Hey, and now you've met me!" Diane reminds me as if to make sure she's included in the interesting group or the weird group, I'm not sure which she'd prefer. But I'm glad to see that she's engaged in my story, and I'm not just boring her to death.

So I gush on. "But things got complicated after a while. After the first few blissful days on the Ranch, reality began to rear its ugly head. The living arrangements where getting increasingly uncomfortable, and the food situation was a serious problem. No meat, no variety, and there is only so much granola you can eat. Artistically, it was a magical time for me, but life on the Ranch was getting to be a strain. Fortunately, I befriended one of the local actors, a guy named Ed, who invited a few of us to his house in St. Helena for some shelter from the stormy personality clashes that had started going on at the Ranch. Starvation tends to make people cranky.

"Ed's parents, Roy and Alice, were incredibly generous and kind. They opened their house to us and made us a part of their family. I had never seen such graciousness and generosity of spirit. All the wonderful dinners and barbecues that they put together for us were really above and beyond. They nourished us, body and soul. Without them, I don't think I would have made it through that season with the company. I could sleep there whenever I wanted, and they would tirelessly listen to me bitch and moan about the hardships we poor stock actors were forced to endure. I feel guilty now when I think of all they did for us and how expensive it must have been for them. At that time I was a taker, and they were the givers. At some point I hope I can repay that. Ed's folks aren't with us anymore, but maybe one day I'll have a chance to be as kind and generous to someone as they were to me.

"I learned later that Ed had a brother who committed suicide a year before the Napa Valley Theatre Company got started. I don't know the circumstance that led to it, and maybe there was some compensation going on to make up for the loss. Whatever it was, I loved these people. To me, they were my California dream, and knowing them, more than anything else, made me fall in love with the Golden State. They made me part of their family and made those four months in Napa one of the best times of my life."

Then it hits me. A real eureka moment. I slap the steering wheel and punch the Prius in the roof. "Bingo! That's it! That's why I had to come up here. I need to go to their house in St. Helena and soak up that energy and fortify myself with that stuff. That's what this whole trip is all about!"

"Cool," Diane says, relieved, I think, that it was nothing more serious like a major heart attack.

We get off the freeway and make our way into St. Helena. I've heard reports that St. Helena, more so than anywhere else in the valley, had become trendy and overcrowded—a tourist trap that would bear no resemblance to the haven I used to know. Again, just like in Yountville, I don't find that to be the case. It's just like I remember it. We drive down Main Street—the barber shop, the hardware store, the ice cream place—all the same. In a sense, St. Helena is my Camelot. And to find it like this makes me feel like my past still exists and has not just vanished into the ether.

I remember the way to the house as if it were yesterday. We turn onto Allyn Street, and I suddenly start feeling nervous. I slow down as if to give myself more time to prepare for the shock that I somehow know is coming. My nervousness is justified. The house is gone. I park in front of an empty lot with a chain-link fence around it and some heavy equipment inside, where the ground is being prepared for whatever is going to happen in there. How odd. Everything else in St. Helena is perfectly intact, just as I remember, except for this.

We get out of the car and walk up to the fence together.

"This is what you wanted to see?" Diane asks.

I nod my head. No need for words.

"I'm sorry," she says and then puts an arm around my shoulder.

"Me too." I wrap my fingers through the chain-link and scan the lot for a hint of a memory, for a feeling. Something I can take with me.

"I can feel it," Diane reassures me. "There's still something here."

We stand there, both staring into the lot. Paying respects, as at a funeral. There is still some sort of energy here. Diane is right. Energy lives on they say, and if you are sensitive enough, you can feel it. And if it's a good energy—maybe you can be guided by it and it can help you find your way.

An engine roars behind us. We spin around and, unbelievably, there is Travis—his hair still caked with blood and syrup—getting off his motorcycle and lunging toward us.

"Little old for you isn't he, Diane?" Travis growls.

"Travis!" Diane squeezes her small body between me and the fence and digs her fingernails into my arm.

How is this even possible? Was he behind us the whole time?

"How'd you find us, you fuck?" Diane demands.

"I tracked you on your cell phone, you stupid bitch!"

Ah, well, there you have it.

He spits at us but is unsuccessful. A string of bloody drool dangles from his chin. I think the hit on the head has done Travis some serious harm. He lists to his left, corrects his balance, and then points a threatening finger at Diane.

"You fucked with me for the last time, bitch." He pulls a gun from the inside of his leather jacket and points it in our direction.

"Wait a minute. Hold on just a second here." That's all I can think to say, but apparently that's enough.

A loud screeching noise from above us, sort of a cross between a jet fighter and a hawk, sends our gazes skyward. The bird-monster from Los Angeles streaks out of the sky and hits Travis's gun hand, ripping the gun away in its mouth along with a few of Travis's fingers. Another bird looming immediately behind, dives in and rips off the top of Travis's head. I hope he is dead when he hits the ground, because the two birds are on him instantly, swallowing chunks of his flesh and tearing him limb from limb.

My heart stops. I am certain that I'm going to die next.

There are a few witnesses on the street walking their dogs. There's an evening jogger with a '70s-style headband flashlight, and a woman who has stopped her Buick right in the middle of the street. All of us are too terrified to move or speak or bark. We can only watch in horror as the bird-monsters continue their meal of Travis. Then as quickly as they flew down, they rise back up into the sky, flapping their giant wings, and vanish into the night.

As soon as the coast is clear, the dogs get brave and start barking like crazy. Diane steps out from behind me, wide-eyed as ever but shockingly unafraid.

"God sent them to protect you," she marvels. Her green eyes sparkle like emeralds.

"I believe that may be true." I pound a fist against my chest just to make sure everything is still working in there.

The other people on the street have begun speaking to each other in hushed, hurried tones. I can see a few of them on their cell phones. All of them are looking in our direction, even the dogs.

"What do we do?" Diane asked.

"Maybe we should stick around for a while…as witnesses, for when the police come."

From the street light, I can see an expanding pool of blood around what's left of Travis's body. He's definitely dead this time.

Diane is pulling on my arm.

"How 'bout let's get a drink," she says. I don't want to talk to any cops.

Now that she mentions it—I probably don't want to deal with the police now, either. Especially with what went down in LA.

"Sounds good," I say.

We lock arms, steadying ourselves against each other again, just as we did earlier today when we were fleeing the diner. Thank goodness the Prius doors unlock immediately this time. We get in and get the hell out of Dodge.

CHAPTER SEVENTEEN

THOSE FRIENDS THOU HAST, GRAPPLE THEM TO THY SOUL WITH HOOPS OF STEEL

Not feeling stable enough to make the drive all the way to San Francisco, I head south to Napa—to at least get some distance between us and what had just happened—and find a Motel 6. The witnesses, if questioned, would surely testify that Travis confronted us, not the other way around, and that the bird-monsters dove from the sky and were the ones that killed him, not the two people who got into a green Prius and drove away like thieves in the night. Yeah, we're pretty screwed.

At the motel check-in desk, Diane tells me to just get one room with two beds and that will be fine.

"I'm his daughter!" she proudly tells the desk clerk, who tries his best to avoid eye contact with us.

If there is a place in my aging brain that might be entertaining a steamy Motel 6 fantasy, that pretty much takes care of it. So we wind up getting one room instead of two (judge me how you will). The Motel 6 is the cheapest place we could find, but it doesn't have a restaurant or a bar, so we get back into the Prius and try to find something. Not far away is a nice little coffee shop that serves beer and wine. This place looks a lot more of the present. In fact, the whole retro '70s thing seems to be fading. I noticed it first when we were leaving St. Helena. As if the drive into Napa were returning us to our own time. I have a sudden hopeful feeling that maybe the whole incident with Travis was left somewhere in the past, and we won't have to deal with the repercussions here in the present.

The voice in my head clarifies things for me.

Fat chance. There's no way of escaping the shit storm that's coming, Buster Brown. Well, there is one way, but we already been over that, ain't we?

I was hoping that Colonel Sanders got lost back there in the '70s as well. No such luck.

We get a booth in the back, and we both order some cabernet. After what we'd been through, Diane must have aged a bit because they don't ask her for ID. The waitress brings our wine, and then we order some food.

"I'm sorry about Travis," I say.

"Why?" She shrugs as if it's no big deal.

"Well, he was your boyfriend."

"No he wasn't. Not anymore." She takes a sip of wine.

"Okay." I leave it alone.

She puts down her glass, and I can see her fighting back some tears and trying to be brave.

"Do you think we can still do a winery tour?" she asks as if she's about ten years old.

It just breaks my heart. She's bringing out things in me I don't think I've ever felt before. Fatherly stuff, I guess it is. She is really attractive—but still, I'm almost positive that it's fatherly stuff.

"I think we better get out of here in the morning, don't you?" I say.

"I guess so," she reluctantly agrees.

"Are you okay?"

"Yeah. Why shouldn't I be? "

Her cell phone rings. She answers it right away. "Hey, Tony... Yeah, I did call. Oh, that's okay, I figured...Listen, do you think I could stay with you guys for a few days? Some stuff went down...I'll tell you later—I'm with somebody...Yeah, I'm okay, I'll tell you about it when I see you...Thanks, I really appreciate it...For just a few days. Tomorrow, is that okay? Great...great...bye." She disconnects the call and drinks some more wine. "Cool, I got a place to stay."

"Good."

I notice her hand starting to shake as she fumbles to put the phone away, and then she lets it go. Like a little kid. She puts her head down on the table and just cries. I want to comfort her, but I'm not sure how or if it would help. I should pat her hand or her head and say, "there, there," but I'd probably just make things worse. I'm just not very good in these situations and prefer to avoid them altogether.

She comes out of it pretty quickly, though. She takes a deep breath, sits up straight, and looks me square in the eye.

Then I do indeed pat her hand in spite of myself.

"The thing is," she says, "for the first time in my life I feel like I'm a part of something really important, or a witness to it anyway. This is a big moment for me. Like something historical in my life. And then tomorrow you'll be gone, and then what? What do I do after this? I just saw something from God! I just saw proof of something that hardly anybody gets to see. I don't want to let that go, you know? I don't want to let you go." She grabs my hand. "I mean, in a way, I was chosen for this, too. Don't you think?"

"Maybe—I don't know what to think."

"I want to be a part of this, Harold."

"But, Diane, I don't even know what this is or what I'm going to do yet."

"Are you going to see that girl?"

"I'll talk to her."

"But if God told you that this is what you have to do, and He told her…don't you just have to do it?" She still has hold of my hand in an ever-tightening grip. "Maybe you're just telling yourself it's not right because you're afraid."

"Maybe," I say again, thinking that she might be on to something.

"He's protecting you so that you get this done."

"So it seems," I say.

She releases my hand and leans back into the booth.

"What a trip," she says then takes a drink and laughs.

The waitress brings our food. It's the same thing I ordered at the pancake house in Coalinga—a California Club. Realizing this, I completely lose my appetite. Diane, on the other hand, dives right in to her greasy cheeseburger with fries. I watch her eat. It's oddly enthralling—the energy with which she goes at it. I'm mesmerized watching her eat. Go figure.

"Maybe I should leave the car here, and we'll walk back to the hotel," I suggest.

"In case they're looking for it?" she manages between mouthfuls.

"Yeah."

"That makes sense."

I finish my wine and look around for the waitress to order another. She must have gone out for a smoke or something.

"The thing is, Diane." Something suddenly comes into focus, and I need to get it out or else I fear I might lose track of it. "My gut is telling me that something else is going on here. There's free will and intuition, right?"

"Yeah?" She stops eating and gives me her full attention.

"Well, my intuition is telling me that things are not what they appear to be, and it's telling me definitely not to have sex with Portia. And it's not because I'm afraid of what might happen after. Well, I am afraid, but that's not the point. The point is, it's about right and wrong. And if there's free will—"

"Yeah…?"

"Well, I aim to use it, that's all. I'm going to trust my intuition. I'm going to stand up for what I believe, no matter what. No matter what anybody says."

"Even God?"

"Yes."

"But what if you're wrong?"

"I'll send the world an apology note."

"But what if what you're thinking has nothing to do with anything, and God just wants you to do what He told you to do or else?"

"Well, then I guess he picked the wrong guy."

"But He's God. He doesn't make mistakes."

"Exactly!"

It occurs to me how similar our conversation is to an Abbott and Costello routine.

"But then what's it all about?" she asks. "If it's not about getting the girl pregnant, what is it?"

"I'd just be guessing at this point," I say.

She inhales a fry. "It's about faith, isn't it? You have to have faith enough to believe. He spoke to you! What more do you need?"

"How's this?" I query. "You know that energy we felt back there in St. Helena?"

"Yeah?"

"It exists because the people in that house felt so strongly about taking care of me and their son's friends. They were completely committed to it. They knew it was the right thing to do no matter what anybody had to say about it. And believe me, their neighbors gave them lots of flack about having all those kids around 24-7. I think if you feel compassion and have a pretty good grip on what's right and wrong, and your nature is to do right by people, then that's what you go with. That's what you put your trust in. That's what you have faith in. It's important for me not to doubt my intuition. Maybe it's a test. That's what I think is going on here."

Diane studies me for a moment and then polishes off her wine. "So it's all about you and not about saving the world?"

"I think they're connected."

"How?"

"I don't know yet."

"Wouldn't it be easier just to screw the girl?" she asks.

"You don't know me that well. It wouldn't be easy at all. It would be awkward and unbelievably embarrassing."

She laughs and I join her, and, man, the laughter is like medicine.

———

We leave the Prius on the street by the restaurant and walk the few blocks back to the Motel 6. The voice shows up in my head again.

Never leave a soldier behind, son…it's not how it's done!

"Did you hear that?" I knew that she hadn't, but I ask anyway.

"What?"

"Never mind."

I know that hearing voices may be symptomatic of depression or psychosis or perhaps a brain tumor. I guess you could say the same about seeing giant bird-monsters. But at least the birds proved to be not just in my imagination but actually flying around and offing people.

Anyway, I'll have to deal with the colonel later. I have no idea what the "never leave a soldier behind" thing is all about, but hopefully the Prius will survive the night without developing any abandonment issues.

When we get into the room, I turn on the TV to see if there's any news about what had happened in St. Helena. Sure enough, the local stations are all over it. They have camera crews out on Allyn Street. Cop cars, ambulances, and a big crowd are gathered at the scene. A reporter talks to the camera:

Witnesses say the man was attacked from above by large birds. It sounds like something out of a Hitchcock movie, Bill, but that's what they're saying here. Authorities have asked for people to stay calm. Police say they're looking for two people who fled the scene. One officer told me earlier, Bill, that what probably happened is that there was a confrontation, shots were fired, and after the man was already dead, vultures came onto the scene, and that's what people saw. Witnesses however report that no shots were fired. It's a mystery right now, Bill. From St. Helena, this is—

I turn off the TV.

"Let's try to get some sleep and get out of here early," I say.

It's been a long time since I shared a room with somebody besides my wife. I did with my sister last year, but not with a gorgeous nineteen-year-old who I wish would be my daughter. This is a lot different and much more confusing. We take our turns using the bathroom and then get into our respective beds without the other one seeing too much. I have another ridiculous sexual fantasy, but it passes like a kidney stone—not as painful, but excruciating nonetheless.

"Harold?"

"Yes?" I say a little too expectantly.

"No matter what happens, thanks for taking me with you."

"I don't think I could have handled it without you, Diane."

"Good night, Harold."

"Good night."

I shut off the bedside lamp. All is blissfully still until my Sherwood Forest ringtone completely annihilates the quiet in the room. I fumble around, trying to find my phone. I get the bedside lamp back on after almost knocking it over, and then the trumpets blare yet again before I'm finally able to get at it.

"Hello?"

"Mr. Geeg!" cries the voice on the phone.

"Yes, Mr. Geeg."

"There're news reports about giant birds killing a guy in St. Helena."

"I know, Mr. Geeg."

"Are you okay?"

"Yeah."

"So it wasn't you who was killed?"

I take a moment before answering, trying to figure out if he's being funny on purpose or just being funny. "No. It wasn't me."

"Okay, good."

"I saw it happen, though."

"Oh shit!" he cries.

"Mr. Geeg, we better get off this line. *Those* people might be listening, you know?"

"I know. You should ditch that phone, I'm telling you. Call me later on a pay phone."

"Tomorrow."

"Goodbye, Mr. Geeg."

"Goodbye, Mr. Geeg." I disconnect the call.

"Who was that?" Diane asks.

"The news is reporting the story in LA."

"That was fast."

"It'll be national by tomorrow."

"They're going to find us aren't they, Harold?"

"We didn't do anything wrong. We'll be okay."

"I hope so—oh shit!"

She grabs for her phone on the nightstand. "I better kill this tracking app. That was so stupid, I can't believe it. I led him right to us."

For what would take me the better part of a day to accomplish, she manages in mere seconds.

"Good night, Diane. We'll be all right. Try and get some sleep, okay?

"Okay. Good night, Harold."

I shut the light off again.

I was dreading an angry knock on the door. An "open up! Police!" But in spite of this, I do manage to get a little sleep.

In the morning I remember the dream I had: Kelly was naked and standing on the roof of our house. I was in the driveway screaming for her to come down. My heart was pounding so hard that I could hear it. She said that I worry too much. Then she raised her arms above her head and jumped—straight up into the air. Kelly flew above the palm trees and took off into the horizon.

CHAPTER EIGHTEEN

ADIEU, ADIEU,
REMEMBER ME

We check out in a hurry and then hustle back to the coffee shop, where we had left the car. Now I've had this happen before in parking garages and one time at a Home Depot—you park the car, do what you came to do, go back to the parking lot, and the car isn't there anymore. Probably my aging brain is to blame, but where I thought I left the car had nothing to do with where the car actually was. The time at Home Depot, I searched and searched and just could not find the Prius. I actually went so far as to notify the store manager that my car had been stolen. He came outside, and we both looked around the lot to no avail. After several minutes of this, he called the police to report the theft of a customer's vehicle. I discovered shortly thereafter, much to my embarrassment, that the Prius had not actually been stolen. I had parked in the back lot on the other side of the building. I apologized profusely to the manager, who was very civil about it and assured me that it could have happened to anyone. I knew what he was thinking, though. I could tell by the flush in his cheeks and the throbbing vein in his neck. What he really wanted to do was hit me over the head with something from the plumbing department.

This time, however, I have a younger, healthier brain with me. The Prius is gone. Diane confirms it. If it were just me, well then sure, I might have parked around the corner or in the next town over, but she knows exactly where we left the car, and the car just isn't there anymore. I check the parking signs, thinking that maybe it got towed for being illegally parked overnight or something. But there are no signs like that on the street.

Then a Napa police car comes around the corner and pulls up next to us.

"Hi," says the cop.

"Good morning," I cheerfully reply.

"Looking for your car?"

I decide to do something that I'm good at. I play dumb. "What car?"

"The green Prius that we just towed."

He gets out of the car, leaving it running in the middle of the street. He walks slowly toward us with a pretentious little smile on his face. He is very skinny for a cop and only about my height. He has bloodshot eyes, and when he gets close, I can smell cigarettes and peanut butter on his breath. A particularly disturbing combination, by the way. The colonel's voice loves to show up at moments like these.

If I was you, for which I am eternally grateful that I am not, I'd make a grab for his gun. Grab his gun, son. It'll make you feel more like a man.

The cop is right in my face now, smirking and smelling terrible.

Are you tough enough, boy? I don't think ya' are, son. I don't think you got it in ya'. Grab the gun, son!

I quickly shake my head and fortunately that clears the colonel out of there. Sometimes this shaking the head thing can look comical—like a triple take. The cop, however, is not amused. He takes a step back, perhaps considering for the first time that I might actually be dangerous.

The cop rests his hand on his holstered weapon. "We just want to ask you a few questions about last night, and then you can get your car back, okay?"

I definitely do not want to make this man nervous, so I try to appease him with an overly friendly and cooperative response, "Okay. Absolutely. No problem."

We get in his car, both me and Diane in the back seat, and start on our way to wherever he wants to take us.

"So, are we arrested?" I ask.

"No, I told you they just want to talk."

"So you tow my car just so we can talk?"

"Well, sir, I guess they *really* want to talk."

"We didn't do anything. We just saw it happen. Just like everybody else who was there."

"You know what? I don't really care. Save your breath and tell it to the detectives."

"We didn't do anything," I reiterated.

"Congratulations," he says. He lights up a cigarette with one of those flip-top silver Zippo lighters. I find this even more offensive than his bad breath.

Diane takes my hand and squeezes it. Quite a grip the kid's got. I believe she is trying to tell me to shut up. I talk way too much when I get nervous.

We drive over this very cool bridge on First Street and then on to the police station, which is not too far from there. I had never spent much time in Napa, so I try to familiarize myself with the surroundings in case I need to make a daring escape later.

The police station is a great old stone building, probably built in the '20s, maybe earlier. It has those big old lampposts out front just like police stations always have in the movies. We are escorted into a back room, where four men in plainclothes and badges on their belts are drinking coffee and apparently waiting for us to arrive. Two metal chairs are positioned in front of an old wooden table. The men are positioned behind the table, standing in front of their own metal chairs. Old Peanut Butter Breath instructs us to sit, and we do. Then we all just stare at each other for a minute. Nobody is smiling or even pretending to be pleasant.

As I mentioned, when I get nervous, I talk. So ignoring Diane's gripping plea for silence, I begin to blather.

"You know, this happened to me once before...down in LA. I was getting all these threatening phone calls from store owners accusing me of writing bad checks. But I didn't write any bad checks, so I didn't know what was going on. Then one day, two police officers from bunco show up at my door and ask me if my name is Harold Goldfarb. I say yes, and they say, 'well, we'd like to have a word with you downtown about all these bad checks you've been writing.' I say, 'oh man, am I glad to see you guys because I didn't write any bad checks, and I've been getting all these really nasty phone calls, and I don't know what's going on.' So they take me downtown to the station, and we go into a little green room, and they're actually trying to get me to confess to writing these checks! I keep telling them that I didn't do it, but they think I'm a con man or something. Then they show me a picture of this guy who's been writing the bad checks. Another guy named Harold Goldfarb—I kid you not! And I'm telling you, he looked just like me. It was so weird. So now I'm freaking out, but I keep telling them that they've got the wrong guy. Then they take me into another room and have me do some writing samples. I guess they had the other Harold Goldfarb's signature—and that was it. That's what got me off. The handwriting didn't match. I'm telling you, though, I was sweating bullets there for a minute. So they apologized, and then they drove me back home. Nice officers. Very nice. A man and a woman. I invited them to come see a play I was in. They didn't, though. So I understand how you might have gotten the wrong idea about this. We didn't do anything is what I'm trying to say."

I look over at Diane, who's looking down at her shoes.

The cops consider us and drink their coffee. Nobody says anything, and the silence is more than a little unsettling. They all have serious expressions on their faces, except for one guy. He's smiling as if he's trying to hold back a laugh. For a cop, this guy has a kind face. Even though he probably thinks I'm a mass murderer, there's something warm about the guy, and I immediately take a liking to him.

"How's it going?" I ask him.

He nods his head at me but doesn't say anything. After a few more somber stares, they all start taking their seats. We look at each other some more, and then the guy in the middle with a remarkably round belly starts the discussion.

"So, what the hell happened in St. Helena last night? Why don't you tell us about it?"

I look over at Diane, who's still studying something on the floor.

"And, you guys are…who exactly?" I figure it couldn't hurt to ask.

"Oh, sure. I'm Detective Joelson from here in Napa and that's Detective Schmitt (the smiling one) from St. Helena and Detectives Williams and Douglas from San Francisco."

"So, we meet again, eh, Diane," Douglas says.

Douglas and Williams from San Francisco look oddly alike. Short cropped hair and mustaches and now both wearing smirks on their faces that remind me of the one that Officer Peanut Butter Breath sports so well.

"Things just got very serious for you, kid," Williams adds.

Diane says nothing. Something cramps up in my stomach, and I'm thinking that I might need to use the bathroom.

"We'll get to Diane's problem in a minute," says Detective Joelson. "But first let's talk a little about last night, okay?" Joelson types something on the laptop he has in front of him.

"But we're not under arrest or anything like that?" I ask as my stomach starts to gurgle.

"No, no—just want to talk, that's all," Detective Joelson says with a slight smile. "We know that you were there last night because another witness gave the police your descriptions and got the license number on the Prius. We're just trying to talk to everyone who was at the scene. Especially to you and Diane because Diane was connected to the deceased, right, Diane?"

Diane still has nothing to say.

"And you were with her, for some reason," Detective Joelson continues. "Why is that Mr. Goldfarb? Are you in a relationship, or were you making a purchase of some kind? And what brings you all the way up here from LA?"

"Okay," I begin. "I'm not sure what I should or shouldn't say in this kind of situation—"

"Just tell us the truth, that's all," Douglas says.

"I'm just going to tell you what happened because we did absolutely nothing wrong here."

"Perfect," Joelson says.

"Would you like some coffee?" Detective Williams offers.

"Ah, the old good cop, bad cop, eh?" I stupidly joke.

"No, not at all," says Williams. "Just offering some coffee is all."

Detective Schmitt is smiling again. At least somebody's having a good time.

"No coffee, thanks. My stomach is a little off all of a sudden. Seriously, is there a bathroom nearby?"

"Down the hall," Schmitt tells me. "The officer will escort you if you need to go."

I look over at old Peanut Butter Breath, who gives me another smirk. I decide it can wait.

"Maybe a Danish or a bagel?" Williams offers, hoping, I think, to make my stomach even more uncomfortable—just to see what happens.

"No, no…thank you, though."

"How about you, Diane, can we get you something?"

Diane still refuses to participate.

Officer Joelson suddenly cuts off the pleasantries with a much firmer tone. "Just tell us what happened."

"Okay, so it's very simple," I say. "I was taking a little break and decided that it would be nice to drive up here for a vacation. I used to work up here years back. Way back. I won't tell you how far back, because I don't want you to feel obligated to treat me respectfully just because of my age." I was hoping for a little chuckle at least, but I get nothing. "Anyway, I'm driving up and I make a stop at a restaurant to get something to eat—"

"Where did you stop?" Joelson interrupts.

"It was a pancake house."

"No, I mean what town?" Joelson corrects.

"Oh! Coalinga, I think it was."

"Isn't that where you relocated, Diane?" Douglas asks.

Diane doesn't answer him.

"Hey, Diane, maybe we can get you in that state prison there. It'd be so convenient. You could just walk over from your house!" Douglas suggests with disturbing enthusiasm.

I lean over and whisper to Diane, "Is this okay? Do you want me to stop?"

"It doesn't matter now," she mumbles.

"Mr. Goldfarb?"

"Yes, Officer Joelson?"

"Please continue."

"So, yes, that's where I saw Diane for the first time."

"Never saw her before that?" asks Williams.

"No."

"So what happened there at the restaurant?" Joelson asks.

A couple of things hit my brain at the same time. Did the Mormon lawyer file charges against me, and did I now have that on my record for all the world to see? And do I really want to tell these guys that I hit Travis on the head with a syrup bottle? And how much do they already know about Diane, and by talking am I about to send her up the river, so to speak? I take a moment to sort all that out.

"Sir…?" Joelson urges.

"Yes?"

"Please continue."

I try to stall. "Do you have a little water or something?"

Williams begrudgingly gets me some water from the watercooler.

"Thank you. I just got a little dry all of a sudden." I drink the water as slowly as I can and then smile at them.

"Go ahead, Mr. Goldfarb," Joelson says with growing impatience.

"Yes, so, Diane was in the booth across from me, and a man comes in the restaurant. It was this Travis guy, and he's angry with Diane. They start to argue. Diane says that she wants out, that she feels trapped. She says she wants to start over, away from all this crap and that she's tired of being his slave. He's screaming at her, calling her all kinds of filthy names, saying that nobody runs out on him—that kind of thing. It was terrible."

"What stuff was she doing with him, do you think?" Douglas asks.

"I don't know, I really don't. I'm sure you know more about it than I do, sir."

"Fair enough," says Williams. "Please continue."

"So, this Travis guy starts grabbing her and hurting her, trying to get her out of the booth. It got very bad, and nobody was doing anything to help, so…I got up, and I did something."

"What did you do?" Williams presses.

"I got her away from him."

"How did you do that?"

About a dozen bad ideas run through my head about what I could say and then that damn voice puts its two cents into the mix.

Oh, they don't like you, son. Go for their guns. It's your only hope.

I do a triple take head shake to clear it out of there. Officer Schmitt has to stifle a laugh.

"Are you okay, Mr. Goldfarb?" Joelson asks.

"I'm fine, thank you. A little tired is all." And then I just let it go. "I hit him over the head with a syrup bottle."

There is silence after that. Joelson types something on his laptop.

"Go ahead," Williams says.

"So I had to take her with me. I couldn't just leave her there. This guy was dangerous. We drove up to San Francisco so she could stay with some friends, but they weren't home, so I took her with me to St. Helena and that's when Travis showed up."

"And then what?" Joelson asks.

"He pulled a gun, and then those birds came."

"The birds killed him?" asks Williams.

"That's right."

"Why did you flee the scene?" Douglas asks.

"Because we were scared."

"Because you didn't want to be implicated?"

"Interpret it any way you want to. I'm just telling you what happened."

"And you had nothing to do with the murder or those things that attacked him?" Douglas continues.

"You mean like were they my trained attack birds or something like that? No, sir. I have never trained or owned a bird in my life. I had a dog once. He shit on our rugs until he was five, and we finally had to get rid of him. So I couldn't even housebreak a dog, gentlemen, let alone train birds to kill."

"So what do you think those birds are? Where did they come from?" Williams asks.

"Maybe they came from God and were sent to punish a very bad man."

"You know what's interesting?" Schmitt asks, and he isn't smiling anymore.

"What?"

"There were eyewitness reports yesterday about unusually large birds, and judging from the recorded sightings, they were making their way up the coast just about the same time that you were."

"No kidding."

"No, I'm very serious," Schmitt says.

"Weird."

"Isn't it?" Schmitt agrees.

"So what do you think about that, Detective Schmitt?" I ask.

"I think you're not telling us the whole story here, Mr. Goldfarb."

"Well, I could tell you the story of my life if you like, but it's really not that interesting. It would bore you to death, and I have too much respect for the police to subject you to that kind of abuse. I don't know what those birds are or where they came from, and I have no control over them. Did I mention that I'm an actor? I'm not that bright, gentlemen."

"But why would they track you up the coast?" Schmitt continues.

"I have no idea. Maybe they're my guardian angels."

There is another pause after that. The line of questioning, if continued, would enter even further into the preposterous or the supernatural, and I guess nobody really wanted to go there.

"You can go, Mr. Goldfarb," Joelson says.

"Thank you, but I'm not going without Diane."

Diane looks up disbelievingly.

"Mr. Goldfarb," says Douglas with a smugness that makes me start thinking about using the bathroom again. "Diane has violated the conditions of her probation, and she will have to appear before a judge for sentencing in San Francisco."

"There was already a warrant issued for her arrest," Williams adds.

"So she's not going anywhere right now," Joelson says as he closes up his laptop. "Travis and Diane were in business together as dealers and as users. Is that somebody you really want to get involved with, Mr. Goldfarb?"

I stand up suddenly, which seems to make the detectives extremely uncomfortable. But I feel a speech coming on, and if there's one thing

I know how to do in this world, it's how to take stage. Oh, and how to play dumb. So two things, maybe.

"Gentlemen, she might have done that once," I begin with great sincerity, "but she doesn't anymore. Doesn't want to. Diane has had a pretty hard time of it. She hasn't gotten any breaks in this life, and she's been dragged into some things that were out of her control. She's nineteen years old for God's sake, and, yes, she's made mistakes. She was set up for it. Gentlemen, Diane needs somebody to care about her. We spent some time together in the last few days. I saw her heart, and I know what kind of person she really is. Diane is a kind, compassionate, good person who just needs a chance to prove it. Yes, Detective Joelson, she is somebody I care about and somebody I'd have no problem getting involved with—in a healthy way—in case you were thinking of it…some way else." I sit down. Not completely satisfied with my performance.

"Well, that was very touching, Mr. Goldfarb," Douglas says. "But Diane will remain in custody here overnight, and tomorrow she will be transported to San Francisco and held there until she can appear before a judge for a violation hearing and further sentencing. That's the law, and that's the way it is."

I take a moment, for dramatic effect, and then stand up again.

"I will hang around then. I will be checking on her, and I will go to San Francisco to talk to the judge. I will be her advocate, and I will stand up and fight for her."

I'm definitely overacting now, but I'm completely sincere about what I'm saying, even if the delivery is somewhat over the top.

Schmitt smiles.

"That is your right, Mr. Goldfarb," Douglas says.

"Get her a good lawyer. She's going to need one," Williams grimly adds.

He is right. Diane will need a good lawyer, but I have no connections up here. I don't even know any in LA. How does one go about finding a good lawyer? The yellow pages? Yelp? To avoid a panic attack, I continue to blather.

"Okay then—I'll be back a little later on to check on things and make sure Diane is okay, and if there's anything she needs…and I guess that's that—for that. Done and done."

I look at Diane, and she's tearing up. I give her a hug.

"Be strong, Diane. I won't desert you, I promise."

"Thanks, Dad," she says.

That really gets to me. I don't want the detectives to see me cry, so I leave the room.

CHAPTER NINETEEN

MY FATE
CRIES OUT

Officer Peanut Butter Breath drives me to an impound lot a few blocks away from the police station. He parks but leaves the engine running. I'm not sure why I feel it necessary to say anything to this guy, but I do.

"Well, I'll be back later on."

"To do what?" he asks as he lights up a cigarette.

Considerate fellow that he is, he rolls down his window, but just a crack. This does nothing to ventilate the car. It seems to just push the smoke to the back seat, where I'm trying not to gag.

"To see her," I say and then clear my throat.

"Well, it's not a hotel, you know. You can't just pop in whenever you want to."

"Oh?"

"Yeah, they have visiting hours. From nine in the morning to ten thirty and from one to three in the afternoon, and you have to sign up thirty minutes before. One half-hour visit per customer. South Jail Women's visits on Monday and North Jail is Friday."

"I thought I could just go down there and see her."

"No, that's not how we do it on Planet Earth anymore," he says, the smirk returning to his face. "And it's not down there where we were. That's the police station. You need to go to the Napa County Jail over on Third Street."

"Really, I thought I'd just go back there."

"You can if you want to, but your friend ain't gonna be there."

"So how do I know if she's in South Jail or North Jail?"

"Probation violation—probably South Jail." He exhales a deep drag, aiming the smoke at the window crack, but it blows back into my face instead.

I cough severely. He doesn't seem to notice.

"And today is Monday?" I wheeze.

"Last I checked," he says.

I try to roll down my window with the power window button, but the window won't budge. "So I could go back and see her today, right?"

"Theoretically...unless they're having a problem over there. You never know for sure."

"Where's Third Street?"

"Two blocks away from First Street," he replies in full-blown smirk.

Normally I like cops, but this guy—I'm thinking about grabbing his gun again, only without any prodding voices this time.

I try to open the car door, but I can't. In case you've never been in a cop car before, they really don't want you getting out until they let you out. He watches me for a while in his rearview mirror as I struggle to get the door open and try not to breathe. Then he gets out and slowly walks all the way around the car and opens the door for me. I jump out of the car through a cloud of smoke.

"Go see that guy in the booth over there and give him this ticket. He'll get the car for you," he tells me.

"Thanks."

"A hundred and fifty dollar impound fee."

"What?"

"I'm kidding, relax. It's on us. Maybe they even washed it for you."

"Really?"

"No, not really."

He reminds me of this skinny kid I knew in grade school. He was sort of the class asshole, and even though I outweighed this kid by fifty pounds, I had no guilt whatsoever the day I beat the shit out of him.

"Have a nice day," he joyfully mocks.

He gets back into his reeking police car and leaves me there with nasty little thoughts in my head.

So I walk over to the booth and give the guy my ticket. He comes out of the booth and walks right past me. I follow him. This guy never says a word to me. One of the meanest, angriest faces I've ever seen. He wears a hairnet and a wifebeater T-shirt and every inch of skin on his arms is covered in tattoos. I walk a safe distance behind him. He definitely has that "Walking Spanish Down the Hall" thing that Tom Waits sings about. We get to the car, and then much to my surprise he smiles at me.

"That cop's fucking classic, isn't he?" he says.

"Yeah," I say. "There are assholes and there are great assholes. That guy—he's just fucking phenomenal."

"You got that right, brother." He laughs and gives me a friendly smack on the arm.

Unfortunately, I get knocked off-balance and stumble awkwardly into the Prius.

"Oh, sorry, bro," he says.

"No, no problem," I assure him. "The ground is a little uneven here."

"Keep your nose clean, my friend."

"Thanks, I will check it often."

He smiles and gives me a nod of approval, which makes me feel very good about him and about myself. But then he gets that serious look again, which I mirror back in self-defense.

"Do I know you?" he says.

"I don't think so."

"I feel as though I do."

"Hmm," I reply.

"Whatever, don't matter—you take care of yourself, bro."

"You do the same. What's your name, by the way?"

"Israel."

"Nice to know you, Israel. My name is Harold."

"Okay, see you around, Harold."

"Yeah, down the road, my friend," I say.

"Yeah."

He looks at me a moment longer, trying to figure out if he knows me from somewhere. Then he turns suddenly and walks Spanish back the other way.

The Prius unlocks on the first attempt. I get in and push the button, and it starts right up. Maybe it is glad to see me, or maybe the Prius just

STILL HARPING ON MY DAUGHTER

doesn't like being institutionalized. I drive out of the lot, not exactly sure of where I'm going but glad to be on my way. I figure I'll check back into the Motel 6. I told you that I have a terrible sense of direction, and I wasn't kidding. I'm completely lost about two seconds after leaving the lot. I pass the jail on Third Street, so at least I know where that is. Whether or not I can find it again—that's another story.

I drive around looking for something familiar. I have the address for the Motel 6 on the receipt they gave me, but the built-in GPS is not working at all now. Things just seem to work or not work depending on the mood of the car. I'm sure the Prius prefers things this way, but eventually I'm going to have to put my foot down.

Finally I pull over and ask a guy on the street if he knows where the Motel 6 is. He looks at me as if I'm crazy and then points straight ahead. It's practically right in front of me. I've always depended on the directional kindness of strangers.

Suddenly I realize that I'm starving. I find my way back to that coffee shop that we hit last night and get myself a breakfast sandwich and a large coffee to go. After that, I make only one wrong turn and then manage to find my way back to the Motel 6.

Turns out that the same room that we checked out of is still available, so I check back in. The desk clerk still avoids eye contact with me through the entire transaction. I'm not sure if it has to do with checking in before with Diane or if there's something mentally wrong with this guy. Pretty creepy, whatever it is.

Once in the room, I lay out my food on the desk and figure I'll make a few calls. See if I can find a lawyer and take care of a few other things that I need to pay some attention to. I take a bite of my breakfast sandwich. I have to tell you, that place makes a nice breakfast sandwich. They gave me a side of fries with it, too. I'm trying to lay off the fried stuff, but what the hell. The world is probably coming to an end before a french fry will have a chance to kill me.

I'm worried about Diane. If Officer Wiseass is right about visiting hours, I figure that I need to get over to the jail by one, and hopefully with some good news about a lawyer. I really didn't like seeing her so down.

Then something goes by the window, and a big shadow crosses the room.

"You gotta be kidding me!" I shout.

I run to the window and catch sight of it flapping away, straight up into the air. Then another one shoots by. It's huge. I stumble backward and almost fall over the desk chair. I get back to the window in time to see them both disappear into the cloudless blue sky.

I sit back down at the desk and stare at the food. If Diane is right and I am wrong and the bird-monsters are actually protecting me so I can make Portia pregnant—if I screw that up (pardon the pun) and my thinking is way off track—then rather than being my protectors, will the bird-monsters become my enemies instead? Will they do to me what they did to Travis?

The thought of my skull being ripped off and my brain struggling for air as I bleed to death in some street somewhere makes me realize that they forgot to give me ketchup for my fries—yet another horror I have to deal with.

Then the bird-monsters fly past the window again. I'm not sure why exactly, but I take this as a vote of confidence from them, that I am indeed on the right track. Probably because if I take it the other way, I would never leave this motel room again for the rest of my life. I admire them as they gracefully turn and swirl, shriek, and then lift their grotesque bodies into the heavens, where they seemingly vanish into thin air. Wow, they are truly magnificent, in a hideous kind of way. I must admit it makes me feel special to have my own personal bird-monsters—that's some heady stuff. Yes, I'd have to say I'm becoming rather fond of them. I think about going out to get them a treat. Some bird seed or a dead raccoon. I'm also starting to worry about their well-being, as any responsible pet owner would. A lot of people must be seeing them out there. They're kind of hard to miss. I hope some idiot with a gun won't decide to take a shot at them. But in reality, the bird-monsters, I have no doubt, are more than capable of taking care of themselves. They are supernatural after all, and probably endowed with powers I have yet to even witness. I'm sure they can handle anything that some human asshole can dish out. So, feeling a little better about everything, I finish my breakfast and then call the number Kelly gave me for the cops who came to the house. When the phone rings on the other end for the fifth time, I'm expecting to be sent to voice mail, but then somebody picks up.

"Officer Rivas," he dully answers.

"Yes. Hello, Officer Rivas. This is Harold Goldfarb."

"Who?"

"Goldfarb? You came to my house in Glendale yesterday? But I wasn't home?"

"Oh? Where were you?"

"Actually, I'm up north right now, in the Bay Area. On a little vacation. My wife let me know that somebody came by, so I'm calling you back."

I can hear typing from his end. Probably looking up the reason for the visit and what he wanted to threaten me with.

"When are you getting back to town?" he asks.

"Tomorrow probably."

"You need to call me as soon as you get back."

"Okay."

"You should not leave town until this gets settled. Do you understand the seriousness of what you've done?" He says this by rote. Like he really doesn't give a shit.

"Not completely, could you tell me. Just so I'm sure."

There is a pause as he searches his computer again to get more information about me. "You have an assault charge pending with the DA in Ventura County."

"Do I?" I say, as if that's nothing compared to the rest of the shit I've done.

"And a restraining order," he says, as if he's somewhat impressed.

"Yes, I've heard about that."

"Do you know the consequences of violating a restraining order, Mr. Goldfarb?"

"I could guess, but why don't you tell me." It seems when you have bird-monsters on your side, it makes you a lot harder to intimidate.

"Jail time. Serious jail time."

"Officer Rivas, I assure you that I have no intentions of getting anywhere near where I'm not wanted."

"These are very serious charges, Mr. Goldfarb."

"Yes, I understand that. I'm very frightened now. Thank you."

"This is not a joke. This is serious. Are you trying to be funny?"

I take a breath. If he says *serious* one more time, I'm going to scream.

"No, I'm hardly ever funny anymore, Officer Rivas. May I ask you a question?"

Now he takes a breath. "Go ahead."

"How will I know or how can I find out if charges have in fact been filed or if they've been dismissed?"

"You will be notified, or you can call the DA in Ventura."

"Notified if they're dismissed?"

"Notified if they are filed."

"Thank you," I say.

"So, you're in the Bay Area?"

"Yes."

"Have you seen those birds?"

"One just flew by my window, actually."

"You're kidding me!"

"I have to run, but thank you for your time, Officer Rivas."

"Call me when you get back."

"I will. Thank you."

I disconnect the call.

The good news is that LA and Ventura Counties are so huge, and so much goes through the court systems there, that I'm starting to believe that nothing is going to be charged against me, especially if Portia won't cooperate. It's very possible that her father's only play was to have the DA send a cop to my house to try and scare me into being a better citizen. Maybe it's the intensity of the last twenty-four hours or being out of town that makes the threat seem distant, but at the moment, in my gut, the whole legal thing just doesn't feel like such a big deal anymore. I can handle it, whatever it is. My confidence and momentary calm surprises me. Maybe I am becoming the better man that I'd hoped to be.

Then something profound comes to me. Well, as profound as I'm capable of anyway : "Your body and your spirit know the right thing to do and how to do it. Leave your head out of it. Life is like acting and acting is like golf. Don't think too much and just swing."

I'm sure I read this somewhere, or some acting teacher who played a lot of golf probably laid that particular gem on me, but it kind of makes sense. And any positive reinforcement at this point will be gladly accepted.

Feeling a little more secure about the bird-monsters and armed with my new bargain-basement self-help philosophy—and a sudden urge to play golf—I grab the TV remote to catch up on the latest news about my favorite pets (sorry, Squeak).

Then the Sherwood Forest trumpets blare. It's Kelly.

"Hey, how do you feel?" I ask. "Did you get to the doctor?"

"I'm here now. I just got done…" She pauses, and it makes me nervous. Like she has some bad news that is going to be very hard to take.

"I'm sitting down in the lobby," she continues, "to catch my breath."

"Is everything okay?" I'm really worried now.

"Where are you?" she asks.

"I'm still up here in Napa, probably for another day."

"You're kidding me!"

"No, I have to tell you what happened."

"I have to tell you what happened, too."

"You go first," I suggest.

"This is really weird."

"Are you okay, though? Tell me that you're okay first, please."

"I think I'm okay."

"Good…so what's happening?"

"Are you sitting down?"

"Yeah, yeah, I'm sitting down." The last time somebody asked me that, God was in my bedroom and the whole world got turned upside down. So I'm thinking this might be pretty good.

"Dr. Bloom thinks I'm pregnant."

When I'm right, I'm right.

"Wait a minute. Wait a minute…" I'm having some difficulty computing what she just told me.

"She took blood and did tests, and then she sent me to a specialist for more tests—they're saying that I'm two months pregnant."

"Have you been seeing somebody else?"

"What? Of course not! And even if I was—"

"It's impossible, isn't it?"

"Considering that I went through menopause like ten years ago? Yeah, I'm pretty sure it is."

"And we just…we did it—"

"Two nights ago and before that I don't even remember when."

"What did Dr. Bloom say?"

"That it's impossible."

"So if it's impossible—"

"Then it's a miracle."

"Holy shit!"

"That's what I said."

CHAPTER TWENTY

MUST GIVE
US PAUSE

When Kelly and I spoke on the phone, there was none of the typical excitement of finding out about something like this. It was more shock and fear. I mean, the implications are really too much to even think about, let alone make baby shower arrangements for. In case she didn't already have enough to freak out about, I filled her in on all the stuff going on in Napa. She listened but didn't say much. I swore to get back home as soon as I could. One more day tops, I promised. I also asked her to try and keep a lid on things and tell the doctors not to start publishing reports or talking to the press or anything like that. We need to keep this quiet for as long as possible. I mean, when this gets out, can you imagine? "Fifty-nine-year-old woman becomes two months pregnant—*instantaneously*!" News like that was bound to draw way too much attention from the Virgin-Mary-on-a-tortilla crowd and who knows who else.

And speaking of miracle babies—why are the bird-monsters following me? Shouldn't they be protecting Kelly?

I become aware of a strong odor, something similar to the water buffalo exhibit at the zoo. But it isn't a water buffalo hiding under the bed. It's me.

I get into the shower, and for a Motel 6, the water pressure is not too bad. I'm lathering up with the lavender-scented soap supplied by the motel, and then my brain gets to whirling.

Was I right about the going with my intuition and not having sex with Portia? Was it really just some kind of test to see if I was worthy enough for the job? But what is the job? Now that it's Kelly who's miraculously pregnant, and assuming that I'm off the hook for getting Portia pregnant, what's the next step? What the hell do I do now?

Having no answers for these questions, I stand motionless in the shower, letting the water run over my troubled head. I go into a momentary paralysis and all thought processes seem to go on hold. I have to do a triple take head shake to get myself out of it. Then I take a deep breath, and I'm back to worrying again.

So what do I need to do? I need to get a lawyer for Diane, first of all. I need to call Mr. Geeg and let him know that he was right about taking this trip. He was right about everything—except what he said about me being crazy.

"I am not crazy!" I shout at the top of my voice.

Yeah, I'm losing it. I'm screaming in the shower. That can't be good. And my God, look at those toe nails! And speaking of crazy—I'm going to be a sixty-one-year-old first-time dad! That means I'll be seventy-six when this kid is fifteen. I better find a good yoga class because something tells me this is going to be murder on my back. Wait a minute—what if it's God's child and not really mine at all? Two months pregnant over-night? Come on. I may have a little left in the tank, but that's ridiculous!

"Kelly is carrying the son of God?" I yell even louder than before. Then again, maybe it's really mine, but time is running out, and God just needs to push things along a little. If He can part the Red Sea, I guess He can speed up a pregnancy. Did He part the Red Sea? Did He send the plagues unto Egypt? Did He deliver the commandments unto Moses? Did He really do all those things in the Bible that I always thought you had to be crazy to believe in?

"Well, who's crazy now?"

I try to calm myself down before the SWAT team crashes through the door.

"I have it all wrong. The world is not how I imagine it to be," I say to myself at a more respectable volume.

I know nothing about how anything works. I am an idiot, and the idiot will become the father of the child who will save mankind. Perfect! Please God, if you can hear me, make this all a dream. Or at least let there be toenail clippers in the vanity drawer. Wait a minute! Is it possible that I'm dead? Maybe none of this is really happening and it's all just some kind of after-life hallucination.

Then a very loud fire alarm goes off in the Motel 6. Lights start flashing and an announcement comes over the intercom system directing guests to vacate their rooms and go quickly and calmly to the nearest stairway exit.

"What in the holy hell!"

I stub my toe on the tub getting out of the most confusing shower of my life. If you could feel that kind of pain when you're already dead, well that just doesn't seem fair. I limp around the room trying to get some clothes on as the announcement continuously repeats.

I finally manage to drag myself and my throbbing toe to the out-side stairway. This Motel 6 is one of those two-story deals, and every room has its own entrance off the outside landing. If I had known I was going to break a toe, I would have definitely gotten something on the ground floor.

From my elevated position on the staircase I see that some of the bushes around the courtyard pool are on fire. The pool itself is situated right in the middle of the parking lot, and the parking lot pretty much surrounds the motel. So this fire is burning, I'd guess, about twenty feet from the motel.

I'm relieved when I hear sirens approaching. Curiously, the bushes are burning in the shape of a large cross, which is interesting and disturbing at the same time. A lot of people have gathered outside at the far end of the parking lot to watch the action. I finally get to the ground level with the other dazed guests. There are only a few of us. I'm sure most of the occupants are out sightseeing and getting drunk at winery tours.

Then I notice that some of the people watching seem to be con-nected to each other, like they're a group. They hold hands and are chanting and gyrating and making quite a scene. They are of different nationalities, men, women, old, and young. Very similar to the group of worshippers that I came across in Griffith Park, except this group seems to have a little more religious fervor.

I start feeling the heat from the burning bushes, and then a few plastic pool chairs catch on fire so I move a little farther away. When I do, one of the members of the group breaks rank and starts rushing toward me screaming in Chinese or something close to it. He is waving his arms in the air. I can't tell if he's having a religious experience or if he wants to kill me. When he gets close enough, and I can see the rage in his eyes. Then I'm pretty sure. He takes a wild swing at me. Before he can connect, my pal Israel from the police impound lot intercedes on my behalf. Israel gets in front of me and pushes the guy back. The man, still screaming Chinese, comes at me again. Israel pushes him harder this time, and he falls, hitting the pavement hard. A fire truck and two police cars come screaming into the lot. The crowd of worshippers, including my attacker, vanish in an instant. They take off in all directions like cockroaches when the kitchen light comes on.

"Israel! Man am I glad to see you!"

"I just got off and heard the sirens and saw the smoke so I came over."

"Thank God for that."

"Who was that guy?"

"I don't know."

"He seemed pretty pissed off, homes."

"He did, didn't he?"

"You know, Harold. I feel like I need to keep an eye on you. Like you need some protection. There's something going on with you, isn't there? What's your story, brother?"

A fireman asks us to move to the far side of the parking lot and out of their way, so we oblige.

"What's wrong with your foot?" Israel asks.

"Oh, I stubbed my toe on the bathtub." The macho façade I was trying to cultivate in Israel's presence pretty much evaporates with the confession.

"Your fly is open, homes," he tells me and then averts his eyes.

"Oh." And now there's no way to ever get it back.

I turn away from him to zip up. The older I get, the more my fly seems to be open. It's like thinning hair and wrinkles. Just another humiliating fact of life. When I turn back, Israel has that serious look again.

"Here." He gives me his card. Magic Shield Security the card says. "You call me if you need me, okay?"

"Thank you. I will."

"I'm serious."

"I can tell."

"I have a feeling about you. I can't explain it." He stares at me for a long moment. Then he gives me one of those punches on the arm. "Call me."

Israel turns and walks Spanish through the parking lot.

The firemen knock out the fire in about ten minutes. The police talk to the motel guests to see if we saw anything suspicious. I don't say anything about the prayer group or being attacked by the Chinese man. Maybe somebody else will. I'm fairly certain that they were the ones who set the fire, but I have enough on my plate already and decide it best to avoid further contact with the authorities.

When we are told that it's okay to go back to our rooms, I hobble back upstairs and check on my toe. It's very sore, but I don't think it's broken. I can move it a little, so I guess I'm okay. I lie back on the bed and try to process things. Apparently, not everybody is rooting for the home team. Do these prayer group people know what's going on? How can they? Why was their response to me so different from the group in Griffith Park?

"What the hell is going on here?" I yell at myself again.

The Sherwood Forest trumpets blare, and I just about jump out of my skin.

"Hello?"

"It's me, Portia."

"Oh, hi." I'm not sure I'm up for going through it with her.

"Where are you?" she asks.

"I'm in Napa."

"I want to come up there."

"No, listen. It's my wife. It's not you. My wife is pregnant."

"What?" she cries.

"We just found out."

"How old is your wife?" she says, as if she can't understand how a woman of childbearing age would be married to the likes of me.

"Fifty-nine."

"She can't be pregnant, can she?"

"She can't. But she is."

"Oh my God."

"Yup, the one and only."

"This is all very confusing," she moans.

"I think it really was a test." I feel obligated to explain. Probably that fatherly thing emerging again. "It's about worthiness and free will or something like that."

"For who?"

"Maybe for both of us."

"How'd we do?"

"I think we're okay."

"What about faith?"

"What about it?"

"If our faith was strong, shouldn't we have done what we were told to do?"

"Maybe faith isn't about just doing what you're told to do. It's about having faith enough to do the right thing."

"How do you know if what you think is right, is right?"

"Faith."

Life really is an Abbott and Costello routine.

"My father can't get the DA to file the charges, by the way. He's very angry with me for not cooperating."

"What about the restraining order?"

"I refused to show up, so they can't do it."

"Thank you."

"Harold, what do you think happens from here? I mean, what can I do? I feel like I'm supposed to do something to help you."

"There will be something, because I know I'm going to need a lot of help."

"I'll do whatever you need. Whatever God commands."

"Yeah, but—"

"I would have done it, Harold. I would have had sex with you. Whatever you need. I know this is for real. I know how important this is."

This throws me. I mean, whatever God commands? Would she kill for God? Would she cheat and lie for God? If he commands her to blow up an elementary school, would she do that, too? She's completely missed the point about it being a test and having faith enough to do the right thing, and that just pisses me off.

"I'll call you when I get back," I tell her.

"I heard about the birds. Are they yours?"

I don't want to be mean to her. She doesn't deserve that. Especially after everything I've put her through. I take a pause before I say something stupid that I'll come to regret. I'm just feeling a little done at the moment. And I'm getting a headache. And my toe hurts.

"I'll tell you about the birds later, okay?"

"They're probably angels sent to protect you."

"I'll call you. Bye, Portia." I disconnect her.

I mean, that kind of thinking is probably how the world got into such a mess in the first place. I flop back down on the bed and stare up at the water stain on the ceiling. It looks like a duck wearing a cowboy hat. I close my eyes and take a breath. And then it hits me.

"I'm the protector!" I shout to the duck on the ceiling. I get up and start lurching around the room. "I've got to put the team together to protect this child from unfathomable craziness!"

A bird-monster flies by the window, and I'm glad to see it.

"Shit! The time!"

I check the clock radio on the bedside table—2 p.m. The fire messed up my timing, and I didn't get a chance to talk to any lawyers for Diane. If I want to see her today, I better get going. I grab my keys, hop into the Prius, and limp down to the Napa County Jail on Third Street. Two blocks away from First Street.

CHAPTER TWENTY-ONE

THE PLAYERS ARE
COME HITHER

I manage to find my way to the jail without too much difficulty, talk about a miracle. The place looks like a big office building. You wouldn't even know it was a jail except on the outside it says Napa County Department of Corrections, so I figure this must be the place.

I walk into the lobby. Not far from the entrance they have a security checkpoint set up. It's like the ones at airports, except here they have real cops with guns, and things feel a lot more serious.

Once I get past security, I head for the back of the lobby where there's a reception area, I guess you'd call it. A woman is stationed back there in a Plexiglas room. She sees me and waves me over. I guess I showed up at a good time because nobody else is waiting to talk to her.

"Hi!" I say loudly into that metal thing in the Plexiglas that I assume I should talk through.

"Hi," she answers in a more normal tone of voice.

"Um, I wanted to sign up to see a friend of mine?"

"For today?" she asks incredulously.

"Yes."

"Cutting it kind of close, aren't you?"

"I got delayed."

"What's your friend's name?" she asks in a perfect monotone.

"Diane."

"Diane who?" a little edge to her monotone now.

It was like somebody hit me in the nose with a pine cone.

"Sir?" she impatiently implores.

"I don't know her last name," I admit.

"Well, that's going to make this difficult then, isn't it?"

"She was just brought in today…"

"Uh, huh."

"For a probation violation, and she's supposed to be transported to San Francisco tomorrow for a hearing. Does that help?"

"One moment…"

She puts on her glasses and starts checking her computer screen. She sighs and makes clicking noises with her tongue. She looks up at me, and I smile at her. She doesn't smile back.

"I have two Diane's who were admitted today," she tells me in an all-business tone of voice.

"Oh, good. That's not too hard then, is it?"

"Both are for parole violations."

"Oh."

"A Diane Farr and a Diane Taylor." She looks at me like I better come up with something quick or else she's shutting down for the day.

"Uh, so, how do I—does it give any more information there?"

"Do you know what she looks like?"

"Yes."

"Well, one of them is black, and one of them is white."

"She's the white one."

"Is this her?"

She turns her computer screen toward me. Its Diane's booking photo. Diane Farr.

"That's her!"

She seems offended by my enthusiasm.

"She's not here anymore," she informs me.

"What do you mean she's not here anymore?"

"They already transferred her to San Francisco."

"But they said they were transferring her tomorrow."

"Shit happens." And now she feels more like smiling.

"Where did they take her?"

"County Jail Number 2."

"Is there an address?"

"One moment…"

She does some typing on her computer and then gets up and goes into another room that is out of view. This woman moves as if it's been a very long day, and she is going wherever she needs to be as slowly as humanly possible. She has a giant ass, by the way. Not that it matters, and I would never judge a person by the size of their ass, but this one I feel is worth mentioning. It really is colossal.

She comes back at an even slower pace than when she left. She sits back down at her desk and adjusts herself for a moment so that the ass and the chair can get reacquainted. Then she slips a computer printout to me through the slot under the Plexiglas. It has a listing of all the jails in San Francisco, numbered 1 through 6, with addresses and phone numbers.

"Thanks." I try another smile.

She is unimpressed by my actor's charisma.

"There's someone behind you," she says.

I turn to look. Someone else is indeed waiting for her time. A thin and dusty-looking man dressed in black. He has a lean, cruel face that is pale, and his eyes seem to glow from under the brim of his fedora hat. I am momentarily stunned by the sight of him. He smiles at me. It's the most unnatural smile that I have ever seen. I turn back to the lady in the Plexiglas room, relieved that my attention can be directed elsewhere, anywhere except on the sociopath in line behind me.

"Well, thanks again," I manage.

"Next." She is done with me.

I move away from the window, fearful of having to look upon that pale, cruel face again, but he's gone. Standing in his place is an ordinary-looking gentleman in work clothes carrying a manila envelope under his arm. I look around the room, but I don't see the first guy. He just seems to have vanished. I look back at my friend in the Plexiglas booth for some kind of confirmation as to what happened to this guy, but she's already occupied by something on her computer screen. I try to shake it off, literally shaking my head to try and clear the image of him out of there. After regaining my equilibrium, I continue on my way. The man in work clothes sidesteps me, as if I'm the scary one, and then takes my place at the Plexiglas window.

I'm limping my way through the lobby when I see someone who looks very familiar. He's wearing a suit and carrying a briefcase. He talks intently with an older man who looks troubled. I know this person, but I can't place him. He has full reddish-blond hair with just the right amount of gray around the temples. Very distinguished looking. He's probably my age but seems to be in much better shape. He does all the talking with the older man, and considering where we are, I assume it's a lawyer-client conference of some kind. The two men finish their discussion, shake hands, and then the older man walks away. The guy in the suit looks up and sees me standing there gawking at him. He takes a step toward me, and the look on his face is probably identical to my own. He thinks he knows me as well. Then he smiles and walks toward me. He's figured it out, and it seems to make him happy, which I'm thrilled to see, considering that the Chinese guy, who also seemed to know me, tried to punch me in the face.

"Harold Goldfarb—I can't believe it!"

When I hear his voice, I get it.

"Rodger Stock? Holy crap!"

I put out my hand, but he ignores that and gives me a big hug instead. Rodger Stock is the stoner I saved from drowning at the Ranch all those years ago during my stint with the Napa Valley Theatre Company. Unbelievable!

"Man, it's great to see you!" Rodger says. "Do you live up here?"

"No, I'm down in LA."

"Still acting?"

"Well, that's kind of a long story."

"What are you doing up here?"

"I came to see somebody who I thought was being held here, but they transferred her to San Francisco. She's got a hearing down there tomorrow."

"For what?"

"A parole violation."

"Does she have a lawyer?"

"No, I was going to try and find one for her. She's a good kid I met on the road who's had a lot of bad luck. I'm just trying to help her out if I can."

"I'm a defense attorney now. Do you want me to handle it for you?"

"Seriously?" I'm practically in tears at this point.

"I live in San Francisco. I was heading back down right after this."

"You'd take the case?"

"Dude, you saved my life. I owe you one."

"I knew that'd pay off one day."

I start laughing—from relief, I think. Maybe things are actually starting to turn my way. Rodger smiles at me, pleased it seems that I'm so happy about running into him.

"Do you have a car?" he asks.

"Yes, I drove up."

"Perfect, I drove up with a friend. I'll just call and let him know. This will be great, we'll drive down, catch up a little, and you can stay at my place tonight, okay?"

"That sounds great, Rodger, thank you so much."

He throws an arm around me and leads me away from the Napa County Department of Corrections.

CHAPTER TWENTY-TWO

HOW LONG HATH
SHE BEEN THUS

We drive back to the Motel 6 so I can get my things, and then we're are on our way. I tell Rodger about the fire and the weird confrontation with the Chinese man. I wonder about how much of my story I should reveal to him. Fortunately, Rodger gives me lots of time to think about it because he never stops talking the whole way to San Francisco.

Rodger, of course, is not the same Rodger that I knew all those years ago. If there was anyone voted most likely not to become a lawyer, it would be he. Back in the day, he would carry *Mao's Little Red Book* in his back pocket. When he wasn't too stoned, he'd preach about what he considered to be the ideal system for fairness and equality. He also wore the people's party green hat with the red star that all respectable revolutionaries were wearing at the time. Turns out that after our Napa Valley Theatre experience, Rodger traveled abroad to visit some communist countries and became disillusioned by what he saw. Far from fairness and equality, he found a lot of misery instead. It sobered him up and a transformation had begun. He did a stint with the Peace Corps in Africa, and when he got back home, his political philosophy took a serious turn to the right. Rodger had decided that capitalism, although imperfect, was the best political system on the planet. Never one to go halfway, Rodger tried to enlist in the army but was turned down because of flat feet. You'd think with flat feet he'd have been a better swimmer, but what works for ducks did nothing for Rodger. So he went back to school, got his law degree, and has been practicing successfully in the Bay

Area ever since. Rodger tells me that he's a small-government, more-freedom type of guy. More libertarian than republican, but a shocking transformation, nonetheless.

"What about religion?" I ask him as we make our way into the city.

"I believe in a symbiotic order," he says. "Not all the Bible stuff, but I think that we're all connected to each other and everything else that's out there. Whatever that is—I believe in that."

"Still a hippie after all these years," I say.

"Yes, some freak remains," he agrees. "Take a right. We'll head down to the jail and see what's going on."

It's a real treat not having to worry about getting lost, and I'm actually enjoying the ride. The Prius seems to be enjoying it as well because it's behaved perfectly ever since we left Napa.

"Do you ever see any of those people from back then?" Rodger asks with a hint of melancholy in his voice.

"No, not really, not so much anymore," I'm sorry to tell him.

"Who was that girl you liked? She had the German shepherd? Jean?"

"Yeah, that's her. Her dog bit me once."

"Hated communists, that dog."

Rodger laughs, a good hearty laugh. For a moment, I see in his face the young man that he once was. Full of talent and fire and lots of drugs. Some of what we once were always remains. I hope so anyway.

"So, tell me about this girl we're going to see. You're still picking up hitchhikers at your age?"

"I met her in a restaurant on the way up here. She was sitting across from me and this guy came in and started giving her a hard time. So I got her away from him."

"How did you do that?"

"I hit him over the head with a syrup bottle."

"You did?"

"Yeah, I had to do something. The guy was on drugs, and he was getting very rough with her."

"And you drove her up here and then what? How did she get arrested?"

I take a moment. I'm not sure how much to say or if I should trust him.

"Come on, man. I'm your lawyer now! You have to tell me what's going on, or I can't really help her."

I guess he's right. And I did save his life once, so…"Rodger, some pretty weird shit has been going on."

I spill my guts and tell him the whole story. About the visit from God, about my wife, about Portia, about what happened with the bird-monsters, and then about how the cops got involved.

There is a prolonged silence after I finish. I'm afraid that I might have blown a good thing by laying too much on him too soon. His expression gives nothing away, and I have no idea what he's thinking.

He surprises me when he finally speaks.

"Did I tell you I was gay?"

I'm so surprised by his response that I laugh.

"No, I don't think you did," I say.

"Yeah. That was part of the problem with me back then. I didn't understand what was going on with all of that."

If all he has to tell me after hearing my outrageous story is that he's gay, well then, I guess I'm doing all right. Maybe he hears a lot of wild tales in his line of work, and this just doesn't faze him much. Or maybe he's choosing to ignore it because it is too weird to deal with, and he doesn't want to ruin the nice reunion that we're having. I'm sure it will come up at some point after he has time to digest what I've told him.

Oh, and about those bird-monsters and the talking to God thing? Are you out of your freaking mind?

Rodger interrupts my internal conversation to ask a question. "Was her probation for a first-time offense?"

"Oh, I'm not sure."

"She probably got a diversion if it was a first time. I can most likely get her on a secondary probation with courtesy supervision, but if she violates the terms of that one, she will go to prison. She can't screw up again."

"I don't think she will. She really wants out of that world. She wants a new start."

"Would you speak at her hearing?" he asks.

"Absolutely." In fact, I would love to. I wouldn't mind another crack at the monologue I did for the cops in Napa.

"Good," Rodger says.

"As a matter of fact, I would be willing to sponsor her."

"What do you mean?"

"Well, she could come to LA," I explain, "and I'd help set her up down there and get her going, and I would be responsible for her. I'd be willing to do that."

"Are you sure? You might want to steer clear of that kind of commitment. You don't really know her that well, do you?"

"I know her. I mean, we just met, but we've been through a lot. I'd like to help her if I can."

"It might be hard to transfer the case to LA," Rodger tells me. "They have a pretty heavy case load down there already. We can try, though."

"Let's try."

"Okay, boss," Rodger says. "I look forward to meeting her. She must be something special."

"Yeah, she's a good kid."

"Take a right here. There's a lot on the corner where we can park." We pull onto 7th Street. "Do you think," Rodger continues, "that our meeting was supposed to happen? Cosmically speaking, I mean."

"If you mean that something guided us to be together? Yes, I'm starting to believe things like that are happening."

"I dreamed about those birds. Before it was on the news."

"Really?"

"Something revolutionary is going on here," he says.

"Just like the old days."

"Hot damn, here we go again! Yee haw!" he shouts like a rodeo cowboy.

Rodger is full of surprises, and it makes me extremely happy to know that he wasn't ignoring the story. In fact, he's probably a big part of it.

———

We park in the ten-dollar lot and make our way to Jail #2. Rodger knows the ropes. We go through security, and then he talks to some people at the reception desk. Rodger seems to know everybody. I decide the most helpful thing I can do at this point is to stay out of the way and keep my mouth shut.

After a few minutes we are led into a room. A cinder block wall with windows separates the guests from the prisoners. In the movies they usually have phones that you talk into, but here they don't, so I guess you can either be heard through the glass, or they have the whole place miked. There are eight windows in this room, but we're the only visitors, so Rodger drags another chair over, and we both sit in front of one of the windows. Two female officers bring Diane into the prisoners' side of the room, and my heart sinks. She's dressed in prison garb with her head hanging low. She is still looking down, as she was when I saw her last. She isn't cuffed, I am glad to see, but she moves as if she were drugged. She sits in a heap and then raises her head to look at us—the whole left side of her face is swollen and bruised.

"What the hell happened to your face?" I cry.

"I ran into a dissatisfied customer," she says.

"My God, are you okay?" I look around for someone to complain to.

"Did they take you to the infirmary?" Rodger asks her.

"Yeah, nothing broken, and I got some pain pills. They say I'm depressed."

"Are you depressed?" I ask.

"Wouldn't you be?"

She puts her head down and starts to laugh. A helpless, defeated kind of laugh that just rips my heart out. She looks back up at us, and she has tears running down her face.

"Who's he?" she asks.

"This is Rodger. He's going to be your lawyer now."

"Harold, you got me a lawyer?"

"I told you, Diane, it's going to be all right."

"I didn't think I'd ever see you again." She sounds again like a ten-year-old, like when we were in the Napa coffee shop.

"Why did you think that?" I ask.

"Because that's just the way it's always been."

"Well, you've got a friend now," Rodger tells her. "You've got two of them."

Then he explains things for us. Diane is to appear before a judge tomorrow at ten thirty in the morning. Usually the first appearance in court is a quick one. A judge records her violation and then schedules another hearing for when her case will actually be heard and sentencing will be determined.

"How long before the second hearing?" I ask.

"Could be a few days or a week," Rodger tells me.

I don't want to say anything, but I have to get back to Kelly. I thought I'd be done with this and back to LA tomorrow. Rodger, somehow, knows what I'm thinking.

"Maybe I can do a special circumstance request and move it along. If not, I will handle things here. You don't have to worry," he assures me.

"What about my testimony?" I ask.

"If we have to, we'll write something out that I can present to the judge."

"Diane, I think you should come down to LA," I say.

"If we can make that happen," Rodger adds. "I'm not sure. Is this your first probation violation, Diane?"

"Yes, it was a diversion," she tells him.

"That's what I thought. I'm sure I can get you a secondary probation. You're not going to do prison time for this, so don't worry about that. Whether I can get a transfer to Los Angeles, we'll have to see. Is that what you'd like to do, though?"

"I would like that a lot," she says with a renewed sense of hope.

"I'll get you set up down there," I say. "You can stay with us until we find something for you. No problem with that."

I begin to imagine trying to explain this development to Kelly. In my imagination, she doesn't like it very much.

"Why are you doing all this for me?" Diane asks.

"Because I need you, Diane. What you said before, I think is true. You're supposed to be a part of this now. Oh, and by the way, it's not Portia. It's my wife who's pregnant."

"Your wife is pregnant?"

"Yes."

"How old is your wife?"

"Old enough that she's not supposed to get pregnant."

"Oh my God! So you were right about the whole thing with Portia. Your gut was telling you the truth."

Diane puts a hand up on the glass that separates us. I put a hand up to meet hers.

Our time is done and the guards come for her.

"We'll see you tomorrow," I say.

"It's going to be okay, Diane. We'll work it out," Rodger assures her with a warm smile.

She smiles back, which I am thrilled to see, but I walk away because it just breaks me up.

They take Diane away, and then Rodger puts an arm around my shoulder and leads me from the room.

"So does your gut say anything about me?" Rodger asks.

"I think you might be gay."

"Seriously, I mean, about all of this," he says.

"Not yet. Right now it just wants a margarita."

"That might be your liver talking."

CHAPTER TWENTY-THREE

GIVE EVERY MAN THY EAR
BUT FEW THY VOICE

We walk back to the ten-dollar lot. Rodger walks quickly. I do my best to keep up, but my toe is really throbbing. I know that when the mind whirls, one's pace tends to quicken. I hope this is the case with Rodger, and he isn't just trying to ditch me.

We get to the Prius, and it takes me three tries to get the doors to unlock.

"You should check the key battery," Rodger says. "That's probably it."

"Probably," I agree, although I know better (the Prius is possessed by demons).

We get into the car, and I push the start button, the car turns on, but it won't go into gear. This is a new development at a very bad time. Finally, after the fifth attempt, the car cooperates. Hopefully, it was just showing off because we have company.

"So, where we headed?" I cheerfully ask as if everything were normal in my world.

"How about my place?" Rodger offers. "I have lots of stuff there to smooth out the day."

"Perfect!" I'm downright giddy about having a friendly place to go.

"Does the car do this all the time?" he asks.

"Pretty much."

"Take a left when you get out of the lot, and we'll head for the bridge. I live in Sausalito. Should take about twenty minutes to get there if the traffic doesn't suck too much."

"Cool."

"I've heard a lot of stories about the Prius," Rodger tells me. "People seem to either love them or hate them."

"You have to be careful what you say around them," I whisper.

"Ever think about getting something else?"

"Shhh," I caution and then pet the Prius reassuringly as you would a troubled child.

"He's kidding," I tell the car. "I'd never trade you in and get something else. It's a good thing when you won't start, a very good thing!"

If you're old enough to get the *Twilight Zone* reference—my sympathies.

The traffic is a little heavy but not too bad. Rodger is good at giving directions, so I'm free to enjoy the drive and appreciate the scenery.

He makes a call on his cell phone. "Hey, I'm bringing somebody over. Do we have enough for three, or do you want me to stop...No, nobody you know. He's a flash from the past. It should be entertaining. Just don't ask him about his Prius...Okay, love you, bye."

"Who's that?" I ask.

"My roommate. He says there's plenty of everything, so we're in business."

"Great."

"Take a right."

And when we do, I see the Golden Gate Bridge majestically materializing through a fog bank. It looks just like a postcard.

"Who do you think that Chinese man was?" Rodger asks.

"I have no idea," I tell him.

"Have there been other things like that happening? Other threats?"

"A few."

"Like what?"

"There was a homeless guy who was very strange. At a gas station. He didn't like me much either."

"Did he say anything?"

"He said that he knew who I was, and if they told him to, he would kill me.

"Really? Well, that definitely qualifies as a threat. You didn't do anything to piss him off? Like try to hit him over the head with a syrup bottle or anything like that?"

"No, nothing like that. There've been some others. Homeless people who seem to know things about me. A guy back in LA, in my neighborhood, he was saying some pretty interesting things. He likes me, though. Gave me that penguin in the back seat."

Rodger turns around to look. "Cute, and my, my, grandma, what large pine cones you have."

"Yes, thank you—they're surprisingly good for protection, and they keep the car smelling like a breath of mountain air, don't you think?"

"Do you have control over those birds?" he asks abruptly, getting serious again.

"I don't know. They just come. The cop in Napa said that they were spotted coming up the coast when I was driving up here."

"They followed you?" He seems impressed by this.

"That's what they think."

"The cops in Napa didn't say anything about not leaving town?"

"No, it seemed like they were through with me."

"Hmm," he says.

We head over the Golden Gate Bridge, and, again, if you haven't seen it or driven across it, do yourself a favor.

Then Rodger throws me a zinger.

"Weren't you the guy who was always talking about UFOs back then?"

I actually have a physical reaction when he says this. My stomach does a leap toward my throat, and my ears start ringing. I'm literally paralyzed for a moment. Like an actor who has no idea what his next line is (and I know exactly how that feels, by the way).

"Yeah, I remember now," Rodger continues. "You had all kinds of stories. Weren't you abducted a few times?"

"Uh, it's possible. I'm not really sure."

"You were pretty sure back then."

"Well, you were a communist back then! I don't hold that against you, do I?" I get a little defensive.

"I'm not holding it against you. Listen, people believe all kinds of things. I don't think it's any weirder to believe in UFOs than to believe that there's a guy with a big white beard who sits in a cloud and watches over everybody. Actually, the UFO thing makes a lot more sense."

This makes me feel no better.

"I don't talk about it much anymore," I say.

"But are you still into it?" Rodger presses.

I had seriously never considered that UFOs might be involved in any of this, but I am considering it now, and my body is reacting with quakes and quivers and increasing nausea. Then the voice in my head shows up. He just can't let an opportunity like this go by.

Hey, I got an idea! Why don't you just drive yourself right into that guardrail? Take out a few joggers and then plunge to your death in that nice big bay down there. Wouldn't that be nice? You can even take your gay lawyer friend with you. Go ahead, son, do yourself a favor. Do us all a favor.

Now I'm starting to sweat, and I'm getting those floaters in my eyes, which usually indicate an approaching anxiety attack.

"Rodger!" I shout. "Say something funny! Quick!"

"Trump Care!" he immediately responds.

That seems to do it. I laugh and that helps break the spell.

"Are you okay?" he asks, probably wondering how emotionally damaged I might have become over the years.

"Yeah, thank you."

"You don't look so good."

"No, I'm fine. I probably just need some food."

I'm about to ask him to pull over so I can get some air, when I realize that I'm the one driving. That's how distracted I am. I try to turn on the radio, but the Prius will have none of it. I take some deep breaths and grip the steering wheel tightly, just to make sure I don't drive into the guardrail as was previously suggested.

"Wouldn't it be weird," Rodger wonders in a curiously casual tone of voice, "if the one you're in touch with isn't who you think it is?"

I grip the wheel tighter. "If it's not God, you mean?"

"I mean, what if it's aliens?"

My stomach does a perfect landing in my throat, and I hope that the Prius will let me roll down the windows in case I have to throw up. This new sensation, however, clears out the floaters and relieves my anxiety attack considerably. So all things considered, it's a good trade.

I choose to avoid the alien question for the moment.

"You know, Rodger, I'm sure I don't have to tell you this, but it might be a good idea to keep a lid on all this stuff for the time being."

"I agree," he says.

"I might want to keep a low profile, if you know what I mean."

"Yes, your life may depend on it."

"Well, don't feel like you have to sugarcoat it for me or anything."

"Sorry," he says, not sounding very apologetic.

"So maybe we shouldn't say anything around your roommate," I suggest.

"We'll just talk about the old days and leave it at that," he assures me.

"Perfect, thank you." I am relieved.

"I wonder how it works, though."

"What?"

"How people are finding out about you."

"I don't know."

"It's interesting that some of them like you, and some of them want to hurt you. It's like two camps are forming or something. You're going to have to be careful about who you trust."

"I am?"

"Sometimes the people you think are your friends are the ones that can do the most harm. 'O beware, my Lord, of jealousy; it is the green-eyed monster, which doth mock the meat it feeds on.'"

"Iago from *Othello*."

"Treachery in disguise and all of that."

"I played Iago once," I am compelled to tell him.

"Really? I don't see you as an Iago type."

"I know. Nobody else did either."

"I'm one of the good guys, Harold."

He pats me on the back. Another softy moment for me. Little gestures of kindness just slay me. I try to keep the conversation going so I won't start falling apart.

"I'm worried about my wife. If I'm having all this craziness up here…"

"You should go back tomorrow. I'll take care of Diane. I promise."

"Thanks, Rodger. I can't tell you how much that means."

"Got your back, old friend."

It takes exactly twenty minutes to get to Rodger's place. We park in a lot, I grab my suitcase, and then walk down to his houseboat on the water (redundant, I know) in a really nice neighborhood of houseboats (once you start being redundant it's hard to stop). I guess Rodger does very well in the lawyer business because, zounds, not too shabby! His (houseboat) neighborhood is laid-back, bohemian, and artsy. People walk by and smile and say hello, and nobody so far as I can tell wants to kill me. The sun is low in the horizon and getting ready to set. Seals are barking, and the seagulls are…gulling? There are lots of boats in the bay, and a cool breeze blows in from the water. For the moment, all is right with the world.

Rodger's roommate, a tall, good-looking guy, maybe a little younger than Rodger, is at the door of their place waiting to meet us. His smile seems a little forced to me, and he moves like a performer. Like everything is choreographed. Rodger is greeted with a hug and a kiss. I am not.

The outside of their place, I guess you could say, is turn of the century rustic. It has a porch with hand-carved railings that run out to the deck, and there are a couple of Adirondack-type rocking chairs, where you can sit and watch all the bohemians go by. Beautiful mobiles made of stained glass, wind chimes that seem to harmonize with each other, and lots of hand-carved wooden seabirds complete the aesthetic. It's a good life out here on the bay.

Rodger introduces us. "Thomas, this is Harold, a long-lost friend. He'll be spending the night with us."

"He will?"

Thomas's smile turns into a slight grimace—not so sure he's thrilled with the plan.

"Nice to meet you, Harold." The forced smile returns to his face, and then he puts out his hand and I shake it.

"Very nice to meet you, too. I'm glad to be here," I say most sincerely.

"Very mysterious all this. I can't wait to hear the sordid details. Come in, come in!"

There are two steps down from the entryway, and then we are standing in the main room. It's much larger than what I had expected. A big dining room table sits in the middle of the room that is already set up for the three of us. Comfortable-looking overstuffed chairs and a loveseat look out onto the bay through a large picture window. The place is furnished in that arts and crafts style. Unlike the outside, the inside is upscale and lavish. Fancy but comfortable.

"Anybody want a drink?" Thomas offers.

"Scotch for me. Harold, what's your poison?"

"Scotch is good. Sounds great."

Thomas heads to another room. The kitchen, I suppose.

"Sit down, Harold, make yourself at home," Roger suggests.

"Do you mind if I make a call first?"

"No, go ahead. Go upstairs. It's more private up there." He points to the stairway, and that's where I go.

Upstairs there are two bedrooms—a guest room and the master bedroom—and there's a bathroom down the hall. I go into the guest room to make my call. There is a big balcony off this room and a sliding glass door that gives you access. The balcony extends out and over the bay. It's like an outdoor living room with a big table and lots of plants and sculptures. They have a huge barbecue and more of those Adirondack chairs—there's even a couch out there! My mother was right. I should have been a lawyer. Or at least married one.

I call the house in Glendale, but there's no answer. As is my nature, I assume the worst. I try her cell phone next. Kelly is not at all smart-phone dependent and sometimes doesn't even take the phone with her when she goes out. This time, thankfully, she answers her cell.

"Where are you?" she instantly wants to know.

"I'm coming back tomorrow. I'm leaving here about noon. Where are you?"

"I'm at the store."

"Everything all right?"

"Peachy, what could be wrong?"

"What are you getting at the store?"

"The usual stuff. Bread, aspirin, pasta, a parenting manual. Do you need anything?"

"No, thanks. Notice anything unusual?"

"In the store?"

"No, in general."

"Oh, you mean the people in cars stopping and pointing at the house? We really need to paint this year, Harold, it's embarrassing."

"Did anybody do anything more than look?"

"What do you mean?"

"Anybody say anything to you or throw eggs at you? Anything like that?"

"No."

"Do me a favor. Until I get back, if you don't have to go out, don't go out."

"What's going on?" She's getting a little nervous now. I don't mean to upset her, but, really, what choice do I have?

"I think people are starting to find out about us. I don't know how they are, but they are."

"Shit."

"We're going to have to be careful."

"There was something on the roof last night," she suddenly remembers.

"What do you mean?"

"Something was walking around up there."

"Squirrels maybe?"

"At night?"

"Raccoons?"

"Bigger."

"Bird-monsters?"

She is silent, so I continue.

"It's probably a good thing, because it looks like they're on our side."

"Is there another side?"

"I'm starting to think that there is."

We talk a bit longer, but then she rushes me off the phone so she can finish her shopping. I make her promise me that she'll stay low. She swears that she will.

Then I call Mr. Geeg and tell him about Kelly being pregnant. I ask him to check up on her until I get back. He says he will, right after he finishes something he's watching on Netflix about the Kennedy assassination. He wants to know if he should stay overnight with her. I say I think that would be great but just not in the same bed. Mr. Geeg asks if I want him to bring any food or weapons. I suggest that he leave his weapons at home and just bring his sense of humor. Keeping her laughing should be all that's required. I hope. He reminds me again about the dangers of using the cell phone. I tell him not to worry about it. It's the least of our problems.

I head back downstairs. Thomas and Rodger are on the love seat together. They seem to be whispering heatedly. They stop when they recognize that I'm coming down the stairs. I take the chair opposite them and pick up the drink that Thomas has set down for me on the coffee table.

"Cheers," I say.

"Everything all right?" Rodger asks.

"Yes, no problem. I do need to get back there, though. I'll head back right after the hearing."

"Good," Rodger agrees.

"What hearing?" Thomas smiles broadly, obviously trying to mask whatever is bothering him.

"Somebody I met on the road is in some trouble. We're going to see if we can get her out of it," I say.

We drink, and I pick at some of the Chex Mix that Thomas has put out for us. I'm actually starving and hope that the drink won't go right to my head and make me start talking too much.

"So." Thomas seems to be sizing me up. "You two were pals back in the olden days I understand."

Rodger raises his glass to me. "He saved my life."

"Well, I pulled him out of the water. Actually, it was somebody else who gave you CPR, if memory serves."

"Oh, that's right! What was that guy's name again?"

"Joe. Pretty sure it was Joe." In fact, I'm positive it was Joe. Joe made a huge impression on me. He was good-looking, cool, and a big hit with the ladies. I'd give anything to walk a mile in Joe's sandals.

"If I'd remembered that Joe was actually the one who saved me, I never would have offered to help you. You lucked out on that one, Harold."

"I was due."

"How did you wind up needing to be saved?" Thomas asks.

"I was stoned and wanted to lie down on the bottom of the pool."

"I hate when you do that!" Thomas says and then smacks Rodger on the shoulder in a playfully affected way.

I'm afraid that I am developing a serious dislike for Thomas.

"I was stoned most of the time in those days. I hardly remember the shows we did," Rodger says.

"They were good shows. They really were."

"Who did you play?" Thomas asks him.

"I was the priest in *Mother Courage*, and the Mad Hatter in *Alice in Wonderland*. What else did we do?" Rodger asks me.

"There were a couple of one-acts and *What the Butler Saw*, right?"

"Right, I wasn't in those. I think I ran sound or lights or something like that."

"You really were out of it in those days, weren't you?" Thomas gleefully snickers.

"Yes, I took my drug abuse very seriously."

"He wasn't that bad. Actually, he was one of the better actors, and he was pretty good with a hammer, too. And weren't you always doing stunts and things, juggling and falling down stairs—stuff like that?"

"Yes, that was me. We did publicity shows for the theater, and I would do clowning stuff like that. I went to clown college, the year before the Napa thing happened."

"You were a clown?" Thomas shrieks.

"Well, I studied to be one."

"What about you, Thomas, what do you do?" I'm curious to know.

"I was a dancer and a model. Now I'm just charming and delightful." And then he strikes a pose.

I raise my glass to salute his good fortune.

"It really was a time, that year in Napa," Rodger says with a contented grin. "From what I can remember of it, anyway."

"Free love and all the granola you could eat!" I'm starting to feel the whisky do its work.

"Love is never really free, though, is it?" Thomas informs us.

"Well, when it's good, it is," I parry.

"Hmm," Thomas doubtfully responds.

Every time he opens his mouth, it just rubs me the wrong way.

We drink in silence for a moment. It's starting to get dark outside. Lights come on across the bay, and the boats that are still in the water put their lights on as well. It's all very peaceful and magical looking, but I'm becoming more and more uncomfortable about being here.

"Is this a single malt scotch?" I ask, although I already know. I feel like I have to say something to snap myself out of a funk that's coming on.

"Yes, it's Oban. One of my favorites," Thomas tells me.

"Very nice," I say and then take another sip.

As I gaze out onto the bay, I notice that in the water just beyond the house, there is a bright-green spot that's swirling around like a pinwheel.

"What is that?" I get up for a closer look. My toe is feeling much better by this time. Must be the scotch. Whatever is in the water is getting bigger. It brightens, dims, and then grows bright again.

My hosts get up and join me by the window.

"Jellyfish maybe," Rodger says.

"I've never seen anything like that before." I'm genuinely awed. "I didn't know they lit up like that!"

"Maybe it's mating season for them?" Rodger wonders.

"You used to light up like that, remember?" coos Thomas.

Then something huge streaks by the window. The three of us stagger back, and then another one follows the first.

"Oh my God! Is that them?" Thomas shouts.

"They followed you," Rodger decides while being awed by the sight of them.

I guess there's no hiding now.

"Are those the things that were on the news that killed that man?" Thomas wants to know.

"I think so," I say.

"Are they connected to you?" Thomas is understandably alarmed by what he had just seen. "Are they connected to you?" he repeats more severely this time.

I'm surprised by his aggressive reaction.

"I knew it! Oh, I don't know about this, I really don't."

A beeper goes off in the kitchen, and Thomas hastily leaves the room.

"We should tell him a little," Rodger says. "He feels like we're keeping secrets from him."

"Okay," I reluctantly agree, but I really don't want to say much to this guy. I don't trust him at all.

"Those things are huge," Rodger says as if they're about the coolest things he's ever seen. "Are they birds?"

"I don't know. They're kind of like birds."

"So they really do follow you?"

"Apparently."

"Maybe the jellyfish told them where you are."

"Sure, why not? If a pig flew by the window right now, it wouldn't surprise me one bit."

"Look," Rodger says pointing out to the bay. "They're gone."

The green spot in the water has indeed vanished.

"Weird," Rodger says and then finishes his drink.

"Does Thomas want me to leave?"

"He just likes things to be normal. This is all a little bit out of his comfort zone. I think if we talk about it a little, he'll be fine."

"Just a little, though."

Thomas comes back in with a platter of food.

"Sit at the table and eat."

A cold invitation if ever I heard one.

We take our glasses and go to the table. Thomas has made enchiladas, and they look delicious. He goes back into the kitchen and brings out a big bowl of corn and a bowl of beans.

"Thank you, Thomas. This looks terrific," I say.

"My pleasure," he says insincerely.

We dig into the food, but there is a palpable tension around the table.

"Were you around when those birds killed that man?" Thomas asks without looking at me.

"I was."

"What do you think this is all about?"

"Thomas, I don't really know what it's all about. I've been pulled into something kind of extraordinary, and I'm still trying to sort it out."

"Is it supernatural?" Thomas continues.

"Well…"

"Is it evil?"

"Come on, Thomas," Rodger starts.

"Are you trying to drag us into this?"

Thomas won't let up.

"I'm not. People seem to get drawn into it on their own. I'm not dragging anybody."

"I don't like this," Thomas declares.

"I'm not exactly on cloud nine about it either, Thomas." I'm trying to be patient with him, but I'm not sure how long I can keep this up.

"I think you are trying to take Rodger away from me."

"Okay, that's enough." Rodger puts a reassuring hand onto Thomas's. Thomas pulls away from him and gets up from the table.

"I have a bad feeling about all of this. I am very uncomfortable about this man being in my house. You take that, and you decide what you want to do about it, Rodger. Excuse me."

Thomas leaves the table and goes upstairs into the master bedroom, slamming the door behind him.

"Shit, I'm sorry, Rodger."

"Don't worry about it. He gets like that," Rodger says, trying to act like it's no big deal.

"Maybe I should go," I offer.

"No, this is my house, not his. You're not going anywhere. You are my guest, Harold. He's a pain in the ass sometimes, that's all. Go ahead and eat. Do you want another drink?"

"Yes, now more than ever."

Rodger goes into the kitchen and brings back the scotch and a bucket of ice.

"Knock yourself out," he says.

"I'll give it my best shot."

A show tune begins to play from the upstairs bedroom. We listen for a moment.

"Wow. How gay is that?" says the gay man, so I assume it's okay to laugh.

We clink glasses and then drink the night away. I pretty much tell the whole story of my life after Napa, and Rodger does the same. My sense is that Rodger will be a valuable friend in what's to come, even though his lover will not. I know this is just a taste of the friction that I will be bringing into the world, and I better get used to it.

It's about one in the morning when we stagger upstairs to go to bed. I feel no pain in my toe, or anywhere else for that matter. Rodger goes in to join Thomas, and I go into the guest room. I did what Rodger had suggested and quite literally knocked myself out. I fall into the bed, and I'm almost immediately unconscious.

———

Sometime later I feel a presence in the room. It jars me awake like a bad dream. Thomas is sitting on the end of my bed holding a large knife and pointing it in my direction. I gasp and shift away from him, slamming myself into the headboard behind me. It might be the alcohol, but I feel the whole house rock a bit when I do this. A framed picture of Rodger and Thomas looking happy on an island somewhere falls off the wall and shatters when it hits the wood floor.

"I want you to leave," says Thomas ominously.

"Okay, Thomas."

"I dreamed about you. You want to break us up and then bring all kinds of hell into the world."

I shift on the bed and try to get up, but he threatens me with the knife so I freeze where I am.

"Take it easy, Thomas. I'll go if you want me to."

"I should kill you and do everyone a favor," he whispers as if he's in some kind of trance.

I knew I didn't like Thomas, but at least now I know it's not because he's pretentiously gay. It's because he's psychotic. He stands up and towers over me, the knife raised above his head like Norman Bates in the shower scene. My heart is pounding so hard in my chest that I think it might break a rib.

Then Rodger comes in.

"What the hell are you doing?" he screams.

"I want him dead!" Thomas screams back.

Rodger makes a grab for him. There is a struggle and lots of cursing and screaming. They slam into walls and into the doorway, kicking and punching. It's horrible. Rodger gets him out of the room and onto the upstairs landing. I'm paralyzed by what I'm seeing and completely useless. The struggle continues to the stairway. I have a fairly good view as they both tumble down the stairs. The thuds and thumps are awful.

I finally manage to get myself out of the bed and rush out to the landing. They are both in a heap at the bottom of the stairs. Rodger is on top. There's a moment of silence and then the screaming starts again.

"Get out!" Rodger roars as he pulls Thomas to his feet.

How they are both not dead from that fall is truly miraculous. I don't see the knife. I don't know what happened to it, but there is blood on both of them. Thomas is sobbing hysterically. Rodger shows no remorse. He is still strong and shoves Thomas toward the door.

I go down the stairs to be useful, or supportive, but Rodger is doing all the work. He gets the door open and shoves Thomas outside and then literally kicks him off the porch and out onto the deck. Thomas falls hard, screaming and cursing at the top of his voice. I get out there just as Rodger begins to stumble and lose his balance. I get an arm around him to keep him from falling. That gets Thomas going even more. He grabs hold of a rock and throws it. He misses us but shatters one of the beautiful stained glass mobiles.

By now the neighbors are coming out to see what all the commotion is about. Thomas, still screaming and crying, picks up something else to throw when a bird-monster dives in from out of nowhere and rips the top of his head off. Thomas's body falls in a heap. His blood is everywhere. The bird-monster soars up, shrieks, and then seems to vanish into thin air. Now everyone is screaming. Rodger grabs me, pulls me back into the house, and quickly slams the door shut behind us.

"You need to get out of here, now!" he demands.

"I—"

"You can't be connected to this. I'll handle it. I'll get Diane taken care of. They'll set a bail and then we'll both go down south."

"I'm sorry, Rodger."

"Don't be—just go! It's too dangerous here."

He is right, of course. We exchange numbers, and I quickly grab my stuff and split.

A lot of people are outside standing around watching. I step over Thomas's body and hustle past them, not making eye contact with anyone. I get the Prius out of the lot just as the sirens are approaching.

CHAPTER TWENTY-FOUR

MAD LET US
GRANT HIM THEN

Well, nothing like a nice relaxing road trip to refresh one's spirit. It's four in the morning and there's no traffic on the 5. I figure I won't call Kelly until I get closer to LA. I don't want to wake her up and scare her.

The earlier violence seems to have cleared my head, and I'm wide awake. I feel no effects from the drinking or lack of sleep. My toe seems fine now, too. Scotch and adrenaline—good for what ails ya'. I pull into the first rest stop that I come across and get gas, a large coffee, and a cinnamon bun. I am determined not to stop again until I make it into town. I wish the Prius would play some music for me, but it refuses. I promise myself not to think too much, but with no radio to distract me, that proves difficult.

Do I need to take Kelly and go into hiding? Will bird-monsters kill anything that looks at me funny? Will I become a fugitive, constantly on the run while trying to raise a family? How will we support ourselves?

I expect at any second to hear the colonel's voice in my head telling me to jump off a bridge or to buy as much gold as I can before the prices go up again. But the voice doesn't show. I guess he figures I'm doing enough damage all by myself.

I drink my coffee and start to sing. I go through every Beatles song, album by album, chronologically. I sing as loud as I possibly can, trying to block out anything else that might be trying to get in.

CHAPTER TWENTY-FIVE

TO BE, OR NOT TO BE—
THAT IS THE QUESTION

I don't hit serious traffic until I get about thirty miles from the city. By the time I get into North Hollywood, the traffic is at a crawl. But even with that I make pretty good time. I call Kelly to catch her at home before she heads off for work. I don't go into great detail about what happened—instead I suggest that she take the day off; she pretty much ignores this. She does seem glad that I'm back, though. I hope I can keep her that way for a while. Jerry did spend the night. I know it wasn't easy for him, because he's allergic to cats. Mr. Geeg is a cat lover, but they turn him into a leaking, scratching, sobbing mess. Usually when he visits, he prefers to stay in the backyard. Anyway, I know it took a lot for him to spend the night in the house. Kelly said he left right before I called, and he was starting to have trouble breathing. I owe him one for that. So in all probability, nobody will be home except for Squeak, and I'm looking forward to telling him all about my adventures in wine country. He'll really appreciate all the bloody parts.

As I get closer to my house, a baffling urge comes upon me. I feel compelled to see the homeless woman again. Her face shows up in my head, and it won't go away. I skip my exit and continue on to the Roosevelt Golf Course instead.

I pull into the parking lot at just about 10 a.m. It's already hot outside, and the parking lot is full. I have an uneasy feeling as I get out of the car. I look around and above me to check for bird-monsters—nothing unusual in the sky. I take a deep breath and walk through the parking lot toward the coffee shop.

Sure enough there she is, angrily muttering and packing her plastic water bottles into her overstuffed plastic bags.

I walk under the corrugated metal overhang and stand across from her at the picnic table that she has commandeered. As ever, a few of the old Korean men sit at a distance reading their newspapers. Not pleased that I have invaded her space, she glares at me. I smile at her and nod a hello. She softens instantly, returns my smile, and then grunts Yoda-like. I take this as an acknowledgment, an invitation to engage. I nod again (not knowing the language she speaks or if she speaks at all). Then I bow to her (for reasons that escape me) and then slowly and respectfully take a seat at her table. She takes a seat as well, still smiling but watching me very carefully. She's as concerned about my mental state as I am about hers. Then she takes a plastic water bottle from her plastic bag and slides it over to me. I don't want to offend her by not accepting her peace offering, but to actually *drink* from that bottle? I'm sure you understand my hesitation. She gestures to me, like a Native American trying to communicate with a pilgrim—*drink* she signs to me. I pick up the bottle but then quickly put it down again. She becomes more insistent, demonstrating (in steps), as if teaching a child how to drink from a plastic water bottle. I decide that this meeting will go no further unless I do what she wants. I have no choice but to drink.

Note to self: always carry Listerine on your person. Do not leave home without it. And a stomach pump.

I take a sip. "Thank you," I say. "Delicious!"

She smiles again and gives me a thumbs up. I return her thumbs up with one of my own. Then something startling happens. She goes blank. Her eyes glaze over, and her head falls forward. An incredibly loud and prolonged *belch* comes out of this woman, the likes of which I have never heard before. I quickly get up from the table, afraid of what is to follow. The Koreans look over for a moment and then quickly disengage again. I am expecting vomit or a heart attack. What I get instead is a voice. A voice that I recognize from when this whole rigmarole began.

"Hellooo, Harold Goldfarb! How go the wars?"

The homeless woman speaks in a voice that is clearly not her own. She is channeling the voice from the burning dresser. Stunned, I sit back down at the table. The Koreans seem oblivious. I can't tell if they don't care or if they just can't hear any of this.

"Who are you?" I ask with an assertiveness that I surprise myself with.

"Oh, I'm sorry," says God or Marvin the Martian, or whoever the hell he is. "I thought that was already established."

"It was, but now I'm not so sure."

"Really?"

"Yes, really!"

"Who do you think I am?"

"Alien?"

"*Habla español?*"

"No, *space* alien."

"I knew you'd get it."

"Well, why did you lie to me?"

"God seemed like a better way to get the ball rolling, and time is short."

"Why should I trust you after you lied to me?"

"Because your intuition tells you to."

I hate to admit it, but in spite of everything, it's probably true. But damn it, I thought I had a biblical-type relationship with the Lord Himself. Now, it seems, it's just with an alien. It's still pretty impressive, sure, but you can understand my frustration.

"But does God have anything to do with any of this?" Letting go of the Lord ain't easy.

"We'd like to think so."

"We?"

"Yes, there are many who are concerned about what happens here."

"You mean about who I get pregnant and the whole world coming to an end?"

"Well, it's an immigration issue, actually. I know that in your country people have strong feelings about immigration and undocumented visitors arriving en masse. It's a difficult problem—how to balance compassion and national security. We know about the walls being built and the tension that is causing. We appreciate the delicacy of the situation, we really do. We've seen the escalating fear and paranoia infecting the entire planet, and maybe we can help with that."

My head is swimming now. "So you're here to help with the immigration problem?"

"Actually, we *are* the immigration problem."

"Wait a minute. I'm not sure I'm following."

"In two months, our home planet will become uninhabitable because our sun is dying. After an exhaustive search of the galaxy, Earth was chosen as the most suitable place to relocate."

"Oh, come on. You're kidding me now, right?"

"No, I do not kid. You have been chosen as our ambassador, or go-between if you prefer, because we felt it best to have a human involved to help smooth the way—someone entertaining and nonthreatening."

I'm not sure how to take that.

"And now with your wife successfully impregnated..."

Only an alien would say *impregnated*, so maybe this is for real.

"You now have..." he pauses as if checking his calendar, "one month to present the situation to the powers that be in your government and negotiate terms for our arrival."

"One month?" I cry as I leap to my feet.

"Yes, if we cannot succeed within the time frame—are you sitting down?"

"No."

"You really might want to sit down for this."

I take his advice and sit back down.

"I, and some like-minded associates, our faction if you will, believe humanity is capable of great things and should therefore be encouraged to realize its potential. The others, our opposing party, believe quite the opposite. They believe that trying to negotiate a positive result with your government or any government on Earth is an impossibility and a waste of time. The other side feels that humans are primitive, violent, suicidal, and incapable of dealing with the great opportunity that this situation presents."

"And this great opportunity is what exactly?"

Now I've already seen enough weird, convincing things regarding the reality of all this strangeness, but, still, I feel like I got cast in a

'50s sci-fi movie that doesn't make any sense. I'm trying to take him seriously. Mankind's future may depend on it, but I have to tell you—it's a challenge.

"Our intention," he continues, "if you will accept us peacefully and voluntarily, is to be most generous with our knowledge, which will benefit your country and your entire planet in ways you cannot even imagine."

"Uh, huh…"

"And you have been carefully chosen to be our representative."

"I'm overwhelmed, really."

"You will be endowed with certain gifts and powers in order to help your people understand the great benefit to be gained through the acceptance of our presence on Earth. In addition, these powers will provide you with some protection. In case there's any trouble from the other side. Or from your own kind…who may wish to cause you harm."

"Wait a second, the other side has to give me a month, right? Isn't that what you said?"

"There is a possibility that some may refuse to cooperate. A minority, I'm sure, but just in case."

"In case of what?"

"Rebellion against the agreement."

"Great. This just gets better and better. Don't get me wrong, I do appreciate your support. At least when you dump me into a world of shit, you're considerate enough to give me a shovel. Forgive me, but I'm sure you can appreciate why I'm feeling some angst at the moment. Can I ask a question?"

"Of course," he says like a kindly mathematics professor.

"I would rather not even ask this, because I'm not sure if I can handle the answer, but assuming that I can even get close enough to talk to anybody in any kind of position of power—what if my government refuses and will not accept your terms of arrival?"

"Then the other side will have been proven right, and human extermination will commence."

"You can't be serious."

"It's very serious. That's the deal."

"Have you thought about maybe trying another country first, where smart people live? What about France or Switzerland—they love aliens! Or what about another planet? They say there're millions of them out there.

"We want Wyoming."

"You want what now?"

"In exchange for Wyoming, we will make life on Earth much more comfortable, and much, much better. Really terrific!"

I take a moment before asking my next question because the alien just did a perfect Donald Trump impersonation and it throws me off a bit.

"And tell me why again that I should believe you can make life better for us here on Earth instead of just bringing a whole new set of problems to an already screwed up world?"

"We have been around a long time. We know things that your species is still thousands of years from understanding."

"But it sounds like you have your problems, too, right? Not everybody is exactly on the same page in your world, either, are they? I mean, you may be way ahead of us in years, but it's not all peaches and cream either—if you get the vernacular."

"Frankly, and forgive my bluntness, you really don't have a choice. Let me be clear—"

"Yes, by all means, let us be clear."

"Our opponents believe that humanity is a failed experiment that has run its course and should be exterminated."

"Right, got it."

"And we believe that humankind, when led by a great leader, can do great things. So you can either take action and side with hope or do nothing and choose assured destruction. It's one or the other."

"No room for negotiations? At least to adjust the time frame a little?"

He doesn't respond to my question. After another moment of silence, the homeless lady suddenly reaches for a bottle of water and takes a sip, most of which dribbles down her chin. After letting that visual sink in for a moment, I attempt to reconnect with the alien.

"And this great leader you mention. Would that be my kid?"

Still nothing back.

"Hello?"

The homeless woman takes another dribbling drink and then contact is reestablished.

"There will be no more time for you if we do not succeed," he resumes. "And yes, when the time is right, your child will become a great leader."

"I have to tell you. I liked your first visit at the house much better. I only had to get somebody pregnant. This is much more complicated now.

"Well, I didn't want to lay too much on you right off the bat. And just so you know, you and Kelly were chosen long ago for this moment. You were carefully selected. You first met when you were children. On our ship. We brought you together, and our genes were mixed with your own. Your child will be a wonder. A much beloved peacemaker and a brilliant political strategist. With guidance and love, the child will usher in a new genesis for humanity, and a long and prosperous relationship between our people and your own."

"If we get that far."

"Yes. You must first clear the way."

"We met on your ship, you say?"

"Yes."

"I don't remember that."

"They never do. It may come back to you, though."

"Oh, good. Why did you mislead me about Portia and tell me that she was the one I had to get pregnant?"

"It was necessary to bring you to your wife at just the right moment."

"So you had that all planned out, too?"

"Yes, I know how you are."

"But why go through that whole trip to Northern California? Why all the trouble with Diane and Rodger and why put Portia through all of this if it wasn't necessary? People died up there because of me!"

"It was necessary. You and they had to experience what happened in order for things to proceed in the right direction. These people are an important part of what's to come, and it was essential for you to make the connections and learn from your experiences."

"I'm not sure what I learned—just so you know."

"It will come to you. I promise."

"Where are the bird-monsters coming from? Are they yours?"

"Yes. The protectors became necessary."

"Aren't people going to go crazy when they find out about aliens wanting to take over Wyoming? Let alone the threat of human extinction? I don't mean to be negative, but I don't think that's going to go over well. I have to tell you, people get crazy about that kind of thing. They freak out and start behaving very badly. A lot of people are going to die when this gets out, I think."

"If things go well, not so many."

"Not so many? Oh, okay, not so many. What a relief. And my child. How will he—"

"It's not a he. It's a she."

"I'm going to have a *daughter*?"

"Yes."

I have an odd reaction to this. I should be overwhelmed by the enormity of what's being laid on my shoulders, but the news that my child will be a daughter makes me absolutely giddy. I'm ecstatic, actually. I'm going to have a daughter! I'm proud and terrified and overjoyed all at the same time. I'm out of my mind about this! I almost forget for a moment that the whole world will probably be destroyed after I screw everything up.

"I have to go," he suddenly announces.

"Why? What's wrong? Do you have a Christmas party to go to or something?"

"Christmas in June? Have they changed it?"

"No, it's a joke. I was trying to be funny. Because it's June. That's why it's funny."

He doesn't say anything, so I continue.

"Listen, before you rush out to do your holiday shopping, I want to ask you something."

"It will have to be quick."

"Okay. Did you see that group in the park? That prayer group?"

"Yes, I saw them."

"Did you keep me from joining them? It felt like a good thing for me."

"I didn't stop you."

"I'm telling you, I got stopped! Like I hit a brick wall."

"You did that yourself. You intuitively knew that it was the wrong thing. They weren't ready for you yet, and you weren't ready for them. You have a naturally strong intuitive sense, and we will help you increase your skills with that. You will have powers and abilities far beyond those of mortal men."

"You got to be shitting me now."

"I do not shit," he replies.

"That must be very uncomfortable for you." There's another silence. He didn't get that one either. "You do realize, do you not, that the line 'powers and abilities far beyond those of mortal men' is from the old *Superman* TV show?"

The homeless lady grunts, and then her eyeballs start to roll around like marbles. Very creepy. I wait a moment for her to settle.

"I have to tell you, I much prefer you in the burning dresser than this putting-people-into-trances-and-talking-through-them thing. A little over the top, don't you think?"

The homeless woman coughs, and then after another silent moment the alien returns.

"What?" he says distractedly. "I'm sorry I missed that last part."

"That's okay. It doesn't matter. Does this woman know about you?"

"Yes. The homeless and the disenfranchised are more receptive to our presence than others. They will be your allies."

"Oh, good, an army of schizophrenics, how can we lose?"

"Not all of them will be friendly to you, though."

"Yes, I noticed. So how bad do you think this is going to get?"

"You will need your friends to get the word out and then, hopefully—"

"Will we need guns?"

"Couldn't hurt! A little protection wouldn't be so badddd" he says in what I do believe is the best Mel Brooks impersonation I've ever heard.

I'm impressed. I never could do impersonations and have great respect for people, or aliens, who can.

"But seriously," he says, treating me to a touch more of his Mel Brooks mastery. "You have talents that will protect you. You won't believe how much!"

"More powerful than a locomotive?"

"You will learn about it in your dreams, relax already!"

Then he drops the performance and goes back to his regular alien voice. "You can be in two places at the same time. You can move between dimensions as well. That's what the protectors do. You can also become telepathic and alter someone else's consciousness."

"Do you do anybody else? As good as Mel Brooks?"

"I got a million of them!" he says in a spot-on Jimmy Durante (that only someone my age would appreciate), then he immediately gets back to business in his own voice. "You will learn how to use your powers, and they will prove to be very useful."

"Like if somebody wants to kill me."

"Yes."

"Will my daughter have this as well?"

"In spades."

"I have to tell you, I seriously don't know if I'm up for this. How can I possibly organize something this big? How do I even begin?"

"We never really know what we're capable of until we wrestle around with it for a while."

"Yeah, well, I've got a pretty good idea."

"You might be surprised."

"I hope so."

"Watch out for the Mormon lawyer."

"I thought he was backing off?"

"I don't think so."

"What's he going to do?"

"Make trouble."

"What about Rodger and Diane?"

"You've done very well with them. Good work."

"Jerry?"

"Major dude. He can heal by the way. He doesn't know it yet, but he is powerful."

"Jerry?"

"Mr. Geeg was made for this. We have visited him before as well."

"And you're sure I'm not dead or dreaming or anything like that?"

"You were carefully selected for this, Harold Goldfarb. Have faith. Have courage."

"But what do I do next? What's the next step?"

"Things will be revealed to you in time."

"Time? There is no time!"

"When change happens. It happens quickly."

"Do you really look like Mel Brooks?

"No, I just thought it would be a face you'd be more comfortable with."

"Very thoughtful of you."

"We're not so different. We will meet, and you will see my real face."

"Okay."

"I have to go now. They're coming."

"Who's coming?"

The homeless woman's head drops to her chest, and she belches again, not as violently this time, but it's still quite a thing. Then she slowly raises her head and smiles. She gets up, starts reorganizing her stuff, and then pulls a small object from one of her bags that appears to be a flash drive. She looks me squarely in the eyes and then slides the object over to me.

"Hold this to your forehead before you sleep tonight," she says in clear, perfect English. "It will help you to find your gifts."

As if on cue, the park police come for her. She grabs her water bottle back from me and stuffs it into one of her plastic bags, and they take her away in their park police minivan.

I look over at the Koreans. It's as if nothing happened. I put the flash drive in my pocket and head for home.

PART TWO

CHAPTER TWENTY-SIX

A HUMAN BEING IS PART OF THE WHOLE, CALLED BY US THE "UNIVERSE"

I suppose one has to ask—are we really worth saving? Maybe the opposing-party aliens are right. Look at all the ugly things that humans have done to themselves and to the planet. All the wars and suffering, the greed and bigotry. Why bother with humans? Why go through the trouble? Enough is enough already. If we survive, we will just spread our misery into the cosmos, and our fear and paranoia will poison everything we come into contact with. It's unavoidable. It's our nature.

But then there is Shakespeare and Einstein and Mozart and all the wonderful painters, musicians, writers, and poets. What genius human beings are capable of! Isn't that worth saving? What about the people who just want to love and live and have families and marvel at the wonder of it all? Like Alice and Roy, Ed's parents from St. Helena. Aren't they worth trying to save? It's so sad and sweet that it just takes my breath away, and it's so completely ridiculous that it's all been dumped on me.

Can I be the kind of father that my daughter will need? Am I strong enough to keep her safe so she can grow into who she needs to be? How many years do I have left? They say sixty is the new forty, but this is really pushing it. Who will step up when I'm no longer strong enough? Am I ready to die for her if need be? Could I sacrifice myself, or will I cut and run like the colonel told me I would?

———

On the drive home from the Roosevelt Golf Course there is much to consider. In the midst of these epic meanderings, I begin to recall some incidences from my childhood that suddenly seem tremendously significant.

Every summer, the Good Humor Man would come through our neighborhood in his white ice cream truck. He would ring his bells, and kids would run out from everywhere to wave him down. It was the most exciting part of my summer day, way back when, and hopefully for some other chubby little kid somewhere it still is. One day I got a Good Humor ice cream on a stick with nuts and chocolate. By the time I got back home, my eyes had swollen completely shut. My mother, as was her way, went into a panic and ran around the house screaming. I remember very clearly going over to the kitchen counter and looking at my swollen face in our shiny chrome toaster. But the thing is, I was looking at myself from above. From the ceiling, I watched myself looking at myself in the toaster. I was outside of my physical body. My actual body couldn't see a thing. My eyes were completely swollen shut. Rather than being terrified by the experience, I was fascinated by it and thought it was the coolest thing that ever happened to me. This was way before anybody was talking about out of body experiences and all that kind of stuff. I remember trying to tell my parents about it and how I could see not with my eyes, but from above myself. They didn't buy it. I was eight years old. The same year that Kennedy was shot, and the same year I had the experience with the strangers in my bedroom.

In the dead of night I woke to find three strangers standing in my bedroom doorway. They were cloaked and hooded with almond-shaped black eyes. I tried to scream, but I couldn't. I was completely paralyzed. They just stared at me for what seemed like a very long time, and then they started to evaporate. I could see through their bodies and into the next room. It was terrifying. Then I felt myself regaining some feeling in my limbs. I got to my feet and ran. I went right through what was left of them and dashed into my parents' room, screaming and crying about people being in my room. My father told me that I'd had a dream and to go back to bed, which I eventually did. It never happened again—that I can remember, anyway. I'm pretty sure now who they were.

Not long after that I became convinced that I could move objects with my mind. I'd put a pencil in the middle of the kitchen table and concentrate as hard as I could to make the pencil move. I would work at it endlessly until my head ached. One day I did move the pencil. But I could never do it again. Nobody saw me and nobody would believe me when I told them what I had done.

A few days later, my sister and I were in the backyard, and pennies fell from the sky. I thought that my father was playing a trick on us. We lived on the second floor of a two-family house, and we had a little balcony off the back that looked out over our tiny backyard. I thought that my father had thrown the pennies from the balcony, but he always said that he had nothing to do with the pennies-from-heaven incident, as it came to be known.

Maybe some freakish storm picked them up and deposited them in our yard. That's probably what happened. I still have one of those pennies. I keep it in a junk drawer in my office.

CHAPTER TWENTY-SEVEN

WHAT DOES A FISH KNOW ABOUT
THE WATER IN WHICH HE SWIMS

The first thing I do when I get home is give Squeak a little love bite on the ear (I'm hoping that other cat owners do this as well, or else I'm going to feel very awkward about revealing this aspect of our relationship).

Kelly, not unexpectedly, ignored my plea to stay home. She never misses work. California could crumble into the ocean and meteorites could fall from the sky, but she'd still get to the office on time. So the next thing I do is call Rodger in San Francisco to see how he's making out up there. He picks up on the first ring.

"Rodger, how's it going?"

He takes enough time before answering to cause me some concern.

"Okay. It's going…okay. We appeared before the judge this morning and the probation hearing is scheduled with the same judge for next week. We lucked out with that one. I know him. He's a good judge. Very fair."

"Fantastic," I say, feeling only slightly less concerned.

"Don't forget to write that letter of support for Diane's case being transferred to LA," he reminds me.

He gives me a fax number, where I can send the letter directly to the judge.

"How's Diane holding up?" I ask.

"All things considered, she's holding up pretty well. Bail's been set, so I'll have her out of there shortly. Me on the other hand…"

I can hear the strain in his voice.

"My clients are bailing like rats from a sinking ship, and my supposed friends are nowhere to be found. The police and the press, though, they can't get close enough. When a prominent defense attorney has a public fight with his gay lover, and then he winds up slaughtered in front of his house—that makes for some pretty good copy. And get this—local TV, just to sweeten the deal, is reporting that I'm a devil worshipper."

"Why are they doing this? There were witnesses who saw what happened. Did they talk to them?"

"Yeah, but how do you pin a murder on a giant bird? Much easier to implicate the jealous gay lover—the lawyer devil worshipper with attack birds from hell. I'd pay to see that, wouldn't you?"

"I'm sorry, Rodger."

He ignores my apology.

"And if that's not annoying enough, my neighbors told the police about someone running away from the scene afterward."

"Shit," is all I can think to say.

"So the cops want to know who that was. I told them it was a friend of Thomas's who was visiting and took off when things got ugly. The police want a name. I told them I don't know his name. That I never met him before."

"Maybe you should just tell them the truth, Rodger. You shouldn't have to lie for me."

"Listen," he says in a calm and reassuring tone. "You can't be connected to any of this. The truth will only muck up the works for much more important things to come. And I know that doesn't sound good. Like some tyrant justifying his transgressions. But, Harold, with this thing…we have to do what we have to do."

I'm thankful that Rodger is on my side, and I'm truly sorry for the trouble I've caused him. But I'm getting that old queasy feeling again. How much lying will we have to do? I take a breath and then lay the latest on him. I tell him about what happened with the homeless lady and that his suspicions had proven to be correct. God is really an alien, and we got us one serious immigration problem.

"Harold, you realize, don't you, that this is the most important thing that has ever happened! Unless you're crazy, of course."

"Don't knock crazy," I say. "It's the only thing keeping me sane."

"I'm going to wrap things up here as quickly as I can. I need to get out. I'm closing my office, and then we'll both go down to LA."

"What if the judge doesn't cooperate?"

"Harold, even if he doesn't, I think this trumps a probation violation, don't you?"

"I guess it probably does."

"You still want us to come, don't you?"

"Are you kidding? I need all the help I can get. And listen, any connections you have—we need to find people who can get the word out."

"I know people here in local government, but with all the bad press going on, they may not want to talk to me right now."

"We'll figure something out. How hard can it be?"

Rodger laughs. "Keep me in the loop," he says.

"I will," I assure him. "Hang in there, compadre."

"Oh yeah—way too wild of a ride to let go."

I disconnect the call. I think about calling Jerry next but figure he's asleep after a sleepless night in the cat house. So I go into the office and write the letter to the judge about Diane. I lay it on pretty thick, and hopefully I'm not making her sound like the second coming. But I mean what I say about her character, and my offer to help her get established in LA is genuine, even if the human race is likely a month away from extermination. Anyway, I fax that off to the judge.

Then I call Kelly. She never picks up her cell at work, so I call her on the office phone.

"Hi," I say. "Are you busy?"

"Yes, it's crazy here. Are you back?"

"Yes, I'm back."

"Thank God."

"I talked to him again."

"Who?"

"God. But he's not really God. He's an alien.

"Uh, huh."

"And the baby is going to be a girl. Part human, part alien—a superkid."

There is silence on the phone, and then she hangs up. Understandable, and I try not to take it personally.

I need sleep. I lock all the windows and doors and put on the alarm system. Squeak leads the way, running serpentine in front of me as he always does when he wants attention.

I get undressed, and Squeak sneaks under the covers with me, curling up against my side. I take the flash drive thing that the homeless lady had given me and set it on the night table next to the bed. I'm hesitant to use it—not sure if I want to go where it might take me. I nudge it around and reposition it a few times on the night table.

"Less thinking and more swinging," I say out loud to myself.

I pick it up and put it on my forehead as instructed by a crazy homeless lady who had an alien speaking through her. In the grand scheme of things, I'm sure I've done dumber things.

I feel nothing at first. "She probably just found a discarded flash drive on the street somewhere," I say to myself.

Then my mind gets still and quiet. Very unusual for me, you may have noticed. I have a peaceful and relaxing sensation. Like when I had a colonoscopy. They give you a drug, and that moment right before you get knocked out feels something like this. Then the drowsiness overtakes me. I manage to put the thing back on the night table, and then I'm out.

I find myself in Jerry's apartment. He is asleep. I watch him for a moment and then concentrate and try to wake him up with my mind.

I have a friend who practices lucid dreaming. From the way he has described it to me, I think that's what I'm experiencing now. My friend takes special vitamins and supplements to help him get to where he wants to go and do whatever he's trying to accomplish in the dream world. I have this thing from a homeless lady. The idea is that with practice you can control your dreams, manipulate them, actually contact other people who are also dreaming, and deliver messages to them. Sometimes you can help them heal from physical or emotional problems. This also reminds me of what I've heard about remote viewing. That's where you can actually visit places, transporting your consciousness to all corners of the globe, or the universe, without ever leaving the comfort of your bed. Our government actually had a program in place to develop these skills so they could spy on whomever they weren't too happy with at the time.

Jerry wakes up.

"Hi," I say.

"What are you doing here?"

"We're dreaming," I tell him, in case he doesn't already know.

"Why are you on the ceiling?" he groggily inquires.

I hadn't realized that I am hovering up here. I try to concentrate on getting myself down to the floor, and I slowly descend.

"You don't have any legs, Mr. Geeg," Jerry tells me.

He's right. Only half of me has made the trip. I try to concentrate on completing myself, but I can't get my legs to show up.

"Listen," I say. "It's aliens, not God."

"Tell me something I don't know."

"Okay," I say.

I float over to him. I take his hand, and it's like I'm downloading information to him.

"Wow!" he says.

"Did you get something?"

"You chew on your cat's ear?"

"Besides that."

"I can heal?"

"Yes! And the alien said that you are very powerful."

"I had a feeling that I might be."

"I need your help, Mr. Geeg."

"I know."

"We will do this together, okay?"

"Yes, of course."

"This is big," I say.

"The biggest," he says, staying amazingly calm about what I'm laying on him. "Do you know what kind of alien he is? Gray, reptilian, those big Nordic blonde-looking ones? The women are supposed to be incredibly hot."

"No, I don't know what kind, yet."

"I don't think I'm allergic to cats anymore. Something just happened with that. I was dreaming about cats before you showed up. I was playing with them, and they were all over me, and nothing happened. No sneezing, no reaction at all."

"Fantastic."

"Remind me to ask him about the thing I saw in the woods by the Hollywood Sign."

"I will. Thanks for being my friend, Mr. Geeg."

"You're welcome, Mr. Geeg. Do you want some coffee or anything?"

"No thanks."

"Okay, good night." Jerry curls up with his pillow and goes back to sleep. I mean, we're already asleep, but I guess he just went to another level of sleep.

I float across the room and go right through the front door (without opening it), and there in the courtyard around the fountain are six little gray aliens squatting in a circle and holding hands. I make a suggestion (in my mind) that they should let me join them. After a moment they make space for me, and all six of them simultaneously, with their tiny little three-fingered doll hands, wave me into their circle. This time I am able to join. I don't freeze up as I did in the park. I sit, or rather position myself (I'm still legless), right in between them. The ones on either side of me each take a hand. Touching them is an odd sensation. Their little hands are not exactly cold but not exactly alive either. That's the best way I can describe it.

Their faces are expressionless and I feel an impulse to put some life into them. I start making mental suggestions, which in this dream state is easy to do. It's as if they are here for me to practice on. I start with the one sitting across from me. I make a suggestion that he sing us a song. I suggest *Mack the Knife*. He gets to his feet and sings, word perfect. I let him get about halfway through (he's no Bobby Darin) and tell him to stop and sit back down, which he does. I applaud his effort, and the others follow suit. When the clapping stops, they go back to meditating or whatever they're doing. The next one I make slither around like a snake. Another one I have do jumping jacks. I have them crow like roosters, snort like pigs, and roar like lions. They are very cooperative and seem to take these abuses without any resentment whatsoever.

Then I hear a whooshing sound. I look up and see a bird-monster circling in a reddish-gray sky. It screams and then dives at us. In a single fluid motion, it swoops down, snatches up one of the grays, and then soars back into the sky.

No, I command in my mind. *Put him back, he's mine!*

It flies back in and dumps the gray right back where it got him from. The bird-monster screams again and then pops out of existence—just vanishes into thin air.

I'm getting ready for some more mind games with the grays when a shadow comes over us. I look up and see saucer ships in formation filing in above us. Their numbers multiply quickly until I can no longer see the sky.

"Do you want to go back now?" I ask my little companions telepathically.

They nod that they do. There must be hundreds of ships up in the sky, but the grays telepathically let me know which ones they belong to. I bow my head and try to wish the grays away. This is much more difficult than the mind games we played before. It's like trying to get the pencil to move on the kitchen table. My eyes start to burn, and my lower back begins to ache. It takes some time, but one by one I get them back onto their ships. They pop out just like the bird-monster did. Then the saucers above me also begin to disappear. Like bubbles bursting, they pop and vanish, and soon they're all gone.

I begin to feel dizzy and a little bit nauseous. As I look around for a place to throw up, I start to bounce like a rubber ball, and then whoosh—I'm on top of Jerry's building. I start transporting myself quickly, going from one place to the next. First I'm on top of Jerry's building, then instantly I'm way up on top of the giant palm tree across the street, and I'm watching myself from where I just was. I can actually see myself dissolving on top of Jerry's building. For a moment I am somehow in two places at the same time. Suddenly I'm in New Jersey at the Passaic Falls. Then I go to New York, to the Village Gate, and I see Mr. Geeg and me as sixteen-year-olds standing in line to get into the club. If my calculations are corrected, it must be 1969. I'm shooting all over the place. It's exhausting, and I'm having a hard time catching my breath. It's as if I'm on a crazy rollercoaster ride that has lost its brakes. I'm losing control of the dream, and I have to get out or I'm quite sure that I will die. I try to focus my concentration, to make it stop, but it just goes faster and faster: Paris, Egypt, France. I'm in a panic, and then, instantaneously, I'm soaring into space. There is no sound. It's beautiful and peaceful, and although I'm in space, I find that I can breathe quite normally.

Just when I'm starting to enjoy the ride, it gets bad again. I come to an abrupt stop and slowly begin to rotate, turning back toward Earth. And then I'm let go, dropped headfirst into a rapid descent, hurtling through space to meet my death. I scream, but my scream is silent.

I feel a pat on my cheek. It centers my focus. Pat, pat, pat—like gentle little slaps on the face. The pats become more insistent, and then they start to sting.

I wake in my bed with Squeak sitting on my chest, smacking me in the face with his cute little paws of death. His claws are needle sharp, and if a fool were to challenge my cat to a game of catch the hand under the blanket, that fool would walk away bloodied and humiliated. Why I continue to play this game with him is a complete mystery to me. But there he is, my champion, punching me in the face and looking concerned.

"Good boy. You're a very good cat," I tell him.

CHAPTER TWENTY-EIGHT

NO PROBLEM CAN BE SOLVED BY THE SAME CONSCIOUSNESS THAT CREATED IT

Maybe I do have some hidden talents, like the alien said. I know that I'm good with animals, and I can drink like a fish, but if I can get this dream stuff going, that'd really be kicking it up a notch. Did I see Jerry? Would he remember seeing me? How does what happens in the dream world relate to the real world? Will I actually be able to do what I'm learning in my dreams?

I manage to get some good sleep after asking myself more questions that I have no answers for. But one may be provided for me in my sleep through a more normal dream that's almost as disturbing as the flash drive experience:

I'm in a line, waiting to check in at a Las Vegas–style hotel. I'm talking to the man behind me who is dressed like Elvis Presley. He has a beard that is perfectly trimmed in that three-day-growth look that's so popular today. This beard, however, is carefully sculpted with swirls and stars meticulously carved into it. The beard runs down his neck, all the way to his chest. I say to him that it must take him a long time to care for such a beard. He tells me that it's worth it because it makes him feel special. I realize then that Elvis is actually Israel, who I had met up in Napa. He takes off his Elvis glasses, and he has eyes like mirrors. I see myself reflected naked in his eyes. Rather than screaming and running for cover, I'm surprisingly comfortable with this. Then he leans toward me and whispers into my ear.

"You see? We're the same, you and me."

Then I get a horrible pain in my leg. In the calf muscle. I have to step away from the line. The pain is excruciating. I start massaging my leg when I notice that it's heavily tattooed, which surprises me because I don't have tattoos in real life. The tattoos are animated—flying saucers and bird-monsters and many of the same tattoos that I saw on Israel's arms. The tattoos are all moving in a circular motion around my calf. I'm trying to rub the pain away when I wake up with the same exact pain that I was having in the dream.

So that answers one question anyway. What happens in my dreams can absolutely happen in my life. But it's probably the other way around. I just had a leg cramp that worked its way into my dream. But when you're desperate for answers—you tend to stretch the logic. I've heard that dreams can sometimes be messages from our subconscious mind trying to tell us something. The meaning of this one escapes me for the moment.

I carefully contort myself to get out of bed without disturbing my hero, Squeak. I've had this happen before, the cramping in my leg, but nothing this severe. After pacing around for a while, the pain begins to subside. I look at the clock—it's 3 p.m. I'd slept soundly until the cramp woke me up. I hope that the new me will be a better sleeper than the old one, and I also hope that if I'm naked and vulnerable somewhere, that I'll be as comfortable with that as I was with Israel in the hotel lobby.

I walk into the kitchen and make some coffee. It feels great to be home. Then I go out to the porch to pick up the paper. Kelly always puts the paper up on the porch when she leaves for work in the morning because the sprinklers go off at seven. Nothing worse than a wet newspaper. I check up and down my street for any potential threats, but things seem peaceful for the moment. I'm excited to see my wife again. It's only been a few days, but it feels like a month. I figure that I'll go to the store and get something to cook for dinner and maybe a bottle of wine. For me, not for her. What kind of father do you think I am?

I have some coffee and toast with peanut butter and jelly and start looking through the paper. Should've let the sprinklers get it. What a mess. The country doesn't trust its leaders, and the people don't trust each other. The Middle East is completely out of control. People are killing each other all over the world in the name of God or drugs or oil. Our intolerance for each other gets worse every day. If the aliens don't wipe us out, we'll probably do a pretty good job of it ourselves.

Hopefully, the aliens coming will inspire us to unify as a species. As humans. No more my group and your group, and we're right and you're wrong so go fuck yourself. Maybe we'll get off our phones for a minute and really start paying attention to each other. I hope so, because I'd like to be around to raise my daughter. My part-alien, part-human daughter. Unreal. Born to lead and keep the peace—between two different worlds no less! What kind of powers will she have? What type of person will she have to be to bear that responsibility? Can you imagine growing up with that kind of expectation hanging over your head? It's child abuse, is what it is! And when word of this really starts to get around—they'll crucify her! Antichrist, devil, monster. How can this poor kid be expected to deal with something like that?

Then I see a story in the California section called KILLER BIRDS BY THE BAY. The article scoffs at the supernatural explanation and assures readers that there is a very logical and scientific reason for what has occurred. They just don't know what it is yet. The writer deals with the story the same way the media always deal with UFO stories. Wink-wink, nudge-nudge, it's all just a lot of crazy people who believe this stuff.

In the interest of self-preservation, I try to think about something normal. I think about Thanksgiving. It's my favorite holiday because it's all about the food and nobody needs a present. Kelly and I do all the traditional stuff, have the cousins over, the whole bit. I get up early to put the turkey in the oven, and I treat myself to a little brandy in my coffee. Inspired by the holiday, I make my way to the liquor cabinet. I check to be sure that Squeak isn't watching and then slip a little brandy into my coffee—just to take the edge off. I know this is probably not a good habit to get into because a lot of overwhelming days lie ahead, and how much brandy can you drink before the neighbors start talking? But as many great drinkers before me have said, "fuck the fucking neighbors." So Happy Thanksgiving, everybody! I refresh my coffee one more time and go out on the porch to take a look at the world. A neighbor comes down the street walking his three dalmatians. I always see this guy on my walks and usually say hello. I never got his name, though.

"Hey, there he is," the guy shouts out to me. "How goes the world?"

I just smile and nod. I have no idea how to answer that, so I go back inside the house, where I won't get thrown by any more confusing questions.

I take a long shower, trying hard not to think about aliens or human extermination or my increasing dependence on alcohol. Then I get dressed to go to the store.

As I'm headed out the front door, I hesitate, trying to remember if anything was left on that should be turned off, and then I see him. Stretched out on my front lawn, his shopping cart parked next to our big elm tree, whose roots are starting to grow through the foundation on the side of the house (but don't get me started). He looks comfortable, with his hands behind his head. His eyes are closed, and he's smiling a gigantic toothless smile. He's humming a tune to himself as he takes in the sunshine. It's the homeless guy who had given me the penguin in the yellow raincoat.

"Hey, my friend! What are you doing here?" I ask.

"Hey, *papito*! I make sure all right for you!" he says with considerable delight.

"How did you find out where I live?" I ask.

He taps the side of his head and grins.

"Well, listen, my friend," I say. "You probably don't want to hang around here for too long. The neighbors get jumpy about things like this."

"Like what, *papito*?"

"Well, they get nervous about strangers coming around."

"Oh, *si, si, si*. Very nervous people start jumping around like jumping beans, eh, *papito*?" He finds this image completely hilarious and laughs loud and hard.

His English, I notice, seems much improved since the last time we chatted.

"It's okay, *papito*!" he continues after he calms down a bit. "I just have to make sure you okay."

"I appreciate that, but somebody might call the police on you."

"How is the baby, *papito*?" He laughs again and waggles his feet in the air.

"I don't know. Why don't you tell me?" This guy has me totally mystified.

"She will be good, *papito. Muy bueno.*"

"Is that what you heard?"

"Oh, ya', *papito.* I hear a lot." He starts to laugh again.

I'm not sure if this man laughs when something is funny, or if he's trying to keep some really bad shit from getting into his head. I can relate to that. Either way, I have affection for him. I walk over to where he lies on my grass and shake his hand, just as we always do when we meet, only this time, I initiate the action.

"Thank you for looking after me," I tell him with real sincerity.

"Have to keep you safe." His grip on my hand tightens. His ever-present smile is replaced with a worried look that I've never seen on him. "You want me move inside with you, *papito?* It be better that way. It safer that way."

"No, no. I don't think that will be necessary." I am sincerely thankful to him, but not that thankful.

He lets go of my hand and leaps to his feet like a man half his age. He goes to his cart and proudly brings back a present for me. It's a cowgirl doll.

"Thank you," I say. "It's very cute."

"Happy, happy?"

"Yes," I tell him. "Happy, happy."

He grabs my hand and shakes it vigorously, the big smile returning to his face.

"What's your name?" I ask him. "You've never told me."

"Oscar Robinson. But you can call me Lou."

"Okay, Lou. But why Lou if your name is Oscar?"

"Because *Lou* rhymes with *Jew*—just like *you!*"

This sets him off into another burst of uproarious guffawing. I can almost feel the neighbors peeking out from behind drawn curtains to see what all the commotion is about. After his fit subsides, he skips over to his shopping cart and starts singing that children's song that I've heard him sing before. A Dr. Seuss kind of thing that rhymes, some parts in Spanish and some in English. He gets his shopping cart and heads down the hill, waving and singing all the way.

Because Lou rhymes with Jew? How Lou knows I'm a Jew I haven't a clue. But there he goes. My new head of security. I get in the car and go to the store. I go to the Ralphs for bargains galore.

———

The Ralphs I go to just redid everything. They made it fancier and prettier, but it takes twice as long for me to shop because I can't find anything anymore. Eventually, I get a bottle of wine, some chicken, sweet potatoes, asparagus, one of Ralphs' fancy, ready-made Greek salads, and some pound cake and vanilla ice cream. That's gonna run me about sixty-five bucks, I kid you not.

I'm standing in the checkout line and there are a few people in front of me. There's a young powerfully built guy with his wife and a baby in a stroller. A wild, disheveled-looking man stands behind them and directly in front of me. He's tapping his foot and nervously folding his arms over his head and behind his back and scratching his ass. He just can't keep still. As he becomes more and more agitated, I know that something is about to happen and that I will probably be getting involved. It always happens like this. The guy could have been in another checkout line or another store, but no. He has to be standing right here—scratching his ass and getting ready to snap. I also notice that he has no items to check out. So what does that tell you? He's standing in line with no basket, no groceries, and no shoes by the way. He's here for only one reason—to make something bad happen.

And then it does.

I will not go into great detail about what comes out of this guy's mouth, but the string of profanities and insults directed at the man in front of us and the entire Armenian population in general is like nothing I've ever heard before. And I'm in theater, so I've heard a lot. So for a disheveled-looking non-Armenian person to start hurling racist profanities like this in a place that is at least 70 percent Armenian—he'd have to be either crazy, suicidal, or looking for somebody to sue for beating the shit out of him.

The man with the family struggles to stay cool. "I've got my wife and kid here. Have a little respect," he says.

But the guy will not stop. He accuses the Armenians of destroying his life and destroying the country. It is outrageously ugly. The Armenian man warns the crazy guy to stop, but he won't. He warns him again and is literally turning red with rage. Finally, our family man can't take it anymore, and he attacks. He pushes the crazy guy back, who falls into the candy display, scattering stuff everywhere. He lands, of course, where else, but right at my feet. The wife covers her face, too horrified to watch, and their baby starts crying. The lunatic pops up, and the profanities continue.

"Let's go!" he shouts. "You want to hit me? Fuck you! Go on and hit me, you sorry-ass faggot Armenian pig!"

People in the store are yelling for someone to call the police. Young Armenian guys are starting to surround the violence. Cashiers are screaming for them to take it outside, and there's not a security guard in sight.

I put my hand on this crazy man's shoulder. He spins around to face me, ready to start swinging.

"Stop," I say. "Just stop."

He staggers a bit as if I had pushed him. But I hadn't pushed him—physically anyway.

"Who the fuck are—"

"Just go," I interrupt in a calm yet firm tone of voice.

He stares at me for a moment, confused, not able to process what is happening to him. Then he lurches away through a very hostile crowd. At the exit door, he turns back to me and tries to say something.

"Who the fuck—?"

I don't let him finish. I point a finger at him, and he seems to choke on the curses that he's attempting to spew. They literally get stuck in his throat, and he starts to cough. Then he runs out of the supermarket.

"I'm sorry," the Armenian family man says to me.

"Forget it," I tell him. "It's not your fault."

"Thank you," he says. "I would have killed him."

The crowded supermarket is completely still and silent. Even the baby is quiet. Onlookers are staring at me, trying to understand what had just happened. After a moment or two, a few people come up to thank me, and a few of the guys want to shake my hand and slap me on the back.

When I get out of the store, thankfully, the maniac is nowhere in sight.

What the hell just happened? What did I do? I mixed up his process somehow. I forced something else to go on inside of his head. Something good and reasonable? Is that what he got? Or was it just that I forced him to do what I wanted him to do? I controlled him. I overwhelmed him with my "powers and abilities far beyond those of mortal men." Holy shit!

If what just happened has to do with the flash drive dreaming stuff, then I have been given a great gift. The responsibility of which is daunting. Could I exchange it for a toaster or something?

CHAPTER TWENTY-NINE

WHEN THE SOLUTION IS SIMPLE
GOD IS ANSWERING

I like to cook. I'm not fancy about it, just basic stuff. I also like to drink red wine when I cook. I know what you're thinking, and you're certainly entitled to your opinion, but red wine (in case you haven't heard the most important news of the twenty-first century) happens to be very good for you. Probably not the copious amounts that I enjoy, but, hey, it's been a rough week. Anyway, I have a few dishes that I make and make very well. This evening's dining adventure is baked skinless chicken thighs coated in Italian bread crumbs, yams, asparagus, and, of course, Ralphs' ready-made Greek salad—low calorie and delicious. I love to cook for Kelly. I just wish she enjoyed my food half as much as I do.

The trick is getting the timing right for how long it takes her to get home. She works in Anaheim, which is about thirty-five miles south of our house. The traffic out here in LA, as you know, is ridiculous. If it's moving faster than a crawl, it takes her an hour to an hour and a half to get home. If it's bad (Fridays are always bad), it can take over two hours. So timing is tricky when cooking dinner for my wife.

This day, I am on my game. She gets home only ten minutes after what I had planned for, so everything is hot and ready when she walks through the door. I'm so happy to see her safe and sound that I get a little teary-eyed. We hug, and I think she's glad to see me as well.

"I love you very much," I tell her.

"I love you, too," she says.

"We should say it more often. Like every day," I suggest.

"That would get a little tedious." She's much more practical about these things than I. "Are you okay?" she asks looking deeply into my eyes.

"I'm okay. How are you?"

"I feel like I'm in a dream," she says.

"We have a lot to talk about."

"I'm glad you're back."

"Me too."

"What's for dinner?"

"Guess."

"Baked chicken, yams, and asparagus?"

"How'd you know?"

"Greek salad?"

"I'm afraid so."

She kisses me and then heads off to the bedroom to change out of her work clothes. She looks tired to me. A little pregnant maybe, if that's possible at this point.

"I thought we'd eat in the dining room!" I call after her.

"Great!" she yells back.

We often just eat in the TV room and watch *Jeopardy* or something, but I thought we needed to focus on each other instead of on Alex Trebek. I should have made a cream sauce. She deserves a cream sauce if anybody ever did.

We sit at the dining room table, and I fill her in on the latest developments. There are questions after that.

"And we met on a spaceship when we were kids?" She's trying to stay calm, but I don't think that will last much longer.

"That's what he said." I know how crazy it sounds.

"But I was in Australia then, and you were in New Jersey."

"They get around."

"And they were already messing with our DNA?"

"Apparently so."

"And you're getting all this through a homeless woman?"

"Yeah, some of it, and here's the thing she gave me." I have the flash drive in my pocket. I take it out and show it to her.

"What's this again?"

"It's the thing that's training me to do stuff in my dreams that will help me control things that happen in the real world."

"Like what happened in the store today?"

"Yes, I put it on my forehead before I go to sleep."

"I see," she says and then takes a moment to massage her temples before continuing. "See, if we hadn't had sex and then the very next day I wake up pregnant at the age of fifty-nine, and if I hadn't read about giant birds in the paper, I could definitely see how somebody might think you're crazy."

"But you don't think I'm crazy, do you?"

Kelly smiles at me sweetly but doesn't answer the question. She looks down at her food and picks up her fork. She doesn't eat, though. She just repositions things on her plate. I'm pretty hungry myself, but if she's not going to eat, I guess I'll hold off as well.

"I'm going to take a leave from work," she says.

"I think that's a good idea."

"We're going to need help?"

"It's coming. I'm meeting people who really want to help."

"And other people who really want to kill you?"

"Yes."

She drops the fork and buries her face in her hands.

"I think I can control the birds now," I say in an attempt to give her some cheerful news.

"Oh, good. When we run out of money and food, they can bring home live cattle for us to eat."

"My friend from up north, Rodger? He's coming down here soon with the girl I told you about."

"The one whose boyfriend lost his head?"

"Yes."

"So there's that girl and the one from the show—that's all straightened out with her now, correct?"

"Yes, Portia knows that it was you who was supposed to get pregnant and not her. But she wants to help us, too. She wants to be a part of it."

"And it's her father that's the Mormon lawyer that wants you to rot in hell?"

"Correct, but she won't cooperate with him. So hopefully we don't have to worry about that one anymore."

"Any other girlfriends I should know about?"

"I think that's it for now. Unless you want me to tell you about Maureen, my first girlfriend from New Jersey?

"Spare me. I couldn't possibly sit through that again. By the way, that cop who came to the house called."

"Really? I didn't think I'd hear from him anymore."

"He said to call when you got back so he knows where you are."

"Okay, I will."

She pushes her plate away and takes a deep breath.

"Are you okay?" I ask.

"I can't eat much. I think I'm starting to feel it inside me. I'm seeing the specialist again on Friday. A geriatric gynecologist that Dr. Bloom sent me to. But I don't know what she can tell me. It's not like they see this kind of thing every day."

"Did you tell them to keep quiet about it?"

"No."

"Why not?"

"Because, the thing is..." She chews on her lip as she does when something weighty is about to come out of her mouth. "Why should we keep it quiet? I think we've got to make some noise, don't we? We've only got a month, for God's sake!"

"I know."

"We need to get this out there! We've got to get the ball rolling and make the connections. We've got to let the world know what's going on! I mean, this is life and death we're talking about. This is human existence. This is freaking extermination!"

"It's a lot."

I'm glad she understands the scope of what's happening, but I'm concerned about how worked up she's getting. I don't want her to hurt something.

"Harold!" she suddenly shouts.

"Yes!" I shout back.

"We have to start what our daughter has to finish," she says as if channeling a prophetic vision. "And you, as much as it pains me to say, are the perfect front man."

"I am?"

"There's something about you that people trust. They're drawn to you. That's why you were chosen for this. You are the father of the revolution, Harold!"

"I'll have to get a beret and grow a mustache."

She completely ignores what I thought was a pretty funny line, but she's on a roll, and I'm smart enough to get out of the way.

"Okay, one month, get the word out, save mankind, and make the world safe for our superbaby. Okay, no problem. Give me a minute. It's coming to me."

With nothing of value to contribute I pour myself more cabernet.

"The press has already started with the birds," she continues. "We just need to take advantage of certain opportunities. We'll need a website. Create a little buzz. That's where I come in. I'll be our press secretary and marketing expert. So long as I'm able, anyway."

"You know what I'm thinking, though?" I carefully interject. "What if the one who's talking to me isn't the good guy? What if they're playing us for some nefarious reasons?"

"*What?*" My question throws her off-balance.

"I just can't get past that he lied to me," I continue. "There's something not right about that."

"Well, he's under a time limit, too, Harold. He's trying to move things along as quickly as he can. You can't really blame him for that, can you?"

She is surprisingly defensive on the alien's behalf. Then she gulps some cranberry juice that I had put out for her so she could pretend that it's wine. See what a thoughtful father of the revolution I am?

"So you're saying that you don't trust him?" she asks and then rubs at her temples again.

"My gut tells me he's sincere, but—"

"Did you say anything to him about this?"

"I asked him why he lied."

"What did he say?"

"Just what you said. That he had to so I would come to you at the exact right moment."

"But you still have doubts?"

"I do. If he manipulated us into this, what else will we be manipulated into?"

She stares at me, or rather through me, before she speaks again. "I don't get the why," she says. "Why go to all the trouble? Why the pregnancy? Why talk to you at all if he doesn't want to help?"

"I don't know."

We drink of our respective juices.

"We have to be confident if we're going to be successful," she decides. "We have to believe him. We don't have a choice."

Then a look of complete astonishment comes over her face.

"Oh my God!"

"What?"

"Now that I think about it, there was a lot of UFO stuff back then in Australia. I remember airline pilots reporting things on the news. I must have forgotten about it. Wait a minute! I think I actually saw something, Harold! In Brisbane! Right outside our house!"

"Sometimes those memories disguise themselves as dreams, and you can't remember if it was real or not."

"Holy…sweet puppies in a tub!"

Kelly has always come up with the most interesting expressions of astonishment. I'm not sure how or where they come from, but she consistently surprises me with them. After saying "holy sweet puppies in a tub," she says no more and seems to drift away into whatever she's remembering from back then.

I eat a little food and give her some space. But her departure is starting to concern me. She's staring at me, but she's really not in the room anymore. I'm worried that I laid too much on her too soon, and she's gone into some kind of mental retreat.

"So you're really going to take a leave from work?" I ask, trying to get her back again.

She doesn't answer.

I take her hand and shake her arm a little. That seems to snap her out of it. She blinks a few times as if coming out of hypnosis.

"So you're going to take a leave from work?" I repeat because I'm pretty sure she didn't hear me the first time.

"Yes, I think I should, don't you?"

"What about retiring?" I suggest.

"What will we do about money?"

"When this gets out, something tells me that money won't be a problem."

"Because people will want to support the cause, you mean?"

"Yes, and if they don't and things don't work out…"

"Then what difference does it make, anyway," she concludes.

"Let's not lose each other when it gets crazy."

"It's crazy already, dear." She reaches across the table and takes my hand. "We won't," she promises.

"Do you want to talk to him?"

"The alien? I think I should, if it's possible. Get another perspective on things."

"He's kind of funny, actually."

"Good. I could use a laugh."

My homeless friend Oscar Robinson makes a sudden appearance. He waves at us through the picture window in the dining room. It's much creepier seeing him at night than during the day. I wave back. He blows some kisses to Kelly and then moves away and disappears into the night.

"What the hell was that?"

"That's our head of security."

"Have I seen that guy before? He looks familiar."

"He's around the neighborhood. He knows about us. He says that he has to make sure we're safe."

"This is weird, Harold."

"The alien said that the homeless are tapped into what's happening. This guy knew about the baby, too. Even before we did. He even knew it was a girl."

"Sweet Mary on a surfboard."

My cell phone rings. I've changed it from the Sherwood Forest ringtone to a jazz riff, but it still makes me jump.

"Hello?"

"Harold?" It's Portia.

"Portia! Hi."

"Are you back?"

"Yes, I'm back. Can you come to the house tomorrow?" I smile at Kelly so she feels included. I don't think she really cares, though.

"When?" Portia asks.

"In the afternoon?"

"I have a rehearsal at six."

"Come for lunch."

"Great!" Portia happily agrees.

Kelly smiles back at me. Thrilled, I'm sure, that I get to have a lunch date.

"How's your father?"

"He's crazy. I'll tell you about it tomorrow."

"I'll text you my address," I offer.

"I have it from the cast list. They want you back, Harold."

"Who wants me back?"

"They want you to come back and play Polonius."

"You're kidding me."

"They can't find anybody else who they like."

"I can't come back."

"Well, if you want to, you can."

"Thanks."

"Everybody here loves you, Harold."

"Tell them that I love them, too." I'm misting up again—I can't believe it.

"I will," Portia promises.

"See you tomorrow, Portia."

"Bye, Harold."

I disconnect the call and polish off my wine.

"That was Portia," I inform my wife, in case she might have missed it. "They want me to come back and play Polonius."

"You've got a better part to play now."

"I'd rather do Polonius."

"Well, on the bright side," she says, "if the world does come to an end, there'll be no more Shakespeare Festivals that I have to go to!"

"Funny."

"I wonder if anybody at the festival has political connections. You should check that out, Harold."

"Okay."

"Did you talk to Jerry?"

"Not yet. Thought I'd let him sleep."

"He was pretty miserable when he left here. He could barely breathe."

"He may not have that problem anymore."

"Really?"

"Yeah, it was something that happened when I used the flash drive thing. He might have gotten cured of his cat allergies."

"How? What happened?"

"I think he did it himself. Jerry is a healer. They gave it to him. He's going to be a big part of this, too."

"Why does that not surprise me."

She picks at her food again but doesn't eat anything. "You know? It was actually pretty clever how he did it," she says.

"What?"

"Got you to think he was God and that you had to make Portia pregnant because he knew how you'd react and that you'd come to me like you did. Kind of brilliant when you think about it."

"It's like all these puzzle pieces are coming together. It's all happening—the thing with Portia and Rodger and Diane and the whole trip up north…I had to have the experience in order to take the next step. And the people I met, I met them because they all have a role to play. It's like he's casting the company. It's very crafty, but you know what's confusing me?"

"What?"

"Why don't the aliens just do it? They would be like gods. People would listen to them more than they'd listen to us, wouldn't they?"

"People would freak out and panic, maybe. I don't know."

"Right, so, they need us to set things up. We introduce the idea of their presence, and then they show up when they feel the planet is ready for them. And then our kid becomes supreme leader of the universe—piece of cake."

"Speaking of which—did you get any dessert?"

"Pound cake and ice cream."

"Bring me some."

"Yes, dear."

CHAPTER THIRTY

GREAT SPIRITS HAVE OFTEN ENCOUNTERED VIOLENT OPPOSITION FROM MEDIOCRE MINDS

We're enjoying our dessert when Jerry appears like a phantom, looking in at us through the dining room window. For a moment I wonder if it's really him or just a representation that he's projected over from the dream world. When he actually knocks on the glass and Kelly sees him, too, I decide that it's probably him.

"We have to get some curtains for that window," she says.

"Hey, can I come in?" he pleads from the porch. "Something weird just happened!"

When something weird happens to Jerry (which is most of the time) his eyes get enormous, as if they might actually pop right out of his head. His face, in the dim glow of our energy-saving yellow florescent porch light is truly unsettling. I consider for a moment that Jerry is actually an alien himself, or at least has some relatives that are.

I get up to let him in. He hugs me, goes into the dining room, kisses Kelly on the cheek, and takes a seat at the table.

"Do you want some cake and ice cream?" I offer.

"No, let me just collect my thoughts for a second. This is pretty weird."

"Okay," I tell him. "Take your time."

"What kind of cake and ice cream?" he asks.

"Pound cake and vanilla ice cream."

"Vanilla?"

"Yeah."

"Do you have any chocolate?"

Kelly comments with a raised eyebrow.

"No, just vanilla," I tell him.

"Okay, maybe just a little."

I move toward the kitchen.

"Are you going to toast the pound cake?" he asks.

A snort from Kelly this time.

"I can if you like," I say.

"That would be nice."

"Okay." I start to go again.

"And some coffee? Do you have any coffee made?"

"I could make some."

"No, if you don't have it made, forget it."

"I'll make some. No big deal."

"Well, if it's no big deal. I'd love some coffee."

I go to fill his order.

"How are you feeling?" I hear him ask Kelly.

"Don't ask. How are you feeling?"

"I'm a little freaked out to tell you the truth."

"So what happened?" I ask from the kitchen.

"Did you come into my dream before?"

"Holy shit!" I cry.

"You did?"

I run back into the room. "Did you see me hovering on the ceiling?"

"Yes!"

"Did I have no legs?"

"Yes!"

"Are you feeling allergic to the cat?"

"No! What the hell is going on, Mr. Geeg?"

So I get him the pound cake, ice cream, and coffee, and we all sit around the table going over the conversation in the dream world. Mr. Geeg remembers everything. I tell him about the aliens in the courtyard and flying into space. I also give him details about the chat with the alien at the Roosevelt Golf Course coffee shop.

Jerry is still feeling no effects from the cat. Usually after about five minutes in our house he's sneezing and his eyes are turning red, but after fifteen minutes of conversation—nothing like that is happening to him.

"So do you think it's true? That I'm a healer?" Jerry asks with gigantic eyeballs.

"Yes, they gave it to you."

"And my first patient was me?"

"Pretty cool, huh?"

"I wonder how it works. I mean, what kind of healing can I do? Is it a putting on hands kind of thing?"

"I guess you'll find out."

"Anything bothering you two that you want me to cure?"

"I'm good," I say.

"See me in a couple of weeks," Kelly suggests.

"Maybe I'll deliver the baby!"

"That is disturbing on so many levels I don't even know where to begin," Kelly says with no delicacy whatsoever—something I really love about her, by the way.

"It's funny. I always thought I had an aptitude for this kind of stuff. Maybe it's what my comedy is all about. Trying to heal people with laughter."

"Oh is that what it's about?" Kelly razzes.

My wife and my best friend have a brother-sister-type relationship. They just love to give each other a hard time.

"How's Squeak?" Jerry asks.

"He's sleeping under the covers in the bedroom," I tell him. "If you put hands on him, make sure you don't put them under the covers because healer or not, he'll rip the shit out of you."

"So listen." Kelly puts a hand on Jerry's arm, stopping him just before his fork reaches his mouth. "We need your opinion on something."

"Okay," Jerry says reluctantly returning the fork to his plate.

"How do we get the word out?

"About the alien, you mean?"

"We want to use the internet and really start reaching out to people with a kick-ass marketing strategy. We have to get to leaders, presidents, congressmen, political types from all around the world. We have to get them to understand the stakes of what's going on here."

"Yeah, but wait a minute," I intervene. "The more I think about it—do we really want to put this out for everybody all over the world to see?"

"Why not?" Jerry asks.

"Because that's going to complicate things, and we only have a month. The aliens want Wyoming, and they'll share their knowledge with us, America, to get it. If we put that out everywhere—"

"Then everywhere else is going to completely freak out because they won't be getting what we're getting," Kelly says.

"Exactly," I say.

"So we can't just blast it out there," Jerry says. We need to find somebody who can get to somebody important without the thing exploding all over the internet. What about starting with some UFO networks? Tap into their resources and connections. You'd be surprised how many government people look at that stuff. And if they're already looking, maybe they'd be a little more open to what we have to tell them, and they would understand the need to keep a lid on it, too."

"UFO groups? Really?" Kelly makes a sour face. "I mean, they're pretty far out there, aren't they? We're looking for some legitimacy here. Not a bunch of conspiracy theory freaks."

"I'll try not to take that personally," Jerry mutters.

"No, no, by all means, take it personally," Kelly says. "I'll be disappointed if you don't."

"You are just a pleasure to be around, do you know that?"

"Thank you. You inspire me."

"Listen," he continues in spite of her. "I think they can really help us. UFO groups are a lot more scientific about this stuff than you'd think. They're not, as apparently you've been led to believe, just a bunch of crackpots and charlatans."

Jerry scoops up the last bits of his cake and ice cream. A small piece dribbles onto his chin and then onto his shirt. He doesn't seem to notice.

Kelly puts a hand on his arm again. They look at each other.

"You got something on your chin," she sweetly tells him.

"Oh." He wipes it off with his hand and then licks his fingers.

"Nice."

"Want to hear what happened at the Ralphs?" I ask.

"Yeah, I love supermarket stories. What happened, Mr. Geeg?"

"When I was at Ralphs, a guy was about to start a fight, but I stopped it. I kind of pushed the idea of stopping, and it worked. You have the healing thing, and I have this. I can suggest things to people, and then they do what I suggest. So maybe if people don't respond the way we want them to—"

"You can control them?" Jerry asks.

"Yes, because a lot of people aren't going to like what we're trying to do. We're going to have enemies out there."

"Is there any more coffee?" Jerry asks.

I bring the pot to the table, and then Jerry summarizes the situation.

"So they are giving us these gifts, these miracles, to get things started, so that people will listen and take us seriously. We tell only trustworthy UFO groups and certain government-type people about the aliens, and hopefully they can keep quiet about it. They're pretty good at that, right? Look at Roswell."

"Oh no. Not Roswell again," Kelly grumbles.

"We let them know what the deal is, and hopefully it doesn't cause a panic and get us all killed. Is that about it?"

"That's about it," I agree. "Get the word out but keep it quiet at the same time. Whether or not that's possible? I don't know. And we have one month."

"Did you hear about the birds?" Kelly asks him.

"They're still on our side, right?"

"I sure as hell hope so," I say.

"You know what we're really going to need?" Jerry asks as he pours himself more coffee.

"What's that?" Kelly answers.

"Somewhere down the road, we're going to need a martyr. To seal the deal, so to speak."

"What? What the hell are you talking about?" Kelly seems particularly bothered by this.

"If you really want to sell this thing, there's nothing like a martyr to get your point across. Think about it. Something this big and this important—there's always a martyr."

"I have to go lie down for a while," Kelly informs us and then abruptly leaves the table.

CHAPTER THIRTY-ONE

WE CANNOT DESPAIR OF HUMANITY, SINCE WE OURSELVES ARE HUMAN BEINGS

I use the flash drive thing again before I go to sleep. Here's what happens: I'm in the Prius. It's foggy outside, like a late-night trip home from Thousand Oaks. The colonel comes in my head clear and loud—*This must end! Drive onto the shoulder, now!* It isn't a suggestion. The voice is commanding me. This time, however, I answer back, *Stop, just stop!* I say it with equal command and considerable determination. And then the voice is gone from my head. The fog lifts, and the morning is bright and clear. A large tractor trailer truck previously hidden in the fog is parked on the shoulder of the road where the voice had pushed me to go. Now that I have pushed back, a weight is lifted, and I know things between me and the voice will never be the same.

———

The morning is brutally hot. It's 90 degrees at 9 a.m. Jerry spent the night in the guest room and had no cat trouble whatsoever. Squeak even visited him at some point and slept on the edge of his bed. Normally he would have had to throw something to get Squeak out of there, but not this time. No books were displaced, and Squeak's self-confidence remains intact.

Kelly is off to work, even after I begged her again not to go. She promises me that she is going to give her notice and then retire—and I'm very happy about that.

Jerry and I do some research on the computer and make a few calls. We find some local UFO societies that we can visit. We also make an appointment with a writer from the *UFO Journal*, a highly respected publication—among UFO enthusiasts, anyway.

Our first destination is the Athenians Society of Hollywood. We are both familiar with the Athenians Society. It's been around for a long time and has branches in several countries around the world. Jerry and I have no branches anywhere, so they must be doing something right. We get in the Prius and head to Hollywood.

"You know what's weird?" Jerry asks.

"Dogs in sweaters?"

"No, what's weird is, what's the difference between us and people in the Athenians Society?"

"Is this a riddle?" I wonder.

"No, I'm really asking you."

"Well, they're probably not as funny as you, and I've done more Shakespeare?"

"According to the website, they believe in an ascended master who imparts wisdom about how humankind can grow and be better and save the planet."

"What, did you memorize it?"

"So what makes our thing more impressive than their thing, and why would people believe our thing more than their thing?"

"The quality of the thing?"

"Why do you always have to make it about sex?"

"Besides," I continue, "aliens made my wife pregnant overnight. That's kind of a big thing—as far as things go."

"True, and we do have X-Men powers and the killer bird thing."

"I wonder how many people already know about us."

"About our thing you mean?" Jerry asks.

"Some people know, and some people just have a notion. They need a little push to remember. Like it's been repressed, and they're just waiting for a spark so they can get at it again. I saw some of that up north," I tell him.

"So once we *spark* 'em, people will recognize our thing—for the *real* thing?"

"Yes, but not everybody will like our thing. Or they will confuse our thing with another thing. You understand this, do you not?"

"You mean the thing about our thing?"

"We're going to have enemies, Mr. Geeg."

"Yes, some will find our thing offensive. Even though..." Jerry carefully works his way through it, "what they think is our thing, is not really our thing?"

"Yes, because the aliens that they're in touch with may be from the other side—the ones who don't like us very much and think that humans are not worth saving. They just want us and our thing out of the way, and they're probably giving the people they're in touch with false information about us."

"About us and our thing?" he asks just to be sure.

"Are we still talking about the same thing here?" I ask.

"I'm not sure, but I remember the last time we did this kind of thing. The thing went on for days." Jerry reminds me.

"Well, the thing is...well, what do we know for sure? We know that the aliens on the other side are not our friends. What we don't know is who they already got to. What we do know is that people seem to have some kind of repressed memory or some premonition of what's about to go down. What we don't know is when people get this *memory spark*, what side of the fence are they going to fall on. Will they be with us or against us?"

"It's going to be hard to tell who's who without a program."

"That's exactly what my friend Rodger said, too."

"Who's Rodger again?"

"He's the guy from up north. The stoner actor turned lawyer."

"Oh, right."

"He'll be coming down soon to help us."

"It's good you took that trip," Jerry says.

"You were right on the money about that one," I tell him. "And what you said about trusting my gut."

"Always trust the gut. In gut we trust," Jerry proclaims.

"If your heart is in the right place, the gut will follow."

There is a momentary silence, and I'm hoping this *gut* word game has come to an end before it really gets started.

"May the gut be with you." Jerry unfortunately is just getting warmed up.

The *gut* thing replaces the *thing* thing and goes on for way too long. Eventually, the weight of the situation settles back down on us again.

"This is our mission in life," I say. "This is what we're here for, Mr. Geeg."

"Yes, Mr. Geeg. I thought it was to have a TV series, but it is what it is."

We drive through Hollywood, which is barely recognizable from the days when Jerry and I used to make the rounds here. You think it's funky now? You should have seen it back in the good old bad days. That was serious funk. Jerry and I shared a place on Whitley Avenue just above Franklin. Rent was ninety-five dollars a month for a room in a building full of drug addicts, hookers, and bad musicians. The people next door were devil worshippers, and the Hillside Strangler killed somebody right across the street. Good times.

"Maybe we shouldn't say anything about the baby," I am compelled to suggest.

"Okay," Jerry agrees.

"Not yet anyway. I just don't want anybody going after Kelly."

"Got it."

"At least until I can really protect her."

"And how are we going to do that again?"

"I have no idea. But I know a guy who might."

"What guy?"

"I met him up in Napa. You'll like him. He's got attitude."

"Good, we're gonna need some of that."

CHAPTER THIRTY-TWO

MAN GROWS COLD FASTER
THAN THE PLANET HE INHABITS

I find a parking spot past the Athenians Society about halfway down the block. Parking in Hollywood is a challenge, to say the least. It's a small spot, but the Prius and I slip right in with only inches to spare front and back. Driving around NYC in my younger days has made me a very good parallel parker. It is rare for me to take more than one try to fit into a tight spot. If the future of mankind depended on my parallel parking, we'd be in much better shape than we are now.

The whole street has a weird vibe. I'm not sure if my feeling is tainted by everything that's going on, but there's definitely an uncomfortable weight in the air. Jerry and I both feel it. It's oppressive and is actually making my sinuses hurt. Maybe it's the heat of the day, but, honestly, I don't think so.

We get out of the car and see a man across the street having a heated conversation with himself. At first, I think he's talking on his phone, as so many people on the street do these days. They seem to be having conversations with themselves, but actually they have an earpiece or a mini-headset or whatever the latest gizmo is to keep us talking and safely disconnected from our surroundings. This guy, though, is definitely talking to himself, or rather shouting at himself or at something else that might be going on in his head.

"Shut up! Be quiet! I hate you!" He punctuates these violent eruptions by slapping himself in the face. He sits on the stoop of an old brick apartment building. The kind with the fire escape on the outside. It's not run-down, like our old place on Whitley Ave. It's actually a pretty nice-looking building, and judging by the stoop sitter's fitful behavior, maybe it's some kind of halfway house kept up by the state. As we're watching this guy, I become aware of a kind of sensory deprivation. There's no sound on this street except for the shouts of the stoop sitter. No birds, no construction noise, no traffic, no wind through the trees, as if we are in a bubble and this whole street is somehow isolated from the rest of the world.

We walk back toward the Athenians Society. The buildings we pass along the way all have a similar look about them. Old brick but well kept up. One place has a sign out front—Child Rescue Home. I don't see or hear any kids, though.

The Athenians Society owns the corner house on this block and some small bungalows that are behind it. The buildings are painted a pinkish color, and their cryptic-looking logo hangs over the front door. There is a tall wrought iron fence that surrounds the property and a locked gate with an odd-looking apparatus attached that makes me wonder if the fence might be electrified. The grounds are immaculately kept, with lots of flowers and tall bushes planted along the inside fence line so that visibility of the property is limited. Although the friendly pink color seems welcoming, there is an ominous compound feel that makes me nervous about getting too close. The desired effect I would imagine.

The Athenians Society looks deserted. Shades are drawn, and there is no activity on the grounds. I don't know if people actually live here or if they just meet here or what. Their website says that office hours are between 9 and 5, Monday through Friday, but the place looks dead.

"Should we go in?" Jerry asks.

"I don't think anybody's in there."

"Is there a bell or something?" Jerry asks as he starts snooping around.

"I don't see one," I say while following him.

"Well, let's go in then and knock on the door."

"Yeah, but what's that thing?" I point to the contraption attached to the gate.

"A camera?" he guesses.

"No, it looks like a sensor or a charge box or something like that."

"What do you mean a charge box?"

"I mean, the gate might be electrified, Jerry!" My uneasiness about being here is starting to get the best of me.

"Hmm." He reaches out with one finger as if to test my theory.

I swat his hand away from the gate.

"They can't electrify a gate in the middle of Hollywood!" he yells.

"But you don't have to get electrified trying to find out," I yell back.

"Well, what do you want to do then?"

"I don't know. We should have called first."

"Just relax," Jerry tells me. "I have the number right here."

He calls on his cell phone, and I scout around a little looking for signs of life. But I'm getting some seriously bad vibes and really just want to get the hell out of here.

"What's happening? Anybody answer?" I impatiently ask.

"It's just ringing," he says.

Then I see somebody peek out from behind a curtain. A young man with a shaved head, dressed in a white robe. He glares at me, and then he rolls his eyes back up into his head. White eyeballs staring. Completely freaks me out.

"Jerry," I hiss. "Come here!"

Jerry comes over, and I point to the man in the window.

"Holy shit!" he croaks.

We can see others are in the room behind this man. They are swaying in rhythm with each other.

"I think they're pushing us to leave. Or to die," I say.

"We just wanted to talk!" Jerry yells out to them.

The man in the robe puts his hands onto the window glass as if to focus his energy out to us. When he does, the curtain pushes back, revealing more of the room inside. It looks like a church. I can see a kind of altar in the background with a large portrait hanging above it. It's a painting of an intense *old* bald man in a white robe who also glares with white eyeballs. I assume this to be their leader or founder, and someone I have no desire to ever meet. The swaying minions behind him are people of all different races and ages. They are well dressed and completely focused on whatever message they are trying to send out to us.

"Look!" Jerry is pointing to the building across the street. At different windows, people are peering out at us with a look on their faces not unlike the intense-looking man in the portrait.

"What, is this whole block possessed or something?" Jerry gets loud at the most inappropriate times. It works great for his comedy but here, not so much.

"Let's get the hell out of here," I say at a more appropriate volume.

We hustle back with throbbing sinuses to the Prius. The car, of course, refuses to cooperate. I can't get the doors to unlock. By this time, possessed looking faces are peering out at us from everywhere.

"What's with this fucking car?" Jerry yells.

"It's not the car's fault! It's broiling out here!" I'm not sure why I try to defend the Prius. But I do.

"You should scrap this piece of shit already, I swear to God."

After the third try, the Prius unlocks. I would burn some rubber getting out of there, but the Prius isn't capable of that kind of pep.

CHAPTER THIRTY-THREE

I AM REMINDED OF THE GERMAN PROVERB:
EVERYONE MEASURES ACCORDING TO HIS OWN SHOES

Our sinuses begin to clear as soon as we get out of there. When your reality shifts like that, it's an unnerving yet somehow exhilarating experience. Probably how Jerry felt when he saw that bear/badger monster in Griffith Park.

My cell does a jazz riff and then the Bluetooth connects.

"Are we still on?" It's Portia.

"Yeah, how's one o'clock? I'm out running around, but I'll be back by then."

"Good. I can't wait to see you!" she says excitedly.

"Okay, bye Portia—can't wait to see you, too." I disconnect the call.

When a young woman says that kind of thing to an old guy like me, well, it makes you kind of stupid, actually. I won't even bother to tell you what ran through my head, especially after our initial humiliating encounter. The persistence of the male ego, even at my age, is a powerful and ridiculous force of nature.

"You know what's particularly disturbing about all this?" Jerry says.

"What? That I'm old enough to be her father?"

"No, besides that. Even if we get to some UFO groups and we can actually get them to listen to us, the UFO groups are the people who will be more threatened by what we have to say than even the nonbelievers will be."

"Why is that?"

"Because when we come along with a different alien story that doesn't jive with their alien story—that's a threat. So we get cast as the lunatics or, even worse, the villains, otherwise their own beliefs become irrelevant."

"We have to be either ignored or destroyed by the people we hoped would help us."

"I think I might have been wrong about the UFO groups, Mr. Geeg. This ain't gonna be so easy."

"No, it surely won't, Mr. Geeg."

The *UFO Journal*'s main office is in New Jersey (oddly enough). Jerry is very good on the telephone. Years of selling everything from jewelry to theater subscriptions has made him an incredibly charming and persuasive telephone salesman. Of course, it's not his mission in life to do sales, but when he has to, he does it really well. Jerry charmed the *UFO Journal* into giving us the number of one of its contributors in LA. So Jerry called this woman, Linda Broomfield, and talked her into letting us come over to her house in Burbank and tell her our story. Hopefully, this visit will be more productive than the last one and a lot easier on the sinuses.

Linda has a little bungalow on a side street right across from the Burbank Studios. It takes us a little while to find a parking spot, but finally I find something that doesn't require a parking permit and is way too small for ordinary drivers to even consider. I, of course, slip in there like a pro.

We walk the few blocks to her bungalow. The neighborhood around the studios is residential. One-story houses on tree-lined streets, and none of the heavy vibes that we experienced earlier. We walk past the Burbank Studios main gate, and I have some pangs for the days when I was a pretty busy actor in this town. I shot a few things at the Burbank lot. Made pretty good money back then, too. I never really enjoyed it much, though. All the waiting around, the egos, the pressure. It made me nervous. I have always preferred stage work. The money sucks, but artistically it's a lot more satisfying. Cameras just never really did it for me.

There is a big messy bougainvillea vine that is taking over the front porch of Linda Broomfield's bungalow, and we have to fight our way through to get to the door. The place looks neglected. The paint is peeling, and her roof is worn down to the tar paper. The next good rain is going to be a big problem for her. Jerry knocks on the door. I shift to avoid a thorny bougainvillea branch but then get poked by another one right in the back of my neck.

Linda Broomfield answers the door with a friendly smile. She's wearing a T-shirt and shorts and is not at all what I was expecting. I thought she'd be a frumpy UFO freak with greasy hair and mustard stains down her front. She isn't like that at all. Linda is about fifty, I guess, with an East Coast vibe about her. Smart and tough and good-looking. Not petite, but trim and well put together—great arms. She wears glasses that give her that studious but sexy look, and her bright, brown eyes sparkle with intelligence and curiosity. But that smile—that's what gets me. So genuine and inviting. She charms us before she even says a word. Some people just have that thing about them. You like them right away. I looked over at Jerry, and I think he more than liked her right away.

"One of you must be Jerry?" Linda says.

"I'm Jerry."

"I am Harold."

"You're bleeding. Did you know that, Harold?" Linda observes.

"Am I? The bougainvillea—it snuck up behind me."

"Sorry about that," she says. "The owners aren't keeping things up so well anymore. I think they're trying to bail on the property."

"You're renting then?" Jerry asks, as if he knows something about real estate.

"Yeah, for about a year now. I'm trying to sell some screenplays."

"California dreamin', there you go!" He elbows me in the ribs for some reason. For emphasis, I guess.

"In the meantime, I write for different magazines, like the *Journal*. I hear a lot of stories."

"I bet you do," I say. "Where are you from?"

"New Jersey," she tells us.

"I knew it! I felt it right away!" Jerry gets very excited by this news and tries to poke me in the ribs again. I sidestep him this time, though.

"You're from Jersey, too?" Linda asks him.

"Absolutely!" he cries in his best New Jersey wise guy accent. "That is so weird that we're all from Jersey! Of course, everybody in LA is from Jersey. We should have our own section of town. Call it Little Jersey, or Hey, You Talkin' to Me Town. They should absolutely name a fault line for us. Call it the Garden Plate."

Linda laughs, and Jerry has a fool-in-love look on his face that I don't think I've seen on him before. When the laughing fades into awkward silence, Linda graciously picks up the ball.

"Anyway, sorry about the mess. It was good here at first, but now it's all gone to hell," Linda tells us.

"Too bad, great location," Jerry says with a goofy, lovesick smile.

"Anyway, enough about me and devaluating property. You've got some serious UFO news for me, don't you?"

"We do," I say.

"Well, come on in. Let's wipe off some blood and get into it then."

"Great!" Jerry and I yelp at the same time."

Her place looks like where a writer would live. Her desk is in the center of the room, and there's a clutter of magazines, scripts, and books. Nothing fancy here, and it's more like an office then a home. Linda is here to work, not to set up housekeeping. We sit in the two folding chairs that she has set up for us in front of her desk and wait for her to return from the kitchen. She brings us cranberry juice in coffee mugs and a wet dishrag for the back of my neck. She sits at her desk and gives us another one of her disarming smiles.

"Cranberry juice. Good for the prostate," Jerry says.

"That's why I like it," Linda agrees. "How's the neck?"

"It's fine," I say.

Actually, it's stinging like a son of a bitch, but I'm trying to make a good impression, so I don't complain.

"So, lay it on me! What have you got?" She opens a desk drawer and takes out a tape recorder. Jerry and I look at each other. He gestures to let me know that the floor is mine. I had thought about what I might say, but I am still uncertain about how to start telling this story so I won't come off like a lunatic. I take a deep breath, but nothing happens after that.

"Just start talking," Linda says. "It doesn't have to be perfect, and believe me, I've heard it all. I won't laugh in your face and take back my towel, I promise." She turns on the tape recorder.

"Okay, thanks. But I have to ask—" I'm nervous about her taking this the wrong way—"can we be off the record at first?"

"Off the record? Do you want me to do a story or no?"

"Well, yes and no. We need your help to get the word out, but not to everybody. Just to certain people. Official people. We're trying to avoid a bad reaction," I tell her.

"Go ahead and tell me what happened, and then we'll go from there." She shuts off the tape recorder. "I'll just take some notes. Is that acceptable to you?"

"That'd be great. Thank you."

"Go ahead," she says with just a glimmer of impatience.

"Okay," I begin. "We have been contacted by who I thought at first was God, but it turns out was really an alien." When the words come out of my mouth, I'm impressed by how ridiculous I sound.

Linda seems unfazed, however. "Did he name himself?"

"No."

"He didn't say what kind of alien? What civilization, what planet, anything like that?"

"No, but he told me that their planet's sun is dying, and they need a new home. They want Wyoming, and they want to work with our government to come to some kind of immigration plan. In exchange, they will share their knowledge with us. Then there's another faction that just wants us out of the way. Wants us exterminated. They don't think that trying to work with us is worth the trouble. Anyway, that's why they're here, and they want me to be sort of the middle man between their people and our people. My wife and I—"

I stop myself. Nothing about the baby. I really don't want to go there yet.

"Excuse me," I say while attempting to regroup. "I'm trying to get this organized in my head at the same time that I'm talking, and I don't want to overwhelm you right off the bat."

"Take your time," she tells me.

"You know those birds?" Jerry interjects. "Have you heard about them, the giant birds?" He's apparently becoming impatient with me and tries to move things along.

"The killer birds by the bay?" she asks.

"They're with him," Jerry tells her.

"What do you mean?"

"They seem to be protecting me," I say. "They follow me."

"Protecting you against who? The other faction?"

"There have been a few people who have wanted to hurt me. I think they have been influenced by the aliens that don't like us so much."

"So the people who were killed up north—"

"They were threatening me."

"You were up there?"

"Yes."

"Do you have proof?"

"That I was there?"

"Yes."

I look in my wallet and find the credit card receipt for the room at the Motel 6. I hand it to her, and she looks it over.

"Go on," she says.

I do. I tell her almost everything. Way too much. I give her the history back to the Jersey days, all the way up to the weirdness with the Athenians Society. I talk for over an hour. She asks me questions as I go, and Jerry fills in some gaps along the way. I tell her everything. Except I'm careful to avoid the stuff about Kelly being pregnant.

"The point is," I conclude, "we need to get the word out to certain powers that be without having this spread all over the place and cause a panic. If it gets out on the internet and goes viral, I'm afraid the situation will become uncontrollable. If other countries find out about what the aliens are offering us in America—I don't think that will be so good either. So we need to get to people who can get to the right people. So that we can effectively save humankind."

"And we only have a month," Jerry adds.

"Well, twenty-nine days," I clarify.

"Twenty-nine days for what?" Linda asks.

"To get the government to allow the aliens to immigrate peacefully," I say. "If we can't do that, then that other faction will be proven right about our worthiness, and then—that's it. That would be the end."

She closes her notebook.

"They gave me this." I have the flash drive dream thing with me and put it on her desk.

"A flash drive?"

"No, it's a tool they gave me. I use it at night. It teaches me things about dreaming. I can do things now that I couldn't do before."

"Really? Like what?"

"I can enter dreams. Other people's dreams. I can influence people's thoughts, and I can move things. I'm really just learning about what I can do. It's still pretty new."

"I can heal," Jerry tells her. "I'm the healer."

"It sounds like they're preparing you for battle," she says.

"I think they gave us these things," I try to explain, "to prove that the situation is real and that there's a lot to be gained by having them here."

"His wife is pregnant," Jerry blurts out.

I give him a disbelieving look.

"I'm sorry Harold, but it's a big part of the story. You can't just leave it out and have it make any sense."

After stewing for a moment, I confess. "It's true. I'm worried about this getting out before I can protect her. I'm sure you can understand."

"How old is your wife?"

"Fifty-nine."

"It happened literally overnight," Jerry tells her. "It's kind of a miracle."

"And it's been medically confirmed? She's for sure pregnant?" Linda asks.

"Yes, and it's developing very rapidly. Not like a normal pregnancy," I say.

"So your wife is carrying a hybrid child?"

"It's a little of me and a little of her and a little of something else."

"It's a hybrid," she reiterates.

"Should love the Prius, then," Jerry says.

"The alien said that she's supposed to be a great leader. A great peacemaker."

"You know that it's a she?"

"Yes."

There is an unmistakable look of alarm on her face. After all I've told her, this seems to affect her the most. Linda puts her notebook back into her desk drawer. When she looks at me again, something has changed about her. There's nothing warm or inviting. The smile that charmed us when we first came in has definitely left the building.

"Have you considered," she begins slowly, "that the ones you're in touch with might not have humanity's best interests at heart? That maybe they're not who you think they are?"

"Yes, I have considered that."

"And that maybe you are unwittingly on the wrong side of this thing."

"We're not on the wrong side. There're only two sides in this. We either succeed with my alien or we fail all of humanity."

"Yes, that's what they'd like you to believe. Let me ask you something. Do you think that you're qualified enough to decide who knows and who doesn't know about this? What if Earth has to defend itself against an invasion? What gives you the right to sign the planet's death warrant by concealing information? And the girl, by the way, is a sign. There are a lot of stories about what a child like this will be coming here to do."

"Like what?" Jerry asks.

"Like the beginning of the end, sealing the deal, the apocalypse. You know, that kind of thing. Your child is not here to bridge any gaps or to be a peacemaker. She's here for them. Not for us. You're being set up, Harold."

"I have to trust my gut that we're on the right track. We're trying to save the world, not destroy it. Believe me, we're the good guys."

"I'm not completely convinced of that," Linda tells me.

The arrogant way she says this really irritates me, and I guess she can read it in my face.

"You're not going to set the birds on me are you, Harold?"

And that just makes it worse. I start to drum my fingers on her desk. I'm frustrated and feel betrayed by this woman. Then the house starts to shake. It feels like a 4.0. Not a huge one, but big enough to make you freeze in your tracks and wonder how bad it's going to get. It goes on for just a few seconds and then it's done.

"Is that your first earthquake?" Jerry asks her.

"Yes," she says uneasily.

"Looks like the power didn't go off or anything," Jerry observes.

"I'm not the man who would raise an evil child," I tell her.

"Did you shake my house?"

"I'm not sure."

"I think you should leave now," she says.

"We're not bad people," I tell her. "You must see that."

But she has nothing more to say. I take a card from my wallet and put it on her desk. I don't trust her, but I don't want to lose her either, and I certainly don't want her as an enemy.

"Call me, when you're ready to talk," I say. "We need your help."

I take back my flash drive and put it in my pocket.

"Are you going to write a story?" Jerry asks her.

She stares at us and refuses to speak another word.

"I think you're wrong about what's going on," I say. "But I promise you, I will keep an open mind about it. If we need to change course, that's what we'll have to do. Just give me a few more days before you do anything."

She abruptly gets up and goes into her bedroom, closing the door after her.

"Shit!" Jerry says. "I thought I had a shot with her."

I fold the dishrag that she gave me and put it on her desk. "Let's get out of here, Mr. Geeg."

CHAPTER THIRTY-FOUR

ONLY A LIFE LIVED FOR OTHERS
IS A LIFE WORTHWHILE

I try to turn on the radio, but why do I bother.

"Maybe she just needs some time," Jerry says.

"I think she's probably already made up her mind."

"She hears a lot of stuff. It must be hard to sort out the crazy from whatever it is that we've got going on. Besides, if you look at it from her position, what if we are evil, and she helps us, and then the world blows up? That might give the paper a bad name."

"Well, if the world blows up, then—"

"Yeah, but you know what I mean."

We drive in silence.

"We're not wrong about what's going on here, are we?" Jerry asks.

"No time to waffle," I remind him. "Got to go with the gut."

"Yes. In gut we trust."

But honestly, I'm having doubts of my own. It'd be impossible not to.

"If we're going to bring people over to our side," Jerry says, "we'll have to come up with something big. Probably something to do with these powers we have."

"Well, that is the point. It's why they gave us these things. To impress people."

"Yeah, but maybe we have to scare them, too. Maybe that's how you get their attention. Did you shake her house?"

"I think I did."

"Cool. Because I'm thinking it has to be big. Like explosions and force fields and rivers changing course. Like we're gods. Gods with big killer birds."

Jerry, I notice, is getting a glint of crazy in his eye.

"Maybe a human sacrifice," he adds.

"We don't want to pretend to be gods. That can't be good. If we get into deceiving and scaring people…you don't really want to do that, do you?"

"Well, if it gets me lots of women and gold and stuff."

"Easy, Mr. Geeg."

"Sorry, I'm lustful by nature."

He pushes the touch screen on the dash, trying to get some music going, but he puts the heat on instead. I move his hand away and turn off the air.

"We're going to need a lot of friends," Jerry says. "Maybe you should throw a block party. Have a barbecue or something."

We get off at San Fernando Road and head toward my house. Everything on the street looks different to me. Probably it's my mood, which is not very good at the moment. I feel as if I'm seeing the world for the first time, as it really is, and it's not a pretty picture. Everything looks weary and worn, and the people seem zombielike, disconnected and ripe for the taking. How many know? How many can be saved? "Love recklessly," a dear, departed friend once told me. I will try and take that to heart. There will be no more hiding from the world. I've been drinking way too much for way too long; avoiding friends and responsibilities in favor of my selfish pursuit of contentedness. Now we're at the crossroads, and for reasons I cannot possibly comprehend, my responsibilities have become humankind's last chance for survival.

"But, Mr. Geeg!" I suddenly blurt out as if to keep from drowning in the enormity of it all. "It's not that we're gods or pretending to be gods, but if we can do these things, and if we do them to help people, to heal and save lives—that's a good thing, right?"

"Sure it is, Mr. Geeg."

"It's what will draw people to us, and then maybe they'll listen to what we have to tell them."

"Right. I get it," Jerry says somewhat defensively.

"I wish this were happening to somebody else. I'd gladly give it all away in a second. But it is meant for us to do, and if we deny the talent, well, that'd just be rude. It's not that we're gods, we're just—"

"God*like?*"

"No! We're not gods and we're not godlike, goddamn it! We're just…we can do some shit, and now we have to save the world! That's it! Okay? Got it?"

"Okay, okay, I get it. Take it easy. Don't flip the car over or make the freeway collapse or anything." Jerry looks at me as though I'm really losing it, which I probably am.

"Sorry," I say, and then my eyelid starts twitching.

"Mind if I smoke?" Jerry asks.

"Yes."

"It'll relax me."

"Don't smoke, please. It'll make the car stink."

"Okay, forget it then. Geeze."

We pull into my driveway, and Portia is sitting on the front porch steps waiting for us. She waves when we pull in.

"Is that her?" Jerry asks.

"It is."

"She's cute."

"Don't scare her. She's sensitive."

We get out of the car, and Portia comes down the steps to greet us. She gives me a hug and hangs on to me for longer than an obligatory hug would require. It's a moment filled with meaning. I'm not sure what meaning it is, but I'm sure it's meaningful, nonetheless. After she finally lets me go, I make introductions.

"Portia, this is Jerry. A very old friend of mine."

"Actually, I'm younger than him by six months. He's the old guy—just for the record."

"Hi, Jerry, nice to meet you," she says with great vulnerability and warmth, and I think again about what a great Ophelia she would be.

"The pleasure is mine, milady." Jerry bows with Shakespearian flourish.

"Let's go in," I offer. "I've got some stuff for sandwiches if you're hungry."

CHAPTER THIRTY-FIVE

GOD NEVER TELLS US IN ADVANCE WHETHER THE COURSE WE ARE TO FOLLOW IS THE CORRECT ONE

I put out some sandwich stuff and a pitcher of iced tea. We tell Portia about our encounter with the Athenians Society and our weird meeting with Linda in Burbank. I'm putting it out there for her that what's to come will probably get dangerous. I want to give her the option of getting out before it gets ugly. But Portia is determined, and committed, and our warnings seem not to faze her at all.

"How's your wife?" she asks.

"Kelly is good," I tell her. "She's giving notice on her job today."

"Good, that's good." She nods and smiles.

"She needs to stay close to home now. She's a lot smarter than I am, and we're going to need her input."

"I can't wait to meet her," Portia says cheerfully.

"How's your father?" I ask.

"He won't let it go." She becomes instantly uncheerful. "He thinks that I've been brainwashed by you, and that you're like a Charlie Manson or something. He's just got it in his head that you are bad. He's obsessed about it."

"What about legally? What's happening with all that stuff?"

"He keeps pestering the DA in Ventura, who is about ready to have *him* arrested for harassment instead of you."

"That reminds me. I have to call that cop later. Remind me, Jerry, would you?"

"Don't forget to call that cop."

"Thank you."

"I'm afraid that he might do an intervention," Portia says bowing her head and wringing her hands.

"An intervention?"

"Yes, because he feels like I'm being drawn into a dangerous cult and that I'm not thinking straight."

"You think he might actually do that?" I ask.

"I've never seen him like this before. I don't know what he might do."

"But how old are you?" Jerry is getting particularly worked up about this latest development.

"Twenty-four."

"So he can't do that! You're an adult. That would be a felony kidnapping!" Jerry sustains his outrage even as he makes himself a second sandwich.

"When they think somebody is in trouble, for drugs and stuff, they just do it. Mormons do that kind of thing."

"I'm sorry, but that is complete bullshit," Jerry says firmly. "You're an adult person. Nobody, I don't care who they are, can just come in and grab you off the street and whisk you away in the night. I mean, that is just ludicrous. Mr. Geeg, are there any pickles?"

Jerry's appetite momentarily trumps his outrage.

"I'm all out."

"Too bad. A pickle would have been nice with this."

"I still have—I don't know if they're dreams or if they're visits," Portia confesses. "But it's confirming that this is the right thing. I have to help you. Whatever you need from me, I'll do."

"Okay, but it bothers me when you say that," I tell her. "I want you to use your own judgment. If I ask you for something and it doesn't sit right with you, don't do it. I need you to be thoughtful, and not just do whatever I need. Okay?"

"Yes, okay. Whatever you need."

Well, that's just spooky. If I asked her to go up on the roof and jump, would she do that, too? Maybe her father is right about her susceptibility to brainwashing. I hope he isn't right about me as well. Trust the gut and all that. I change the subject.

"How's the show going?"

"I can't even focus on that. I really understand now why you can't come back to play Polonius. I'm thinking of leaving, too."

"Don't leave. You should play Ophelia."

"Maybe I should, but I don't think I can right now. Nothing is more important than what's going on here. This is all that matters now."

She reaches out for my hand. I reach out for my iced tea instead, and, yes, I did put a little brandy in it. Baby steps.

"You should let her stay at the house, Harold." Jerry's generosity extends way beyond himself.

"Have you had any inclinations about your role in this?" I ask her.

"I think I'm supposed to bring people over to us. Oh, and I can do this:" She waves her hand over the butter knife, and it flies across the room and sticks in the wall above the hutch.

"Huh," Jerry says.

"Is that a recent thing you can do?" I ask.

"Yes, I'm a quick study."

"He can make earthquakes and make people do things," Jerry tells her.

"I think I have that, too," she says. "I'm not so good at that, though. I tried it on my father, and he didn't even flinch."

"I can heal," Jerry tells her with a mouth full of sandwich.

"Oh, and I know how to deliver a baby," Portia adds. "I'm trained as a midwife."

I go over and take the knife out of the wall. It just doesn't match the wallpaper. Roy and Alice from St. Helena and their crowded house of actor refugees come into my thoughts. I know that Kelly likes her privacy, but there isn't going to be a whole lot of that pretty soon.

"So the big question is," Jerry begins, "how do we get the right people's attention without causing a worldwide panic? I'm thinking that it has to be something big. Probably something to do with these new skills that we have. Any thoughts on that, Portia?"

"It's got to be like, well, why do people believe in UFOs and God and magic? What is it that they're looking for in all that? Why is *Star Trek* so enduring? Whatever that is, that good that people are looking for, we have to satisfy that need. If we can do that." She smiles sweetly for us. "Then we can save the world."

"That's impressive," Jerry says.

"Very good," I agree.

CHAPTER THIRTY-SIX

THOSE WHO WOULD PRESERVE THE SPIRIT MUST ALSO LOOK AFTER THE BODY TO WHICH IT IS ATTACHED

Portia takes off after lunch to run some errands and then make the trip out to Thousand Oaks. She says that she's going to talk to Tom (the director) about leaving the show. I urge her again not to, but she insist that it's the right thing to do. I'm glad that she's sticking to her guns, regardless of what I tell her. Makes me feel less Charlie Manson-ish.

Jerry and I sit in my office and debate if there's any benefit in calling more UFO groups, considering the previous disasters that occurred. We decide to try a few more because what else is there to do?

We find a local organization called The UFO Research Group that has some affiliations with MUFON, which is the big nationwide UFO investigating body. I've heard that MUFON is, in reality, one guy in a cluttered room taking lots of phone calls. But I guess it does actually have some agents (of dubious credentials) who go out and look into stories that they deem worthy of investigation. I hand the phone to Jerry, master of the cold call, but, unfortunately, he gets a recording. It's still fun listening to him leave a message, though.

"Hi, my name is Brad Hansen. I'm calling because a group of extremely serious and well-intentioned individuals, myself included, have been contacted by, and have received an urgent message from, an alien life form. We have proof of this contact and would be very interested in confidentially, and exclusively, sharing our experiences with your most reputable organization. Again, we have received a message of extreme importance. Our number is 818-730-XXXX. This was a very close encounter and the events that are already developing will have great consequences for the entire planet. Again, my name is Brad, and I look forward to sharing with you what may be the most monumental thing that has ever happened. I look forward to hearing from you. Hopefully, before it's too late."

He hangs up the phone and then gives me a questioning look.

"Brad Hansen? Why'd you use a phony name?"

"Oh, it's my phone sales name," he explains. "I think I might have laid it on a little thick. Did you think it was too much?"

"No, it was good."

"A little too serious. I should have put a little humor in there."

"UFO people don't respond to humor."

"I threw in *confidential* and *exclusive*," Jerry says, "so hopefully they won't say anything to anybody before they talk to us first."

"I got that. Good work."

"Should've tried to sell them a theater subscription or some stationary supplies. Maybe make a little money off this deal."

"Did you remind me to call that cop?"

"A couple of hours ago. Want me to remind you again?"

"No, that's okay."

I take the folded-up number out of my wallet and give Officer Rivas a call. He picks up right away.

"Rivas."

"Yes, Officer Rivas, this is Harold Goldfarb, I spoke to you a couple of days ago."

"Are you calling regarding a parole violation?"

"No, you called me, and I was out of town? You told me to call when I got back? We spoke when I was in the Bay Area?"

"So?"

"Well, I'm back."

"What did you do?"

"I think you called to warn me about something. I'm not exactly sure."

"Have you been charged with anything?"

"I don't think so. I haven't heard anything."

"There are no warrants? Nothing like that?"

"Last time we spoke you looked me up on your computer and told me to behave myself."

"Are you behaving yourself?"

"Yes, I am."

"Well, let's keep it that way then!" and then he hangs up.

I am either off his computer list or Rivas has had enough for one day, and it is, after all, happy hour somewhere. Whatever it is, I'm not going to worry about Officer Rivas anymore because he certainly isn't worrying about me.

We make a few more calls, including one to Sacramento and one to a California congresswoman. We leave a lot of messages because nobody is answering their phone. Then I try to check in with Rodger up north, but he's not picking up either. I do get hold of Kelly, and she tells me that she gave notice at her job, and she'll be in meetings all day trying to help the company figure out how to survive without her.

Jerry decides that he needs to take a break and goes home to work on a blog that he's writing. Since Kelly said that she would be a few more hours at work, I ignore my conscience and decide that it might be nice to have a drink in a bar with other people around for a change. It might be my last time to enjoy this kind of escape, and tomorrow will be a much better day for kicking old habits and becoming the better person that I long to be. There's a little place not far from my house that specializes in craft cocktails. High-end stuff and very expensive. Of course I don't go there, but I thought you might like to know about it. I go to the Mexican place instead. At happy hour they always put out some free cheesy snacks to keep you thirsty. I love Mexican places.

———

It's too early to be crowded, so I get a good spot in the bar. A little table in the corner. I cruise the happy hour food and fix myself a nice plate. I get a margarita (happy hour half price). I'm doing a remarkably good job of ignoring my drinking problem, when a neighbor sits down with me at my table.

"Hey, how you doing?" says the neighbor.

"Okay, how's it going?"

"I've seen you around, walking in the neighborhood. My name is Steve Hammond. I'm over on Cleveland Avenue? I have the dalmatians?"

"Oh, of course, Steve Hammond. What an unexpected surprise." And then I pretty much ignore him and pretend he isn't there. I'm hoping my rudeness will give him a hint, and he'll go away. He doesn't.

"You're on that website, aren't you?" says Steve Hammond.

"What website?" I begrudgingly reply.

"What do they call it? You know that neighborhood site? For the neighborhood?"

"Oh, yeah, I look at that once in a while."

"Did you read about that homeless guy?"

As soon as he says it, a shiver goes down my spine. Steve reaches out and grabs a waiter—literally.

"Can you bring me a margarita, no salt? Another for you, my friend?"

"Okay," I agree.

"Make it two," Steve tells him.

"No salt on mine either, please." No salt on the glass makes us afternoon drinkers feel better about the other abuses, I suppose.

"And put it on my tab, por favor," Steve tells the guy.

Hey, I'm beginning to like neighbor Steve!

"Thanks, Steve," I say with new appreciation.

"My pleasure. What did you say your name was, again?"

"I didn't, but since you bought me a drink, it's Harold." Steve gives me a vigorous handshake.

"So tell me about this homeless guy."

"It's that guy in the neighborhood. I'm sure you've seen him. He has the shopping cart, talks to everybody, always happy."

"Yeah, I know who he is."

"He's dead."

"What!"

"They found him in the alley between Sonora and Grandview. His throat was slashed."

"Are you sure?"

"Hell yeah, I'm sure. Everybody is talking about it. That's why I'm here. I don't go drinking in the middle of the day for nothing. Everybody in the neighborhood is freaking out."

I pick up my drink, and my hand is shaking badly.

"Who would do something like that," Steve says. "I mean, somebody cut his throat! For what, some old newspapers and soda cans? What's going on out there? That kind of thing isn't supposed to happen in Glendale!"

"Steve, I think I have to go now. I'm not feeling well."

"But I just ordered drinks!"

"Never buy drinks for strangers, Steve. You just never know what they're capable of."

I throw some money on the table. I leave the restaurant, shaken and angry and racked with guilt.

CHAPTER THIRTY-SEVEN

IN THE SERVICE OF LIFE
SACRIFICE BECOMES GRACE

I'm heartsick as I slowly drive through the alley, looking for something, anything that can connect me to him again. I see discarded yellow police tape, and that makes my stomach threaten to bring up something cheesy from the Mexican restaurant. It must have happened the night we saw him in the dining room window. The first thing I think of are the bird-monsters. Not their MO, however, to cut throats. They prefer taking the entire head. Besides, Lou, or Oscar Robinson, was on our side, and if I am sure about anything in this world, it is that the birds are on our side, too. So who would have done this?

Then I see some brownish-red splotches on the concrete and spattered on the side of a building. My stomach lurches again. If somebody killed my friend because of what he felt compelled to do for me, I need to start taking our security a lot more seriously.

Something moving next to a dumpster catches my eye. It's about the size of a squirrel and seems to be bobbing up and down. I stop the car to look, but I can't make out what it is. I get out and walk toward it. It's a bobblehead Einstein doll, and I'm certain that it's from Oscar Robinson's shopping cart. I check around to see if anyone is watching, and then I take it. I get back into the Prius and place Einstein between the penguin and the cowgirl in the back seat.

I drive out of the alley and make my way home.

———

The first thing I do when I get back home is go into my office and turn on my laptop. While I'm waiting for the computer to boot up, I look around at the photos that hang on my office walls. Pictures dating back to the seventies. Jerry and me from our first comedy act and all the other partners I've had and the shows I've done over a long career. It's the story of my life but looking at it now seems only to add to my depression.

The computer seems ready for me, finally, and I check the neighborhood watch site to see if anyone has posted information about the murder. But there is nothing there that I don't already know. Next, I call the Glendale Police Department. After being shuffled around to several different departments, Officer Howard gets on the phone. I have actually met him before. He does the community watch talks for our neighborhood. I went to one of the meetings that they hold at the local Boy Scout Center. He's probably in his fifties with the shiniest bald head that I've ever seen. I remember wondering if he used polish to make it so reflective. Anyway, Officer Howard always seems genuinely concerned about keeping the neighborhood safe. He knows a lot about coyotes and mountain lions, and he has lots of stories about funny things that have happened in Glendale. He brings printouts with him with useful tips about how to keep your person and your property safe from thieves and wild animals. But he doesn't seem to know much about what happened to Oscar Robinson.

"Are there any suspects yet, Officer Howard?"

"I don't believe so. Not yet."

"No clues or anything?"

"Well, I'm not really at liberty to discuss that. The case is under investigation. Are you a relative of the deceased?"

"No, I'm a friend," I say with a quivering voice.

"There have been a lot of people calling about him. When information becomes available, I'll be happy to share it with you. I'll also be posting on the neighborhood watch website, so you can check in there."

"Do you think there was more than one person involved?"

"We don't know that yet, sir."

"Please, call me Harold. We've met before at a community watch meeting."

"How about that!" He brightens considerably. "Well, hi then, Harold, and it's nice to talk to you again."

"Was there a note, anything like that?"

"Harold, I'm sorry, but I can't discuss it at this time."

"Where did they take the body?"

"The downtown morgue."

"The Los Angeles morgue?"

"Right."

"Why did they take him down there?"

"That's just where they go in situations like this. No family, nobody to claim him. That's where they go."

"Will he be cremated?"

"Yes, that's the standard procedure."

Cremation bothers me. Not for religious reasons but because it's so final. You hear stories all the time about people who are declared dead but actually had something going on where they only appear to be dead, and then they pop up on a table somewhere wondering what the hell is going on. With cremation, you don't pop up.

"Thank you, sorry to bother you, Officer Howard."

"I'm sorry for your loss, and it's no bother at all."

"Goodbye, sir."

"Goodbye, Harold."

Squeak comes over and jumps on my lap. I feel emotionally drained and suddenly very tired. He gets up on my desk so we're at eye level, and then he hits me in the nose with a right cross. He knows my moods and how to get me back on track. And he's a lot cheaper than therapy.

"Thanks, buddy." I scratch him under the chin, and he purrs like a motorboat.

I search my wallet for the card I was given earlier. Squeak walks over the keyboard and types *fedr t y zaaag*. Smart cat. He squeaks like a mouse and types in German. I find Israel's card, Magic Shield Protection, and give him a call. He picks up on the second ring.

"Israel, it's me, Harold. The guy with the—"

"Hey, brother, I thought I might be hearing from you."

"Listen, man. I need your help."

"Where are you?"

"I'm in LA. In Glendale."

"Hold tight, I'm on my way."

He takes my address and says that he's been meaning to take a trip down south anyway, and he has lots of contacts here that we can take advantage of. Israel says that he'll be here within twenty-four hours.

Looks like I have a new head of security, although I'll never forget the old one. I put the bobblehead Einstein on my desk on top of my table clock so that whenever I check the time, I will be reminded of him.

Thank you, Oscar Robinson, wherever you are. I am truly very sorry.

CHAPTER THIRTY-EIGHT

WE DO THINGS, BUT WE DO NOT KNOW WHY WE DO THEM

I'm not hungry because of the trip to happy hour and the stuff I nearly puked up in the alley, but I want to make something nice for Kelly. I do a vegetable stir-fry (with tofu) served over brown rice. If I spice it right, it's not half bad. If I don't, it's all bad. I taste it, and I think I got it right. It's all about the cayenne.

When she comes in the door, Kelly looks tired and pale and, I swear to God, about four months pregnant.

"I feel terrible!" she announces.

"I made some dinner for you. Vegetable stir-fry!"

Somehow, she gets even paler, runs into the bathroom, and starts throwing up. I assume this to be a symptom of the pregnancy and not a critique of my culinary skills. I go to check up on her.

"Are you okay?"

"Go away! Just leave me alone for a minute!"

She throws up again.

I go into my office and call Jerry.

"Hellooo?" he answers in his ninety-year-old grandmother voice.

"Mr. Geeg, what are you doing?"

"I just finished my blog, and I've been doing some research on energy healers."

"Good. I think I have your first patient."

"Who?"

"Kelly. She's in the bathroom throwing up."

"I don't normally do house calls when there's vomit involved, but because we've all been abducted by aliens, I'll make an exception. What I'm going to do when I get there, I have no idea, but I'll be there in about an hour."

"Thank you, Mr. Geeg. I swear to God, she already looks about four months pregnant."

"Wait a minute," he says. "There's somebody at the door."

"Mr. Geeg! Wait!"

"What?"

"Check first and make sure you know who it is."

"Why, did something happen?"

"Yeah, I'll tell you later."

"Okay, I'm going over now…I'm looking through the peephole… It's my neighbor, and she has a plate of cupcakes. She makes cakes and brings me some once in a while. I've had her cupcakes before. They're dry, but I don't think she's trying to kill me."

"Okay, just be careful out there. Keep your eyes open."

"I'll see you soon."

"Be careful, Mr. Geeg."

"Okay, Mom, I will."

I go back to the dining room and wait for Kelly. I think about putting a plate out for her but decide that might not be such a good idea. After a few more minutes, I hear the toilet flush, and then she drags herself in to see me. She looks pissed off but a little healthier than when she first walked in.

"Look at this!" She lifts up her shirt, and her flat stomach isn't flat anymore.

"And that's just from today!" she cries. "It's killing me, Harold. I feel like all my insides are being churned up!"

Then she collapses in a chair and lays her head down on the table.

"Are you hungry?" I tentatively ask.

"Fuck you."

That's pretty much what I thought she'd say.

"Harold." She raises her head, her eyes are pleading and wet. "I think this is going to kill me. That's why Dr. Bloom sent me to the specialist."

"It won't kill you."

"It's taking everything from me. A body can't stand this. It's too fast, and I'm too old. I think they're just using me as a vessel, and when the baby comes, I'm done. I'm scared, Harold. I think I'm going to die."

"You're not going to die," I reassure her.

"Oh, really? And how would you know?"

"Because..." I struggle for a comforting explanation. "Because...it wouldn't make any sense. Pregnancies are just hard at first, and this one is probably a little harder, but I'm sure you're not supposed to die. That would be counterproductive. The kid needs a mother, right?"

"If you're trying to make me feel better, it's not working."

"Your appointment is Friday?"

"Yes, if I live that long."

"Well, let's go tomorrow instead. Maybe they can give you something to make you feel better."

"They've never seen anything like this before, so how are they supposed to know how to help me? And wait till they get a load of this!" She pulls up her shirt again. "In just five days, Harold! This is ridiculous!"

"I'll call them in the morning."

"I have to tell you, Harold. I am freaking out right now. And I hate aliens, I hate you, I hate my job, and I especially hate stir-fry vegetables!"

I give her a moment to recover herself.

"So what happened at work today, dear?" I ask as if today were like any other day.

"There's so much work to do and they're panicked about how they're going to replace me. My stomach started growling and gurgling right in the middle of the meeting. Somebody actually gasped. I don't know what to say to people anymore. I'm going to try and do as much as I can from the house—on the phone and the computer. I don't think I'm going back. I'm done."

"Good. I'm glad."

"I'm actually feeling a little better now," she admits.

"See!"

"Is there any more ice cream?"

"Yeah."

"Any raw meat?"

"Seriously?"

"No, I'm kidding. Unless there's buffalo liver. I'll have some of that."

"We're all out."

"Damn."

She surprises me with a smile. A grimacelike smile. I'm not sure if she's trying to be sweet or if she wants to stick a fork in my neck.

"And how was your day, honey?" she asks like a vacuous '50s sitcom mom.

"Well, you know the homeless guy who looked in the window and was our head of security?"

"Let me guess—he wants us to do his laundry now?"

"No, he's dead."

"What?"

"They found him in an alley over by Grandview."

"Oh my God! Do you think it has to do with all of this?"

"I think it might. I called the police to try and find out what they know, but they weren't saying anything."

"Jesus!"

"So I called this guy I met in Napa, and he's coming down. He runs a security company."

"Do you think we should get a gun or something?"

In the past, Kelly has threatened to leave me if I ever got a gun. What a difference a day makes.

"I have a feeling Israel has lots of guns," I say.

"Who's Israel?"

"He's the guy. Our new head of security."

"Are you sure he's on our side?"

"I'm pretty sure."

"You're pretty sure? He's coming down here with artillery, Harold! You should be a little more than pretty sure, don't you think?"

"Well, it felt like he knew me the first time we met. And he wants to help us. That's what happens with the good ones...I think."

"Wonderful, we've gone from *pretty sure* to *I think*. I feel almost completely not better now, thank you very much."

"We don't have time for background checks and references. I gotta go with my gut. It's all we have right now."

"Please, don't talk to me about guts." She pulls up her shirt and looks again at her own. "Jesus! That's just ridiculous. When can I see the homeless lady that the alien talks through? I've got some questions, and at this point she can probably help me more than any doctor can."

"When do you want to?"

"Tomorrow."

"Okay, we'll go down there."

"Ice cream, please." She bats her eyelashes like a little angel.

I kiss her on the cheek.

"If there's none left, I'm killing the cat."

"Do you want me to sprinkle some bacon bits on it?"

"That's disgusting—but, yeah, that sounds pretty good."

I have to laugh at that one, and that gets her going too. I head toward the kitchen.

"Harold, do you think this pregnancy might change my personality?"

I take the Fifth.

"We should get some bars on the windows," she says as I'm preparing her treat in the kitchen. "Maybe run a few volts through the metal. We'll just put it on at night, though, so we don't kill the mailman. I don't want to get the mail any later then we already do."

"Jerry's coming over," I tell her as I sprinkle on the bacon.

"Again?"

"Yeah, he's going to start treating you with his magic healing powers."

"That should be annoying."

"Give him a chance. Couldn't hurt."

"Easy for you to say."

"Maybe that's why they gave it to him. Maybe it's for you."

"Lucky me."

I put her ice cream on a silver platter and present it to her with a bow.

"Madam, your dessert," I say like a stuffy English butler.

She ignores my theatrics, grabs the dish, and dives right in.

"I get the feeling we're outnumbered," I tell her as she devours the stuff as if it's her first meal in a week. "So we have to figure out how to make our enemies our allies and get them to come over to our side. Jerry thinks it's going to have to be something big. Something really explosive to get the public's attention. But we don't want to scare them, and we don't want to cause a panic. I think we have to find a way to seduce them with the positive. Portia said something interesting: Whatever the good is that people are looking for—we have to satisfy that need. If we can do that, she said, we can save the world. Whatever we do, though, it better be good."

"Or else we're toast?" she drops the spoon into her now empty bowl.

"I think so."

"First of all, we have to lose the sides." Her brow furrows with concentration, and she taps her fingers together like Oliver Hardy used to do. "If we can't get people to come together over something like this? Then forget it. It's all over."

"Funny, I thought for a minute that you were talking about my sides—my love handles."

She lets that sink in for a moment and then starts to laugh. And I mean really laugh. Wild abandonment–type laughing. It goes on for at least a minute. I'm glad to see her laughing again, but it really wasn't that funny. Then she stops and gets immediately serious again.

"Actually, toast sounds really good," she says.

I go to make her some toast.

———

When Jerry arrives, he has Kelly lie down on the bed and then sits down next to her. "I had a revelation on the way over here about how to do this," he says.

"Touch my tits and I'm going rip your lungs out, and your stand-up comedy days will finally be over."

"I'm going to touch you all over, actually," Jerry says.

"Okay, that's it!" She tries to sit up, and we both push her back down again.

"Let him do it," I tell her. "It's only Jerry. You've known him for thirty years."

"Yeah, but I've never been in bed with him before."

"Who knows, you might like it," Jerry suggests.

"Are you trying to cure me or traumatize me?"

"Ha, ha. That's hilarious. Now shut up for a minute because I have to concentrate." He closes his eyes and takes a deep breath, exhales, and then opens his eyes again. "Are you ready?" Jerry asks her.

"No," she tells him.

"Tough." He puts his hands on her forehead. "I'm sending you pure-white healing light—"

Kelly snorts judgmentally.

"Starting in your forehead…a bright and soothing light that's going to melt away anything that's bothering you. Starting here—"

"Don't touch them. Either one," Kelly warns.

"Shut up, Kelly, and just feel the goddamned light!" When he wants to, Jerry can be intimidating, and Kelly backs off a bit. He lays his hands on her again, this time with a little attitude. "I'm trying to work a miracle here, so cut me a little slack for Christ's sake," he mutters.

"Okay, okay. Go ahead and get it over with, then," she says.

Jerry takes another deep breath. "Everybody just try to relax and concentrate," he says. "It's kind of a group effort. Ready? Here we go. Everybody focus and believe. Close your eyes, Kelly."

She actually does, which I find promising and somewhat of a miracle in itself.

"The light is moving down your body. Relax and feel its energy and its warmth. Down to your neck. Down to your shoulders."

When he moves his hands down to her shoulders, Kelly opens one glaring evil eye.

"Hey…!" I firmly warn, as only the father of the revolution can.

She quickly closes the evil eye.

"Down to your arms and your chest, but I promise I won't touch your tits," he assures her.

"Better not," she says.

"But it's going there as well. Not my hands—but the energy."

He moves his hands up and down her arms and then onto her stomach. "Feel it…warm and comforting in there. Healing light."

I watch her face start to relax and show some color again. Jerry keeps his hands on her stomach for a few moments, and then he looks up at me with huge eyes and a shocked expression.

"I just felt it move," he whispers to me. "I can't believe it. Come over here and feel this, Mr. Geeg!"

As gently as I can, I reach over and feel her stomach. It's true. The baby is already moving. I'm in awe and slack-jawed.

Kelly's face seems to be glowing now.

Jerry continues, both of us with hands on her belly.

"And the light is going into your legs and your knees, and you are at peace in the white light, and all is well. Your ankles and your feet—relaxed and completely comfortable now. Bathed in healing white light, protected and safe from harm."

Kelly is asleep. I can tell by the baby rhino snores. We both back off and stand at the bedside watching her. Jerry and I have a special Mr. Geeg finger handshake that only Mr. Geegs would know. It's kind of an ET thing. Just the index fingers touch. I don't know how that got started, but we always do it, and we do it now.

"How'd you learn to do that?" I ask him.

"I don't know. I was looking at a bunch of stuff, and that's what stuck."

"Good job, Mr. Geeg."

"Thank you, Mr. Geeg."

We leave Kelly peacefully snoring away and go in and have some vegetable stir-fry. We make plans for the next day, and Jerry decides to spend the night again. Squeak comes in to say hello and jumps onto Jerry's lap. His allergy is definitely gone, no doubt about it.

Later, back in the bedroom, I do the flash drive thing on my forehead before I go to sleep. It's another vivid and disturbing experience: Kelly and I and Oscar Robinson are in a kind of tent. Me and Kelly on one cot and Oscar Robinson on the other. It has a prisoner-of-war-type feel about it. There's a light bulb hanging down from the center of the tent. Oscar is humming the tune that he always sings whenever I see him. We're all lying there pensively, waiting for something.

"Can you save me, boss?" Oscar Robinson asks me.

"I don't think I can, Lou. Not anymore."

"It's okay. Don't feel bad, *papito*."

"I want to sleep," Kelly says.

I get up from our cot and turn off the light. When I turn back toward them, Kelly is holding a baby in her arms that is wrapped in a blanket. I want to go to them, to see its face, but a siren goes off, and I can hear boots marching toward us, and then the light comes back on by itself.

"They're coming for me, *papito*."

"Do we die now?" Kelly asks.

The baby starts to cry. But it isn't like a baby's cry. It's like a woman mourning, like a keening. I go to the door and put my hands against it.

"Stop—just stop," I calmly command.

Kelly and Oscar Robinson are weeping. I try to block their cries from my awareness and stay with my hands on the door, concentrating on the marching boots. The light in the tent goes out again, and the marching noises stop. I go over to the window. It's pitch-black outside, but when I put my hands up on the glass, it becomes light outside. I can see beautiful snow-covered mountains. The troops that we heard marching toward us are now running away along the base of these large mountains. Then the tent begins to shake. Rocks and snow tumble down upon the retreating troops, and then a river of water rushes down and washes them all away.

I get back on the cot and turn toward Kelly.

"I killed them all," I say.

"I know, honey, now go to sleep."

What am I becoming?

CHAPTER THIRTY-NINE

THE END COMES SOMETIME:
DOES IT MATTER WHEN?

We get up early and gulp down some coffee. Kelly has cranberry juice and ice cream and is feeling much better than she did last night. Then the three of us drive out to Roosevelt Golf Course with questions for the One Who Starts Dresser Fires. Jerry sits in the back with the penguin and the cowgirl. Kelly rides shotgun. We hit bad rush hour traffic, and Los Feliz Boulevard is a parking lot, so it's taking forever to get there. Jerry is squirming around in the back seat like a restless school boy, and I'm about to ask him what his problem is, but he beats me to it.

"I don't want to freak anybody out, but I think we're being followed."

"What do you mean?" I ask.

"I mean there's a guy following us, Harold! He picked us up in Glendale, and he's been behind us ever since."

"He might just be going to work or going to play golf or something. A lot of people head this way from Glendale. It doesn't necessarily mean that he's following us."

"Believe me, he's following us."

"Maybe we know him. What's he look like?" Kelly asks.

"He looks like an angry old priest—do you know any of those?"

"How do you know he's a priest?" I ask him.

"Uh, because he's wearing a priest's collar?" Jerry satirically clarifies.

I try to turn on the radio—no dice. I take a right onto Hillhurst Avenue, and we head up into the park.

"Is he still behind us, Mr. Geeg?"

"No, he kept straight." Jerry takes another look behind and then slumps back into his seat.

"See, I told you."

"Okay, I thought he was following us, so shoot me."

I'm not sure why I was so unwilling to entertain the notion that we were being followed. I think it has to do with what's hard to face about the dream last night, the part when Oscar Robinson wanted to know if I could save him. In real life I could have—but I didn't—so I think he let me save him in the dream instead. "Don't feel bad, *papito*," he had said. But I do feel bad. I should have paid more attention that day he stretched out on my lawn. He asked if he could come into the house so that he could protect Kelly and me. But it was Oscar who needed protection. He knew he was in danger, and he was trying to tell me, but I was too self-absorbed, too blind to understand what he was really asking me for.

I have essentially no experience with this kind of violence. The prospect of having to deal with it, perhaps continuously, with a potential threat always lurking—it's a shock to the system, really. I'd rather push it away and ignore it, as in this case with the priest, just pretend it isn't happening. I've had my ridiculous Dirty Harry fantasies, but this is real and this is now. I can no longer pretend that bad things can't happen. I have to develop a new mind-set, and I'd better do it fast. Man, did I pick the wrong day to quit drinking.

Jerry notices that I'm uneasy and scanning the road for potential trouble.

"What are you looking for?" he asks.

"Nothing. I like this street, that's all. With these big trees. Eucalyptus, I think they are. I like the overhanging branches and the way they come together up there. It's like driving through a tunnel."

Jerry is unimpressed with my bullshit about eucalyptus trees.

"He might've taken Vermont into the park," he says. "It intersects Hillhurst just up ahead. He might've passed us just to throw us off track."

"He might have," I agree.

"See any big birds in those trees?"

"Not yet."

In the rearview mirror I see Jerry take the penguin and put it onto his lap. He looks like a scared little kid back there.

"Does he have a name?" Kelly asks.

"Who?"

"The alien."

"Oh, I never asked."

I pull into the golf course lot and park the car. There is a palpable weight in the air.

"Just keep your eyes open," I say. "If you see something suspicious—"

"Scream and run like hell?" Kelly guesses.

"Well, make some noise or something, and don't assume that it's probably nothing—"

"Because it's probably something," Jerry accurately concludes.

"Yeah, unfortunately it probably is," I say.

"What is this?" Jerry asks.

"What?"

He reaches across from the back seat and holds a giant pine cone in front of my face. "This."

"Oh, that? Take that with you. It's a priest detection device. It locates angry priests, and then you can hit them with it."

"Oh yeah," he says. "I think I saw one of these in the Sharper Image catalog."

"Let's do this already," Kelly urges.

We get out of the car and walk toward the coffee shop and the picnic tables under the corrugated metal overhang. The old Korean men are reading their newspapers—but no homeless woman.

"Where's the pine cone?" I ask feeling even more vulnerable than I did before.

"It's in the car," Jerry says.

"You didn't bring it?"

"You were serious?"

"Yeah, I was serious!"

"Oh. Well, I didn't know. It's so hard to tell with you."

"All right, don't worry about it. Let's go inside and see if anybody's seen her."

"I have to tell you. I'm getting a very weird feeling about this place," Kelly says.

One of the Korean men smiles at Kelly.

"Forget it. I'm pregnant," she tells him.

The Korean man quickly goes back to his paper.

———

My Armenian friend is inside pouring coffee for a foursome in the booth where I had sat the last time I was here. We wait at the entrance searching the room for trouble, like nervous cops on a drug bust waiting for a guy to come blasting out of the bedroom. That's a little much, but you get the idea.

"Hello, my friend!" she says loud enough to make the three of us jump.

"Hey, my friend!" I reply, trying to match her volume and enthusiasm.

I've known this woman for ten years but don't know her name. We just call each other friend. "Familiar but never vulgar." That's a line from a Polonius speech in *Hamlet*, when he's giving his son advice about how to deal with the world. I use lines from that speech all the time, and people consistently have no idea what I'm talking about.

"Table for three?" asks my friend.

"No, not this time," I tell her. "I just wanted to ask you something."

"Okay."

I make introductions first. Everybody exchanges hellos, but she still doesn't say her name. Maybe it's a name that's hard to pronounce if you don't speak Armenian, and she is sparing us the trouble and herself the annoyance of having to listen to us butcher it.

"We just wanted to know if you've seen that homeless woman who hangs around here," I ask.

"The crazy lady?"

"Yes, have you seen her?"

"Not for a few days now."

"Really?" my sense of dread intensifies.

"Maybe she found a new restaurant to bother," she says shrugging her shoulders.

"Yeah, maybe she did," I say.

"Go, sit. I'll get some menus."

"No, we're not staying," I tell her again.

"No?" she seems insulted by this.

"Next time," I promise. "It's a great breakfast here," I tell Kelly and Jerry, hoping to make her feel better about our not staying.

"Okay, next time," she says. "Always good to see you, my friend, and nice to meet your family, too."

"I'm just a friend. No relation."

"Oh, you look like brothers."

"We grew up in the same town," Jerry tells her. "Something in the water makes us all look this way."

She smiles, not quite getting the humor, then goes back to her waitress stuff.

We go back outside and stand under the overhang.

"Bummer," Kelly says.

"I hope nothing happened to her," I say, but I'm fairly certain that something has.

The Korean man is smiling at Kelly again. She gives him a smile back that reminds me of the smiles I saw when I did a show at the Napa State Hospital for the Criminally Insane. The Korean man quickly goes back to his newspaper.

"Let's get out of here," Jerry says. "Something is wrong. I'm getting a headache, and I never get headaches."

Just as we get to the Prius, I see the priest coming toward us. He's coming fast and is very determined.

"Get in the car!" I push Kelly toward the Prius.

"What are you doing?" Kelly protests.

"*Get in the car!*"

It takes only two tries to get the door to open, and then I pretty much throw Kelly inside, slamming the door shut after her.

"Lock it!"

I hear the car doors lock just as the priest attacks. He has an ancient-looking knife with a nasty curved serrated blade. It's a knife made for killing and nothing else. He doesn't say anything. He just starts swinging. I can hear Kelly screaming from inside the car. His first swing nicks my arm, not bad, but I can feel it starting to bleed under my sleeve. He takes a backswing to come at us again, and then Jerry and I both lunge at him. Jerry grabs the hand with the knife; I grab his other arm and pin it behind his back. After that, I'm at a complete loss about what to do next. Then I hear the birds scream. I look up. Two of them are streaking toward us like dive-bombers.

"No...stop!

"What do you mean stop!" Jerry cries.

The birds take my command and veer off.

"She has to die!" the priest yells.

Jerry knees the priest hard in the groin. He falls to the pavement and then miraculously, two park rangers pull up in their van, get out, and rush toward us. The priest is in agony and vomits at our feet. That makes us back off. He takes the opportunity to try another swing at us, but the rangers intercept, easily disarm him, and the knife clatters onto the pavement.

"What the hell happened here?" the first ranger demands.

"He attacked us," I say.

"Good timing," Jerry gasps. "You guys are the best park rangers ever!"

"They have to be stopped," the priest groans. "The woman is carrying a demon who will release torment on the earth like has never been seen before." Then he throws up again.

"Jesus Christ!" the other ranger cries.

"You're bleeding, did he cut you?" the first ranger asks.

"He got me a little. It's not bad."

The priest somehow breaks free and charges the car.

"Shit!" the second ranger yells.

The priest gets to the back seat window and tries to punch through. Kelly screams and recoils. We all jump on him this time, and I get kneed in the back by one of the rangers, which hurts more than the knife did. Jerry and I back off, and the rangers get the priest onto his stomach, cuffing his hands behind his back.

"They have to be stopped!" the priest roars.

"Let's get him in the van!" the first ranger orders as they start getting him to his feet. "We'll call LAPD, and they can take a report."

"They might want you to come down and file charges," the other ranger adds.

"I'm not filing charges."

"He tried to kill you, man!" Jerry cries.

"No charges!" I yell to the priest. "Do you hear that? No charges! We are not trying to do you any harm! We are not your enemy! You have been lied to. We're all on the same side, do you understand? We all want the same thing!"

In a very stressful moment, I have to say, I definitely take the high road. I'm momentarily impressed with myself, even though the priest is not. He continues to scream about evil, and the end of times, and I'm sure if given half a chance he'd take my peace offering and shove it right back down my throat. There is no reasoning with a madman.

The rangers drag the priest to their van, but he just won't let up, "The demons will rise up…" blah, blah, blah, and yadda, yadda, yadda.

I scream back, "We want to save the world, not destroy it!" Seriously, I just don't know when to quit.

The rangers get him in the van, and the priest shows no more resistance. He looks defeated now. I almost feel bad for him, which is ridiculous, I know, but I can't help it. After they get him secured, the first ranger comes back out to talk to us.

"The police will insist that you go to the hospital and get a doctor's report on that injury. It'll be important for the case."

"Okay," I say.

"Are you sure that arm is okay?" he asks.

"It's fine. Stings a little, that's all."

"What was that stuff about saving the world and all that?"

"I don't know," I lie. "He was talking crazy, and I was talking crazy, and the whole world is crazy, so…my wife is pregnant, and he thinks there's a conspiracy or something. No demons or devils, I promise!" I laugh nervously. "Probably just the heat, and that can make people a little prickly sometimes—Edith Prickley! Remember her from the old SCTV show? Man, it's hot out here, though, isn't it?"

If I were listening to myself in another person's shoes, I would definitely think that I was talking to a deranged individual. No doubt about it.

"Your wife is pregnant?" He leans down to take a peek at her in the car. "A little late in the game for you two, isn't it?"

"I guess it's a miracle. What can I tell you?"

"How did he know she was pregnant? Do you know this guy?"

"I never saw him before," I say growing weary of his questions.

"What's your name, sir?"

"Harold," I tell him, because I don't have the energy to play games anymore, and I'm actually starting to feel a little weak.

The ranger becomes very still with a puzzled look on his face. "Do I know you?" he asks.

"No, I don't think so."

"I'd swear I've met you before. I'll be in the van, make sure we don't have any more trouble with this guy. Just hang out for a minute until LAPD gets here." He studies me for a moment. "That's really strange. Do me a favor, call me if I can help you with anything."

He gives me his card, and I do appreciate the offer. Being an actor in LA, I feel compelled to give him one of my own cards. It's been a little slow lately, so I have thousands of them sitting in my desk, so any chance I get—I reach for my wallet, and then the knife wound starts to demand attention—a sharp pain from my shoulder all the way to my fingertips. I still manage to get him a card, though. He looks at it, then looks at me with that same puzzled expression. He's remembering. Something got triggered, he got the spark, but he can't quite place it yet. Or maybe he's considering what the priest was screaming about and whether or not they had just put the wrong guy in handcuffs.

"Are you sure you're okay? Do you want me to call an ambulance for you?"

"No, no. I'm fine, really."

He gives me one more questioning look and then moves away toward the van. I don't know if he saw the birds or if the birds didn't want to be seen, but they are both sitting up in the pine trees, in plain sight, right across from where we are standing. I look over and wave them away. They immediately take off and disappear into the sky. My arm is really burning. I walk back to the Prius and notice that we have drawn a crowd from the restaurant and the nearby putting green. I don't know how much they saw, but judging by their shocked expressions, they saw enough. My Armenian friend comes running over to me. She has a wet soapy towel.

"Here, put this on it. I put some medicine on there. Rub it in the wound."

Strangely, her voice sounds far away, even though she's standing right next to me.

"You nice very lady nice you." I recognize that my words came out in a strange order, but I have no idea how to correct myself. Then I start feeling lightheaded, and I'm seeing floaters in my eyes. Probably from all the excitement, I think. Then my legs start shaking, and I'm getting dizzy. "I have to down sit now for me," I manage.

"Come inside!" my friend says with great alarm.

"No, sit the car. I'm okay. Just need to down sit, I mean—"

"Let me get you something. What do you need?" I distantly hear.

"Orange…"

She rushes off. I stagger toward the Prius and manage to get myself inside, literally right before I collapse. I'm sweating like a pig, and the spots in my eyes are now big black blobs. I can barely see anything at all.

Jerry gets in the passenger seat. "You don't look good, Mr. Geeg," I think I hear him say.

"I feel very…I think just sit minute here."

Kelly says something—I'm not sure what, but I can recognize the panic in her voice.

"I'm…" now, it's getting hard to breathe. "Oh shit." Even my own voice sounds far away.

And then everything goes black.

CHAPTER FORTY

BIOLOGICAL PROCEDURES CANNOT BE EXPRESSED IN MATHEMATICAL FORMULAE

I see myself from above. I'm put on a stretcher and wheeled into the hospital, where I'm poked and prodded. Then I take off into a dream. Or I might be dead. I'm walking in long hallways that are filled with ghost shadows that crawl along the walls and slither on the floor. Some of them are grotesque and others I think might be kindly, but once they find me, they latch on and won't let go. I'm not sure if I'm one of them, or if I'm the person they've come to haunt. A bright flash transports me to another place. It's a ruin of crumbled buildings and wrecked landscapes as far as I can see. Another flash and I'm in a canoe on a peaceful lake, and the shadows are rushing toward me along the surface of the water. Another flash and I'm in a hospital bed, with tubes attached to my arms. Kelly is there crying at my bedside. Another flash and I'm a very old man walking in my neighborhood. I hold the hand of a young girl who is dressed in black. Part phantom and part human. She blinks in and out of existence, but her crying always remains. Another flash and I'm soaring through bright clouds, trying to escape it all, but there are hundreds of ghost shadows in pursuit. If this is death, then death is exhausting.

I wake up in a hospital bed. Sitting in chairs across from me are Jerry, Kelly, and Israel. "What time is it?" I ask.

"The prodigal son returns!" Jerry cries.

Kelly gets up and gives me a hug.

"It's 6 p.m.," Israel tells me.

"Israel, you made it!"

"I did. A little late, though, looks like."

"He called on your cell," Jerry says. "I picked it up and told him where we were, and then I made a few calls to Australia. I hope that's okay."

"I'm glad you're here, Israel."

"We'll make some plans to keep you safe, bro."

"So how are you feeling?" Kelly asks.

"Actually, I'm feeling really good. I probably slept better than I have in about ten years." I take Kelly's hand and kiss it. "How are you?"

"I'm okay, don't worry about me. Dr. Bloom is coming to see you again in a minute. I called her right after it happened, and she told me to make sure that you came here to Verdugo Hills so she could see you on her rounds. She's been on top of it ever since you got here."

Kelly and I both have Dr. Bloom on our HMO plan. We like her. She is thorough and never talks down to you. We both feel comfortable with her and think of her more as a friend than as our doctor.

"How long do I have to stay here?" I ask.

"She's coming in to talk about it," Kelly says. "You've been sleeping a lot."

"I was kind of in and out. Weird dreams. But I remember them doing tests, and I remember joking around with the nurses."

"Yes, I was told that you were so annoying that they're going to discharge you."

"I'm getting discharged before I even get a hospital meal? That doesn't seem fair."

"You got it, but you were asleep. So I ate it for you," Jerry explains with a wry smile. "Don't worry, you didn't miss much. Except for the pudding. I have to say, that was the best damn pudding I ever ate. Absolutely delicious."

"What flavor?"

"Vanilla fudge."

"I can't believe you ate my pudding."

"I feel terrible about it if that's any consolation."

"You saved my life today, Mr. Geeg."

"I did?"

"If you didn't do what you did to that priest—no telling what might have happened."

"Yes, when there is need for some serious groin kicking, I will not hesitate." Jerry smiles and shares a fist bump with Israel.

"So what happened in the car and on the way over here? I must've blacked out. I'm still alive, right?"

"It was a little iffy for a while, but you are alive," Kelly assures me.

"You threw up in the Prius," Jerry lets me know.

"I did? I don't remember that."

"I for one will never forget it," Kelly says.

"So who drove the car here?"

"I did." Jerry raises his hand as he answers the question. "I got hands on you for a couple of minutes, but Kelly wanted you to get to the hospital, and she was too nervous to drive. I'm not good enough to drive and cure at the same time yet."

"Did the car behave itself?"

"It got us here. Does the air conditioning usually go on by itself and randomly switch from hot to cold?"

"It does."

"Well, then, yes—the car behaved perfectly."

"So...what happened?"

"When you started to turn green and unresponsive," Kelly begins, "that's when I insisted we go to the hospital. Jerry went and told the rangers that something was wrong. They wanted to call an ambulance."

"But I told them not to bother, that I would take you," Jerry adds.

"They didn't like that idea very much," says Kelly.

"I told them it'd be faster. They got a little testy about it, but I didn't give them much time to argue. You really looked like shit, Mr. Geeg."

"Yes, I'm known for that."

"On the way back to the car, I picked up the priest's knife and took it with us to the hospital. Just had a feeling about it. Turns out that was about the smartest thing I could have done."

"When we got to emergency, they started doing tests right away," Kelly adds.

"The maniac priest put snake venom on the blade of his knife! Can you believe that?" Jerry cries.

"But they're really good about snake bites here," Kelly says. "Being in the foothills they see it all the time."

I'm impressed by how Kelly bounces off Jerry and vice versa. They're a good team, and it makes me happy just listening to them.

"So they gave you anti-venom, and because I picked up the knife, they knew exactly what they were dealing with."

"Do you remember the police coming by to talk with you?" Kelly asks.

"I remember, but I was still a little foggy, and I thought it might be a good idea not to say too much right then."

"Good idea," says Israel.

"They talked to us, too," Kelly tells me.

"They told us—you're not going to believe this, Mr. Geeg—that the priest is the head of a fundamentalist snake-handling church. I mean, seriously?"

"You wouldn't believe some of the shit going on in this town." Israel shakes his head disdainfully, and I wonder about what kind of shit he's talking about.

"He's being held at the Sunset Station Jail," Kelly says. "They're going to hold him there until he goes to trial. They wanted to know why he would come after us."

"So what did you tell them?"

"We played dumb," Jerry says.

"He's almost as good at it as you are."

"Israel met us here, and I filled him in on what's been happening," Jerry explains, and then they give each other another fist bump.

"I'm up to speed, bro," Israel tells me.

———

Dr. Bloom comes into the room in her street clothes. I've never seen her like that before. I'm used to the white lab coat that she always wears in the office. It strikes me as funny for some reason. If you saw her on the street, you'd never think she was a doctor. You'd think she was a sculptor or a pottery maker who lives alone with a lot of cats. She's about my age and not at all unattractive but keeping up with the latest fashions and having her hair done just isn't her thing. I like that about Dr. Bloom.

"What are you smiling about?" she asks me.

"Nothing, I'm just glad to see you."

She sits on the bed and pats my leg. I think she's glad to see me, too. She checks me over as we talk.

"One day you're going to have to tell me what's really going on here. Impossible pregnancies and recovering so quickly from a deadly snake bite—those kind of things keep me up at night."

I look over at Jerry, healer extraordinaire. He winks and smiles. I guess for even the short time he had hands on me, that must have been enough.

"We're still figuring it out ourselves," I tell her.

"It seems, whatever it is, it's not exactly a healthy lifestyle choice."

"No, so it seems," I agree.

She looks in my eyes and feels around my throat. "You're not feeling confused or disorientated."

"No more than usual."

"No shortness of breath or trouble breathing?"

"No, I feel pretty good. I'm hungry, but that's about it."

There's a stern look on her face as she checks my pulse.

"I'm putting you on antibiotics for ten days. And drink lots of water. As much as you can. Very important for you to stay hydrated now."

"How much water?"

"Eight to ten full glasses a day."

"That's a lot of water. I'll be going to the bathroom all the time."

"Yes, you probably will. Drink a lot during the day so you don't have to keep getting up at night."

"Good idea."

"That's why they pay me the big bucks. Do you want to go home?"

"Yes, please."

"Not that I'm particularly surprised at this point," she says, "but the amount of venom that got into your system from a snake like that? It should have killed you before you ever made it to the hospital. I really have no idea how you recovered so quickly, but there's no reason to keep you here any longer. Why don't you come into the office tomorrow, though, just to be safe? Why don't you both come in? We'll make it a party."

"We will," Kelly promises.

"Are you seeing the specialist, Kelly?"

"Yes, I'm going in on Friday."

"Good."

"But I'm really feeling much better now."

"Amazing," she says.

"Incredible," Jerry adds with a satisfied grin.

Dr. Bloom gets a puzzled look on her face. I can tell that something is happening to her. Like what happened to the ranger before. She's starting to remember something but then snaps herself out of it and turns her attention back to me. "If you start feeling weak or woozy, don't wait. Go to emergency right away."

"I will."

"I'll arrange for your release with the desk. Get dressed, and they'll send somebody in here with a wheelchair."

"I don't need a wheelchair."

"I know, but that's how they do it. Don't give them a hard time about it or they'll inject you with something."

"What will they inject me with? Might be worth it."

"See you tomorrow, and don't be a wise ass."

She pats my leg again and leaves the room.

"Where are my clothes?" I ask.

"You threw up on the stuff you had on, so I brought some clothes from home," Kelly tells me.

She goes to the little dresser by the bed and takes some stuff out of the drawer for me. She brought a lot of stuff.

"Did you think I was moving in?"

"Well, I didn't know how long you were going to be here, and you know I always over pack."

"So now I have to make a fashion decision on top of everything else?"

"Poor baby," she says and then kisses my cheek.

"Well, let me get dressed then." Nobody moves. "Can I have a minute?"

"I've seen him naked before, and it's nothing I want to see again," Jerry says, already on his way out the door.

"I concur," Kelly quips, and she and Israel follow him out.

I start getting dressed and have a sudden uneasy feeling about Israel. He seemed preoccupied and distracted while we were talking. I'm sure he's just concerned about what he's getting into. Or maybe his trip down here is motivated by something else entirely. Hopefully I'm not about to let the fox into the henhouse.

I get dressed and really feel like nothing ever happened to me today. Ten minutes later we are gathered back in the room when an orderly comes in. The guy is either at the end of his shift or taking heavy doses of some kind of muscle relaxant. He has the wheelchair and discharge papers for me to sign.

"We can wheel him out," Jerry tells him.

The orderly mumbles something and then shuffles out of the room. I'm thinking quaaludes.

Then we hear some shouting from down the hall.

"Wait here," Israel orders. He leaves the room, I assume, to make sure things are safe out there.

"You're sure about this guy?" Kelly asks.

"Pretty sure," I say, but I'm really not sure about anything anymore.

Israel comes back looking bothered. "It's something in a room down the hall. Nothing to do with us."

"What is it?" I ask him.

"It's a kid screaming and crying, but it's not a kid."

"Harold!" a pained young voice calls out.

"My creep-out meter just jumped off the scale," Jerry says.

"What do you want to do?" Kelly asks me as if I might actually know.

"What floor are we on?"

"The tenth."

"Let's jump anyway."

"I've never seen anything like this before," Israel says.

"Like what?" Jerry asks with increasing anxiety.

"It's like a little kid in an old person's body. This kid has the face of an eighty-year-old man."

"Harold!" the child's voice calls out again.

"God, I hate hospitals," Jerry moans.

———

Israel pushes me in the wheelchair as we make our way down the hallway. There's a commotion by the room at the end of the corridor. A woman is crying in the hallway, while the child screams from inside the room.

"Harold!"

The woman, the kid's mother I assume, walks toward us. She looks worn out, as if she hasn't slept in a month.

"Are you Harold?"

"I am."

"He wants to see you."

"Okay."

I get out of the wheelchair. Israel puts a hand on my shoulder, encouraging me to sit back down.

"It's okay," I tell him. "I can handle being on my feet. You can wheel me out later if you want."

And then the four of us go into his room. The door shuts behind us, seemingly of its own accord.

None of us can speak. We heard a child's voice, but we're looking at a tiny, frail old man. The sight of this takes a moment to process.

"Can you save me, Harold?" he asks.

"What's your name?" I finally manage.

"Joshua."

"Hi, Joshua."

"Hi, Harold. Are you going to help me?" He struggles for a moment with a pain that seems to take his breath away. "The man said that you would."

"Did he? Okay, I will if I can."

"That's good. Do you have a cat? He told me about him."

"Yes, his name is Squeak. We call him Squeak, because he's a cat that squeaks like a mouse."

"That's funny." Joshua giggles, reminding us that he's just a kid.

"He's a pretty funny cat."

"Maybe I could meet him someday."

"Of course you can," I say. "I think he would like you."

"No, he won't. People are afraid of me. He'd be afraid of me, too."

"He wouldn't, Joshua. He'd be your friend."

"He would? Because I'd be his friend, too."

"Joshua, this is Jerry and Israel and my wife, Kelly."

"Hi," Joshua says.

"We're glad to know you, Joshua," Kelly tells him.

"I don't hurt anymore. Not since you came in," he bravely tells us.

Kelly takes my hand and takes a deep breath.

"I know that you all have something important to do now," he says. "But thank you for coming to see me. I really feel much better now."

Then Joshua's chin falls forward onto his chest and the next voice we hear doesn't belong to Joshua anymore.

"Hellooo, Harold!" the alien cheerfully begins.

"You gotta be kidding me!" Jerry's eyeballs are about ready to pop out onto the floor.

"It's good to see you all together. Do you have questions for me?"

"Can you help this kid?" I ask him.

"Jerry can help him."

"Me? How can I help him? I'm good, but I'm not that good."

"Give him your hand, and your heart will take care of the rest," says the alien. "There are things you can do now. Demonstrate your powers and show the world what good the future may hold."

"Who are you? Where are you from?" Kelly asks him.

"If he says New Jersey, I'm jumping out the window. I don't care how high up we are." Jerry takes a seat, changes his mind, and stands up again.

"I come from a place across the galaxy. We were once like you are now. Only better looking and much smarter at science and math." The alien laughs a high, breathy kind of laugh that is extremely unpleasant to listen to.

"Are we going to make it?" I ask. "Are we doing this right, so far?"

"The more you can be who you really are, the more successful you will become."

"Excuse me, I don't mean to be rude, but what the hell does that mean, exactly? Give it to me straight. Some jerk just tried to kill me to get at my wife. It's getting pretty serious around here, in case you haven't noticed."

"Okay, what I mean is, Harold, your true nature is to be kind and loving. Let that guide you and it will serve you well. Trust your intuition. It will get you where you need to be."

"What is your name?" Kelly asks him.

"Call me Sid. It'll be easier."

"Am I going to survive this pregnancy, Sid?"

The lights in the room flicker and then there is nothing.

"Sid? Are you there?" Kelly is understandably alarmed by the disconnection. "I'm not going to survive, am I? Is that what you're afraid to tell me?"

The lights flicker again, and Sid is back. "Whoa, sorry about that. A little interference."

"Sweet Jesus on a shingle! So am I going to survive this pregnancy or what?"

"Yes, yes. Of course."

"How long will it take?"

"Six months."

"But will we make it for six months? Will we survive that long?" Kelly probes.

"We're counting on it."

"But do you know?" she continues.

"I can't see that. I don't know, but I'm confident that you will," Sid says.

"That's not exactly what I was hoping to hear," she tells him.

"Sorry. We'll know more soon. When I know, you'll know."

"Well, do you have any tips?" Kelly asks. "Any special things I should eat or vitamins I should take? Things to avoid?"

Sid goes into his spot-on Mel Brooks impression again. "Stay away from too much vitamin C, but take all the B complex you can, and zinc, and protein. Lots of protein, and starting next month, no more hockey or tackle football." He laughs again, and the sound of it makes me cringe. "Seriously, though, folks—cranberry juice and ice cream for breakfast is very good for you and the baby right now."

"Really?" Kelly seems pleased by this.

"Are you nuts? Sugar is a killer. Everybody knows that!"

"Oh, okay…what about probiotics?"

"What do I look like, a doctor?" he bellows. Nobody laughs, if that's what he was expecting. "Sorry," Sid says back in his normal voice. "I was just trying to lighten it up a little—jeez Louise, is this an audience or an oil painting? Is it getting hot in here? No respect, I tell ya'. No respect at all."

It's the best Rodney Dangerfield I've ever heard. I am so glad that other people are in the room to witness this strangeness, because no one would ever believe it. Then Kelly gets back to business.

"What will the baby be?"

"A girl," he says.

"I know that, but *what* will she be?"

"Oh. She will become a benevolent warrior."

"A warrior?" Again, Kelly is not thrilled by what she hears.

"She will take what you have secured for her. She will lead with wisdom, with kindness, and with great strength of purpose. She will never hesitate to act and she will never have doubts about the right thing to do. She will be the bridge between two worlds."

"Well, it's not from my side of the family," I throw in.

"But if you can't see it yet, how do you know that's how it turns out for her?" Kelly asks.

"That is the hope. That is the plan."

"Are you trying to spare us some very bad news? Or do you really just not know?" I have to ask.

"I know what will happen if nothing is done. I know that there is still hope."

"Can't you space jump to find out?" I suggest.

"What's space jump again?" Jerry whispers in my ear.

"When you transport yourself to different places or different times. You can do that, can't you, Sid?"

"There are events that still need to transpire before we can clearly see what the future may hold. Besides, you will be able to do that for yourself in short time."

"If there is time—" I know he knows more than he's telling us.

"Yes...parsley, sage, rosemary, and thyme."

Weird. Anyway, Sid won't budge, so I move on to something else.

"What happened to Oscar Robinson?"

"They got into his head, and he couldn't take what they were telling him."

"Who got in his head?"

"Voices from the other side."

"And they killed him?"

"In a sense. He killed himself to protect you. They were trying to turn him against you."

"Jesus! And what about the other one, the woman?" I ask.

"The other one is gone, too," he sadly confirms.

"They're murdering them? Can't you do anything to stop it?"

"We're trying."

"Try harder!"

"We will, I'm sorry."

"What if they try that with us? What do we do?" I ask.

"Push them out. You can do it now. You are much stronger than you realize."

"Yeah, but what about us?" Jerry cries.

"Don't fear them, that's the key. You can push them out, you all can. They are not established here yet. They are like spirits. If you are resolute, they cannot overwhelm you."

"But what if they do overwhelm us?" Jerry demands.

"That must not happen."

"But what if it does?"

"Then you must remove yourself from the situation."

"You mean." Jerry gulps. "Literally?"

"Yes."

"Like Oscar Robinson did?" I ask.

"Yes."

"Oh my God," Jerry groans.

"But always keep a sense of humor. Did I mention that? It's very important." Then Sid sings a little for us. "Always look on the bright side of life...la da, la da dee da, dee da."

Again, Sid stuns us with the absurd.

"So, what's next?" I ask, though I'm not sure I can take much more.

"Save this boy, and it will help save you. He will become an example and an inspiration for your people. We'll talk soon. Follow your intuition. I've got to run. I'm sooo late."

"What did you mean about being spirits and not being established here yet?"

He doesn't answer.

"Sid?"

He's gone. His energy, or whatever he is, has left the room.

Joshua comes back. He raises his head and smiles at us. "Is he gone?" he asks.

"I think so, Joshua," I tell him.

"Did he give you what you wanted? Did he say what I should do?"

We all look at Jerry, and with very little hesitation, he steps up to the plate. "He wants you to get better, Joshua." Whatever panic Jerry had felt before is gone. He is focused and ready to perform. "He wants me to help you do that, okay?"

"Okay," Joshua readily agrees.

Jerry goes to Joshua's bedside and takes his hand. He doesn't say anything about warming lights. He closes his eyes and concentrates. Joshua leans back onto the bed, and then he literally starts to glow. He smiles and peacefully falls asleep. We watch as the color comes back into his cheeks, and he actually starts to look younger.

Jerry, for as long as I have known him, has had a great capacity to open his heart to anybody in trouble. He is a generous man, and contrary to an occasionally gruff exterior, he has a heart of gold. It's what's so appealing about his comedy, I think. The alien chose well. Jerry is meant to heal.

We leave the room. Joshua's mother and their doctor are waiting for us.

"Who are you people?" the doctor asks.

"I'm Harold and this is—"

"No, I mean *who* are you?"

"Nobody, we just want to help," Jerry tells him.

"What happened in there?" the doctor asks. "We couldn't get in. I was about to call security."

"I tried to do something for him, that's all," Jerry tells him. "We never touched the door. Did anybody touch the door?"

"Nobody touched the door," Israel confirms.

"It doesn't matter anyway," Jerry says to the doctor. "Because the important thing is that Joshua is going to get better now."

"That's not possible, and it's cruel!" the doctor admonishes. "Joshua has progeria, and he will not get better. You are giving this poor woman false hope, and that is wrong and it's irresponsible."

"Well, doctor," I say. "Hope is not the worst thing that could happen to this kid. And it's a distinct and completely irresponsible possibility that Joshua is going to feel a whole lot better now."

"That is impossible," the doctor insists.

"Yes, it is," Jerry agrees. "But impossible ain't what it used to be."

The doctor pushes past us with a disgusted look on his face.

I have heard of progeria. It's a rapid aging disease. I saw a kid with it when my father was in the hospital many years ago. Kids who have it usually don't live to see their thirteenth birthday. After suffering through all manner of physical and emotional traumas, the child usually dies of heart failure. If there is a God—what the hell was he thinking?

"I guess people just see what they want to see," Jerry says.

"Will you let us know how he's doing?" I ask Joshua's mother.

"Yes, of course."

"What's your name?"

"Jane."

"Here, Jane." I give her a card. I've given out more of them today than in the last fifteen years. "He wants to come over to meet my cat. So give me a call when he's feeling up to it."

Jane hugs me and then goes over and hugs Jerry as well. She hangs on to him for a moment and then whispers a heartfelt thank you into his ear. She seems to know that Jerry is the healer and that he may have just saved her son's life.

"Come on, we should go," Jerry says trying to keep his emotions in check.

"Will I see you all again?" Jane asks."

"Oh yes, you haven't seen the last of us," I say. "We'll be seeing each other quite often, I do believe."

"Thank you," she says again and then goes into Joshua's room.

"Kind of makes it all worth it, doesn't it?" Jerry says.

That gets me going again. I've been curiously emotional since this whole thing began.

"Come on, let's go home." I start down the hallway, but then Israel speaks up.

"Hey, boss!" he points to the wheelchair. "Get in. I'll give you a ride."

"Oh, yeah." I get in the chair.

"Think I might be staying around for a while, brother. If that's what you want me to do."

"Absolutely," I say, but my intuition is screaming at me to beware.

CHAPTER FORTY-ONE

CONVICTION IS A GOOD MAINSPRING...

When we get to the house, Squeak is sitting by the front door and greets us with an annoyed series of high-pitched squeaks. He is not pleased about the lack of attention of late. He considers Israel suspiciously and then hisses at him. After that, he regards him with indifference. I take this as a positive sign only because I'm desperate for positive signs. I give him a Temptations chicken treat (Squeak, not Israel), and then he goes to his favorite chair to chill out. I'm sure it will be a comfort to those I try to sway over to my way of thinking that I make my decisions based upon the reactions of a cat. I've used turtles in the past, but they are slow to make up their minds and tend to waffle.

I make some iced tea and bring out some cheese and crackers and some cold El Pollo Loco chicken. I'm starving. We chow down for a bit, and then Israel starts asking questions.

"How long have you been here?" he asks while scoping things out.

"Almost twenty years," I tell him.

"Nice place." He gives a nod of approval.

"Thank you. We like it," Kelly says.

"You have an alarm system?"

"Yes," I say.

"Are there sensors on all the windows and doors?"

"No, not all of them. Just the ones in the back and the ones hidden from the street."

When I had it installed, I thought that would be all I'd need. The vibe I'm getting from Israel is telling me something else.

"No bars on anything?"

"No, no bars."

I get the feeling Israel is going to try and sell me something in a minute.

"Have you seen anybody watching the house?"

"I have," Kelly tells him.

"So people are finding out about you. Do you have a gun?"

"No," I answer. "Do you?"

"I do."

"Do you think I should get one?"

"I think you should," he says with a hard look.

"Lord…" Kelly groans.

"Judging by the fact that you just got out of the hospital because somebody attacked you, and people are watching the house—yeah, I think you should have some protection."

"I have a metal bat."

"You need a gun."

"How do I do that?"

"I'll get you some."

"Some?" Kelly cries.

"Yeah, I think so," Israel confirms.

Out of habit, I go to the liquor cabinet and take out a bottle of bourbon.

"Anybody?" I offer.

Nobody bites. I look at the bottle. On another day, when life was simpler, I would fortify my tea without hesitation.

"Do you think that's a good idea? With the antibiotic and almost dying a few hours ago?" Kelly asks in the way she does when she wants me to feel really stupid.

"I'm thinking about it," I say as I continue to stare at the bottle.

"Okayyy." She stretches out the word the way she does when she wants me to feel really guilty for being really stupid.

I've been hiding behind this stuff for long enough. And frankly, I'm sick of it. I'm not running away from a promise I made to myself. I'm not running away period. The voice in my head is dead wrong about me. I put the bottle away, and I feel good about doing it. I sit back down at the table. Kelly and Jerry seem stunned. I guess I've developed quite a reputation over the years.

"Do you have other people? Are there places you could move around to?" Israel asks.

"What do you mean?"

"I mean, it may not be wise to stay in one place for too long."

"Really?"

"Really."

"He's right," Jerry agrees. "Oh, and before I forget, here's your phone. You better charge it. It went dead right after Israel called."

"Oh, yeah, I better do that."

I take the phone from Jerry and go into the kitchen.

After the phone is plugged in to charge, I check for messages. There are two. The first one is from Rodger. He says that Diane is out of jail, and they will be heading down to Los Angeles, regardless of what the court decides. He asks me to call him when I get a chance. He says that he and Diane are getting along really well and that they are both eager to be getting out of town. The other call is from Portia. I listen to it twice.

"Hi, Harold. I got tipped off about an intervention from a friend in Utah. I think it's happening tonight. I'm going to rehearsal because I hope I might be safer there. If you can't reach me, or you don't hear from me, you know what happened. My family's address in Salt Lake is 527 Eighth Street West. The church address is 78 E. Temple. He's obsessed, Harold. I've never seen him like this."

I call her back right away and get her voice mail. If she's in rehearsal, it's understandable that she wouldn't pick up. Or something already went down. I call the stage manager next.

"Ira," I cry. "I can't believe I actually got you!"

"Harold, how's it going, man?"

"Ira, listen, is everything okay over there? Did anything weird happen with Portia tonight?"

"No. Unless you mean her father showing up in the middle of rehearsal and taking her outside to talk, and then she never comes back."

"Shit!"

"Does this have to do with you, Harold?"

"I'll talk to you later, Ira. Thanks."

I disconnect the call and go back into the dining room.

"We have a problem."

CHAPTER FORTY-TWO

...BUT A BAD JUDGE

"We have to drive," Israel tells us.

"That's a long drive," I reply.

Kelly is already checking distances on her tablet.

"It's ten hours," she says.

"Why do we have to drive?" Jerry challenges.

"Because if we fly, I can't bring a gun," Israel says.

"You're bringing a gun?" I ask just to be sure I heard him right.

"It may get ugly. I don't want to use a gun, brother, but it is what it is."

"Okay," Jerry begins. "I have to ask because somebody really should..." He takes a hit on an imaginary cigar, exhales, flicks imaginary ash, and then continues. "We have a lot to do and very little time to do it. And to take a road trip at this point...can we afford to do that? And if it turns ugly with yelling and shooting and getting overheated, are we sure that's such a great idea at this point?"

They all look to me for something convincing. I give it my best shot.

"Portia is meant to be a part of this. She needs to be here with us and away from her father, who's definitely getting messages from the other side. The aliens gave her skills just like they did us. She's part of the team, and you never leave a soldier behind."

It occurs to me that the colonel told me the same thing about the Prius back in Napa, when I abandoned the car by the coffee shop. I'm stealing lines from a psychotic voice that lives in my head, but he stole it from someone else, no doubt, so whatever works. I trudge on.

"I just think it's a good precedent for us to set. That we take care of our own. It says a lot about the type of people we are. If we're trying to get the word out about our good intentions, and we want people to listen to what we have to say, then we should definitely rescue Portia. And plus, she's a midwife. And plus, she can fling objects with her mind."

After a brief moment there are nods of agreement.

Whew.

"So are we all going?" Kelly asks.

"No, too complicated. We're going to have to move fast," Israel says.

"So who's going then?" I ask.

"You and me," Israel says without hesitation.

"But that leaves me and Kelly here by ourselves. Is everybody okay with that?" Jerry, I think, is hoping for more options.

"I will bring some people in," Israel tells us.

"Who?" Kelly starts rubbing at her temples again.

"People who will protect you. Have you ever used a gun, Jerry?"

"No, I'm strictly a kick-'em-in-the-balls kind o' guy."

"I'll leave a gun here and show you how to use it."

Kelly abruptly takes her tablet and leaves the room.

Israel looks after her for a moment before continuing. "We should count on two days going and two days coming back. We find out where they're holding her and then get in and get out fast."

"You're sure about this?" Jerry asks me.

"It's got to be done. I'm sure about it," I say.

"It might be a trap, Mr. Geeg."

"Oh, it's definitely a trap." Israel confirms.

"It is?" I guess I didn't get the memo.

"They know that you'll come for her. They'll be expecting us."

"Oy vey," I say.

"We'll be all right, bro." Israel gives me a reassuring punch on the arm. "Been in way tougher spots than this before, so don't sweat it too much. No big deal."

"So you two go rescue the girl, and me and Kelly hold down the fort. I'm not worried, seriously." Jerry leans back in his chair, looking nothing but worried. "Kelly and me, we're a great team. Any disturbances that occur will be immediately neutralized by Kelly's quick wit, and my disarmingly handsome bone structure. And if that doesn't work, we'll start blasting. What can go wrong?" Jerry tries to laugh, but it comes out as a hysterical-sounding snort instead.

"Rodger will be down, probably before we get back," I say, hoping to build up his confidence. "As soon as he calls, I'll let you know."

"Who's Rodger again? I know you told me, but I've been under a lot of stress lately."

"He's the lawyer. And he's pretty tough, too."

Israel puts a hand on Jerry's shoulder. "Can you cut hair?"

"Can I what now?"

"I don't want to go like this. I should look a little more Mormon."

"There's a good pair of scissors in the top drawer of the desk in the living room," I say.

"I'll try it, no promises, though. You might turn out looking more like a skin head than a Mormon," Jerry warns.

———

I go in to see Kelly, who's lying down in the bedroom. I get onto the bed. We hold each other and talk quietly.

"I think I quit drinking."

"Really?"

"When I get back, I'll call the Midnight Mission and donate all the booze."

"What if Israel is not really here to protect us?" Kelly asks.

"I think he is. If I'm reading the cat right."

"You're going to be on the road alone with him in the middle of nowhere, and he's bringing strangers into the house. Is that smart?"

"Probably not."

"What if you're wrong?"

I have no idea how to answer her question.

———

Later, there's a knock on the door. Israel lets in two of his associates. One of them is huge, 6'4" at least, and all muscle. The other one is my height, about 5'8", but he is also huge in a different way: very broad shoulders and no neck. He looks like a muscular square. They both have that long-haired renegade look—like Israel had before Jerry got at him. They each carry a large duffel bag.

270

"What happened to your hair, homes?" the tall one asks.

"It got cut. I'm trying to look more conservative," Israel tells them.

"You look like a cancer patient or something," the other one says.

Jerry steps in from the other room, ominously clicking his scissors like the demon barber of Fleet Street. "Who's next?" he says with a wicked grin.

The tall one smiles. The other one doesn't.

———

We sit around the dining room table and get acquainted. The tall one is Jose, the short one is Javier. Kelly comes in to meet them, and they are courteous and respectful, but it seems a little forced to me.

"For how long will you need us here?" Javier asks.

"Not sure exactly," Israel tells them. "Depends on how long it takes. Maybe four days. Maybe more."

"What's in the bags?" I ask.

"Clothes and food and some things like that," Javier says.

"And some protection," Jose adds with a hint of a smile.

"What kind of protection?" I press.

They both look at Israel.

"Guns?" Kelly nervously guesses.

"Yes," Israel answers. "Let's get away from this window, and I'll show you."

"Israel, are we going to be charged for this protection?" I feel compelled to ask before the weapons' parade begins. "Should we talk a little about how much all this security is going to cost?"

"There is no charge for this, brother. This is a duty. This is a righteous obligation. We are here because we believe in your mission, and we believe that we are supposed to be a part of it. I dreamed of this. This is my penance. My redemption."

"What do you need redemption from, Israel?"

"Well, I'll tell you, brother. I used to be down here in LA. We actually started the security company when some other business interests went badly for us—imports and exports and overseas commodities. We were dealing with some unsavory-type individuals, and the business was becoming increasingly...volatile. So we got out. Unfortunately things have a way of catching up with you. We were doing really good with the security company, when some unpleasantness from the past started showing up."

"Very nasty business," Jose adds.

"It got a little rough, and some people got hurt," Javier says with a grin, which I find extremely disturbing.

"That's why I was up north. My compadres here kept things going, and thanks to them, we still have the business."

"We do celebrities," Javier says.

"You do celebrities? What do you do to them?"

Kelly, I'm fairly certain, is thinking that they shoot the celebrities, and then mount their heads in a basement somewhere.

"He means that we protect them. We don't *do* them. We work for them," Israel clarifies.

"Oh," Kelly says, somewhat relieved.

The way that Jose and Javier are looking at Kelly has me approaching freak-out mode. They have half smiles on their faces. Like shit-eating grins; two school boys with a nasty secret. Something is wrong here.

"I'm not a perfect person, but I'm trying to be a better one," Israel confesses. "As soon as I saw you, I knew that this was my calling. This is more important to me than money. Do you know what I'm saying?"

"I do," I tell him. "What about you guys?"

"What about us?" Javier asks.

"Are you okay with this?"

"What's with those birds?" Jose throws in. "Can you talk to them before you leave? Let them know that we're okay?"

"If you're okay, they will know."

"We're okay, but just tell them anyways. I don't like birds."

"You don't have to worry about them," I promise.

"Okay, homes, we're cool, then. I haven't seen nobody in my dreams or nothin' like that, but we're down. You don't have to worry about us."

Jose is either a very bad actor, or he just doesn't give a shit what we think. The look of resentment on his face is easy to read. But it's more than that. He seems disgusted by us. He smiles at me again, and if there is such a thing as an ugly smile, that was it. I feel quite certain at this point that Jose and Javier are definitely not here to protect us.

"Come on, let's look at this stuff." Israel grabs one of the duffel bags, and we follow him into the living room.

Jerry, Kelly, and I sit on the couch. Jose and Javier flank Israel, who kneels by a duffel bag on the floor. Javier walks over and pulls the living room curtains closed. Kelly, I already know, is very suspicious of them. Jerry just seems excited about seeing some guns. I have to stop this. I have to get them out, but I have no idea how. A million thoughts go flinging around in my head, but the only thing that sticks is the image of the three of us shot dead on the living room floor. Israel has deceived me. He's just better at it then his partners are.

"Let me show you what we've got," Israel says. Javier comes back and joins his associates.

We are sitting ducks in my own living room, waiting patiently to be executed. I flash on how angry I would get as a kid when I heard stories about the Nazis exterminating the Jews. Why didn't they fight back? How could they just let that happen? Why were they so defenseless? I feel that same anger rising in me now. Then Squeak comes into the room. He sits down next to the couch, stares at our guests, and starts to howl. One long sustained yell unlike anything I've ever heard come out of him before. Squeak stops everything.

"What the fuck is his problem?" Jose sneers.

"He doesn't like you," I bluntly tell him.

"I don't like him either. I hate fucking cats," he says.

Squeak leaves and goes toward the bedroom, but he never stops yelling. It is a continuous howling protest. A terrific performance, brilliantly unnerving and heartfelt.

Then there's a thump on the roof.

"What the fuck is that?" Javier cries.

"They're here," Kelly says with a great sense of relief.

Then there is another thump, and another one after that. I never thought I would see fear in these guys, but I was seeing it now, and I had to take advantage.

"Don't open that bag, Israel. This is not going to work out."

"We're here to protect you," Israel protests.

"Really? I don't think so. And no way am I leaving my wife alone with your crew here, either."

"They work for me," Israel says.

"But who do you work for, Israel?"

"I come all the way down here when you call, and you still don't trust me?"

"I want you all to leave right now. Take your shit and get out."

"Little harsh there, homes. Might want to turn that down a notch," Jose suggests.

And then the house starts to shake.

"Earthquake?" Javier croaks.

"No, Harold's doing it," Jerry says with absolute surety. "You better get out. I've seen him do this before. He'll bring the whole place down on you. Get out now before he starts flinging knives and shit, and the birds crash through the window and peck your eyeballs out."

"And it sounds like there're three of them. Isn't that nice? One for each of you," Kelly adds with her own version of an ugly smile.

"Fuck this, let's get out of here." Jose is seriously spooked. "Are they going to attack us when we go out there?"

"Only if you try to hurt us," I say. "If you do, they'll rip your heads off."

"You're reading this wrong, bro," Israel says while remaining unnaturally calm.

"Come on, let's get out of here!" Jose has had quite enough. He grabs a duffel bag and heads for the door. Javier follows him. The shaking is intensifying, and stuff is starting to fall off the walls and the bookcases.

"If those birds attack, I'm coming back in, and I'm going to kill you all," Javier threatens.

A book flies across the room. Javier ducks just in time.

"If they attack, you'll have a hard time aiming because you won't have a head," Jerry tells him.

"You may think you're doing the right thing, but you're not. You don't understand what's really going on here," Israel says.

"Okay, Israel, last warning. Now get out!"

Israel reluctantly goes to the door, and then the three of them run out to their cars. We get up from the couch and rush to the dining room window. The birds circle low above them, snapping at them with claw and beak until they are in their cars and driving away.

"Can you stop shaking the house now, please?" Kelly asks with a distracted politeness that I find particularly unnerving.

I'm not sure if I can stop the shaking, but after a moment things do start to settle down. We all watch as the birds circle above the house in lazy but deliberate circles.

"Good birds," Jerry says. "Very good boys."

"Anybody want to go to Utah?" I ask.

CHAPTER FORTY-THREE

ALL SEEMING ACCORD
CLOAKS A LURKING ABYSS

The dining room table has become strategic headquarters. After doing some calculations, we decide to stick to the plan and drive to Utah. To get a flight for three and a flight back for four would cost a fortune. The Prius will be very good on gas and hopefully won't cause us too much trouble. We can split the driving and all get a little sleep on the way. Plus, Kelly could overpack without being charged extra for it. The downside, of course, is who might follow us.

It's about seven hundred miles to Salt Lake City. About ten hours of driving time. We'll take the 210 to the I-15 all the way through the desert and then into Utah. I try calling Portia again but can't get through. I think about leaving a voice mail but decide against it—just don't know who might be listening. The plan is to get there as quickly as possible, scope out the scene, find out who's holding her and where, and then execute a quick rescue. Just like Israel had said. That's the best we can do before we have more information. Hopefully, some of my newfound abilities will compensate for the lack of firearms.

After all that gets settled, Kelly checks for restaurants along the route, Jerry eats pound cake while reading up on Mormons, and I make some calls.

First, I try our neighbor Ellen who we have a mutual cat-watching relationship with, and fortunately she's available to come over and help us out. Squeak doesn't care much for Ellen. She tries to play with him, but he doesn't seem interested in having much to do with her. His aloofness is probably a result of how much he hates it when we go away. Squeak has some kind of extrasensory kitty perception. He knows we're leaving about a week before we do. He'll start moping around the house, complaining, and strategically puking up hairballs so we either sit on or step in one. Maybe that's what he was doing earlier when he started howling in the living room. Same thing when we have to take him to the vet, except he does his complaining from under the bed. So Cate Blanchett could be coming over to feed him, and he'd ignore her, too. I don't mention any of the drama to Ellen and hope to God that nothing weird goes down, so she won't have to deal with anything more disturbing than cat puke.

I call Rodger next but miss him again. I do leave a message, though. I let him know that we have to hit the road for a few days to rescue Portia. I tell him that if they are heading down before we get back, they're welcome to stay at the house, and I let him know where we hide the extra house key. Also, I say that I'll leave a note on the kitchen counter with the security alarm code written down so he can deal with the house alarm before it goes off.

"Mr. Geeg! You just left security information on his cell phone, dude! You should never do that!"

Of course he's right. Jesus! I'm telling you, I still think they got the wrong guy for this job.

"You better call Ellen back and let her know that lawyer is coming down," Kelly says, only momentarily looking up from her tablet.

So I call Ellen back to let her know about Rodger, and as soon as I hang up with her, my jazz riff ringtone starts to swing.

It's Jane, Joshua's mother. I put her on speaker.

"I don't know how to say this—it's like I'm in a dream," she says.

"What happened, Jane?" I ask.

"All his symptoms are vanishing. He's starting to look like a little boy, and I'm taking him home tomorrow! I thought he was going to die tonight, and now I'm taking him home!"

"That's wonderful, Jane!" Kelly cries.

"It's a miracle, isn't it?"

"We're not sure what it is yet," Jerry says.

"He wants to know if he can come see your cat."

"Of course he can," I assure her. "Except we have to go away for a few days. We're leaving tonight. Can I call you when we get back?"

"Yes, yes, please do. And thank you. Thank you so much."

She hangs up, and we all sit with it for a moment.

"We are definitely doing the right thing," Jerry says and then blows his nose into a napkin.

I check outside for potential trouble. Satisfied that the coast is clear, we grab our stuff and hit the road.

CHAPTER FORTY-FOUR

EVERY MAN HAS HIS OWN COSMOLOGY AND WHO CAN SAY THAT HIS OWN THEORY IS RIGHT

Kelly looks bigger than she did fifteen minutes ago. She assures me that she feels great and insists on doing the driving. I'm in front and Jerry is in the back. We cruise along the 134 to the 210, watching hillsides go by that look mysterious and unfamiliar in the evening shadows. Then Kelly's stomach starts making noise. It's sort of a growl and a wheeze at the same time with some clicks thrown in.

"Wow that was a good one!" Kelly declares.

"Are you okay?" I ask.

"I'm great. Feel like a million bucks!"

We come around a bend in the freeway and head into Pasadena. I'm glad we decided to leave at night. There's hardly any traffic, and hopefully we'll be harder to spot on the road—if somebody should be trying to find us.

The Prius bucks and the cabin lights dim and then brighten again.

"Did you feel that?" Kelly cries. "Did the car just lurch, or was that me?"

"That's the car. It does that," I say.

"How long has it been doing that? You should get that checked out, Harold."

"I will," I promise.

Rather than going into the whole saga about my continuing frustration with the Toyota service department and its refusal to believe that the Prius enjoys a good lurch from time to time, I just leave it at that.

"I have a question," Jerry says.

"Yes, Mr. Geeg?"

"Do you think Israel is going to come after us?"

"I think he probably will."

"Do you think the birds are following us?" he continues.

"I hope so."

"What if she's not even in Utah?" Kelly wants to know. "They could have taken her anywhere."

"I know she's in Utah," I say.

"How do you know?" Jerry asks.

"Because I do. Same reason I can shake houses and talk to people in their dreams."

"But that's not really the same thing, Mr. Geeg."

"Close enough."

My head is starting to pound.

"Well, maybe when we find out where she's being held, you can shake the house, and they'll run out, and we can just grab her and take off," Jerry suggests.

"Or," Kelly adds, "we can pretend to deliver a pizza or flowers or—wait a minute! How's this? We pretend to be the gas company and say that there's a leak. Yeah, I like that!" Kelly pounds on the wheel, getting curiously pumped up about her imaginary scenario. "When they run outside, we run in, and bam! We grab her!"

"But it'd be easier just to give them a mental suggestion, right Mr. Geeg? Just tell them to turn her over to us. You can do that, right?"

"No, no," Kelly protests. "The gas company one! That's a sure thing! We'll have to get the uniforms. But we can steal those from a supply place. I think that's the way to go, I really do."

A needle-sharp pain starts jabbing at me right behind my left eyeball.

"Ow."

"What?" Kelly asks.

"Nothing, I just had a weird pain," I tell her.

"Where?"

"Behind my eye. It's okay."

"Are you sure? Do you want me to fix it for you?" Jerry offers.

"No, thanks. It's nothing."

"I have to call Dr. Bloom tomorrow," Kelly says. "And I have to cancel that appointment on Friday, too. Remind me, okay?"

"Okay."

"Bloom is going to ask me what's going on. What should I tell her?"

"I need to sleep now. Do you mind?"

"No, go ahead," Kelly says. "I can drive all night."

"Before you leave us, Mr. Geeg, may I address the elephant in the room for a moment?"

"I resemble that remark!" Kelly quips à la Groucho Marx. "I shot an elephant in my pajamas once. How he got in my pajamas, I'll never know!"

And then she starts to laugh. A hard, loud laugh that goes on for an uncomfortably long amount of time. It's hard to tell if she's laughing because she loves the Groucho joke, or if she's just losing her mind.

Jerry lets her calm down a bit before continuing.

"Do you think these things we can do will go to our heads? And we'll start making bad decisions because of it? I mean, don't get me wrong. I love this healing thing, and watching you get inside people's heads and shake up houses…nothing I'd rather do. But I guess the elephant I'm talking about—"

Kelly giggles.

"Knowing myself as I do, and my tendencies toward being addictive and self-indulgent—which I know you can relate to, being somewhat addictive yourself—is it possible that these powers are going to ultimately do us more harm than good?"

"You mean by making us into gods?"

"Well, by making us into monsters is probably what I'm getting at here."

"If we fail, we fail!" Kelly dramatically proclaims from out of nowhere. "Lady Macbeth, am I correct?" Kelly looks at me, the Shakespeare expert, for verification.

"Yes, Lady Macbeth, you are correct."

"Bingo!"

She raises her hand looking for a high five. After a slight hesitation, I oblige her. Then she starts to whistle and drum on the steering wheel.

Not a care in a very frightful world. Kelly's personality definitely seems to be going through some alterations. I know that women can have mood swings when they're pregnant, but this is way over the top and more than a little disconcerting.

"Are you sure you're feeling okay?" I ask her.

"Stop asking me that! I feel great!"

She tries to turn on the radio. Nothing but static.

"Fucking piece of shit radio!"

I've never heard her talk that way in my life.

"I mean, these things we can do," Jerry says, getting back to his elephant in the room. "How do you not let that get to you? I just hope we can handle it. We need to check each other on that so we don't start blowing things up just for the fun of it. That's all I'm saying."

I put my head back and close my eyes. In spite of the increasing pain in my head, I fall asleep almost instantly.

CHAPTER FORTY-FIVE

BODY AND SOUL ARE NOT TWO DIFFERENT THINGS, BUT ONLY TWO DIFFERENT WAYS OF PERCEIVING THE SAME THING

I'm not sure how long I slept. But the thing that's happened before, happens again. I'm watching myself from above. I see Jerry looking quite concerned as he tries to wake me but can't. He tries moving my arm that my face is resting against. When he does, my head falls against the window, but I stay asleep. Then I feel myself going into a dream— exit stage right:

I'm in Linda's house, the writer from the *UFO Journal*. She stands behind her desk, and I stand opposite her. Her house is shaking and starts to fall apart. The whole place is falling down around us. Huge beams tumble down from above, but there seems to be some kind of shield around us, protecting us from harm. The walls come down, and there's nothing left standing. She takes my hand and leads me out. The tangle of bougainvillea vines part for us, and we make our way clear of the house, not into the streets of Burbank, but into a beautiful meadow, where Portia and Kelly are waiting for us. Then the three of them walk with me to a door that stands alone in the field suspended about a foot off the ground. They back away as I open the door and go through. Israel sits in a chair next to a bed, a gun in his lap.

"Am I dreaming?" he asks.

"Yes," I tell him. "I need you, Israel."

"I know. I'm trying," he says.

"Good, I'm glad," I say.

"You only have one leg, brother."

"I'm trying."

Then I float up and evaporate into the ceiling.

I'm returning to the Prius again and back into my body when I see us get cut off by a red Jeep. Kelly swerves to avoid a crash, and we skid off into the desert. That snaps me all the way back, and now I'm fully awake.

My eyes focus through the front window. I see the Jeep make a crazy U-turn and pull up right in front of us. When the dust settles, I can see that Israel is behind the wheel and pointing a gun at me. He jumps out and comes toward us, keeping his gun aimed at my face.

"Shit, what do we do?" Jerry cries.

"Get out! All of you!" Israel orders.

"It'll be okay," I lie.

We get out of the car and stand shoulder to shoulder in the desert. Israel stands in front of us with his gun still aimed at my head.

"Israel," I begin. "This is not a good idea."

"Harold, be quiet. I have to tell you something about what's really going on here, and I need you to listen very carefully. Can you do that?"

"Yes."

"No birds, no earthquakes. No nothing till I'm done, okay?"

"Okay." I'm feeling agreeable.

"I'm going to tell you what's really going on here, and it's not going to be easy for you, but you have to hear this." Israel lowers the gun. "Everything, all of this, is not what you think it is. She's not real, he's not real…not in the way you think they are. And I am a messenger from your other self. I somehow have joined with your consciousness, and I need to deliver a message to you before it's too late for you to get back."

"Get back? Get back where, exactly?"

He raises his gun at me again.

"Don't talk. Just listen," he commands.

"Sorry."

"Your wife is not pregnant. She's sitting with you right now crying in a hospital room, where you've been for the last forty-eight hours."

"What the fuck, Israel?" Jerry says as he steps forward. "What am I if I'm not me? What the hell are you talking about, man?"

Israel points his gun at him. "Shut up."

"Oh, right, okay." Jerry steps back and rejoins the lineup.

"You are Harold's interpretation of you," Israel continues. "His idealized interpretation. The way he'd like things to be and not what they really are. Here he has power. Here he is wise and caring, and he's willing to sacrifice for a worthy cause. Here he can be the person that he always wanted to be."

"He's insane," Kelly whispers and then grabs my hand in a vicelike grip.

"The truth is I'm trying to save you, Harold. If you stay here, you will die. The reason your wife is pregnant here is because you had a daughter. You and the other Kelly. She was a sweet, beautiful, talented girl who was also a manic depressive. She was twenty-four years old, and three days ago she killed herself. The shock of it wrecked you. It was too much, and then you tried to kill yourself as well. You went into the garage, closed the garage door, got into your car, and ran the engine. A neighbor got suspicious and called the police, and they got you out of there. You're in a coma, lying in a hospital room. Everything going on here, with this pregnancy and God and the aliens and all these young women that you're trying to save—it's all about you trying to make some kind of peace with yourself. But you have to go back, Harold. There are people who need you. Your wife needs you, bro. She's won't make it without you. Do you understand?"

"I don't know anything about this, Israel. I'm sorry, I really don't."

"Of course you don't! That's why you're here, because you don't want to see it. But it's the truth, and the only way for you to get back is for me to kill you."

"You know how crazy you sound, don't you, Israel?"

"I know."

A bird-monster shrieks from above us.

"But I tell you what, bro. After this bird kills me and I come back again, maybe then you'll start to remember. I'm the good guy here, Harold, and you need to go home. There's shit to do, brother."

The bird-monster rips Israel's head off. The three of us watch for a while, remarkably unfazed by the horror of what just happened. Then we get back in the car and continue driving to Utah.

CHAPTER FORTY-SIX

I NEVER THINK OF THE FUTURE—
IT COMES SOON ENOUGH

Whatever Israel's motivation might have been, and why he didn't just shoot me when he had the chance, I really have no idea. The result of the encounter, however, is an odd sense of disconnection—from myself and everything around me. I'm doing the driving at this point in kind of a trance. Israel successfully got me doubting myself again. His story was madness, it had to be. But this whole thing is madness and who can say where the truth lies. Reality is what you choose to believe, isn't it?

Kelly sits next to me, staring out of the passenger-side window. Jerry taps me on the shoulder from the back seat and then leans in between us.

"For the record," he says. "I'm definitely real and not some figment of your imagination. I yam what I yam." And then he laughs like Popeye the Sailor.

"You're not actually considering what he said, are you?" Kelly admonishes with a kind of shocked indignation.

"No, of course not," I answer defensively.

Jerry jumps back in and tries to heal the situation. "Nobody is considering anything here, so everybody just relax." He puts hands on us both.

Kelly brushes him off her shoulder as if she's swatting away a fly.

"Okay, fine, be that way. But, just to clear the air, and for the record, I am quite confident that I do exist, that we are riding in this car, and all this weird shit that's going on is, in fact, going on." He picks a piece of lint off my shoulder and flops back into his seat.

"And if this ain't pregnant, I don't know what the hell is," Kelly adds. "And if we had a child before, I'm sure I would have known something about that, wouldn't I?" She grabs my face and kisses me hard on the mouth. The car swerves over the yellow line, and we narrowly avoid a collision with a truck coming from the other direction.

"I don't know what you're thinking—but cut it out! You're not alone here, you know? So let's not overthink this thing, okay?"

"Okay," I gasp. "But what if Israel shows up again after we just saw his head get ripped off? What should we think about that?" I have to ask.

"No more talking now! Quiet!" She goes back to staring out the window. Her reply is so cold, so unlike her, that it sends a shiver through me. I look at Jerry in the rearview mirror. He has the penguin in his lap, and he's picking at its eyes. I'm not sure what he's trying to do, but it consumes his full attention.

We drive in silence again. As much as I hate to admit it, the two people that I care most about in this world suddenly seem like complete strangers to me. I look up and notice that the sky is red. Of course it is. Why the hell not.

My cell phone rings. I let it go. I'm not in the mood.

"Please answer that before I go insane," Kelly suggests.

"Do I have to?"

The look on her face compels me to answer the call.

"Hello?"

"Call me when you get back," says a female voice.

"Who is this?"

"It's Linda Broomfield from the *UFO Journal*."

"Oh, hi," I say with absurd casualness.

"I have information for you. Things I couldn't tell you before, because you wouldn't understand, not until you went through this first. I've been getting messages, too, Harold."

Then she hangs up. It was on the Bluetooth speaker, so everybody heard the conversation. It's probably because we're tired and over-loaded, but nobody chooses to say anything after that.

We just drive on, into whatever. Death doesn't seem like such a big deal anymore.

CHAPTER FORTY- SEVEN

THE DISTINCTION BETWEEN PAST, PRESENT AND FUTURE IS ONLY A STUBBORNLY PERSISTENT ILLUSION

I'm beginning to seriously consider that Israel was telling the truth.

I look over at Kelly and Jerry. They're both fast asleep, as if they've been unplugged. The sky is doing an aurora borealis kind of thing (in the desert, mind you), and then my phone rings again. Kelly's stomach rumbles and groans like a garbage truck trying to get up a steep hill, but neither she nor Jerry stirs from their sleep.

"Hello?"

"Harold!"

"Yes?"

"It's me, Rodger!"

"Oh, hi, Rodger," I say with tired enthusiasm.

"Where are you?"

"I'm driving to Utah."

"I'm with Diane. We're headed your way."

"You are?"

"Are you hanging in there?"

"Oh yeah, I'm pretty good."

"We're coming to help you. To save Portia."

"Okay."

"If you see a rest stop or a restaurant, stop there and call me. We'll hook up, and we can make some plans."

"Great."

Diane shouts a cheerful "Hey, daddy-o!"

"Hi, Diane." I try to sound glad to hear her, but it's hard to get up the energy.

"Can't wait to see you!" she gushes. "Everything is going to work out now, so don't worry. Okay?"

"Okay."

"I don't think we're far behind you," Rodger says. "Can't wait to catch up on all that's happened."

"Me too," I say while wondering how what he's telling me could possibly be true.

"Call me!"

"I will."

"Are you sure you're okay?"

"Peachy," as Kelly likes to say.

"Good. Talk to you soon, compadre!"

"Hey, what color is the sky where you are?" I ask.

"Blue, not a cloud. Why?"

"Nothing."

"Okay, see you soon."

I disconnect the call, and Kelly begins to stir.

"Who was that?" she asks in a semiconscious tone of voice.

"Nobody," I say.

"Good."

She instantly goes back to sleep and snores like a baby rhino.

CHAPTER FORTY-EIGHT

ALL MEN DANCE TO THE TUNE
OF AN INVISIBLE PIPER

I see a sign for a Denny's not long after I get off the phone with Rodger. The area we are in is still desolate. Nothing but desert and highway for as far as the eye can see, but the Denny's parking lot is full. People must be coming from miles around. I park the car, and Kelly and Jerry spring back to life at exactly the same time, as if an internal alarm clock had gone off in their heads.

The three of us enter Denny's and stand by the cashier's station waiting to be seated, just as the sign tells us to do, but no one comes to assist us. Not far from where we're standing is the Denny's counter with its eight cushioned stools that face the kitchen. One customer sits at the counter. A very old man eating soup. Maybe he is sick or mentally deficient in some way, but watching this old man eat his soup might be the most disgusting thing that I've ever seen. I would rather see a bird-monster rip somebody's head off then have to watch this old man eat his soup. A string of snot comes from his nose and drips into his bowl. He does not seem to notice this. He simply stirs his soup, slowly mixing his snot into the bowl, and then very carefully brings the trembling spoon to his eager mouth and slurps the stuff down.

Watching this is a horrifying yet mesmerizing experience. A waitress busies herself behind the counter, ignoring both us and the grotesque scene playing out at her station.

"I'm not really hungry anymore," I say.

"Come on, we have to eat!" Kelly leads the way, boldly ignoring the Please Wait to Be Seated sign, and marches off to find an open booth.

Jerry and I follow like ducklings. I guess being pregnant with the child that will become humankind's salvation gives one a certain gravitas.

"Some soup would hit the spot, wouldn't it?" Jerry says as we work our way into the booth.

So we sit and wait for a server to come, but it's like we're invisible. I wave at the counter waitress, but she continues to ignore us. I look around for somebody else to call to our table and notice that all the customers, mostly young women, are on their cell phones except for the snot eater at the counter.

I call Rodger and let him know where we are.

"What's the deal here?" Jerry complains loud enough to attract some attention. "Does anybody work here or what?"

Kelly scoots herself out of the booth. "I'll get some menus," she says with considerable annoyance and a deep stomach growl.

"Rodger, we're in a Denny's."

"I just saw the sign," he tells me, "we'll be right there."

How he got behind us so fast, and how he knew our route, I have no idea. But I'm not in an asking questions kind of mood. Especially questions with answers that won't make any sense.

Kelly flops some menus down on our table and gets back into the booth just as a crazed young man with long dirty hair, wearing a Led Zeppelin T-shirt enters the restaurant carrying a gun.

"Everybody freeze!" commands the man in an oddly high and squeaky voice. Actually, he sounds a lot like Mickey Mouse, and despite the seriousness of the situation, Jerry looks like he's about to laugh.

The gunman points his weapon at the counter waitress and shouts, "Open the register!"

The waitress faints, and the old man continues eating his soup.

"Jesus Christ!" Mickey squeaks.

I'm not sure if he's referring to the passed-out waitress or the old man, but either way he is becoming increasingly agitated. He tries to open the register but can't.

"Fuck! Fuck! Fuck!" Mickey squeals.

If there are other employees at this Denny's, they must have been hiding, or they ran out the back. It is just us customers and this crazy gunman with the mousy voice. He comes into our area next, recklessly waving his gun around. Nobody even bothers to put down their phones. They just kind of freeze—as if someone pushed a button and put them on "pause." I'm not sure if it's his voice or all the other stuff that's been going on, but it's just hard for me to take this guy seriously. I, for one, am much more disturbed by the old man than the gunman.

"Give me your wallets!" he squeaks and then whips out a pillowcase with racing cars on it—making his dangerous-gunman credibility even more suspect. He continues squeaking at us as he walks through the dining room collecting valuables in his pillowcase. "I'm not fucking around here! Don't try anything, or I'll kill everybody in the place!"

There is a little lisp when he says *place*. Sort of a cross between Mickey Mouse and Mike Tyson. By this point, the three of us are just trying not to laugh. Then he's at our table looking flustered and nervous.

"Give me your money!" he says in his highest, squeakiest voice yet.

Kelly snorts, and Jerry tries unsuccessfully to hold back a laugh. I just look at him and smile.

"What the fuck is so fucking funny?" he screeches. "I don't think you want to fuck with me, motherfuckers!" The way he says *motherfuckers* is really classic. Like a Disney character gone to the dark side. All eyes are on our table, waiting for something bad to happen.

"Stop it," I calmly tell him. "Just stop."

"What did you say?" He points his gun at my eye, but I just don't care anymore.

"Put the gun down on the table. Leave the bag. Then turn around and go home."

He looks pitifully confused, and begins to tremble, and then his eyes fill with tears. Whatever it was that I pushed him toward, it completely overwhelms him. He struggles against it for just a moment, and then he goes completely blank. He puts the gun down on our table and drops the pillowcase full of loot onto the floor. He turns around and leaves the restaurant.

"Nice job, honey!" Kelly says, kissing me on the cheek.

I push the gun over to Jerry. "Hide that. We'll take it to go."

"Oh, man." he handles the gun like a hot potato and struggles unsuccessfully to fit it into the waistband of his pants. "So what am I, the muscle for this outfit now?"

"Just put it where nobody can see it," I tell him.

"Easy for you to say!" He isn't having much luck getting the gun to fit anywhere.

"Give it to me before you shoot something off," Kelly tells him.

They make the switch under the table, and then Kelly puts the gun into her purse.

I was expecting some kind of reaction from the Denny's crowd. Some applause or a slap on the back or maybe some better service at least. There was none of that. I put the pillowcase on the table next to us and people gradually begin to drift over to retrieve their stuff. They seem unable or unwilling to express any gratitude. A few of them smile, but that's about it.

Employees begin to pop up from back in the kitchen area to see if the coast is clear, and then things continue as before. Everyone retreating back into their own private cell phone bubbles.

I get out of the booth to check on the passed-out waitress. She's just coming around, and I help her back to her feet. Another waitress makes an appearance and gives her a glass of water, then sits her down at the counter next to the snot eater, who doesn't seem to realize that anything out of the ordinary had just occurred.

"Anything you guys want, it's on the house," the second waitress tells me.

"Thank you."

"You're a goddamn hero. It's the least we can do."

"I appreciate that."

"Anything except the rib eye steak. Everything else is okay. The soup is split pea today."

The old man lets out a tremendous belch and then goes back to slurping.

"I'll pass on the soup," I tell her.

I walk back to our table and get back into the booth.

"How about that, a free lunch!" I tell them.

"If you don't starve to death first," Jerry mutters.

"And a whole room full of young damsels," I say. "Like the whole place was put here just for me to save them."

"Interesting," Kelly says as she looks around.

Rodger and Diane storm in, and some damsels gasp, anticipating yet another confrontation.

"It's okay, they're with us!" I announce to the room.

We scoot over so that Rodger and Diane can join us.

"I can't believe that we're actually here!" Diane cries. "This is all so crazy!" And then she gives me a furious hug.

"We're getting married!" Rodger happily informs us.

"Who's getting married?" I'm a little thrown by this.

"Me and Diane."

"I thought you were gay?"

"I am. Well, I'm both. I'm a people person. When it's right, it's right, and love is love."

He kisses Diane in a way that lets us know that he's not fooling around. Love has transformed Rodger and Diane, and I have no idea who they are anymore.

I make introductions at the table. Diane is intent on hugging everyone and not afraid to climb over the table to do so.

"I just want you to know," Diane says to Kelly, "I'm going to do everything I can to help you, whatever you need. I'm here for you. For always. No matter what!"

"Great." Kelly's stomach growls as if to comment on Diane's offer.

"So you're the lawyer, right?" Jerry asks Rodger.

"Yes, or I was one up till a few days ago. Now I'm working exclusively for you guys."

"Kind of like a mob lawyer," Jerry says.

"Yeah, I guess so. Kind of like that." Rodger seems fine with the idea.

"We don't have insurance or benefits or even salaries, but if things work out, you can have Africa," Jerry generously offers.

"I have Africa," Kelly deadpans.

"How about Paraguay?" Jerry counters.

"Deal!" Rodger laughs and seems delighted by the offer.

"Everything is moving so fast," Diane exclaims. "It feels so unreal, doesn't it?"

And then as if on cue, the front door flies open and a stream of people dressed in vaudevillian costumes enter the dining area. The men are wearing baggy suits, and the women are in burlesque outfits. They have instruments and all manner of props and gags with them.

An attractive woman in a skimpy sparkling outfit steps forward to make the introductions.

"Ladies and Gentlemen! We are the Comedy Commandos! Indulge us a moment, if you would be so kind. Get off your phones and leave the world behind!" She bows and takes a few steps back.

Jerry grabs my arm. "That was the name of our first act! The Comedy Commandos, remember? We did that vaudeville show at the Attic Theatre downtown! What the hell?"

A large woman in opera-type armor with a horned helmet steps forward and strikes a dramatic pose. I'm expecting something grand from her, but what we get instead is a Tiny Tim–like version of "Tiptoe Through the Tulips," accompanied by a little person comic in baggy pants playing a ukulele. The performance is oddly charming. Like a Fellini movie.

The big woman takes a bow and then steps back as two more baggy-pants comics come forward. They do a soft-shoe dance and they speak in unison:

"We got all the jokes, and we dance like the wind."

Two more little people come in front of the dancing comics and place a bucket on the dining room floor. Then, also in unison, they joyfully announce:

"And if you like what we do, please put something in!"

If this isn't already strange enough, what happens next is really just too much. Either this is the best damn Denny's in the universe, or somebody else is controlling our reality at the moment. The dining room and the light from outside go dark. A spotlight suddenly illuminates two more baggy-pants comics walking in place but with such skill that you'd really think they were walking down the street. The effect is enhanced by what seems to be a set, or a projection, that suddenly appears behind them. It's a moving cityscape perfectly synchronized with the comics' movements. After letting this marvel sink in for a moment, they go into their routine:

"I have a $500 bill here, and it belongs to you if you can answer one question," the first comic says.

"Okay," says the other.

"What's the last thing your wife says to you before you go to sleep?"

"That ain't hard."

"You win!"

A rim shot from somewhere punctuates the joke, and then the first comic starts another bit.

"Hey, I didn't get a chance to congratulate you on your new baby."

"I'm not too happy with the kid."

"Why, what's the matter?"

"He has red hair."

"What's the matter with red hair?"

"Nothing, except I don't have red hair. My wife doesn't have red hair. No one on either side of our family has ever had red hair."

"May I ask you a personal question?"

"Sure."

"How often do you make love to your wife?"

"Oh, once every six months."

"That's it then!"

"What?"

"Rust!"

Another rim shot, and then the spotlight goes out.

Someone behind us starts to applaud but abruptly stops when no one else joins in. The rest of us are just too stunned by what we had just seen.

The spotlight comes back up again, and the set has changed. It's a traditional vaudeville stage. Standing in front of a red curtain is truly the most beautiful woman I have ever seen. She seems to be naked except for the large feather fans that she covers herself with. She moves the feathers around, teasing and seducing us. When she speaks, it's a breathy Marilyn Monroe–type voice:

"I know you want to touch me,

You never get enough.

So take this can of powder,

And, baby, do your stuff."

A can of powder suddenly appears and hovers in the air in front of her.

"Here is my suggestion,

And I know you won't be rough.

So slap me, hit me, beat me

With my pretty powder puff."

With an elegant flick of her wrist, her feather fans instantly turn into giant powder puffs.

"Let me feel you do it gently,

Caress me, don't attack.

I love it when you touch me

As you powder down my back."

She turns her back to us, and she is naked. The spotlight goes out in time to just give us a taste.

We applaud and the spotlight comes back on again.

The song "Let's Misbehave" starts to play, and an amazing Busby Berkeley–type dance number begins. It defies imagination. It seems as if the dozen or so performers that had first entered Denny's have now multiplied into the hundreds. Different city scenes—bars, hotel rooms, street corners—all become the playground for this sexy, whirling, frenetic dance number. One moment tops the next with lavish costumes and dancers of the very highest caliber. "Let's Misbehave" seamlessly morphs into "42nd Street." The intensity and pace builds and builds until I feel almost breathless in its presence. Suddenly, all the players shift their focus to us, their audience. It's like looking down a busy street in NYC, and everyone on that street suddenly turns from whatever they were doing to focus on you. The walls of Denny's seem to have vanished, and we have somehow been transported into this other world. Then they all strike a pose for the big finish. They sing the final line of the song in a soaring, powerful harmony—"on Forteee-Secconnnd Streeeet." The force of it literally pushes me back into my seat. They hold the last note for an impossibly long time. When you think it will start to wind down, it just keeps building in power and volume. And then, walking down the center of the boulevard, two figures start moving toward us. The man has a short, uneven haircut, and they are both in modern clothes, so they really stand out from the rest. I can't make out the man's face, but I'm sure that it's Israel. He is holding a young woman's hand. She's looking right at me as if she is here just for me. When she smiles, I think my heart will burst. If that is Israel, then—

The spotlight goes out and everything is instantly silent.

There is a moment of pitch-black, and then the Denny's lights and the light from outside blink back on. The Comedy Commandos are gone. The only thing left is the tip bucket, where the two little people had left it.

No one moves or says anything.

The old man at the counter starts to clap. "Holy cow! Holy cow what a show!" he says with the energy of a much younger man. He begins to spin on his stool. Faster and faster, around and around, and then he shoots straight up. He flies through the air and makes a perfect landing right behind the Comedy Commando's tip bucket. It's an impossible feat for a world-class athlete, let alone a feeble, snot-eating old man.

"Aren't they something, folks? Come on, let's hear it for 'em!"

The old man leads his stunned audience in a round of applause. Once he gets us going, he begins to rigorously rub his nose as if he's trying to hold back a sneeze. I'm expecting another stream of snot to appear at any moment. He starts pulling on it, and the nose stretches out like Pinocchio's nose. Then his face begins to distort. He pulls and pulls, and then his whole face comes off. It's an amazingly realistic old-man mask, and underneath it is a handsome young man with the warmest smile I've ever seen.

"Give what you can my friends. It's good for the soul."

He walks through the room with the bucket. Everyone else is dumbstruck, but I can't stop crying.

The handsome young man makes his rounds, stopping at our table last.

"It's okay," he says to me. "You're almost home now, Harold. Almost home."

After he collects our donations, we watch him walk through the door and then vanish into the desert.

"Are you okay?" Kelly asks me.

"Did you see that girl?"

"Which one?"

"Never mind. Doesn't matter. I'm fine now."

"I'm not!" Jerry shouts. "I mean, what the hell!"

"Aliens," Rodger says with absolute certainty.

"You think they were aliens?" I ask.

"They're all aliens," Diane says.

We look around the place, and everyone is staring at us and whispering into their cell phones.

"Let's get the hell out of here," Jerry suggests.

And that's what we do.

CHAPTER FORTY-NINE

WHAT A PECULIAR WAY THIS IS
TO WEATHER THE STORMS OF LIFE

We step outside and find that the landscape has completely changed. Across the road where once there was only desert, now there is a neighborhood—a block of middle-class homes with lawns, flowers, and wind chimes.

"I do believe," I say, "that this is the end."

"The end of what?" Jerry cries.

We hear a familiar screech. Four bird-monsters circle above us like vultures waiting for something to die.

"Holy shit." Jerry marvels at the sight of them.

"This can't be real," Kelly decides, grabbing my hand in another vicelike grip.

"What are we supposed to do?" Rodger asks in a panic.

The front door of the house directly across the way swings open, and Portia attempts an escape.

"Help me, Harold! Thank God you've come!"

Three men rush after her. They grab her and start dragging her back inside.

"No, let me go!" Portia screams.

Another man comes out of the house and yells at us from the porch.

"Get the hell away from here, do you understand? You have no rights here. I will not allow my daughter to be corrupted by your kind of evil. Now get the hell out! I won't warn you again!"

"What do we do?" Diane cries.

I pull my hand away from Kelly's and start walking toward the house.

"What are you doing?" she screams.

"This time I'm going to be there when she needs me."

"What are you talking about, Harold?"

"Our daughter, Kelly! I'm talking about our daughter!"

"Stop!" somebody commands from the house.

I don't stop. I will not be stopped. Windows fly open in the house and shots are fired. Bullets explode in the dirt all around my feet, but I keep going. I hear sirens approaching and more people yelling for me to stop. TV news vans suddenly arrive, and cameramen jockey around to get the best angles of the live action.

The house starts to shake. A man crashes through the window as if he'd been shot out of a cannon. In an instant, a bird-monster is on him, ripping him to shreds. More shots are fired, and people are screaming. Bullets are flying all around me, but none can touch me. More men flee from the house, rushing past me as I move relentlessly forward.

"This is the police," someone announces through a bullhorn. "Stop or we'll shoot."

"No! No more shooting! Stop it. Just stop!" I respond.

A bird-monster goes after a fleeing man, but I'll have none of that either. "No more—stop!" The bird-monsters all fly off into a blood-red sky.

When I get to the front porch, Portia's father is there to meet me. He points his gun at me.

"I warned you. Please, I am not a bad man."

"I know you're not. Just stop. Sit down and be calm. It's over now."

He drops his gun and sits in a rocking chair on the porch.

"Thank you," I say, but he will not, or cannot, respond.

I go inside. Portia and Israel are sitting on the couch together. Portia smiles at me. Israel has a gun in his lap. The house shakes violently, and stuff is crashing all around us.

"You get it, now?" Israel asks me.

"Yes, I think so," I answer.

"Daddy, it's going to be all right now," Portia says.

"It is," Israel says. "It's going to be like waking up from a bad dream. But I have to kill you first."

"Okay," I say.

Pennies begin to fall from out of nowhere like a gentle rain. Portia is smiling, but there are tears running down her face.

"I'll miss you," she says. "And thank you for saving me."

Israel gets up and points his gun at my eye.

"Just an instant," he says. "Just a flash, and then you can go home."

"I want to go home, Israel."

"I know. Then let's go home now."

A shot is fired from behind me, and Israel falls to the floor. It's Kelly. I didn't hear her come in, but she's shot Israel right between the eyes. I turn to her in utter disbelief.

"Why did you do that?"

"Because, Harold, if he was a part of your own consciousness, it wouldn't have worked. It'd be like trying to kill yourself twice, and that kind of defeats the purpose. Let's go home, Harold. I've missed you. I need you, okay?"

"I love you, Kelly."

"I love you, too, Harold."

And then she shoots me.

PART THREE

CHAPTER FIFTY

GOOD DAY
SUNSHINE

When I open my eyes, I find myself in a hospital bed hooked up to all kinds beeping instruments. There's a nurse standing at the end of my bed typing on a computer that's on a dolly. My throat feels dry and raw, as if somebody had shoved something down there and wasn't very gentle about it.

"Could I have a glass of water, please?" I croak.

"Oh, decided to come back to us, did you?"

"Yeah, apparently so."

She comes over and pours me a glass of water from a pitcher that's on the little dresser next to the bed. She puts a straw into the plastic cup and hands it to me.

"Is my wife here?"

"Yes, she went to the cafeteria. She's been here the whole time."

"How long?"

"Two days. How do you feel?"

"Pretty good."

"Do you know your name and where you are?"

"I think so."

"What's your name?"

"Harold."

"Do you know where you are?"

"I'm not dead, right?"

"Right."

"And judging by how bad this water tastes, I'd say I'm in the hospital."

"Well, it's been sitting there for a while."

"How's my wife?"

"I'll get her. I'll get everybody. Don't go anywhere."

"I won't."

I remember everything from wherever I had just been. The dream world or whatever it was. I remember what happened in the real world, too. My daughter's death and all the frantic crazy things that happened afterward.

Then, two bald doctors with matching goatees come into the room.

"Mr. Goldfarb, how do you feel?" the first one asks.

"I'm hungry."

"Good. That's good. We'll get you something."

"Thank you."

"Do you know what happened to you?"

"Uh…" I feel something well up, and then I lose it a little. It's odd. I don't feel particularly emotional at the moment, but I'm crying anyway.

"Sorry," I say to the doctors.

"It's fine. It's good. You've been through a lot," the first one says as if he's talking to a ten-year-old.

"I tried to kill myself?"

"Yes."

"I lost my daughter?"

"I'm very sorry for your loss, Mr. Goldfarb."

"Am I going to be okay?"

"Yes, to tell you the truth…" the second doctor begins as he sits on my bed and puts a hand on my shoulder. A nice gesture I suppose, but I don't find it particularly comforting or reassuring, if that was his intent.

"We aren't exactly sure what happened to you. It wasn't a coma, per se. You just went away for a while and hopefully to no ill effect."

"I think you are going to be fine, Mr. Goldfarb," the first doctor adds with a detached indifference. "After you go through a proper grieving period, you'll be just fine."

What the hell is the proper grieving period? I hate to be so judgmental after just returning from the dead, but I don't like these guys very much. Either one of them.

"You won't be trying anything like this again, will you Mr. Goldfarb?" the second doctor asks with an odd little chuckle.

"Please, call me Harold."

"Okay, Harold."

"We want you to see a therapist for a time," the first one says. "And we'll prescribe some medications to help even out the mood swings for you."

"What mood swings?"

"Well, after what you've been through—it's a lot to handle."

Then Kelly comes into the room. She looks exhausted and a lot thinner than the last time I saw her. The doctors back away as she rushes to my bedside.

"I'm sorry," I say pulling her close.

"I thought I lost you both!"

"I'm back. It's okay now."

"I love you so much!" Then she breaks down, and so do I.

"I love you, too," I tell her.

And we keep saying it over and over, hanging on to each other as if our lives depended on it.

CHAPTER FIFTY-ONE

THE RIVER'S FAR TOO WIDE WITHOUT YOU

The loss of a child, especially by suicide, is about as bad as it gets. Her name was Rebecca, and she was my pride and joy. She was beautiful, talented, and absolutely one of the funniest people I've ever known. I had no idea that she was in so much turmoil, and that will haunt me for the rest of my days. I don't think you ever really get over something like this. I don't think I ever really want to.

The bond between survivors can either strengthen or shatter. For Kelly and me, we seem to be pulling together. We will be okay, or as close to okay as you can. I did not do therapy or take any drugs. I had what I needed in my wife, and she had me. There's an eighteen-year-old bottle of Macallan in the liquor cabinet, but I think my drinking days may be over.

It's been two weeks since my return and besides becoming occasionally confused about what's real and what isn't, there seems to be no residual effects from my mini coma. That's the term the doctors finally came up with, but the truth is that nobody really knows what happened to me. I haven't talked to anybody about it, either. I don't know how to. It's reasonable to assume that these dream memories are just a carbon monoxide–inspired hallucination, but I'm having a hard time convincing myself of that.

Apparently, after returning from my daughter's apartment on the day of the tragedy, I got very drunk. On the drive home I ran into several cars and nearly hit a pedestrian. I've had a lawsuit filed against me by the pedestrian, my driver's license has been suspended, and if I hadn't tried to kill myself, I'd probably already be in jail for drunk driving.

A funeral service is held at a Lutheran church on the campus where I do Shakespeare in the summer. The service is conducted by both a Rabbi and a Lutheran minister who is a dear friend of ours. The day is filled with laughs and tears and lots of love from people who are much better friends than I probably deserve. Tom (my favorite director) is there and offers me the part of Polonius in *Hamlet*. It's a great part that an actor should be thrilled to play. I couldn't care less, and I turn him down. Jerry is there and some other people who were in my dream.

It's strange to see them again in the real world after what transpired in the other place. Especially with Jerry. We aren't as close anymore, as we were in the dream. Jerry has always been a true friend, and I— probably not so much. It's my MO, I'm afraid. If there is an injury, a funeral, a divorce, a surgery, or a dependency problem, that's when I'm most likely *not* to be found. I'll show up a little later when things have settled down, but in the heat of the moment, when I'm needed most…Jerry, on the other hand, has always been there for me, and if there's some resentment he feels toward me, I would not be surprised. If Rebecca died because of the things I missed in my greedy pursuit of contentment—I don't know how I could ever come to terms with that. I don't know how to make that right.

After the funeral, Kelly and I go to bed and cry in each other's arms. Then we make love, and it's as wonderful as it was in the dream. Afterward, Kelly is snoring away (a sound I have come to cherish) while I'm wide awake and staring at the ceiling. I really am an insomniac, unfortunately. I'm just lying there, thinking about God knows what, and guess who shows up?

It's a great roaring blaze from the dresser top to the ceiling. This time I'm more confused than horrified. There are images in the fire. His usual biblical crap, and then Mel Brooks's face appears and begins to speak.

"Hellooo, Harold!"

"You gotta be kidding me," I say.

"It's no joke," he says somewhat sheepishly—his Mel Brooks face frowning in the flames.

"What do you want? Do I have to make somebody pregnant?"

"You just did, so we can skip that part at least. Harold, are you sitting down?"

"Wait a minute. Are you telling me that Kelly really is pregnant?"

"She is now, yes. Just like before. I don't know the best way to say this, so I'll just say it. Everything you remember about aliens and the immigration problem. Everything that was in your dream? Well, it wasn't actually a dream. It's all true."

"It is?"

"Consider it a kind of training exercise. I know how you were suffering, and I must apologize for the intrusion, but I had to enter into your subconscious. To move things along. I had no choice because, as you recall, time is short."

"Uh, huh."

"So just to be clear, in case you've forgotten. You are the representative. You have the power to save the human race. And you have one month to do it."

"And my daughter?"

"Your daughter will be a great peacemaker. We must protect the future for her, for us, for the whole of humanity."

"No! I mean my other daughter, you son of a bitch!"

The image in the dresser fire blinks out for a moment. I guess he wasn't expecting that kind of reaction from me, and it must have thrown him.

"Oh, yes, I'm very sorry about Rebecca," he says with what seems like genuine empathy.

"Did she know about this? Was she a part of it? Did she hear the voices in her head?"

"Yes. I'm truly sorry for your loss."

"I don't want to talk to you anymore, Sid. You should have told me she was in trouble. I might have been able to help her. I don't know what you are or if you are, but you should have told me.

"I'm sorry. It was a mistake."

"I think you should leave now."

"I'll have more to tell you very soon."

I roll over on the bed, turning my back to him, and bury my face in the pillow.

"Stay well, Harold. There is much to be done. It is bigger than one loss. It's bigger than all of us."

"Nothing is bigger to me than she was," I say into the pillow.

"You need time."

"I need you gone."

And then there is silence. I turn to see if he's left. No fire, no smoke, no trace of him at all. I get up to use the bathroom. There's a flash drive on the dresser top where Sid just did his burning bush routine. I take a piss and then get my bottle of Macallan from the liquor cabinet. In the kitchen I put two ice cubes in a glass and pour myself a drink—but I hesitate. I examine the glass and then heave it into the sink. Broken glass everywhere. I clean up the mess and then go into my office and start writing the whole thing down.

———

In the morning, Kelly kisses me, and I kiss her back. She's dressed in her work clothes.

"I'm going in today," she tells me.

"So soon?" Are you sure you're ready?"

"It's been two weeks. I'm ready. I think work will be good. Get back to some kind of normal again. Besides, there's a ton of stuff I need to catch up on."

"Okay," I agree.

"I'm not feeling so great, though. Think I might be coming down with something."

"So stay home then."

"No, I have to get out. I'll be fine. See you tonight." She kisses me again and takes off.

———

What Sid told me slowly starts sinking in, no matter how much I try to push it away. I knew that it had to be more than a dream—a lesson maybe, but I never dreamed it could be this. Is it possible that the powers I had in the dream have transferred over to the real world?

After Kelly takes off for work, I go back into the office and continue writing my recollections from the dream. The more of this I do, and the fresher the memories become, the more I'm compelled to make a confession to myself. In spite of everything—the angst, the confusion, and the tremendous loss—like an actor who's been off the boards too long, my God I miss the action. I miss Jerry, I miss the bird-monsters, and if I'm able to do the things I did in the dream, if the world is truly on the brink, I guess I better snap out of it and get busy. Can I be more like the person I was becoming in the dream? A more alive and involved version of myself? Then my phone rings. I still have that Sherwood Forest ringtone, and it still makes me jump.

"Hello?" I answer.

"Oh…Harold?" says a young woman's voice.

"Yes?"

"My name is Portia, and I'm playing Ophelia in the show?"

I'm too stunned to speak, so she continues.

"I spoke to Tom, and he asked me to call? I know that you can't drive right now and all, but we happen to be neighbors? So if you want to do the show, I could give you a ride out there?"

"Portia, that is really so kind of you, but there're a lot of reasons why I can't do the show this year. I really appreciate the offer, though."

"I dreamed about you. Isn't that weird?"

I'm speechless again and so is she. I sense that there's more she wants to tell me about this dream, but I'm hoping that she doesn't. If I have to listen to her say one more thing as a question, I'm going to scream. The Portia in the dream didn't talk that way, but the real one—oh my God!

"Anyway," she resumes. "If you change your mind, the offer still stands?"

"Okay, thank you, Portia."

Weird.

———

When Kelly gets home from work, she doesn't eat much. She goes to bed early complaining of stomach pains and says that she's very tired.

After I'm sure she's sleeping (I can tell by the snores), I put a pencil in the center of the dining room table. I concentrate on moving it with my mind, as I did when I was a kid. After about three seconds, the pencil shoots off the table and nearly spears poor Squeak as he's walking by. Maybe tomorrow I'll shake the house.

I think about using the flash drive that Sid left for me, but I don't. Still, my dream that night is pretty rich:

I'm standing alone at the crossroads of some desolate place. A man in black approaches with a dog. The man has a lean, cruel face, and his dog is huge. No breed that I recognize. It stands at least four feet tall with very long legs and a lean, muscular body. His snout is scarred and wide, and his smallish eyes are dark like shark eyes. His fur is dark brown, almost black, and dust comes up from his back as he walks. The man smiles at me, but there is nothing friendly in his smile. "So we meet at last," says this man with a Kentucky gentleman's Southern accent.

His dog trots over to me. He sniffs me. His sniffing becomes more and more aggressive.

"He likes you. He don't like everybody, you know?"

His dog pushes me with his nose, toying with me, and then he starts to bite.

"Hey!" I cry.

Little nips at first, and then he's on top of me. Eating me. I see chunks of my flesh being ripped away. I don't feel pain, but the sight of this is horrifying.

"Stop him!" I scream. "What is he doing to me?"

The man in black laughs. "He's just having a little lunch with you is all."

Then he whistles, and it sounds like a siren. The dog backs off and returns to his master.

"Who are you?" I plead, as I lie there bleeding.

"Oh, come on now, son. You know who I am. I'm the one that you need to stop. But you're going to run like a gazelle, aren't ya'? Just like you always done. Ain't got it in you, son."

He snaps his fingers. Thunder cracks, and the sky lights up with fire. My ripped-away flesh has somehow been restored, and I'm no longer bleeding to death.

"You rest up now, son. You're going to need your strength. Everything you got."

And then he continues on his way, whistling that tune that Oscar Robinson, no, his name was Lou, wasn't it? Anyway, it's that kids' song that he sang in my dream. The dog walks in perfect time with his master, and then they vanish into nothing.

CHAPTER FIFTY-TWO

SHELTER FROM
THE STORM

In the morning Kelly kisses me on the head, and I kiss her back.
"Go out and do something today," she says. "Go to a movie. Take a
walk. It's supposed to be beautiful today."

"How are you feeling?"

"I'm going to take off early and see the doctor. I have a four o'clock
appointment."

"What's going on?" I ask as if I didn't already know.

"Cramps, stomach pains. I don't know what it is."

"Maybe you should stay home, and we can go together."

"No, I'm fine. I'm sure it's nothing."

"You're sure?"

"Yeah."

She pats my shoulder, kisses me again, and then takes off for work.
I'm pretty sure about what's going to happen at the doctor's. After that
goes down, I'll have no choice but to start the conversation I've been
doing my best to avoid. Squeak comes into the bedroom and starts
squeaking, and I know he won't stop until I get up. Having no real say
in the matter, I do as I'm told. Squeak jumps up on the bed (rather than
in his pass-out chair). He goes under the covers, where he'll remain for
the next several hours.

I scan the morning paper, looking for anything unusual, like giant
birds. All I find is what I always find: greedy deeds, squabbling, and
accusations. The aliens have learned to negotiate their differences. It's
probably why we're on the eve of destruction and they're pulling all the

strings. They must know who we are. They're seeing all our crap. Why does Sid still want to give us a chance? What am I missing?

Being easily susceptible to a negative disposition—and the fact that I haven't had a drink in ten minutes—has apparently put me in a dark place.

I wander around the house, distracted and unable to concentrate. I make a pot of hot water because I forgot to put coffee in the filter, and the cat food somehow winds up in the dishwasher. I should get some air. I haven't walked since my return because I'm apprehensive about what I might see and how vulnerable I'll be to whatever might be out to get me.

I muster some resolve and decide to walk anyway. Besides expecting an alien child and having to save humanity, I also have a court date rapidly approaching. So there's a lot to think about, and my walks are usually the best way for me to do that. My mostly inaccessible attorney assures me that he's developing a surefire strategy to keep me from rotting away in a state prison.

Mr. Berman, who's handling my case, is planning to play upon the sympathy of the court. He will plead, rightfully, that my irresponsible behavior was the result of the tragic loss of my daughter. The tremendous grief caused me to momentarily lose my ability to reason soundly and behave like a responsible citizen. In seeking the mercy of the court, he will assure them that I'm now completely recovered and utterly ashamed of my reckless behavior. He tells me that rather than prison time, he will request that I perform mandatory public service and attend weekly counseling sessions. If the court deems it fit for me to receive spankings or electric shock treatments, so be it. I'm willing to do just about anything to avoid wasting time in jail when I have no time left to waste. All in all, I believe Berman's argument is reasonable and valid. I will, in fact, never do anything like that again. I'm sure with what the future has in store for me, my reckless behavior will only be getting worse.

Earlier, I made a list of all the things that I wanted to get done today, but I can't find it. So I put on my sneakers, set the house alarm, and head out to take a restorative walk through the neighborhood. I have to come back inside, however, when I realize that I still have my bathrobe on.

After that gets straightened out, I go back outside. I check to make sure my fly is zipped up and then take a deep breath of the sweet morning air. Kelly was right. It's a beautiful day, spectacular in fact. The sky is bright blue with puffy white clouds that are shaped like animal crackers. The neighborhood dogs are barking, the birds are singing, and I actually feel an unfamiliar twinge of hope.

Then something heavy lands on the roof.

CHAPTER FIFTY-THREE

I GET BY WITH A LITTLE
HELP FROM MY FRIENDS

Of course I know what it is. I think about not even turning around to look, but I do. It reminds me of that scene from *The Exorcist* at the beginning of the movie when they're in the desert and the dogs are fighting. The camera pans up to this creepy-looking statue. It has wings, and it looks like several different things rolled into one—devil, human, beast—and 100 percent evil. That's what it reminds me of.

The bird-monster spreads its wings, and my God it is impressive! Even more so in real life. It doesn't look directly at me. It scans the neighborhood. Either looking for trouble or for lunch. It's gruesomely magnificent. My hit man. My personal enforcer. My Dirty Harry.

"How you doing, big guy? Good to see you again. Kill anything lately?"

The bird-monster cocks its head and looks at me with huge red eyes. In the dream, I think they were yellow eyes. I prefer the red. Makes it fiercer. The beast starts picking at something with its gigantic yellow beak and pulls a squirming black thing out from under a wing that it quickly chomps and swallows. A little snack that it was saving, I suppose. Then the bird-monster takes off. Straight up like a rocket and vanishes from sight—spectacular!

I feel energized by the visit. There is something about seeing the bird-monster in the flesh; at least I know that somebody has my back. I feel instantly better about everything. Maybe the impossible is possible, and I can actually pull this off.

I start my walk, and the weight of Rebecca's death suddenly lifts from my shoulders. I can breathe again. I know this is only a temporary refrain and that dramatic mood swings may be an indication of something serious, but I'm cherishing the moment nonetheless. Maybe she didn't die in vain, and her memory will inspire me to work a miracle in her name.

I take my usual route. Straight up the hill and toward the mountains. You'd think after what I'd been through that I would tire quickly. That isn't the case. I feel really strong. When I get to the top of the first hill, I see a familiar sight. An overpacked shopping cart parked wheels to the curb as if it were a parked car. And there he is, Oscar Robinson (or Lou to his Jewish friends) alive and well and chatting it up with a gardener who reacts to him much as I do, with nods and smiles, agreeing but not really understanding much. The gardener, I know, speaks Spanish, and he doesn't seem to understand him either, so that confirms something for me. Oscar Robinson probably is crazy and speaks a language all his own. Or maybe it's Portuguese. Regardless of his mental state, I'm so glad to see him alive, standing there cheerfully chatting away, I can't even tell you. I have tears.

"Oscar Robinson!" I cry. "So good to see you again, my friend!"

But he is not so glad to see me. He glares for a moment and then starts backing away.

"Hey, Lou! What's the matter?" I yell as I begin to approach.

"Not now! *No bueno.* No good, *papito!*" He grabs his cart and starts to run. Items tumble to the ground as he goes.

He wants away from me as if his life depended on it. The gardener looks at me suspiciously and then goes back to his work.

"What in the holy hell?"

I continue my walk. I find the cowgirl doll that must have fallen from his cart lying akimbo in the street. The doll's head is cracked, and the nose is broken off. I carefully pick it up as if it's a delicate treasure.

Why is he afraid of me? What does he know? Whose voice is he hearing in his head?

It would seem, then, that the dream world and the real world are connected but not necessarily in sync. If I take what I learned there and apply it here as gospel, I could make some serious blunders.

After setting the doll on the curb near where I found it, I start to jog. Then I start to run. I don't stop until I get all the way through Brand Park and then all the way back to my house.

On the bright side, I'm in a lot better shape than I thought I was. Is it possible that they've done something to me physically? I just ran three miles, and I should be close to death, but I feel great. Are they getting me ready? Am I their Terminator—the older model? I get myself some orange juice and call my lawyer. I'm put on hold and forced to listen to a Muzak version of "Bridge Over Troubled Water". It must be the extended version. Mr. Berman finally picks up.

"Harold, how goes the world?" he cheerfully inquires as if we're best friends.

"Don't ask," I answer as if we're not.

"Listen, something's come up here at the firm," he says.

"Oh? And what might that be, pray tell?"

"Well, an unhappy individual at the state department has some questions about a case I'm working on," Berman chuckles. "Can you believe that?"

I absolutely believe it and don't bother to answer his question.

"So there's an investigation going on, and until these ridiculous allegations can be resolved, the firm has no choice but to place me on a temporary leave, and I'll be turning my caseloads over to another attorney here. It happens from time to time. More of an inconvenience than anything else."

"For who? You or me?"

"Your case is on Friday, right?"

"Yeah, *this* Friday. Maybe you should write it down so you don't forget."

"Relax, everything is under control. Nothing to worry about. One of our best lawyers is taking over your case. Hold on, he just came in."

And just like that I'm back on the "Bridge Over Troubled Water". My mind starts to drift. I'm thinking about my list of things to do. "Maybe it's in the freezer?" I wonder out loud. "Did I go in there for anything?"

Then somebody picks up.

"Harold!" a familiar and enthusiastic voice inquires.

"Yes. This is Harold."

"You'll never guess who this is," he says.

I know exactly who it is. I just can't believe it.

"It's me! Rodger Stock! Do you remember? From the Napa Valley Theatre Company?"

"Of course I remember you, Rodger. I remember you like it was yesterday."

"Good! Because I'm your new lawyer, buddy!"

Bizarre.

We set a meeting for tomorrow night at his house in the Pacific Palisades to discuss my case and catch up. If he lives on a houseboat and has a boyfriend, I don't know what I'll do. I really need a drink. I take a shower and go to the store instead. I take an Uber.

———

Ralphs is not too busy. I go up and down the aisles getting what I need for my world-famous low-fat chicken burritos. I'm expecting trouble, like there was in the dream Ralphs. I'm hoping for it, in fact. A little something to practice on. But nothing happens. No crazy people. No robberies. Not even a screaming infant to comfort. Bummer. I'm really in the mood to tweak somebody's consciousness.

When I get back home, I make the low-fat burritos that Kelly enjoys almost as much as my baked chicken. I set the table in the dining room, and I arrange the flowers I bought. I'm hoping that Dr. Bloom might have already broken the ice for me, but she probably doesn't know anything yet. Besides, I'm sure I would have gotten a frantic phone call from Kelly if the doctor had already told her that she was pregnant. Anyway, I try to make things extra nice because the conversation we're about to have is going to be a difficult one.

When she comes in, she looks pale and tired, just like in the dream. She smiles at me, sort of. She isn't quite at the I'm-going-to-stick-a-fork-in-your-neck stage, but I suspect that she'll be getting there soon.

"Chicken?" she asks.

"Actually, I made burritos. Low-fat chicken burritos with Mexicorn on the side!" I try to make this sound as delectable as possible.

She grimaces.

"You got flowers?" she asks, more surprised than impressed.

"I did."

"How come?"

"Just thought it'd be nice. So, how'd it go at the doctor?"

She gets a puzzled look on her face. "Let me change first," she mumbles and then shuffles away down the hall.

I look through the dining room window and see two gardeners staring at the house from their truck across the street. I don't recognize them from around the neighborhood, and the way they're staring makes me uneasy. I decide to go outside and see what's going on.

I go through the front door and walk toward their truck. They are unconcerned that I'm approaching them. They just continue to stare, trancelike. It reminds me of the Athenians Society in the dream, where the whole street seemed to be under some kind of spell. The memory of it makes me shiver.

"Can I help you guys with something?" I ask.

"Need some fertilizer for the yard, señor?" the driver asks.

"No, I don't think so," I suspiciously reply.

"We have extra from another job. Give you a good price."

"No thanks."

"Are you sure?" the other one asks while still staring intently at the house.

"Yup."

"There's a big—there's something on your roof, mister. Does it belong to you?" the driver asks.

I turn around to look. The bird-monster is back, perched and scanning the neighborhood. I wave a hello, which it completely ignores.

"Yeah, it's mine," I tell them. "You want it? I'll give you a good price."

"They're seeing them in Mexico, too. My family has seen them," says the driver.

"It's a bad sign," the other one says and then finally manages to look away from the bird. He glares at me directly, a mix of fear and what I take to be an accusation of some kind.

"Why is it a bad sign?"

They don't answer my question, so I repeat myself.

"Why do you say that it's a bad sign?"

The driver starts the truck.

"Why is it a bad sign?" I ask for a third time.

They drive off. Whatever they know about bird-monsters, they aren't sharing it with me.

They're seeing them in Mexico? What's going on in Mexico? I'll have to check that next time with Sid. If he's still talking to me after I told him to get lost.

I turn back toward the house. The bird-monster extends its gargantuan wings and flaps them enough to rise a few feet into the air and then land again on the roof with a sizable thump. It never looks at me directly but checks up and down our block and then starts picking at its feathers again. Not really interested to see what it might pull out of there, I go back inside.

Kelly is sitting at the table looking only slightly more comfortable. "What did they want?" she asks.

"They wanted to sell me some fertilizer."

"Did a branch fall on the roof or something?"

"No."

"I heard something up there. A thump."

"I'll tell you about that in a minute. Are you hungry?"

"Not really. But I should eat."

"I'll make you a plate." I go into the kitchen.

She talks as I get the food ready. "So, Dr. Bloom says it's probably nothing, but she wants me to see a specialist. There's a stomach flu going around. She said if I was younger, she'd think that I was pregnant."

"Really?" I say, trying to sound surprised.

"Yeah, she said the way my stomach has extended, it looks like I'm a couple months pregnant. But it's probably gas. I've got some other stuff going on, though, that pregnant women get. I remember from Rebecca."

I can hear in her voice that she's getting emotional.

"But she said she won't really know anything until the blood work comes back. I just hope it's not a tumor or something."

I bring the burritos to the table.

"What would you like to drink?" I ask.

"Cranberry juice."

"You're pregnant," I suddenly tell her, much too abruptly, I'm afraid, but I just couldn't hold it in any longer.

"Ha, ha. Very funny."

"I'm serious."

"Shut up," she tells me.

"I saw it coming in the dream."

"It's not possible for me to be pregnant, dear. What are you talking about?"

"Let me get your juice."

I go back into the kitchen when an idea comes to me.

I return to the dining room, put the juice down for her, and then gently take her hand.

"I have to show you something," I say.

"Harold, maybe you did have some brain damage and it's just showing up now. Maybe they missed something."

"Come on outside for a minute."

I get her to her feet and take her outside. We walk down the porch steps, and I turn her to face back toward the house. The bird-monster stares down at us. Kelly gasps. Then it takes off. It circles the house one time and then shoots straight up, vanishing into thin air.

"Whaat in the name of..."

I wait for the tag.

"Sweet Gandhi in a steak house!"

There it is.

"I have a lot to tell you. If you weren't pregnant, I'd get you drunk first."

"Holy shit! I just remembered something," she says slapping a hand to her forehead.

"What?"

"A dream I had. I was standing on the roof, like that thing was just now. I was naked and pregnant and then I jumped. But I flew! I could fly—"

"I had the same exact dream! I was there. I was watching."

Being my wife for thirty years and knowing me better than anybody, she asks the twenty-four-thousand-dollar question.

"Does this have anything to do with aliens?"

"Let's go in. I have a lot to tell you."

———

I run the whole thing down for her. She doesn't say much. She eats a little bit of the burrito, drinks her juice, and then goes to bed. I can't tell what she thought of it all. She did recall the UFO activity in Australia when she was a kid. The rest of it, though—she needs time, and I want to give it to her. For a day at least. I haven't seen the violence yet that I saw in the dream, but I'm worried about safety. Hers, mine, and everybody else's. When I suggested that she give her notice at work—that's when she got up and walked away.

I want to try and enter Jerry's dream tonight. Judging by how distant our friendship has become, it might be the best way to break the ice with him. If it works.

———

Kelly is already asleep as I get into bed. Her snores haven't reached baby rhino proportions yet, but she's getting there. I nudge the flash drive around with my finger. I have it on the nightstand next to the bed. I'm excited and nervous about using it again. Finally, I pick it up and put it on my forehead. I get drowsy very quickly, and then I'm off:

I get out of bed feeling weightless. I know I have become a projection of myself. My spirit self? I'm not sure how to classify it. It surprises me that I'm still in my bedroom and not in Jerry's apartment, where I had planned to go. I'm not worried, though. I intuitively know what to do next. I just walk, or rather float, forward, and then I'm going right through the wall.

Instead of Jerry's apartment, I find myself on the deck of a large, deserted cruise ship. The ship is in the middle of the ocean with no land in sight. Up a stairwell from a lower deck comes a scream. Jerry charges up the stairs in a panic. He goes past me at full speed, and then suddenly comes to a stop. His legs are churning, as in a cartoon, running as fast as he can but not going anywhere. Then this horrible thing comes up the stairs after him. Long stringy hair and an ancient warty witch's face.

It wears a black cloak covered in blood and guts, fingers, eyeballs, and matted hair—as if she had just butchered something. The witch is cackling. Her arms extended, long fingernails clutching at the air preparing to do some terrible harm.

"Get away from me," Jerry screams. "I don't love you anymore!"

Never did understand Jerry's taste in women.

"Don't say that, sugar. Come to Mama," she says in a raspy old witch's voice.

I step in. Float in, rather, right in between them. I'm nose to nose with the most horrible face—and the most gruesome breath—that I've ever had to endure.

"Get out of my way," she hisses through what's left of her rotting teeth. "Or I'll gut you, roast you, and use your bones to take the pudgy one's eyes!"

"Stop, just stop," I calmly tell her.

She freezes with a pained expression. Then she screams (as only a witch can). She runs to the side of the ship and leaps—dives over the railing, her bloody robe billowing behind her. That breaks the spell and frees up Jerry. He rushes over to the railing. I float over and join him there.

We watch her robe bob in the water. That's all that's left of her.

"How'd you get here?" Jerry asks.

"I was in the neighborhood. Mr. Geeg, I'm sorry that we haven't been closer lately. I'm sorry I haven't been as good a friend as I should have been," I sincerely tell him.

"It's a two-way street, Mr. Geeg. We get caught up in our own stuff. It's cool. Good friends can go a long time apart, but when they get together again, it's right back to where they left off. Like they never missed a beat."

"That's good to hear," I say.

"Thanks for saving me from that thing."

"You're welcome."

"I think it was part my mother and part my last girlfriend."

"You like strong women. Nothing wrong with that."

"And I'm sorry about Rebecca."

He takes a moment. I know her death shook him. They stayed close through the years. He was like an uncle to her, and a comedy mentor as well.

"How are you and Kelly doing? Okay?"

"We're dealing with it," I say.

"Yeah, that's all you can do." And then he sadly stares off into the water.

"I need your help, Mr. Geeg," I tell him.

"Aliens?"

"Yup. It's a big one. This is for everything."

"I knew this day was coming," he says.

"They gave us both powers. It's how I can do this."

"And I'm a healer, aren't I?"

"How'd you know?"

"I had a feeling. This is what we've been waiting for all these years, isn't it, Mr. Geeg? This is our moment."

"I think so, yes."

"I have to wake up now. I have to go to the bathroom."

"Okay, call me tomorrow," I tell him. "So we can compare notes."

"You'll be all right here?"

"I should be. I'm pretty good at this now."

"Goodbye, Mr. Geeg," he says.

"Goodbye, Mr. Geeg."

We do our special finger handshake, and then he starts to dissolve. I look out over the water and enjoy the view for a moment. Then the railing I'm holding onto begins to disappear, and the deck starts to vanish from under me. I have to leave. Jerry's dream is fading away. I float across the disappearing deck and go right through the bulkhead.

I open my eyes, and I'm back in my bed. Squeak is sitting on my chest staring at me. I raise the blanket so he can go under the covers. Kelly has stopped snoring. I gently shake her until she snorts so I know that she's okay. Then I roll over and fall easily to sleep.

CHAPTER FIFTY-FOUR

YOU DON'T NEED A WEATHERMAN
TO KNOW WHICH WAY THE WIND BLOWS

I slept well. Kelly wakes me with a good morning kiss.

"How do you feel?" I ask.

"Nauseous and large." She pulls up her shirt and is absolutely bigger than she was the day before.

"Do you believe me now, I ask?"

"It's too weird to believe. Something is moving in there, though. I don't know what moved, but it moved."

"Do me a favor. Don't go into work today?"

"I'm swamped, I have to. What are you going to do?"

"I've got some research to do and some people to see. And then I'm going to try and save the human race."

"Don't save it all at once. You'll throw your back out."

"Please think about what I said, about the job. At least take a leave."

"Petite young women need bathing suits, Harold. You don't want them running around on the beach naked, do you?"

A highly trained raised eyebrow tells her what she needs to know.

"That's what I thought you'd say. Oh, and I wanted to ask, because I'm not sure I heard it right. No big deal or anything, but you say you can move objects with your mind?"

The bedroom TV switches on by itself.

"Huh…call me at lunchtime," she says on her way out the door.

———

I get up and have my coffee at the dining room table. I scan the paper, looking again for anything unusual that somebody might have seen. But there's nothing. You'd think with a bird-monster dancing on my roof, somebody might have noticed. I check the neighborhood watch website on my phone, but there's nothing there either. Just missing cats, coyote sightings, and something about a raccoon that got into somebody's house and ate all the dog food. I get out my laptop, because it's easier for me to surf on it, and start searching around for the *UFO Journal* in New Jersey. I find it right away, but their list of contributing writers has no mention of a Linda Broomfield. Maybe her name was different in the dream. I feel certain that she does exist, however, and my intuition is telling me that we need to team up in order to survive what's coming.

I look up from my computer and there's Jerry with his big eyeballs staring at me through the dining room window.

I open the door for him.

"Hello, Mr. Geeg," I say.

"Hello, Mr. Geeg," he replies.

"Coffee?"

"No. I'm nervous enough already."

We do our finger handshake and then sit down at the table.

"So you can talk to people in their dreams and save them from witches now?"

"So it seems. Wanna take a ride? I'll tell you all about it."

"Okay…" he says warily. "But before I lock myself in a car with you, what else are you capable of these days?"

"I can enter people's thoughts and make them do things or not do things, depending on my mood. And I can move objects with my mind."

"And aliens gave you this?"

"Yes."

"Interesting," he says.

"It's been in the works for a long time."

"I knew about the healing thing, by the way," Jerry says.

"In my dream you saved a little boy."

"Yes, that rings a bell."

"Let's go. I'll explain in the car."

"But wait a minute. So, you're calling it a *dream* now? I thought it was a coma."

"No, I don't think that's what it was. Everything that happened while I was there—while I was dreaming, or whatever you want to call it—it was a training exercise. That's what he told me."

"Who told you?"

"Sid, the alien."

"Sid the alien? You got to be kidding me."

"You ain't heard nothing yet. Come on, let's go."

"Where are we going?"

"I want to see if somebody I met in the dream really exists. I think she's really important to how this all plays out. If she's like she was in the dream, you're going to like her. Definitely your type. Do you mind driving? The state of California doesn't want me behind the wheel for a while."

"My car smells like cigars."

"I know. I can smell it from in here."

"She's my type? I didn't know I had a type. I'm usually not that particular."

"She's a writer, really smart, and good-looking. You were infatuated with her in the dream."

"I was in your dream a lot, it sounds like."

"We were partnered up, Mr. Geeg. Just like old times."

"Maybe all the weird stuff that happened to us back then—"

"Was getting us ready for this? Yeah, I think so. Oh, and Kelly is pregnant."

"You're kidding me now, right?"

"No, I kid you not. This is big, Mr. Geeg."

"And this woman that we're going to see? Did I make her laugh? In the dream, I mean?"

"Yes, you were tasteful and hilarious. If she actually does exist, a steaming hot romance is sure to follow."

"I'm a desperate man, Mr. Geeg. You shouldn't tease me."

"I wouldn't," I assure him.

"Okay. Truth is, just the possibility of a little action, even if it's from somebody else's dream, well, that's good enough for me."

Jerry is up and out the door before I can even grab my keys. For a large man, when motivated, he moves very quickly.

———

Jerry has a minivan. He's no longer allowed to smoke cigars in his apartment because the neighbors have complained about the stench. The area where he lives is a smoke-free zone. So the only place left for him to enjoy a cigar is in his car. Even with the windows rolled down, the smell is overwhelming. I try not to breathe, but you can only keep that up for so long. So ignoring the smell as best I can, I start telling him the story of what happened in my dream.

Jerry listens and doesn't say a word. When he starts to weave into oncoming traffic, I suggest that maybe we should pull over before I go any further. He insists that it's okay, that he drives like this all the time. Why this makes me feel better, I have no idea. I get through the rest of the story, and Jerry, for the most part, stays in his designated lane. As I suspected, thanks to his own history of weirdness, he takes it all very well.

Twenty minutes later we arrive in beautiful downtown Burbank. Safe, sound, and reeking of cigars.

We find a spot to park and start walking. My memory of the house is still quite vivid. I know that I'll recognize it when I see it, and sure enough, there it is—just a short block up from the Burbank Studios. The same worn-out tan color and the decaying roof. The bougainvillea, although overgrown, is not as out of control as it was in the dream, and I'm hopeful that this time around I might avoid getting stabbed in the neck by a three-inch thorn. We make our way up the dilapidated steps and onto the porch, when my stomach flutters and I start getting anxious.

"This is a make or break moment right here, Mr. Geeg."

"It is?"

"If Linda Broomfield is in this house—"

"Then it's really happening?" Jerry guesses.

"Oh, it's really happening. Kelly is pregnant, bird-monsters are on my roof, and we can do things that people normally shouldn't be able to do. I know that it's happening. It's just a matter of how Linda Broomfield is going to fit into it. And if she's with us or against us."

"And if she's against us?"

"Then I got a bad feeling."

"How bad?"

"Like, game over, man."

"Bill Paxton from *Aliens* bad? Shit, that's really bad."

We stand there on the porch, staring at the door. I'm struggling, trying to find the resolve to take the next step.

"Do you think she'd still go out with me, though? Even if she's against us?"

I take a deep breath and taste cigars. Then I knock. Nothing happens. I knock again, a little louder this time.

"If she's not here," Jerry begins, "does that mean—"

But the door opens, and there is Linda Broomfield. Bright eyes, warm smile, and in excellent condition. Pretty much a carbon copy of the dream Linda. Except this Linda is black.

"Hi, I'm Linda Broomfield. Glad you could make it."

It takes me a minute before I can speak, so Jerry jumps in.

"I'm Jerry from New Jersey. I believe in aliens, probably been abducted a few times, and I can heal, by the way. Not like a dog, mind you, but I'm very fond of animals, in case that's a deal breaker for you."

Linda laughs. He did it again.

"Hi, Jerry," she says. "Come on in. We've been waiting for you."

"You knew we were coming?" I finally manage.

A shadow crosses over us from above. I look up and see a bird-monster circling.

Linda gets serious, "Please, we better go in."

It's the same place, just as I remember it. Except now, seated around us in a half circle are twenty or so men and women of various colors and expressions. I recognize many of them from the dream, which is disconcerting, and when I lock eyes with the guy directly in front of me, that really takes my breath away. It's Israel. Long hair, tattoos, the whole bit. He stands up and starts to applaud, and then the others follow his lead. There is an escalating frenzied excitement. They cheer, stomp, whoop, and holler, and a few of them are openly weeping for joy.

After the overly emotional display diminishes, Linda brings in folding chairs for Jerry and me. When we sit down, the others do as well. On a scale of 1 to 10, this is pretty high up there on the creep-out meter. If the intent is to welcome us and make us feel at ease, it's not working.

We all smile and nod pleasantly at each other for a while. Then Israel gets up again and starts toward me. Not knowing what to expect, or if I need to defend myself, I remain seated and just hope for the best. He throws his big arms around me right there where I sit and gives me a serious man hug. Then I get a little slap across the face. An "I love you, bro" type thing, I hope. Then he smiles and goes back to his seat, so I figure we're okay.

The nodding and smiling continues. The two Mexican guys who were bird watching outside my house are here. Except now they wear suits and don't seem like gardeners anymore. Officers Schmitt and Joelson, two of the detectives from my dream police station in Napa, are here. The girl who was being robbed in Brand Park, the one I rescued, is also here. So is Portia and the guy from the Kabbalah Center (who showed up at my door like a Jehovah's Witness). There's an older couple who bear an uncanny resemblance to Roy and Alice, my saviors from St. Helena. They are both looking up at the ceiling and waving their arms in the air. The others, I don't recognize. Linda takes her own chair and joins Jerry and me at the center of things.

"Thank you for coming," she says.

"You were expecting us, it seems."

"Yes."

"How?"

"Well, I invited you, remember?"

"From the dream?" I ask.

"Yes." Linda smiles at me, and her eyes sparkle.

"So, you were in my dream? You remember what happened there?"

"We all were in some parts. I'm sure you have a lot of questions, and we're going to try and answer them for you today," she says.

"Just so you know," I say while leaning in toward her. "It's funny, but in my dream you were white. You looked exactly the same. Except you were white."

"Interesting," she responds. "I didn't see myself that way."

They all make some noises, as if weighing the implications of this, and that makes me a tad paranoid. I just considered it a curious wrinkle to the rest of the strangeness going on, but because Linda was white in my dream…do they think I'm a racist? I don't think I am, but you never know these days.

Jerry picks up the slack. "So everyone here knows about what's going on, then?"

"These people know more about it than anyone else in the world," Linda says.

"And we're cool?" he continues. "Nobody wants to kill us or anything like that?"

There are giggles from the group. It reminds me of when Dorothy landed in Oz, and the Munchkins laughed about what she didn't know about witches.

"And just out of curiosity"—Jerry's on a roll—"can you people do things like Harold can? Shake buildings, change people's minds. You know, stuff like that?"

I modestly clarify. "Well, I don't know yet if I can really do all that stuff. That's just some things I could do in the dream, so…"

The guy from the Kabbalah Center stands up to speak. "Hi, guys! Please rest assured, we definitely don't want to do you any harm."

More good-natured tittering from the group.

"In fact, Harold, we are here to help you."

He's wearing the same suit he wore in the dream. Linda was white, but this guy's suit is a perfect match—go figure.

"We have some abilities, but none of us can do what you guys can. Many of us were able to enter the dream, though. And a few of us were able to see what the aliens were downloading…into Harold's subconsciousness."

"Downloading?" Jerry asks.

"Yes, that's what they were doing. Harold was being programmed. For their own greedy purposes."

"I was?" I feel blindsided by his assessment of the dream. And to have all these people here who seemed to have shared in something that I thought was my own—I guess I feel a little violated as well. The rest of the room seems to be in agreement with the evaluation, however. They're all smiling and nodding again.

"Seth, is that your name? Like it was in the dream?" I'm impressed that I remember his name. I'm usually terrible at that.

"Yes, great to see you again," he responds. "I'm so glad I was able to get in and meet you in there. I wish I could have done more."

"And how exactly were you able to do that?"

"We met you in our own dreams and then were able to follow you into yours. That's why so many people already know about you. It was like an invitation. Like we were meant to see what was going on. I don't know how you did it, how you reached out to so many of us. Maybe it was a cry for help, so that people could see what's coming. Anyway, that's how I found you and how I met these people here—I met them in your dream."

"Must give us pause," as the melancholy Dane would say.

"Are you really with the Kabbalah Center?" I ask.

"I am. I wanted to tell you more, to warn you because we're able to pick up on things now. Things they don't want us to know. Linda and some of her contacts have been able to decipher the dream code, and we now know what their real purpose is. But it might have been dangerous to try and communicate that to you. I'm not as good at it as you are—the dreaming. I didn't want to screw anything up."

"What do you mean for their greedy purposes?" I finally get around to asking.

"Well—" he starts, but I immediately cut him off.

"You know what? Before we do that, and just so we understand each other, let me tell you what I know, or what I've been told, and you tell me where I have it wrong or where we disagree."

No one objects, so I continue.

"We have to contact persons of power within our government and let them know about the aliens, the plight of their planet, and their desire to relocate to Wyoming so they can save themselves, correct? But if we can't get them situated here peacefully within a month, then the deal they have with their opposition, the opposing party, or faction, or whatever you want to call it, then they take over and we go…extinct. Do I have that right? So there's the one side that thinks we are a total waste of time and wants to wipe us out, and the other side that thinks we're terrific and wants to give us a chance to broker a deal. If we're successful, they will share their technology, teach us how to do all kinds of cool stuff, and make the planet a better place for everybody. Is that not the same thing you're hearing?"

"And, if I may," Jerry interjects. "Harold is the go-between with special powers. So that we can impress the government with what is possible if we cooperate and play nice."

There is a gloomy silence.

"Those are all lies," Seth tells us. "There are no different parties. There is only one agenda. The truth is not what you've been led to believe."

"So you're telling me that the alien who's been talking to me, Sid— he lied to me? About everything?"

"They have no interest in helping anybody here," Israel says with that stern look of his. "They want to use us and suck us dry, bro. This is an invasion, plain as that."

"But the voices that I hear in my head that my daughter heard? Who is that? Isn't that the other side that wants us gone and drove my daughter to suicide?"

"It's a setup, bro! They want us grateful to them for saving us so that we're docile and trusting. There is only one side. There is us and them. Period."

"It's a lot to take in," Linda kindly tells me.

There's an understatement if I ever heard one.

"Harold." Linda leans in close. "We have information from sources all over the world. We know how they operate and what the real reasons are for their coming here. The aliens are not our friends. I know you sensed that already. What happened to your daughter is not something a friend would let happen, is it? They are telling you that the goal is to bring peace and make the world a better place. What they really want to do is use you to spread fear and division. They want to divide and conquer, pit nation against nation so they become the only ones for us to trust. Harold, you are their main weapon of deception."

Portia stands up next. "Hi, Harold?" she says with youthful insecurity. "I'm Portia? We spoke on the phone?"

She's doing that question at the end of every sentence thing again, whether it's a question or not. I do my best not to let it aggravate me.

"Yes, hi, Portia. I recognize you from the dream. And from the phone."

"Oh, good! I just wanted to say that they have given you gifts to make you indebted to them? To make us all indebted to them?"

Then the girl from the park stands to throw in her two cents.

"They want to seduce you with power! They want you to do their bidding and spread their lies!" Park Girl is a lot feistier than she was before. "They want you to use your powers to sell their phony story. It's the greatest deception of all time!"

Park Girl is getting a little hysterical. Officer Schmitt helps her back to her seat and pats her on the back.

"Do you remember me saving you from that guy in the park?" I ask her because I'm dying to know.

"What?" My question seems to snap her out of it a bit.

"Remember, you were being robbed, and I hit the guy in the nose with a pine cone?"

She looks at me blankly.

"In the dream? You were on your lunch hour?"

"No. I was a lawyer, and you saved me from a disgruntled client."

Okay…so people were able to enter my dream, but the experience they had with me was not necessarily the same one I had with them. I'm getting a headache.

Then Linda gets close again. She takes my hand, demanding my attention, and she's making me incredibly uncomfortable.

"But the aliens are not as clever as they think they are," she says.

Smiles and nods and hallelujahs from the assembled.

"They make mistakes. They have weaknesses. And they can be defeated."

The group cheers.

She gets closer still. Her eyes glow with energy and purpose.

"They're advanced technologically, but they are arrogant, and that makes them vulnerable. And they really don't understand us."

There is a general grumble of agreement.

"What don't they understand?" Jerry asks.

Portia answers Jerry's question with another question. "Human intuition and the survival instinct?"

"But the powers they gave you can be turned against them, bro!" Israel shouts.

"You are the key, Harold," Linda insists with her face still close to mine.

"You can turn them away!" the excitable Park Girl cries as she jumps up to her feet again.

"We will be your soldiers!" Israel declares as he shoots up from his chair as well.

Then they all rise in a unified show of frenzied commitment. If I wasn't creeped out enough—that really puts the cherry on top.

The only ones left seated are me, Jerry, and Linda.

"So just to clarify," I say, turning to the group and away from Linda and the spell I think she's trying to put me under. "What do they want, specifically? Besides Wyoming?"

"Everything!" Israel cries. "They don't want to share the planet. They want to control it and control us. They will use us as a slave race, and when they're done with us, we will be discarded like garbage! They will suck the planet dry, and then they'll move on to the next conquest and leave the corpse of our world behind."

"Okay—got it. Thanks."

"Señor," the imaginary gardener says. "They have already been in touch with the Mexican government. After they take Wyoming, they will bring in our laborers to help them build their cities. In return, they have promised Mexico that they will destroy the United States and then return the continent to the rightful owners."

In a world of crazy, I seem to have found the mother lode.

"They have made promises like this all over the world!" Park Girl excitedly adds. "They have begun to pit us against each other to build on the mistrust that already exists."

"Time is running out, brother," Israel says. "People will begin to panic. They'll be at each other's throats. That's what the aliens want— to get us to the point where we'll have no choice but to submit to their authority."

"And then we will become extinct," Linda ruefully adds.

"We have to drive them out," Israel says. "We need you to join the fight—you are the unifier." Israel looks at me expectantly as if the fate of the world depends on what I say next. "We can't do it without you, bro."

There is a pause. The group looks sad as they nervously wait, hoping for my positive response to what they have proposed. Then suddenly they all sit at the exact same time.

And then the colonel shows up in my head.

I know we're not exactly on speaking terms, but I just wanted to drop by and wish you luck, son. If you figure out what these crackpots are talkin' about, give me a holler, will ya'? Don't really make no difference, though. Not at this point. The fat lady's already singin', son. You're cooked. You better start runnin', boy—

"Stop. I'm done with you. Just stop!" I say this out loud when I probably should have used my inner voice. Now the group looks more worried than sad.

Jerry taps me on the shoulder.

"Are you okay, Mr. Geeg?"

"I've been better," I say.

Is it possible that these people are right? Is that why the colonel just showed up, because he's worried about this meeting? Is that why he told me to run? Sid, if you're hearing any of this, I think we need to talk. Anyway, when in doubt, blather.

"Here's what I'm thinking," I begin. "Let me talk to Sid about these concerns—"

"There is no compromise to be made with them!" the Mexican shouts.

"Uh, huh. Well, you know," I continue, being careful not to offend their rabid fanaticism. "I understand that you're all very nervous and excited about things, but let me talk to him again. I'll let him know your concerns and see how he responds."

I'm getting looks of utter discouragement. I continue in spite of this.

"Maybe we're misreading the message. There seems to be a lot of different stuff coming through, so…let's not jump the gun. Let's be sure about things before we go starting a war or something, okay? Let me talk to Sid, and maybe he can add a little more perspective to things."

Horrified gasps come from the group.

"Well, I'm sorry, but we want to be sure, don't we? Because it's a little confusing right now. It's possible, and please don't freak out about this, but it's possible that what Sid told me is still true, and the information you're getting is from the other faction. I don't know how you people are so sure about things, I really don't. Personally, I think there's more going on here that we're not even seeing yet. That is a possibility, isn't it?"

More murmurs and rumblings.

"A few things," Linda patiently begins.

I don't even want to look at her, but I gradually do.

"First, you must never tell him about us. Second, if you're thinking about a negotiation, that will never happen. From their end or from ours. Third, in case you don't know, they aren't even here yet."

"They aren't here? Where are they?"

Again, Linda's clear, bright eyes peer into mine. "They are projecting themselves. Like what you can do. They are more spirit than flesh and blood. They are manipulating events from a distance. In a month, they'll arrive. Their goal is for the world to be in chaos before they even get here." She is determined, magnetic, and unwavering. "They are planning an invasion. There will be no negotiating."

"Excuse me." Jerry taps Linda on the arm, unwittingly disrupting her hold over me. "What about the birds? They're real, aren't they? There's one circling above this house right now."

Linda turns to Jerry and smiles as she speaks. "That is a kind of projection as well."

"A projection that can rip off people's heads?" I challenge.

"That was in your dream?" Portia says as a question from across the room. "They haven't done anything like that here? They represent the threat of violence? But they can spy and overhear things? And then the aliens can tap into what they see?"

"And we would not like them to know about this meeting." Linda glares at me, and I glare back. My fear about whether Linda would be on our side and what the consequences would be if she was not...not only am I frightened about it, but I'm getting a little angry as well.

She softens her tone before continuing. "We're doing what we can to block them out." She gestures over to the older couple who have never stopped waving at the ceiling. "That's Sherman and Doris. They're trying to run some interference for us."

"To block them from hearing us?" Jerry will believe just about anything, but I can tell that he's struggling with this one.

"Exactly," Linda confirms.

Sherman and Doris take a break to smile at us and then immediately go back to work. The similarity is really stunning. It's as if Roy and Alice have come back to life and are trying again to give me shelter from the storm.

"What about my daughter that's coming? Do you know that my wife is pregnant?"

"That must end," Linda says. "It belongs to them. We can't let that child be born."

That does it. No more Mr. Nice Guy. The house starts to shake. More horrified gasps, and then everything goes black.

CHAPTER FIFTY-FIVE

YOU'RE BREAKING MY HEART
YOU'RE TEARING IT APART SO FUCK YOU

I'm not sure why everything went black and is still black. Somebody might have hit me over the head, or I might have jumped back into a dream or a coma. Maybe I went into escape mode and did a little time-space jump. I mean, could you blame me?

Breathe. Wherever I am, I can still think, so maybe I can take advantage of this little visit into blackness and get some things sorted out.

Okay, it comes down to one of two things. The weirdos at Linda's place are telling me that the alien is not to be trusted, that Sid is lying, the real alien agenda is to take over everything, and I am essentially their secret weapon designed to wreak havoc on all of mankind. Or Sid is our only salvation—we go with him or we're outa here.

I've said it before and I'll say it again—why me? To be honest, if I were to consider for a moment that what the cabal of weirdos told me is true, then *why me* is really not so hard to understand. I'm actually the perfect choice. I'm not famous or smart or particularly talented. I am, in fact, uniquely qualified *because* of my stunning mediocrity. Give me a little power and some extraordinary talent, and, baby, I'm your man!

But wait, not so fast. Maybe I'm not the man I was. Maybe Sid's training coma backfired and instead of making me their powerful but mindless Manchurian Candidate, I've become a better, stronger, clearer thinking version of myself. Thought they had Barney Fife but they got Dirty Harry instead. Didn't see that one coming, did you, Sid?

Okay, stop patting yourself on the back so much; you'll give yourself a hernia. What we need to do here—I have no freaking idea. But I won't give up my daughter! Never will I do that. So screw Linda and her weirdos. They're not touching my kid! No way am I losing another one.

So where does this leave me? It leaves me stupid and alone in the dark, literally and figuratively. So let's start over.

The world is in a very dangerous place. And I mean even before all this alien crap went down. Humans are at each other's throats all over the planet. We just can't seem to evolve past it. We are an immature species with big weapons and greedy hearts, and if left to our own devices, we probably won't survive our self-destructive nature. So assuming that Sid is being honest and we do what he says, and if that might give us at least a chance at survival—maybe that's the only way for us. Maybe human beings need an outside power to take control of our big brains and damaged psyches—to dictate terms and teach us how to behave. They'll cure us of disease, help us heal the planet. No war. No starvation. No strife. What's not to like?

And if Linda's people are right and Sid is lying, and the alien's plan is to destroy us no matter what we do…maybe I'm missing something here, but what difference does it make? We're heading in that direction anyway. So why not go along with Sid, then? Besides, I'm sure that resistance is futile. Every sci-fi fan knows that. What could we possibly do against them? They're smarter, more advanced, and they do great impressions. We wouldn't have a chance. Sid's proposal is the only real possibility we have for survival, and then hopefully we get to live in a world where no one will be in want of anything ever again. It'll suck for country music, but we have to make sacrifices somewhere—

Oh my God! Wait a minute…suddenly I'm jumping out of where I am, and I'm not in the dark anymore. I'm back at Linda's place, unconscious, and lying flat on my back on the floor. Everyone in the group is gathered in a circle around me. I'm watching all of this from above. I'm not in my body. I see faint cords, or threads, attached to each person in the group and then connected to me, going into my head and my arms. Some people in the group are smiling and seem very happy about this. Linda and Israel are arguing, and some others look pitifully confused. What are they doing to me?

Then I'm back to black.

"What in the holy hell!"

Great, now along with everything else, I feel like I've just been raped. Were they taking something from me? Or connecting something? I have no idea what that was. Jesus Christ, that creeped me out. Okay, keep it together. Breathe...

Okay, so it's Sid's way or no way at all, that's pretty much what we're talking about here. But damn it—it's just not right! "Do what we say and all will be well. If not, we exterminate you?" What the hell is that? Play ball with us, or else? It's arrogant, it's ignorant, it's imperialistic, and it completely sucks! So pardon my French but fuck you very much! It's our planet! Our destiny! We produced Einstein. Shakespeare. Dylan. Martin Luther King. Gandhi. Human beings are worth it! What have you got, Sid? Lies and threats and promises of a utopian future as long as you're calling all the shots? And what about Rebecca? I should trust you after that?

Okay, now we're getting somewhere—well, not really. Breathe. Inconceivable, I know, but now I'm more confused than ever. I'm going to have to talk to him again, that's all.

"Sid, where the hell are you? Where the hell am I? We need a heart-to-heart, buddy. There's more to this than you're telling me, isn't there? If you want me to do this for you, Sid, you've got to level with me now. You've got to convince me. The ball's in your court. So what do you say?"

I don't know where he is. In my gut I still want to trust him, but I need some answers. And then, maybe after that, I can come up with a plan to unite everyone on Earth, for one purpose or another, and then hopefully save the world from extermination.

Jesus Christ! I can't even balance a checkbook!

———

I wake up in a hospital again. Jerry and Kelly are sitting in the room staring at me.

"Here we go again," I groan.

"Are you okay?" Kelly asks.

"What happened?"

"You passed out," Jerry tells me. "The house started to shake, and then you just fell over. I called 911, and they brought you here."

"Where is here?" I ask.

"Verdugo Hills. I called Kelly and picked her up at the house," Jerry explains while enjoying my vanilla fudge pudding.

"Then I called Dr. Bloom," Kelly says.

"Of course you did."

"Harold!" an agonized voice calls from down the hall.

"What the hell is that?" Jerry cries.

"I think that's why we're here."

It's like a script that you've already read, but it's been revised and you're reading it for a second time. The characters and situations are similar, but not exact, so you have no idea where it's about to go.

"Harold? Are you here yet?" the child's voice pleads.

"Mr. Geeg, I think you're up. We're here so that you can heal somebody."

"We are? I usually just do that kind of thing by appointment only."

"And I'm pretty sure we're going to talk to Sid now, too."

I start to get out of the bed, but my head is not quite right yet. I feel a lot of pressure in my forehead and have to lie back down.

"Give me a hand. I'm still a little shaky."

They both come over to help me up. Kelly's stomach growls angrily.

"Oh man," she complains. Then she grabs hold of my arm with a grip that could crush steel. In one effortless motion she gets me to my feet as if she is lifting a pillow.

"Been working out?" I ask.

"No. Why?"

"Quite a grip you got there, honey."

Her stomach gurgles like a five-gallon bottle of Sparkletts does when you put it into the dispenser.

"You better take it easy, Harold," Kelly lectures. "You've been unconscious for a while, you know?"

"I'm fine now."

"You still look a little gray, and it's not a good color for you. Oh, and I did see the specialist today. But, you realize, that for me to be pregnant is completely ridiculous and impossible."

"So, what happened?"

"They said I'm pretty much pregnant."

347

"Impossible ain't what it used to be," Jerry says, exactly as he said it in the dream.

Then I start to lose my balance. Kelly corrects that for me, effortlessly supporting me with her grip of steel.

"My body is acting like it's about four months into it," she says, hardly aware that she just kept me from falling. "But I feel pretty great, actually. I feel really strong. Except for the occasional bouts of projectile vomiting, I'm feeling really good."

"Harold!" the child calls again but more insistently this time.

"Do I have clothes here?" I ask.

———

The young voice continues to call as we make our way down the hallway. As our pace quickens, my head starts to feel only slightly more connected to the rest of my body.

"I want Harold!"

As we get close, the child's mother comes out of his room to meet us. Much as in the dream, she's a wreck. Worn out and at the end of her rope.

"You're Harold?" she asks. Her eyes are desperate, and her voice quivers from the strain of what she's been through.

"Yes. I'm Harold."

"You'll see him?"

"Of course."

She steps aside to let us in. I talk to Kelly and Jerry first—to give them a heads-up.

"It's an aging disease. It's a little kid who looks like an old man." I turn back to his mother for confirmation, "That's what it is, isn't it?"

She confirms with a nod.

"Are you Death?" she asks.

The question leaves me dumb. Jerry covers for me, again.

"He's not Death. He's just an actor."

"He said you would come. I didn't know you were an actor, though. Have I seen you in anything?" she asks, expectantly.

"Probably not," Jerry tells her.

I lead the way in, hoping to circumvent any further discussion of my woefully insignificant résumé.

He is a perfect match for when I saw him in the dream. Though it still takes a moment to regroup after first taking sight of him.

"Hi, Harold," he says. "We've been dreaming about you."

"You're Joshua?"

"Yes."

"Joshua, this is Jerry and my wife, Kelly."

"Yes, I know," he says as cheerfully as he can.

Kelly and Jerry smile at him but are unable to speak.

"Are they afraid of me?" Joshua asks.

"No, they just want to help you. They feel how you hurt, that's all. They're not afraid of you, Joshua."

"I don't hurt so much since you came."

"Good," Kelly manages, "that's very good, Joshua."

"The man said that you would help me. You saved me in my dream, too. Jerry did when you brought him to me," Joshua says with a child's hopefulness.

"We're going to try, Joshua," Jerry tells him.

"Who's Mr. Geeg? He told me there would be a Mr. Geeg here, too."

"I'm Mr. Geeg," Jerry says.

"I'm Mr. Geeg, too."

"You're both Mr. Geeg?"

"It's something we call each other, but we can't remember why," I tell him.

"It's very annoying, actually," Kelly confirms with a roll of her eyes.

"That's funny," Joshua seems genuinely delighted by our Geeg-ness. And then his head suddenly falls forward onto his chest.

We brace ourselves for contact.

"Hellooo, Harold!" Sid's voice comes from Joshua's body and vibrates powerfully all over the room. Sid is getting stronger. The implications of which are unsettling.

"You got to be kidding me," Jerry whispers.

"Holy lisping Moses!" Kelly marvels.

"Glad you all could make it!" Sid roars.

"No need to shout, Sid. We can hear you just fine," I let him know.

"Am I loud? Sorry, I can adjust that."

CHAPTER FIFTY-SIX

ALL ALONG
THE WATCHTOWER

Sid adjusts his volume, and things start off quite civilly.

"It's nice to have you all together," Sid says. "To see you three again is a real shot in the arm."

"Again? Have we done this before?" Kelly asks.

"More times than you realize. From when you were young."

"See, I told you I was young once," I say. As is so often the case, Kelly ignores my attempt at humor.

"And your name is Sid?" she asks, instead.

"Not really, but Sid is good for now."

"Well, Sid, we have some questions," Kelly tells him.

"Great! That's what I'm here for!" Sid says, seeming eager to please. "I know things are happening quickly now, and you're getting some conflicting input. We don't need any distractions at this point. So anything I can do to clear up any doubts or apprehensions—I'm more than happy to do that."

I'm not looking forward to the conflict that I know is coming. Sid already seems aware that something is up. I'm concerned about what his bird spies might be telling him, and here's a terrifying thought—what if he can read my mind? Is he in my head right now?

"You sound so human. Like the guy next door," Kelly says.

"We've been studying you for a long time. We've picked up a thing or two."

"Are you humanlike?" Kelly asks. "If our baby is part you, and part us…"

I flash on that dream I had when I met the man in black, who I assumed was the colonel.

"She will be humanlike enough to pass," Sid tells her. "People will be comfortable with her. She will be a leader who will be much beloved. You will be very proud."

If there are no other parties involved, as discussed earlier, and if the aliens are really of one mind, then—is the colonel Sid? I know he loves to do impersonations. Is Sid the Southern voice that torments me, and did he drive my daughter to suicide?

"Holy crap!" I suddenly blurt out loud.

"Is there a problem, Harold?" Sid inquires.

I take a moment to gather myself.

"Well, we've been hearing some things, Sid," I begin, hoping that I'm not about to annihilate the whole human race ahead of schedule. "It's not necessarily what I believe, but it's what we're hearing out there. That your intentions are not exactly what you've explained them to be. I mean, to be clear and frank about this—"

"I will be as frank as I can. And then I'll be Harry," he says with an odd chuckle.

This time I'm the one to ignore an attempt at humor.

"We're hearing that there really are no factions among you. That it's all one way of thinking about things, and what you're thinking doesn't exactly have our best interests at heart."

It comes out a little sooner than I would have liked. I thought I'd ease into it a little more. But there it was, so here we go.

There's an electric silence; I can feel it on my skin. Then the room starts to rumble.

"Are you doing that?" Jerry whispers harshly in my ear.

"I don't think so," I whisper back.

"Earthquake?" Kelly asks.

"I think it's him," I say.

Then it stops, except for a picture on the wall that continues to bounce around for a few more seconds.

"There are cults that are misrepresenting us," Sid finally says. "There are shadow organizations that you need to be wary of." Sid's volume is up again, and another side of his personality is being revealed. "They are the ones not to be trusted! They are *liars*! They are *worshippers of greed*!"

The windows rattle. Sid has suddenly turned into Ned Beatty's thundering, godlike chairman in *Network* (if you're old enough to remember that one).

"If you listen to them, you will be misinformed, led astray, and distracted from the task at hand!"

I ask him a question with an inside voice that I'm hoping he cannot hear. "Can you hear my thoughts?" For lack of something more creative.

There is another pause. Whether it's to consider my silent question or just to compose himself, I can't tell.

"We've given you powers to reveal the truth to the world," Sid continues in a much more relaxed tone of voice. "Some pretty cool stuff, don't you think? And wait till you see what Kelly can do! Don't waste time overthinking things. I wish there was more time to sit around with donuts and coffee and throw it around, but, unfortunately, there is not."

"But in reality, Sid, we couldn't really do that because you aren't even here yet, are you? You're like a voice projection, or something like that?"

"It's different for us. Physically we are in transport, but we are quite present in this form as well. You are not talking to a projection. This is me in a form that you don't understand. No offense, it's just not in your range of understanding yet."

"The birds are not physical then?" Jerry asks.

"They are capable of becoming very physical. They are here to protect you."

"And to spy on us?" I ask in a somewhat accusatory tone.

"That's an ugly way to put it." Sid sounds offended by the question. "We are just trying to stay as informed as possible."

Then the room starts shaking again, but this time I'm pretty sure it's me.

"Use this boy," Sid continues in spite of my power play. "Heal him and show the world what you can do. It will open the door to communication and cooperation. It will demonstrate our goodwill and all that we have to offer."

"Are there other children?" Kelly asks.

"Only one. You will come to know him."

"Any other countries involved. Like Mexico, maybe?"

I wait a moment, but Sid does not respond.

"I mean, are there other kinds of deals going on? Other arrangements? Frankly, I'm a little concerned about what we're hearing, and since time is short and we've all got places to go, let me just put it out there. I'm not sure if you're trying to make peace, or if you're just setting us up."

The shaking in the room intensifies. There is motion to it. Things start jumping around on Joshua's nightstand, pictures are banging against the wall, and it's getting hard for us to stand without losing our balance. The shaking is now accompanied by a distinct earthquake-type rumble.

"Whoa, easy, big fella!" Sid jokes, but I can sense concern in his tone.

"What's your take on it, Sid?" I feel an advantage, so I press on.

"Lies," he says.

"Is this an invasion, Sid?"

"Boy, oh boy." Sid laughs in that particularly disturbing way of his. "They are really filling your head with a lot of crazy stuff. You better stay away from those crackpots, I'm telling you."

Crackpots! So there you have it. The colonel called them that too.

Kelly takes a seat as the shaking gets even more violent. Sid and I are both doing it. Testing each other. He's letting me know that he is not to be trifled with, and I'm trying to tell him the same.

The rumbles get louder, and whatever you have to say has to be said loudly. Hence, the return of the Ned Beatty effect.

"Do you think I'd go through all of this," Sid thunders, "put in all this time if that's what it was? We've been developing a way to do this peacefully. That is the goal. That's why we started looking all those years ago for the right combination. For the right people to make it work."

"Why did Rebecca have to die?" Kelly shouts above the din.

"It was not our intention."

"So why did it happen?" Kelly is pressing now, too.

"It was an unfortunate miscalculation of her mental state. The new child will be stronger. She will be brilliant. She will be better."

Kelly shoots to her feet in a rage. "She will not be better!" She manages to get herself across the room and right up into Joshua's face. "I'll cut you some slack because you're not from around here, but that's not the smartest thing to say to a grieving mother, and don't you ever say that again!"

In response, the rumbling dies down, and then all of the shaking stops. I think it was me first and then Sid. Kelly pretty much snaps us out of it.

She steps away from Joshua looking flustered. She just yelled at a little boy in an old man's body who really has nothing to do with any of this. It's not an easy thing to assimilate. She steps in between where Jerry and I are standing, and we all wait to see how Sid will respond.

"Yes, there is still much to learn," Sid calmly admits. "I hope we can learn from each other." The rumbling starts again. Kelly smacks me hard on the arm. I'm again impressed by her strength.

"Ow."

"Well, just cut it out then," she admonishes.

The rumbling stops.

"I hope you will think this over carefully," Sid says. "Make the connections. I promise you that my intentions are honorable. I only want to avoid misery and suffering. That's my goal. Please save this boy. That's the first step. Time is short. I have to go."

"How do I save him?" Jerry pleads.

"You know how," Sid tells him.

Joshua's head rises from his chest. Sid is gone. You can feel it.

"Did he tell you what you needed to know?" he feebly asks.

"He wants you to get better, and he wants me to help you," Jerry says.

Joshua perks up, "I knew it!" I knew it!"

"Do you think Sid is lying?" Kelly whispers to me.

"I'm having a very serious déjà vu moment right now," Jerry whispers on my other side. "I've done this before, haven't I, Mr. Geeg?"

Jerry goes to Joshua's bedside and takes his hand. "Kid, we all want you to get better, and I think we have the power to do that for you. I'm going to send something through to you. We all love you, Joshua. We think you are a special boy. So here it comes. We're sending all our love and energy and everything that's good…Uh, Mr. Geeg?"

"Yes, Mr. Geeg?"

"All my hairs are standing up."

It's true, he is looking very Don King–like.

"Keep going. Don't stop! You're doing great!"

"Whoa! Do you feel that, Joshua? It's happening right now. You're already getting better! You are going to be strong and healthy, and let me be the first to congratulate you because we took a vote, and you, my little friend, are now an honorary Mr. Geeg!"

Joshua reaches out for a hug, and Jerry gives him one.

"Joshua, you need a nap now. A reboot. And when you wake up, young Mr. Geeg, the whole world will be a lot better."

Jerry turns back to us with a look of absolute wonder on his face. "Something is tingling here. Something is definitely going on."

"Keep holding his hand, Mr. Geeg!"

Joshua smiles, and just like in the dream, I see it start to happen again. Color comes to his cheeks, his eyes sparkle, and then he starts to glow. He takes a deep breath, and then a contented sigh. Joshua closes his eyes and falls into a peaceful sleep.

Jerry gets up from the bed. He looks tired but completely awed by what's transpired. We do the special handshake, and then Kelly gives him a hug that nearly knocks the wind out of him.

———

We go back into the hallway and find Joshua's mother waiting for us.

"Is everything all right?" she asks.

"Yes, everything went really well," I tell her.

Jerry takes her hand, "I think he's going to get better. It was an amazing thing. I…I don't…" He struggles to find the words. "Something pretty amazing just happened in there!"

Then an upset nurse rapidly approaches. "What are you doing out here? You need to go back to your room this instant!"

"I'm fine now," I insist.

"We have more tests!"

"Maybe tomorrow."

"You shouldn't be walking around like this! I'm calling for help. You can't just—"

I put a hand on her shoulder. "There is no problem here. It is fine for me and my friends to go now. It's the best thing, really. Stop worrying. Stop. Just stop."

After a confused moment, she smiles and continues down the hallway as if she had never talked to us at all.

"Damn, Mr. Geeg," Jerry is impressed.

"Are you angels?" Joshua's mother asks.

"No. I'm a comic, he's an actor, and she's in bathing suits."

"What is your name?" I ask her.

"Jane," she tells me.

"Jane, that's right." I give her a card. "I think Joshua is going to get better now, and then we need to sit down and talk. Call me. I'll explain what's going on," I say, although I'm fairly certain that she already knows.

"Bless you. For him and for me. For all of us," she says.

"Go in and see him," Kelly suggests.

"I almost gave up hope," Jane says and then gives Kelly a hug. "Did you feel those earthquakes? It's the beginning—the connection. Isn't it wonderful?" Then she goes into the room to see her son. We hear her gasp as the door closes behind her.

I guess I didn't get the memo. The connection? What connection?

As we turn to leave, we find Israel blocking our way. He holds a big flower arrangement with Get Well Soon balloons attached.

"You're leaving?" Israel asks, surprised to see me on my feet.

"Yes, I'm much better now."

"Good. Good. I just want to tell you. From me and the others. We mean you no harm. Whatever you think is best is what we'll do. We're on your side in this. Is this the wife?"

"Yes, this is the wife," Kelly confirms, her eyes narrowing into slits.

"Something is happening," Israel says. "We debated about the baby after you left. Linda was wrong. She shouldn't have said that to you."

"What about the baby?" Kelly asks.

"They're worried about what the baby will be like. What her agenda might be," Jerry explains.

"Her agenda? It's a baby!"

Israel smiles, and it's as disarming as Linda's smile was in the dream. I feel instantly connected to him. Like a brother. Like the way it is with Mr. Geeg.

"Some crazy shit got said," Israel says. "Some big mistakes got made. But we need to be together on this. That's the most important thing because there's something new coming through—a lot of us picked up on it right after you left. Before, we were getting things from Linda. But now, it's different. Now, we're all getting it. It's a feeling. I'm not sure how to describe it, but it's different than it was before. It's like some switch just turned on, bro. I hope it's not a trap, but it feels like something good is coming. Linda didn't buy it, though. She got angry, and she left."

"Linda left? Where did she go?" I ask.

"I don't know, but she was leading us in the wrong direction. Things are changing now, really fast. She didn't like what was happening. It got ugly, bro. We were wrong for following her. Like you said, more information is coming through. This whole thing—something big is about to happen."

"What's going to happen?"

"Not sure, but time is up, and it's coming. It's very big."

"I thought we had a month."

"Something got rescheduled, bro. We're having another meeting, and you need to be there."

I'm not sure if he's going to let us pass him or what he's going to do. I don't want to force anything or try to control him. I just want to get out of here to think.

"Israel, we have a few things to do right now, okay?"

He gives me his card, and Christ Almighty, it's a security company! My head starts to ache again.

"We'd like another chance. I need to protect you. The whole world is at stake, brother."

He extends his hand and I shake it.

"Did you feel those earthquakes?" he asks.

CHAPTER FIFTY-SEVEN

BABY YOU CAN
DRIVE MY CAR

We manage our way out of the hospital without further incident. Kelly drives Jerry's minivan. The smell of cigars is just as strong as it was before. Jerry rides shotgun, and I'm in the back.

"It's a good thing I'm driving, or I'd be throwing up on myself by now," Kelly says.

"It's the only place left for me to smoke so cut me some slack," Jerry says.

"You shouldn't be smoking those things, anyway. They're just as bad as cigarettes, you know?"

"You wouldn't want me walking the streets viceless. Believe me, that wouldn't be good for anybody."

Kelly sticks her head out the window and takes some dramatically deep breaths. Jerry takes a cigar out of his shirt pocket and defiantly puts it into his mouth. Kelly grabs it and throws it out the window.

"Hey! That's a twenty-five-cent cigar!" Jerry cries and then turns to me in the back seat. "Even after I perform a freaking miracle, she gives me shit."

"She's an ungodly heathen," I say.

"Yeah, but are you sure you did it, or did Sid do it for you?" Kelly challenges.

"I did it. I got all tingly, didn't I?"

"Harold, do you think Sid is manipulating things?" Kelly makes eye contact with me in the rearview mirror. "Did he make you pass out so you'd have to go to the hospital, so that what happened would happen? How much control does this guy have over us?"

"I don't know. I was shaking a house at the time. I might have passed out from exertion."

"I think he set the whole thing up," she says.

"So that Jerry saves Joshua?" I ask.

"Yes, of course," she responds, as if it should be obvious.

"Makes sense," I agree. "And now we go out with our godlike powers and parade the miracle kid around."

"Gotta hand it to him," Jerry says. "Good point of sale."

"Absolutely," I say. "Get ourselves on a late-night talk show. Cause a world-wide panic. Execute their game plan, and then they execute us. Or we make it easy for them and execute each other. Yeah, I think you're probably right. He set the whole thing up."

After I have successfully sucked all the air out of the room—or the minivan in this case—a silence ensues.

Jerry turns back to me again with bulging eyeballs. "But wait a minute. The guy, Israel. He said things were changing. That something good was coming, didn't he?"

"Yeah," I answer, "but he also said it might be a trap. It might just be the next phase of the invasion. Get us trusting and comfortable so that we're easier to defeat."

"So, what are we talking about then?" Jerry asks. "Going to war with them?"

"I hope not, Mr. Geeg, but maybe we can push back a little. Make them think twice about getting into something with us."

"How are we going to do that?" Jerry cries. "Join up with Linda's people and start waving at the ceiling?"

"We use what they gave us against them."

"Yeah, okay, great. That explains everything. Thank you." Jerry throws up his hands and sits back in his seat.

"We push back. You saw how he reacted in that room. Sid did not like being challenged. When we questioned him, he changed—he got really angry."

"Yeah, but that doesn't necessarily mean that he wants to destroy us!" Jerry says, turning back to me again.

"I'm just saying that we might want to prepare ourselves for the possibility that we're being set up, and Sid might have just given us an indication of vulnerability."

"An indication of what?" Kelly asks.

"An indication of vulnerability," I repeat.

"Listen, General MacArthur. Can you dumb that down a little?"

"I mean, we saw that he can get rattled. Maybe there's a way to take advantage of that."

Kelly's stomach makes a loud grinding noise. I guess we're getting used to it because nobody bothers to editorialize.

"Okay, just so I'm clear," she continues, "and before I start sending out baby shower invitations. Sid is *not* our friend now? Because I thought we were swinging the other way a minute ago."

"Now wait a minute," says Jerry with a confused-looking grimace. "What I don't get is this. Why would they give us all this power if they don't want to help us? Okay, scratch that, forget it. It's because they just want us to *think* that they're helping us, is that it?" He doesn't wait an answer. "Okay, but wouldn't they have taken it into consideration that we might turn on them? And then, like you said, use what they gave us against them? They're very advanced, Mr. Geeg. You'd think they would have thought about that kind of thing, wouldn't you?"

Jerry takes another cigar from his pocket.

"Maybe they gave us just enough to impress," I say, "but not enough to cause problems for them."

"Okay, so how do we fight them then? We don't even know what they are yet! They're way ahead of us technologically. They'll wipe us out in two seconds, and then we lose everything: the healing, the mind manipulations, all of it! And I have to tell you, I'm getting very attached to this healing thing. It's good for my self-esteem, and I'm not so sure I want to give that up right away. There's really no point in fighting them, is what I'm trying to say. There's no upside."

"What about the baby?" Kelly asks.

"We'll figure it out," I say.

Kelly pounds on the steering wheel.

"Those people from this meeting you went to, who you're now apparently starting to agree with, they didn't think the baby is such a great idea because she's going to be part us and part them and grow up to be some kind of alien protector of the realm. So what exactly are we talking about here, Harold? *What happens to the baby?*"

I have never seen her get this explosive before. Except in the dream, when I could hardly recognize who she was anymore. I'm sure it's the pregnancy doing a number on her.

"Relax, nobody is touching the baby," I promise.

"Damn straight they're not," she fumes.

"But wait a minute!" Jerry intervenes. "Israel said they were rethinking the whole thing about the baby, didn't he?"

"He did," I agree.

"Oh man," Jerry moans. "And what about Linda? She left because she didn't like how this new nice feeling thing was going, right? She was the militant one, so doesn't her leaving mean...what does it mean?"

"I don't know, Mr. Geeg. I heard the same stuff you did. If I knew, I'd tell you. I'm just considering the possibilities, is all."

"Well, what does your world-famous gut tell you?"

"The gut is undecided. I'm not sure what the gut is doing right now."

"This is getting unreasonable," he complains. "As in, this shit is impossible to figure out. I'm not kidding, man. This is something a sober man just shouldn't have to deal with."

"I'm not giving up this baby," Kelly reiterates.

"What time is it?" I ask.

"Six thirty," Jerry answers.

"I'm supposed to meet Rodger at seven thirty."

"Who's Rodger, again?" Kelly asks with increasing agitation.

"He's my new lawyer who turns out to be an old friend. Berman is off the case. He's up on some charges, so he's on leave from the firm."

"Oh, that's just peachy!" she cries, and then smacks the steering wheel again.

Jerry almost says something to protect his car, but he doesn't. A wise decision, I'm sure.

"I'm supposed to meet him at his house," I continue.

"Where's his house?" Kelly demands, and I'm starting to worry about her blood pressure.

"Pacific Palisades," I tell her.

"Well, I guess that's where we're going then."

She makes an insane U-turn that nearly puts an end to us before the aliens even get a crack at it.

"It'll take about an hour and half to get there with this traffic," she says, apparently unaware that she nearly flipped the van and missed causing a major accident by about a fraction of an inch. Then she reaches over and grabs Jerry's second cigar from his mouth and throws that one out the window, too. "I'm pregnant with what might be the most important baby ever to drool on the earth, do you mind?"

"Fine," Jerry concedes. "Sure you wouldn't like me to drive for a while? You seem a little tense."

"I'm fine. Don't be ridiculous."

My head is really starting to throb, and I'm getting sharp pains behind my eyeballs again.

"Maybe we can put this trip off," I suggest. "I can call and reschedule."

"We have to go, Harold. We have to deal with this kind of stuff, too, don't we?"

"Do we?"

"Your court date is on Friday, and you haven't even met this new guy yet! Drunk driving and fleeing the scene of an accident after nearly hitting a pedestrian? That's serious stuff, Harold! You could go to jail!"

She's probably right about the meeting with Rodger being important but probably not for the reasons she's thinking. The court date really seems insignificant to me at this point. Just a waste of time and energy.

"Uh, Mr. Geeg?" Jerry is looking back at something behind us.

"Yes, Mr. Geeg?"

"Your boyfriend is following us."

"Which boyfriend?"

"Israel, bro. And he's got two friends with him. Big, nasty-looking, head-bashing types."

I look back and wave at them. Israel waves back. The others do not.

"I can't believe this," Kelly groans.

"Anybody have an Advil or anything? My head is killing me."

Jerry leans into the back seat with his arms reaching out for my head. "Come here, let me heal that shit for you."

CHAPTER FIFTY-EIGHT

LIFE IS VERY SHORT
AND THERE'S NO TIME

Jerry gets his hands on me. I think he's trying to make a point about what he's capable of and what he can do without any help from Sid. He puts his hands on my head, around the temples. Then he moves them around all over my face and then on top of my head. I do believe he's trying to locate where I'm feeling the pain.

"I'm getting that tingly thing again," he says. "And I mean that in a completely nonsexual way."

"It's behind my eyes, too," I tell him.

"You don't have to tell me where it is! It's not like I just started doing this yesterday, you know! Actually…it was yesterday, wasn't it? Anyway, white light and love for my good buddy Mr. Geeg. Easy now, here we go."

I catch sight of Kelly in the rearview mirror rolling her eyes.

"Oh, yeah. It's coming off you now. I feel it in my fingers and…bam! That's it! Bingo bango! Congratulations, you are officially healed." He very abruptly returns to his seat and starts shaking out his hands as if he's trying to get rid of something sticky. Then he turns back to me with a big grin on his face. "How do you feel?"

"Uh, actually, I feel pretty good. I really do. It's pretty much gone."

"Pretty much?" he starts reaching over for me again.

"No, I'm good, I'm good. Thank you."

"See that?" he boasts to Kelly.

"You're really better?" she asks.

"Yup. I gotta say. My hair must look like shit, but I'm feeling pretty good."

Kelly puts up a hand, and Jerry high fives her.

"But if you smoke in this car," she tells him. "I don't care how many people you cure, I'll still have to kill you."

The traffic gets so bad on the freeway that we decide to ignore the GPS. We get off and try the side streets. That isn't much better, but at least we're moving.

"I think we lost him," Kelly says.

Jerry turns to look. "Nope, there he is. He just got behind that truck for a minute."

"Shit!" Being followed does nothing to improve Kelly's mood.

As we're creeping along, we come upon a park on my left-hand side. In an open space are a group of people. They are well dressed and of all colors. Déjà vu all over again. They're in a circle meditating and swaying together, a few of them are waving their arms in the air, like the Napa Valley ringers back at Linda's place. I notice that there's some movement in the trees. Like a breeze coming through. Again, I'm reminded of my dream and how the trees moved in Brand Park after I broke up the purse-snatching incident. It's a still, hot day with no wind anywhere. Except for here. Are they doing it? Putting out some kind of energy and making the trees move? I get that tingly feeling that Jerry is so fond of. A few of them suddenly turn toward us and smile. If we weren't pressed for time, I would have insisted that we stop and talk to these people. I feel an affection for them, and this might sound a little odd, but it's like they are my children. It's that kind of connection. I return their smiles and wave as we drive away. Despite my doubts about God, I feel very Popelike all of a sudden.

My headache is back with a vengeance. I keep quiet about it, though.

CHAPTER FIFTY-NINE

DREAM
WEAVER

The going is painfully slow. Kelly gets on and off the freeway several times. She can't shake Israel, though. I call Rodger to let him know that we will probably be a little late arriving. My headache has evolved into a throbbing in the back of my head. It doesn't really hurt that much. The rhythm of it actually starts to relax me, and I fall asleep. Here's the dream:

I'm driving the Prius, and it's a very dark night. I'm preparing to get onto a freeway entrance ramp when I notice a car pull into the driveway of a building on my right. There's a parking gate where you have to take a ticket to access the underground parking for the building. I catch sight of the driver of the car. It's the man in black. He takes his ticket and the gate opens to let him through. I stop the Prius and then drive up to the gate. I push the button to get a ticket, but the gate won't open. I honk my horn. The man in black turns toward me, and something in his face changes. Just for a second—it's a friendly face. It's Mel Brooks's face. I yell as he drives forward toward the underground parking entrance, "Hey, Sid! Wait a minute! I want to talk to you!" He doesn't stop, but I see him smile, and then he starts to laugh. His laugh thunders in my head—as if he's laughing right in my ear. Then he drives into the underground parking and disappears from view, but his laughter remains—like the Cheshire cat's smile. I put the car into reverse and get back onto the freeway entrance ramp. The night grows darker still, brutally black. Just as I merge onto the freeway, my headlights go out. I'm desperately turning them off and on to no avail. I'm driving in total darkness with that horrible laugh still echoing in my head. I'm driving blind, and then from behind me comes the blast of an air horn.

I wake with a start. My heart is pounding so hard I can hear it.

"Hey, are you all right, Mr. Geeg?" Jerry asks.

"Bad dream," I gasp.

"We're almost there," Kelly says.

The GPS tells her to turn right onto Crestview Road—a narrow, partially paved road that winds up the hillside. I'm so glad to see the sunlight, I can't even tell you.

If Sid is also the man in black, then I have been driving blind. I guess that's what we're talking about here. God, if you exist and you're listening, a little help down here.

CHAPTER SIXTY

THE TIMES THEY
ARE A-CHANGIN'

It's not a house boat, but it's equally impressive. We turn off the dirt road onto a circular driveway that leads up to the front of Rodger's house. The place is palatial: all white, three stories, with big columns out front. It looks ridiculously out of place in the wildness of hills. A big freaking white mansion sitting where it just shouldn't be. Like somebody levitated a plantation from the Deep South and dropped it on a Los Angeles hillside. It's like something you would see in a dream, the thought of which makes my head throb even more.

Israel's Jeep comes skidding up behind us. He beeps the horn and waves, in case we didn't notice, I guess.

"Now what?" Jerry asks.

"I'll talk to him," I say.

"Be careful, Harold!" Kelly warns. "You don't know what they're going to do. Not everybody is your friend, remember?"

"I'll be careful. He wants to protect us he said, didn't he?"

"That's exactly what I'm talking about, Harold. You don't know that. You don't know this guy."

"Don't worry, Mr. Geeg," Jerry tells me. "I got your back."

Jerry opens his door for me. The back passenger door is broken, so I have to squeeze through from the back to get out. Jerry, I guess, figured that he had my back just fine from where he was sitting. So squeezing my way out of the car, considering Jerry's size and my throbbing head, isn't the easiest thing to do. I trip on something on the way out and completely lose my balance. Next thing I know I'm lying facedown

on the gravel driveway. I hear car doors slamming and a lot of rushing around. Before I can fully register what has happened, and how
embarrassing it is, Israel is already helping me up, and everybody else is
standing around looking concerned.

"Are you okay, bro?"

"I'm fine."

"What happened?" Jerry asks as if he were out of town when I fell
out of his car.

Israel is either dusting me off or slapping me around. I can't
tell which.

"I'm okay! I'm okay!" I have to push his hands away to get him to stop.

"Sorry, bro."

Interestingly, I am completely unscathed from the fall. No blood,
not a scrape, not a scratch.

"Why are you following us?" Kelly suddenly demands.

"Because that's the job," the taller of Israel's friends tells us
with a smirk.

"What is this place?" the shorter one asks.

"I have to see the guy that lives here," I tell them.

"Do you know this guy?" Israel asks.

"He's my lawyer."

"Must be doing pretty good. Look at this fucking place," says the
shorter one with an ugly laugh.

Kelly takes an aggressive step, getting closer to Israel than I think he
feels comfortable with. "Are you going to follow us everywhere now?"

"We need to protect you," he says, taking a step back. "I don't think
you realize how important you are to everything."

I have a sudden dream flashback. I'm in the desert—literally, I'm
actually there. Israel is pointing a gun at me, and then a bird-monster
swoops in and rips his head off.

I have to do a triple take head shake to clear it, and then I'm back.

"Are you sure you're okay?" Israel nervously asks.

"I'm fine," I say, glad to see that he still has his head.

I'm uncertain if my dreams are a reliable source for deciding who to
trust and who not to trust, and I'm not sure what that little trip to the

desert was all about. Was it a reminder that in the dream, Israel was the one who was telling the truth? I want to trust him. I want to believe that when he smiled at me in the hospital, the connection I felt with him is something I can trust to be genuine. My intuition seems to have gone on hiatus. I guess if he kills me, then it'll be easier to make up my mind.

And speaking of killing and trust, I wonder where my bird-monsters are. Are they done with me now because I'm not the team player that I was programmed to be? Maybe they're regrouping with a new strategy, and the next head to roll will be the one that's currently connected to my shoulders. Why wasn't I hurt when I fell face-first onto the gravel driveway? Was that another alien demonstration to show the benefits of cooperation?

The front door of the mansion opens, and Rodger comes rushing toward us.

"Hey, there he is!" Rodger cries.

Before I can offer a hello, I find myself in a powerful bear hug.

"Harold, Harold, Harold! You look exactly the same, only forty years older!"

I'm not sure how to take that, so I leave it alone.

"Who are your friends?" Rodger asks.

Introductions are made. Turns out that Israel's intimidating-looking friends are Daniel (the short one) and Rafael (the tall one). They look like Israel's guys from the dream, but their names are different here. I'm trying not to prejudge them based on what happened in the dream, but considering the vibes they're putting out, that isn't an easy thing to do.

"We have a meeting," Israel explains, "a very important meeting."

"Right, the meeting." I say.

"We have to make sure you get there, okay? Everything depends on it."

"We're security for Harold and his family," Daniel sternly adds.

"We'll keep an eye on things out here," Rafael says as if he's pretty sure that he might have to kill something.

"You have security?" Rodger seems impressed by this.

"Apparently so."

Then he throws an arm around my shoulder and leads us into the mansion.

Holy crap, what a place! I'm thinking Rodger must have something on the side, like drug trafficking or gun running because this is ridiculous. Rodger shows us around as he chats whimsically about the past. We follow him like awed children. A huge dining room-living room area on the first level is adorned with the most amazing art collection I have ever seen. It reminds me of stuff they have at the Norton Simon Museum in Pasadena. I mean, real antiquities. He has statues and sculptures from before Christ walked the earth, and if some of his paintings are originals, then something fishy is definitely going on here.

We go up a staircase to the upper level, where he shows us a screening room and a game room with pinball machines and all kinds of cool arcade-type amusements. Toward the front of the upstairs landing is a really nice bar. Like in a fancy hotel. We make ourselves comfortable there in big overstuffed leather chairs. There's a huge picture window that extends up from the first level all the way to our level on the second floor. The view of the Pacific Ocean and coastline is breathtaking.

"You've come a long way," I tell him.

"Yeah, but once a freak, always a freak."

"Are you by yourself here?" Jerry asks. "Need a roommate?"

"We're putting the house on the market. My wife wants to move to Italy."

Ah! So maybe old Rodger married into this opulence.

"She should be coming up in a second. I told her about the whole Napa thing. Are you hungry? Drinks?"

Kelly and I say that water will be fine. Jerry requests something sparkling. Rodger gets up to accommodate us. After that gets taken care of, we all get comfortable with our drinks and some cheese and crackers that he brings out. Then his wife comes in.

Rodger gets up to greet her with a hug and an uncomfortably long kiss. It's Diane from my dream, an exact copy—except she's black. There seems to be a pattern developing here—the significance of which completely escapes me. Things are not always black and white? What may seem to be one thing is oftentimes another? I haven't a clue. After some more kissing, which brings the rest of us to the brink of sarcasm, Diane comes over to join us. When we lock eyes, there's an instantaneous connection. Like old friends, but friends who have never actually met—a bewildering reunion, indeed.

So, we sit watching the Pacific Ocean sparkling in the setting California sun, and then Rodger gets down to business.

"So we're going before the judge on Friday, and then we have to save the planet. Not necessarily in that order."

"Save the planet?" I innocently inquire.

"I guess the cat's out of the bag," says Jerry.

"What are we talking about, Rodger? I ask. "What have you heard?"

"I didn't hear it. I just know it. Because I was there. And so was Diane. Your dream somehow got into a lot of heads. People all over the planet, I would imagine."

"How many people do you think?"

"I'm not sure, but I know a lot of them are waiting for you to get in touch."

"They are?"

"Got a plan?"

"Nope."

"You know that we're talking aliens here, correct?" Kelly asks.

"Correct," Diane confirms.

Kelly gulps down her water. Her stomach does a low rumble. "Sorry. There's nothing I can do about that, so—"

"You're really pregnant?" Diane asks.

"You know about that, too?"

"We do. Pretty crazy."

"Here's a thought that came to me in the car," Jerry begins and then takes another cigar from his pocket. He seems to have an endless supply, like a magic trick. He puts it back, though, after Kelly gives him the evil eye and a stomach growl. "What if after we impress the government with what's happening and if it's ultimately agreed upon that the aliens are not really looking out for our best interests, what if we set something up to trick the aliens and make them believe that we will blow up the planet before we'd ever let them have it? That we would be willing to die and take them with us before giving it up. So it's a better-get-out-while-you-can kind of deal."

"Excuse me one second." Diane crosses her eyes and shakes her head, getting just as confused as the rest of us are. "Let me make sure we're all talking about the same thing. The one you're speaking with…"

"Sid?" I offer.

"Yes, Sid. His name is Sid—that's unreal. Anyway, he said that they want you to impress everybody with the things you can do? With the healing and the mind-control stuff, correct?"

"How do you know all this?"

"We're not entirely sure. We just do," she says.

"Yeah, that sounds about right. Anyway, he wants us to show what the benefits would be for humanity. That the world would be a much better place if we do what they want us to do."

"And what do they want us to do?"

"He told me that we have to arrange a peaceful understanding with our government so the aliens can relocate to our planet before their sun explodes. We have one month…well, we used to have a month. I'm not sure what it is now. Oh, and they want Wyoming."

"I thought it was Montana," Rodger says.

"No, pretty sure it's Wyoming. Anyway, if we fail to negotiate this for them, then the other faction of aliens, who don't think humanity is worth saving, will take charge, and it will be all over for us. But some people think it won't matter what we do, that this is an invasion and there is only one side, Sid is lying, and the real alien agenda is to just take over—to use us to get what they want—and then they'll wipe us out. But now, this group we've been in touch with, they're getting new messages and changing their minds about everything. Now they believe that what they thought it was, isn't anymore. That whatever is going to happen is going to happen very soon, and that instead of this being the end, it might be something good."

Diane leans back into Rodger's arms to gather herself. She has a giddy, confused look, which is completely understandable.

"Fascinating," Rodger says, just like Mr. Spock from *Star Trek*. "Here's what we're getting, if you'll indulge me, and then we can talk about court on Friday."

"If there is a Friday," I say. "But please, go ahead; no pressure."

Rodger smiles. I guess he's used to pressure. "What we're looking at here, the reason that we all have memories from something that you thought was a dream is because we're dealing with a separate reality."

"A separate reality? Really?" Jerry is getting frustrated. He runs his fingers through his hair, and he's got that Don King look going again. "Like Carlos Castaneda in the Don Juan books? That kind of separate reality?"

"Kind of like that, but without all the peyote. It's more like an actual alternate existence, probably several of them. That's why different people might have had different experiences, but the memories we're all having now, we're having them, so we can deal with what's coming around the bend."

"Huh," is all I can think to say.

"What happened there," Diane says, "was what would have been if some things went differently. If other choices were made. There I was a lost kid with no future and an abusive boyfriend. Here I'm the daughter of wealthy architects and art collectors. Separate realities existing side by side with just a thin thread of a connection. You somehow got ahold of that thread, Harold. And you took a bunch of us along for the ride."

Rodger tries to clarify. "We are being forced into a new way of seeing reality. We have to evolve our understanding in order to survive the threat of extinction."

"So we evolve when we're forced to evolve?" Kelly asks.

"That's what I'm thinking," Rodger confirms.

"But what are we supposed to do with that? What are we evolving to do?" Kelly questions again, apparently picking this stuff up a lot better than I am.

"To connect with each other. In the here and now so we can save the future." Diane says.

There is a moment, and then Jerry loses it a little.

"Okay, wait a minute, please. I'm trying to sort this out," Jerry says with a mouthful of crackers and cheese. "What do the aliens know? Do they know about this evolution thing? Are they good? Are they bad? Is Sid lying? Is he telling the truth? What the hell is going on here?"

Some of the crackers spray out of his mouth and land on the table.

"Sorry," he says. Kelly hands him a napkin, and he starts cleaning up the mess.

"Jerry," Rodger calmly explains. "I think the evolution thing is a side effect of the perceived threat. It comes with the territory. The aliens might have triggered it, but it's possible that they had no idea that this would happen. Or maybe they did. I'm not getting anything about what their motives are, one way or the other." Rodger leans back and kisses his wife.

Jerry puts the used napkin on the end of the table, changes his mind, and puts it in his pocket instead.

"Here's what I do know." Rodger leans forward again, and the rest of us lean in as well, sensing this should be pretty good. "There is a sort of technological treason that has poisoned the planet. A few corrupt and greedy power brokers are pulling all the strings and causing all kinds of hell on earth. There is no need for war or famine or pollution or all the other catastrophes that we are watching unfold on a daily basis. The technology already exists to solve all of these problems. We don't need aliens to fix this stuff. We have the means, but it's been kept hidden so that the maniacs in power can continue their stranglehold and reap the profits while keeping the world in turmoil. These few people are getting very rich off of unnecessary suffering. The people need to take back the power in order to save the planet. I would think the aliens would be aware of the struggles going on here. They know that if things don't change, we're pretty much done. Whether or not they know that they've inspired a major evolutionary shift? Your guess is as good as mine."

Now that's the old radical Rodger I used to know.

"It's a revolution, Harold!" Kelly cries. "You are the father of the freaking revolution!"

Same thing she said in the dream.

"Whether the aliens have purposely inspired us to change," Rodger continues, "or if they unwittingly ignited it, either way, a change is coming. A big change that may be the only way to save ourselves from our self-destructive ways and may be the only way for us to deal with an alien invasion."

Rodger finishes his explanation and then leans back into his seat and kisses his wife again. The rest of us lean back as well.

I have no idea what to say after hearing this.

Kelly breaks the silence.

"What about the baby? I'm not going to give it up."

"In the dream...or the other reality," I explain in case they don't already know, "we had no kids. Here, we've already lost one and now this. So you can understand we don't want to lose this one. It seems that some of the people—especially Linda, the ex-leader of Israel's group—are worried about the baby. About what she's going to be and what she's here to do."

Diane reaches over and takes Kelly's hand, who is surprisingly accepting of her show of support.

"If the aliens know about possible outcomes for our future," Rodger begins, and again I'm thinking this should be pretty good. "If they've seen something from another reality or from the future, and they know that in order for us to survive, something has to happen to inspire an evolutionary change, then the baby is a positive. If their intention is to destroy us, and because everyone is sensing that whatever is going to happen is going to happen very soon, then the baby doesn't make sense. Why bother with all that? The only way she will even appear is if the outcome is hopeful, change happens, and then steps are taken to assure the survival of the species. I think the reason for her presence on Earth is to help secure and protect our future, not to destroy it."

"Thank you," Kelly says, with a sigh of relief.

"You're welcome," Rodger answers with a reassuring smile that I recognize from the dream.

"You think Sid might be manipulating us but manipulating us for our own good?" I ask.

"I think that's as reasonable as anything else. And with that being said, I really don't think we need to go running around talking to governments and spreading the word and all that stuff. I think the less the world's lunatic leaders get involved, the better. The word is already getting around by itself to the people who really need to know."

"Something will happen at exactly the right time," Diane says. "Just like you came to me, Harold, in the other reality. You saved me then, and I think you'll do it again."

Rodger's assessment is uplifting, but my headache is getting ridiculous. I'm seriously wondering if I'm going to live long enough to see how this all turns out.

"Anyway," Rodger says. "On a more trivial note, we have a court date to deal with!"

"Just let Harold tweak their brain waves a little. That should do it," Jerry suggests.

"Good idea," Rodger agrees. "But just in case Harold has an off day—what Berman told me is a pretty logical defense. I don't think there's anything to worry about, even if no brains are tweaked. I can't see jail time for this. The court has already shown itself to be sympathetic to the situation. We need to show an attempt on your part to rehabilitate yourself. Some classes or AA would be good. Religious counseling—that kind of thing. We're definitely looking at a continuation of the suspended license and some community service, but jail time? I don't think so."

"I'll go to a Kabbalah meeting. I know a guy."

"Just tweak their brains, honey," Kelly says, echoing Jerry's suggestion. "We've got bigger fish to fry."

"Maybe the judge will already be tuned in to what's happening. He might just throw the whole thing out." Rodger says.

Considering how my head feels, I hope Rodger is right. Tweaking brains at this point might be too much for me to handle.

"Those guys outside? Can we trust them?" Rodger asks.

"Nobody has fired any shots yet," Jerry says.

"Can we go with you to this meeting?" asks Diane. "I'd be curious to see what's going on with these people."

"Fine by me," I say. "It might be good for them to hear what you're thinking. See if it clicks for them."

"For the record and for what it's worth." Jerry gets up to get some more soda at the bar. "I think we're going to be okay. I don't know how, and I don't even completely understand what's going on here, but I agree with Diane. Somehow, something is going to happen." He raises his glass to us. "Brothers and sisters—to the future in whatever reality that may be."

"To the future," we say as one.

"Give me a minute. I have to change." Diane jumps up and moves off toward another room.

"Seen any birds around?" Rodger asks.

"They were at my house and at that meeting we went to, but I haven't seen them since."

"No blood yet?"

"No. The people that Israel's with think the birds are projections, that they don't really exist, but they can spy. They say that the aliens are coming. They're not here physically, but they can somehow project themselves."

"Like astral projections?" he asks.

"Yes, except you can see them. Like a 3-D projection."

"Can you do that, too?"

"In dreams I can."

"Have you tried to go into space?"

"I've done it in the other place. Not here, yet."

"Amazing. Great time to be alive, isn't it?"

I'm not so sure I agree. I fumble for a witty response but come up with this instead. "You don't have any scotch, do you?"

"Of course. Do you want one?"

"I want three actually, but no, no—I shouldn't."

"I've got a twenty-one-year-old Macallan."

My eye starts twitching in perfect time with the pounding in my head.

"No, I'm...I'm...I thought I sensed a Macallan over there. Twenty-one-year-old, you say? Wow...but I'm good. Seriously, forget I brought it up. Just glad to know it's there. Makes a house a home, doesn't it?"

"In case of emergency—open bottle," Roger jokes.

"Yeah," I say with a quiver in my voice.

Then we wait to see what Diane puts on.

CHAPTER SIXTY-ONE

ON THE ROAD
TO FIND OUT

We go outside and find Israel sitting on the hood of his car. His partners, Daniel and Rafael, lie dead and pushed off to the side of the driveway, both of them shot in the head. The rest of us are, needless to say, stopped in our tracks.

"What the hell happened, Israel?"

Israel jumps off the car and starts quickly toward me, his hands raised in a peaceful gesture.

"Harold, breathe, relax. It's going to be handled."

"But what happened?"

"They weren't who I thought they were. They were here to hurt you. There are forces at work—it's complicated. They were with Linda. They are plotting things, bro. They are working for the people who don't like you very much."

"What people?"

"People who don't like where this is going."

"I have dead guys in my driveway," Rodger suddenly seems to realize.

"It will be taken care of. There will be no trace of what happened. We should go."

———

Rodger has a two-seat Mercedes convertible, which doesn't seem like an appropriate vehicle for what we have going on here. We decide that there's safety in numbers (which may or may not be true), so, in spite of the smell, the five of us ride together in Jerry's minivan. Israel says that he will personally take Rodger and Diane home after the meeting and provide security for them on the property. Jerry drives, and Rodger rides shotgun. Diane sits between Kelly and me in the middle section. She sits with her knees almost to her chest, and the little sundress that she had put on has hiked up—way up. Kelly and I steal a few glances but for different reasons.

Israel leads the way in his Jeep, and we follow him down the mountain and back toward Burbank. Nobody speaks. We just left two dead men, and now we're obediently following the man who killed them. Go figure.

We get down the mountain and onto city streets, and in spite of the carnage we just saw, I feel a kind of excited anticipation. Maybe it is Rodger's optimistic assessment of things or that I just turned down a twenty-one-year-old Macallan, but I've got a sudden undeniable feeling that whatever is coming is definitely not the end. My intuition seems to be engaging, and I think Israel might have been right. I can sense it in the air. We drive by the park again. The group I saw earlier is much larger now. They're in a big circle. Kids are running and playing all around them. There is that same electricity that I felt before, only it's stronger now.

"Would it be all right if you drop me at home before going to this meeting?" Kelly asks.

She surprises me with this, putting a damper on all the good vibrations.

"You want to go home?"

"Yeah, I'm not feeling very good."

"Probably shock," Jerry suggests.

"Is it the baby?" Diane asks.

"I don't know. I'm tired and just feeling off."

She stares straight ahead and avoids making eye contact with any of us.

"Do you want me to stay with you?" I ask.

"I just want to sleep. You go ahead. Just drop me off first."

"You can't be by yourself after what just happened!" Jerry cries. "That's crazy talk!"

"I'll be fine. Believe me, I can take care of myself."

"Israel will go crazy if we deviate from the plan," Jerry insists.

"He'll just follow us, and then you can tell him what's going on."

"Are you sure?" I ask. "I don't like this. I think I should stay with you."

"No! You need to be there, Harold. I'll be fine."

"What about a hotel. We can drop you someplace where nobody will know where you are."

"I don't want to talk about it anymore," she says. "Just drop me at the house. End of discussion."

No one challenges her further.

We drive quietly for a while. I think about Rebecca and how stubborn she could be. Just like her mother. Once she got something in her head, for better or for worse, she would have to see it through. I've been wondering about how much she knew and how much she understood about what is happening. My sense is her suicide was not about escaping "the voice" or being unable to deal with a new reality. I'm afraid that she did it for me. Rebecca was well aware of my propensity for avoiding confrontation and hiding behind my cocktails. She understood how high the stakes are and how important my involvement would be for finding a positive outcome. I believe she decided that her suicide might be the only thing to motivate me to see things through. My daughter took her life for me, for all of us. As tragic and painful as that may be—I must never let her sacrifice go to waste. Jerry said in the dream that we would need a martyr. Unfortunately, he was absolutely right.

"Does anybody feel different?" Jerry's question brings me back from my contemplations. "It's like before you go on stage. It feels something like that."

"Like going to a reunion and seeing people that you haven't seen in a long time?" Rodger offers.

"I feel it. I've got butterflies," Diane says.

Kelly's stomach makes a noise like my old Datsun used to make trying to get up a steep hill.

"Sweet Jesus on a tortilla," she says.

We veer off. Instead of taking the Burbank exit, we continue on into Glendale. My phone rings almost immediately.

"Where are you going, bro?"

"We're taking Kelly home first. She's not feeling well."

"What's the matter with her?"

"She just needs some rest. Baby stuff."

"I'll backtrack and follow you."

"You don't have to. We'll meet you there."

"I'll follow you," he insists.

"How'd you get my number?" I ask him.

"Seriously?" Israel seems amused by the question.

I disconnect the call.

"That was him. He's going to follow us," I tell them.

Except for the strange noises coming from Kelly's stomach, it's quiet all the way into Glendale.

When we get to the house, we pull into the driveway behind Kelly's car, and Israel pulls in right behind us. I am hoping to see a bird-monster sitting on the roof, but no such luck.

Israel is not happy at all about Kelly being by herself in the house and insists on giving her a gun. Kelly protests, but Israel won't relent until she takes it. He gives her a brief demo in the car about how the thing works, and then makes a call to have one of his guys come over to watch the house. Then I walk her up to the front door.

"You'll be okay?" I ask again for about the eightieth time.

"I'll be fine."

"Sure you don't want me to stay with you?"

"Stop already. I want to sleep. If you're here you'll just keep me up."

"I was hoping the birds would be here. For protection."

"Just can't find good help anymore."

I give her a hug. Her hug back is strong.

"Do you feel Rebecca? I ask in her ear. "I feel like she's here. Like she's watching."

"I always do," she whispers back.

She unlocks the front door and goes inside.

I know the next time I see her, everything will be different.

CHAPTER SIXTY-TWO

HERE COMES
THE SUN

We follow Israel back into Burbank. Rodger, Jerry, and Diane get involved in a discussion about shared consciousness and alternate universes. Rodger thinks that déjà vu is an actual memory from something that we lived through before, or maybe a premonition of things to come.

"A wheel within a wheel," Jerry says. The others agree with him. I have no idea what he's talking about.

Diane goes on to suggest that the aliens might actually be from another time. That they might be humans from the future, trying to protect themselves from something that we are about to do in our time.

I become distracted from all this heady stuff by watching the people on the street and feeling a deep connection to them—all of them. I'm becoming convinced that Rodger is right. The real crux of this thing is our reaction to the threat. No one is panicking. Nobody is throwing rocks through windows and grabbing flat-screen TVs. People are tuning in, and they are definitely picking up on something. They feel it coming. My head continues to throb as we follow Israel into Linda Broomfield's driveway.

Israel knocks on the door: three knocks, a pause, and then two more. Someone I don't recognize opens the door. There are more people in the room now, but Linda is gone. They are waiting for us and stand to applaud as we come in. A little boy walks toward us. Jerry recognizes him immediately. It takes me a minute. It's Joshua. He seems completely healthy now, with no signs of the trauma that had ravished him.

"I'm part alien!" Joshua proudly tells us.

"The wife isn't coming," Israel announces to the group.

There are groans of disappointment from the room.

"She isn't feeling well," I tell them, hoping they won't take her absence personally. In a way, I'm glad she isn't here. I'm not sure Kelly could have handled hearing Israel call her the wife again.

"Daniel and Rafael are gone," Israel announces. "Linda got to them."

More mutterings from the group. I don't know if they grasp the meaning of *gone* or not.

"We've reconsidered things since we saw you last," says the imaginary gardener in the fancy suit. "Linda was having a hard time adjusting to developments. She maybe isn't who we thought she was. She has an agenda that we didn't know about."

"What kind of agenda?" I ask.

Nobody responds to the question, which I find disturbing, but I become distracted from this particular worry because Joshua is pulling on my shirt sleeve.

"I'm a hybrid, Mr. Geeg! Just like your daughter will be!"

He takes his seat and rejoins his mother who is smiling and waving at me. He's a hybrid? So did Jane go through the same thing that Kelly is going through now? Is Joshua the other one that Sid was talking about, and now he's here to do—what exactly? Jane nods and smiles at me, as if she's reading my thoughts. She shrugs, as if to say, "I don't know either."

I introduce Rodger and Diane to the group, and then we sit as well. As before, there is a lot of nodding and smiling at first, but nobody is sure about how to get the ball rolling. There are more familiar people joining the group now. Portia has brought a guest, whom I recognize from the dream, the handsome Richard Ramirez, if that's his real name. Ira, the stage manager for *Hamlet*, is here. The older couple who remind me so much of Roy and Alice from Napa Valley are still here, but they're not waving at the ceiling anymore. At the sight of them, Rodger's normally composed face takes on a stunned *holy shit* look. More of the strangers from the dream are here, too. The waitress Del, from the '70s Pancake House, the park police cop, the Korean guys from the golf course, and some of the townspeople who were incidental in the dream but have all managed to find their way here. *"The actors are come hither, my lord!"* said Polonius to the melancholy Dane. Eventually the smiles all begin to fade, and everyone looks at me expectantly, as if I have the answer. Everybody knows, it seems, that we are embarking on an important moment, but nobody, myself included, has any idea how to get there.

"Well, what do we know?" Jerry begins. "We've moved on to something new now, correct? It's not about stopping or fighting anybody anymore. Are we all on the same page about that now?"

"It's a collective consciousness thing," Rodger says.

"Are we supposed to direct energy?" Diane asks.

"Direct it where? How do we do that, exactly?" Jerry inquires, his eyeballs growing huge.

"Harold, any thoughts on this?" Portia asks as a question that is actually a question.

My head is pounding, but I'm watching Joshua carefully. He is beginning to mumble and laugh—a delighted little kid's laugh.

"Uh, wait a minute," I say.

Joshua begins speaking in different languages. He isn't completely in the room anymore, and I can certainly relate to that.

"I think we should focus on Joshua and see if we can get to where he is," I say quietly, afraid that he may hear me and get distracted.

"The collective consciousness!" Diane cries, obviously not worried at all about disturbing Joshua.

What happens next changes everything.

When I focus my attention on Joshua, a connection is made between me and Joshua and then with everyone else. I am the conduit that others are able to follow to Joshua, and then Joshua takes us the rest of the way. We become united. It's the communion I had longed for. We are able to follow him like ghost shadows. We are making connections everywhere, all at once—individually and collectively. It's like riding a wave. It's a feeling of connectedness and belonging, and it's washing over the whole world. We are coming together as a species to defend ourselves and to expand ourselves.

There is a visible wave that rises up from the center of our circle and then shoots up through the ceiling, which somehow becomes transparent. I'm not sure if the others see what I see. But I watch our wave soar up into the sky, where it is joined by countless other waves from countless other gatherings. Then in a burst of color, like an aurora borealis, this energy shoots into the cosmos. It's a statement to the universe that we have arrived. We are uniting, and we'll be okay. It is breathtaking. We followed the child and the child has shown us the way.

And then in a flash. I'm out of the room.

CHAPTER SIXTY-THREE

THE MAN IN THE
LONG BLACK COAT

I find myself in Brand Park, or a version of it, anyway. It's like a bomb went off. The Brand Park library is in ruins and the big pine trees are uprooted and scattered about like toothpicks. When I look up, the sky is a reddish-black color.

I hear a rustling from behind. I spin around and standing there is a tall man in a black suit. His eyes are almond shaped and catlike. His skin is very white with some subtle scaling, like an albino snake I saw at the zoo once. He wears a fedora hat. His pure-white hair is long and extends down to his shoulders. I can't tell his age.

"Hellooo, Harold!" he says.

"Sid?"

"In the flesh. Well, sort of."

"We meet at last," I say.

"I promised that we would."

"Where are we?"

"We are in an alternate reality. If things went a little differently, this is what would have happened."

"Rodger was right."

"Yes. There are countless possibilities. Many outcomes and consequences to our actions."

"Are we safe?"

"For now."

"Are you the man in black? From my dream?"

"I am. I'm sorry, but he was necessary."

"Why?"

"So that your species could save itself from itself. You needed to make an evolutionary step before things got beyond the point of survivability. Like this place did. Humans need to experience the threat of extinction in order to progress. You need a man in black. An unfortunate reality for your species."

"Score another one for Rodger."

"Must have been all those drugs he did in the seventies."

"Or maybe you clued him in a little?"

"Maybe a little," he says with a smile.

"Were you also the voice in my head?"

"Yes."

"Why were you so mean? Why were you trying to destroy me?"

"I was trying to prepare you, Harold. If you could turn back that voice, you would be able to handle the rest of it. For what was and what is to be."

"So how am I doing?"

"Your father would be proud," he says, and he's got me tearing up again.

"Are you still going to...do you still need to move here to save yourself?"

"No. That was never the issue. I was just here to help."

"So there is no danger of an alien invasion?"

"Not at the moment."

"Thank you."

"It's my job."

"You do this all the time?"

He shrugs. "It's a living," he says, exactly how Mel Brooks would.

I'm thinking about what "not at the moment" means, when something howls. I see some branches fly up, and then a big head peaks out from behind some decimated pine trees. It's the dog-monster that had me for lunch. My shock at seeing it here is suddenly interrupted by an epiphany of sorts. I'd be willing to bet that my dog-monster is also the bear/badger thing that Mr. Geeg saw in the Hollywood Hills all those years ago. Then my eureka moment is shattered because the thing is now galloping toward us, and I hope to God that he's already eaten.

"Don't worry. He won't hurt you," Sid assures me.

The beast arrives at his side and rubs up against his master. I take a few steps back. Can you blame me?

"We have to go."

"Oh? Have some Christmas shopping to do?"

He puts out his hand, and I shake it. He has three long fingers.

"I thought I had a month? What changed?"

"You didn't need it. You were able to connect much sooner than I had anticipated, and people didn't panic. They were ready for this."

"I'll miss you, Sid. I always liked you. Even when I thought you were going to wipe us out."

"Down the road we'll meet again."

"I hope so."

Reluctantly I release his hand. I really don't want to let him go. I want to ask him about Rebecca. I want to ask him about so many things.

"Watch out for Linda and watch out for Portia's father, too," Sid says.

"What's going on with Linda?"

"Linda works for the people who were hoping this would have a different outcome. She and the people she represents are very dangerous. Portia's father is delusional about what he thinks God wants him to do. You will still have many challenges."

"I can handle it."

"I know you can. Catch you on the flip side, Harold Goldfarb."

"What about the birds? Will I see them again?"

"They've moved on to another assignment."

"I'll miss them too."

"We'll see how it goes. They might be back."

He smiles, the dog winks, and then they both begin to dissolve. Sid waves a farewell, and then they are gone. I start to laugh. From relief, I think. I laugh and laugh. I can't seem to stop. Then things start to dissolve all around me. Or maybe I'm dissolving. I can't tell which. And that just makes me laugh even more.

CHAPTER SIXTY-FOUR

I DON'T KNOW WHY YOU SAY GOODBYE, I SAY HELLO

I'm back at the meeting, right where I had been before I left. And I'm laughing my ass off. When I finally notice that everyone is staring at me—that snaps me out of it.

"Are you okay, Mr. Geeg?" Jerry asks.

"I'm fine," I say. "Have I been here the whole time?"

"What?" Jerry is confused by the question.

Of course I've been here. I just did a little out of body time-space jump, that's all. Sid must have guided me to get to where he was. My actual body never really left the room.

"I just talked to Sid," I say.

"What? You did?" Jerry gets very excited about this, as does everyone else. They move in close to hear what I have to say.

"We're safe now. It was never about aliens. It was about us. Sid was assigned, I think, to protect us from ourselves. He was here to inspire change, and what just happened here is a new beginning—for everything. A whole new way of doing business."

There's silence, and then the room erupts into a great cheer.

My headache is completely gone. I noticed it when I was talking with Sid. It's as if the pressure was building, and the mass connection of our group with the groups from around the world was the release. I wonder how many headaches were cured by what just happened.

Food and wine are brought in, and the mood is jubilant. I stay away from the wine and go for a diet Coke instead. It's decided that regular meetings should be scheduled to keep the lines of communication open, keep track of each other, and stay abreast of what's developing on the planet. I know the struggle isn't over. The shadowy powers that Rodger and Sid talked about, that Linda is connected to, they're probably plotting right now to squelch the progress that was made today.

Eventually, people start filtering out. Rodger comes up, and I get another one of his big hugs.

"Well done, Harold," he says.

"Rodger, you were right about everything."

"I had some help, I think."

"Crazy," I say.

"I'll call you tomorrow, and we'll go over details about the court date. But that all feels so yesterday, doesn't it?"

Diane comes up and whispers in my ear, "I knew you'd find a way."

"I had a lot of help. By the way," I suddenly feel obligated to tell her, "Did I mention that in the other place you were white?"

"I was?"

It's still bugging me, I guess.

"Interesting," she says, sounding just like Rodger, when he sounded just like Spock. "It might have something to do with how isolated we've become, so we can't experience the reality of who people really are. Maybe it was a warning or a lesson for you. When you see the world through a narrow lens, you really don't see very much at all."

I take a moment to ponder the significance of that.

"I guess I need to get out more," I say.

She laughs and sounds just like she did in my car outside of Coalinga when we first met in the dream. Then she grabs me in a powerful hug, plants a kiss on my cheek, and moves away to join her husband.

Before my back has a chance to catch its breath, Israel has me in a serious bro hug.

"I told you, I'm the good guy. Believe me now?"

"One hundred percent," I tell him. "Did your guy get over to the house yet? Everything okay over there?"

"Of course, one of my best guys, no problem. I'm going to give your friends a ride back. And don't worry. I already got that mess cleaned up over there."

"Oh, good. That's good," because really, what else could you say?

"You call me. Day or night. You need me, and I'm there for you. Got it?"

"I will. Oh," I whisper to him, confidentially, "Do you want your gun back?"

"Hang on to it for a while. Keep your eyes open, bro. Use your mojo if you have to."

"I will," I assure him.

He punches my arm. Not enough to hurt, but hard enough to show respect.

The three of them leave. Diane blows kisses until she's out the door.

Portia and Richard Ramirez come over next.

"Howard, this is Richard? He's in the show?" Portia questions.

"How's it going?" I ask as we shake hands.

"Good, I mean, what a day!" Ramirez says. "And I'm so sorry you're not able to do the show. Would have loved for you to be my dad, and Tom's been raving about you. Maybe next year?"

"Maybe, but I think I might be retiring from show business. I'm going to be otherwise engaged, I do believe."

"Thank you for what you've done, Harold," Portia says.

"Thank you for what you will do," Ramirez adds.

They're a nice couple and I'm flattered that they want me to play their father, but I truly don't look anything like either one of them. Nobody would have bought it. So I guess things worked out for the best—on the theatrical side as well.

"By the way," Portia says. "My father has not been reacting well to all of this? He's very upset about me getting involved with this group? And I just want you to know that he's been saying some threatening things?" she continues to question, and I hope I'm not grimacing as she does.

"I'll keep an eye out for him."

I wonder what Portia's experience was and what reality she landed in. Did she get all the stuff about Sid pretending to be God and what he said we had to do together? I'm also wondering if she uses so many questions when she does Shakespeare. My dream Portia didn't, and I couldn't wait to see her do the show. This one—not so much.

"He must have felt some of this today?" she says, interrupting my reverie. "I hope he did? So that maybe he'll calm down a little?"

"Anyway, nice to meet you, Harold," Richard Ramirez says, while shaking my hand again.

"It's funny," Portia continues. "I feel like we've known each other forever, but we really just met today—for the first time? And from when we talked on the phone?"

"Yes, it's funny," I have to agree.

Portia hugs me, and I do believe she's about to get emotional as they head for the door.

The older couple, Sherman and Doris, come up next to say good night. When they get close, the resemblance to Roy and Alice is really uncanny.

"Just want to say thank you," Sherman says.

"We're all just doing our part," I modestly reply.

"Well, you've taken on more than most. Don't be shy about that now," Doris gently scolds.

"We just appreciate it, son."

"Have we met before?" Doris asks. "I feel as if we have."

"Somewhere we probably crossed paths. And I want to say…that I appreciate what you've done. It's inspired me," I sincerely tell them.

"No, we just blocked some negative energy, that's all," Sherman says with a wave of his hand, as if shooing away my sentimentality.

"And radio transmissions," Doris adds. "All of a sudden we can do that, too."

"No, I mean—"

"We know what you mean, son. We're all connected to each other, somehow. Past, present, and future," Sherman says.

"We just remind him of someone, Sherm. That's all."

"Anyway," Sherman tells me. "You're like a son to us, really. We lost a child, too, you know?"

"Maybe that's it, then," I say.

"Good night, Harold," he says.

Doris hugs me, and Sherman gives me a firm handshake that I get a little electric shock from.

"Sorry," Sherman says. "I'm still a little charged up."

CHAPTER SIXTY-FIVE

MY BABY DONE WROTE ME A LETTER

Jerry gives me a ride back to the house.

"Now what?" he asks.

"I guess we just see what develops."

"I wonder how many people were involved in this."

"I think a lot."

We pull into my driveway. I flash on Rebecca again, and the pain comes rushing back as fresh as the day it happened.

"I wonder where Israel's guy is?" Jerry asks.

"Her car isn't here," I suddenly realize.

"What?"

"Why isn't Kelly's car in the driveway?" A wave of panic comes over me. Was the guy who Israel sent over here also corrupted by Linda?

"Maybe she went to the store."

"She said that she wanted to sleep."

"So maybe she slept, and then she went to the store."

We go inside. She isn't in the house, and neither is the cat or Israel's security guy. I look in the bedroom. The bed is still made. Her dresser drawers are opened and a lot of her stuff is gone.

"What the hell?" Jerry cries.

"She left."

"Yes, I can see that! But where did she go? What the hell is she doing?"

"She took Squeak," I say.

"She took the cat? Why would she take the cat?"

"Come on."

We walk through the house looking for clues, and we find a note in the kitchen. I read it out loud:

"Harold—it's not safe. I don't want to say where I've gone, but it's where we've been before. The big house. The big family house. The house made of lox. I told the security guy to leave. I lied—I said I was going to my sister's and that you were going to meet me there. I love you. Don't call. Don't trust the cell. Just find me. You'll figure it out. I have Squeak. He got me good when I put him in the carrier. People are watching. Be careful. Love you, Kelly."

"The house made of lox?"

"What's that mean?" Jerry asks.

Then it hits me. Like a pine cone in the nose. "I got it!" I shout.

"You do?"

"It's her friend's cabin," I whisper, in case somebody might be listening. "Her father was big in the fish business."

Then a voice booms out from the radio. "Hellooo, Harold!"

We both jump, and I think I might have to change my underwear.

"Sid?" I ask the radio.

"'Tis I. Hi, Jerry."

"Oh hi, Sid," he responds, as if nothing is particularly out of the ordinary.

"I just want to say one more thing before I go. Got a minute?" he asks.

"Sure, go ahead," I say.

"Please understand that everything that happened was necessary to get us to this point. The changing stories, doubting the message, and not knowing who to trust. Human nature dictated the method to obtain the desired result. But your daughter's death, that surprised me. I never would have made that a part of the strategy. I want you to know that, Harold, and that I am truly sorry for your loss and how you suffered. But she did not die in vain. She inspired you to return from the coma, to persevere, and you will continue to do so. Rebecca will live on in the people you nurture. You are capable of great things, and now you have the tools to get there, in large part thanks to your daughter and what she has inspired you to do."

"Thanks, Sid. I needed to hear that just now."

"I know you did," he says.

"Will Kelly be okay? Will the baby make it?"

"All signs point to yes."

"Wasn't that a Magic 8 Ball answer?" Jerry whispers to me.

"Yeah, pretty sure it was," I whisper back.

"You may rely on it!" Sid happily adds.

Sid's sense of humor is always surprising.

"When will you be back?" Jerry asks him.

"I don't know, but I'll be watching."

"Will we keep our powers? Can I still heal?"

"Yes, your skills will strengthen and serve you well. Look after Joshua, and he will look after you. He is key."

"Is Joshua a part of you?" I ask.

"Yes. Treat him as your own. He will be your son now, too. Welcome to your future, my friends. I have to go. I'm sooo late."

The radio starts playing Stevie Ray Vaughan's version of "Voodoo Child," which I find to be very cool and apropos.

"Damn," Jerry says while staring at the radio.

"What?"

"That fucker could play some guitar, couldn't he?"

We listen for a minute to Stevie's genius.

"Yeah, humans do have some stuff about them," Jerry says.

"Want to go see Kelly?"

"Can I stay with you guys for a while?"

"Plenty of room up there."

I pack a suitcase, lock up the house, and put on the alarm. On the way out we find a penguin in a yellow raincoat sitting on the front porch steps.

"Hey, I remember him," Jerry says. "He was in the dream, wasn't he?"

I pick up the penguin and feel myself getting emotional again. "I think a friend of mine just figured something out."

We drive to Jerry's, he packs a bag and then we head for the House of Lox.